Doubled

Again

FOR LITERARY HEAT

www.BarbarianSpy.com

This book is copyright © 2013
habu asserts his right to be known as the author of this work.
Published by BarbarianSpy in 2013
Cover design © S Bush 2013
Cover image: Symbol (manipulated), copyright: Ola-Ola at depositphotos.com
ISBN: 978-1-922187-65-9
All rights reserved

BarbarianSpy
Jindalee St
Toronto, NSW 2283
Australia

Doubled

Again

The second gay DP anthology

from

habu

Table of Contents

Introduction

One of the rarer niche fetishes to find in gay male erotica stories is the act of double penetration (DP), two men inside another man at the same time. The fetish is one that frequently is included in the writing of habu, if only as a minor element of a story. In *Doubled Again*, coming three years after the initial launch of his successful and recently reissued *Doubled* anthology, habu provides a collection of his most recent writings that include gay male DP scenes.

Combined in this twenty-four story anthology, with forty-eight double penetration scenes, are new, never-before-published stories focusing directly on DP sex, including "Bangkok Defection," "Club Doblar," "Handed On," and "Horrid Bliss." Habu has also ferreted out DP scenes from his longer marketplace e-books for your focused enjoyment. These includes scenes from his "Death in . . ." books, featuring a willing DP participant, promiscuous detective Clint Folsom. Scenes are also included from the novellas *Gotta Keep Trying*, *Gilded Cage*, *Brambleton*, and *The Indian Prince*. The remaining short stories provided are ones where, typically, the sensuality of the story climaxes in a double penetration scene.

If this is one of your fetishes in gay male stories, you need not dig for it yourself. Habu has provided yet another meaty DP collection for your reading pleasure.

Bangkok Defection

I froze in the middle of talking about the next season of the Bangkok Chopin Society at the ambassador's residence, as the ambassador walked into and around the side of the room to get into another room. I don't know if I audibly gulped or not, but none of the women—and the few men—sitting in a circle of upholstered chairs and couches in the commodious room obviously meant for entertaining seemed to notice. The ambassador himself, though, as if he'd heard me react to his presence, turned at the door of the room he was entering, and looked directly at me. If he had a reaction of surprise or concern, he was too much the trained diplomat to give one. He just inclined his head a bit, gave me a controlled smile—I had every impression it was directed at me—and then turned and left the room.

I returned my attention to the meeting, having been invited there by Lidka Basher, the ambassador's wife, because the East European country sponsoring the annual Chopin competitions in Warsaw this year was mustering all of the international Chopin societies that had formed and inviting their chief executives to sit on the presidium of the next competition. I had, in a convoluted way known only to such social organizations, been roped into the presidency of the Bangkok Chopin Society for the coming year, and thus was being invited to Warsaw. I had had no intention of attending and had told my seniors at the American embassy as much, fearing that I'd done something wrong in even being approached by a communist-country embassy, this still being during the Cold War. But my seniors showed no concern at this nondiplomatic contact and made clear that they had other ideas altogether.

"We would like to get close to the ambassador of that country, very close," the chief of station in the embassy had told me. "You are to foster, not avoid this contact."

That was a surprise. But this was my first posting. I knew I had a lot to learn about this spying game. So, I'd come to this meeting, intending to follow my chief's directive but not really make the contact he wanted me to make. I'd tell him that I hadn't even seen the ambassador, that he wasn't part of the committee. But now that I had seen him, I planned on saying it was just fleeting—that I hadn't had the opportunity to talk with him. Fate had other plans, though.

I perhaps would have known about the ambassador if the chief of station had shown me a photograph of him, even though the contexts were so different that maybe I couldn't have recognized the photo. But he had neglected thus far to do so. He, however, seemed already to have known that I would make contact with Ambassador Bacher and even how that would transpire.

Luckily, I wasn't expected to make more of a contribution to the embassy residence meeting on Chopin Society activities, because my mind kept wandering back to where and when I'd previously encountered the ambassador.

It had been in the sauna of the men's gymnasium club I went to in Bangkok—a very special sort of club that flourished in hedonist, "whatever" international cities such as Bangkok.

I was sitting in the lap of the Indian doctor who had originally seduced me in that sauna some months earlier, facing away from him, toward the door of the sauna, and riding his cock, when the man I now knew as Ambassador Jacek Bacher came into the sauna. He stood there, tall, thin, graying hair at the temples and on his chest, and distinguished looking—perhaps in his fifties, but handsome and well muscled—with just a towel wrapped around his waist, and watched me rise and fall on the Indian's cock with interest and curiosity rather than surprise. Other than a twitch in his cheek muscles, the man initially didn't move while the doctor held my waist in his hands and helped guide me—up and down, a couple of revolves, with me leaning forward then, putting my weight on my feet, and the Indian doctor slamming his long, long, thin cock deep up into me a few times, me huffing at the depth he managed, before pulling me back to rise and fall on the staff myself.

After a few moments of observing, Bacher's towel dropped and he fisted his cock, which looked to be thick and long in contrast to the thin, wiry, tallness of him. The trimmed bush at his groin revealed that he'd had darker hair as a younger man, and his ball sac hung low and heavy. I looked on, mesmerized, the heavy gold signet ring on the middle finger of the slender-fingered hand he was stroking himself with catching my attention, as his cock lengthened and thickened impressively before my eyes.

The two—the Indian doctor and the stranger I didn't then know from Adam—must have known each other well, because the Indian doctor spoke up in his singsong voice that had helped seduce me and then to do whatever he wanted me to do. "Come, Jacek, join me inside him. He's a delicious piece. He knows the double."

And, indeed, I did know the doubling, thanks to the Indian doctor, who had spent months developing me to be able and willing to take anything he suggested.

The man hesitated, but only for a moment, as the Indian doctor's hands went to the underside of my calves just below the knees and he lifted and spread them, rolling my pelvis up to where the man would be able to see the root of the Indian's cock inside me as well as the rim of my hole clutching the cock.

"Are you sure?" the man asked in a husky, heavily accented voice in a mix of guttural tone but perfect British diction. Despite the question, I knew he would have me because already that long slender finger with the signet ring was inside me and along the upper side of the doctor's buried cock, and he was rubbing the rim of my opening with the gold metal. I gasped and reached down and, cupping his balls with one hand and his dick with the other, pulled the cock toward my hole.

"Fuck me, oh, god, fuck me too," I murmured, letting him know that he was more than welcome to join the Indian inside me.

"He will open right up for you," the doctor assured him. "I have trained him to double."

And, indeed, the Indian doctor had trained me to take two men at once. At first men with thin cocks like his, but eventually rough thugs with thick cocks. And, if truth be known, I had come to thoroughly enjoy the feel of two cocks inside me at once, especially liking the feel of two active dicks, moving in and out in a countermovement, rubbing against each other, the men breathing heavily and groaning at the effort, as I speculated which of them would come first. This was barely a year before the scourge of AIDS reared its ugly head—a time when every man in Bangkok was still barebacking. Every man pursuing an even more ultimate fuck.

Of course I had reported this sauna encounter to my seniors at the embassy—I had done so the first time the Indian doctor had seduced me here in the sauna and then taken me to his home and fucked me three ways from Sunday, only letting me go when I was crawling across the floor toward him, begging for the cock. I knew that there was no keeping secrets from the secrets specialists in the embassy. And I had expected to be sent home in disgrace. But, to my surprise, my seniors had been pleased and had said that they had known I would succumb to the wiles of other men—even if I hadn't known it or, even if suspecting it, had had no intention of falling to it. My seniors said that now I would be even more useful to them and that I was to continue seeing the Indian doctor and letting him train me to male sex.

It was then that they explained to me that the oldest techniques of spying were based on sex, on fulfilling someone's sexual desires to the point that they belonged to you, whether willingly or not. My tradecraft training hadn't been accelerated, the station chief told me, because of my great intellect and natural abilities, but because I was blond, cute, cut, and fit the profile of a man who could be fucked by another man—and still fuck women, as needed.

They left little doubt that after I was fully trained for it, I would be using it to further my government's interests, whether the target was male or female.

I have thought on more than one occasion since then that the Indian doctor was actually in the employ of my seniors in the Agency, and that the most important part of my Agency training occurred here, in Bangkok.

Having been assured by both the Indian doctor and me that I would take his cock along with the Indian's, the tall stranger hadn't waited for a second invitation. He was crouched between my raised and spread thighs and, with grunts and groans, was allowing me to guide his cock to my entrance and force it inside me, above that of the Indian's. I let loose of the cock when the bulb cleared my sphincter muscle, not being sure I could take him further and grabbed his ribs as if to push him away. But he was forcing his way deeper into me and I just gripped his sides hard and began to pant.

He faltered, but I whimpered, "Yes, yes," to egg him on, wanting this fuck, wanting to please my Indian teacher. Being willing to endure how it started for where I knew it would lead. I moaned and whimpered as I always do at the first entrance of even one cock, until my opening and channel had got the measure of what I had to take. But the Indian doctor was whispering encouragement in my ear between moments of sucking on the lobe and even biting it to move the pain I was enduring while the tall stranger was saddling his outsized cock.

I realized that the Indian and this man had done this before, though, because, once saddled, the Indian's cock remained dormant, although still hard, inside me as the stranger bottomed and began to stroke. The stranger wrapped one fist around my cock and stroked me and grabbed my waist with the other hand, while the Indian continued to hold my thighs raised and spread.

Harder, deeper, faster, the stranger fucked, his balls making a slapping sound on my butt cheeks that reverberated around the wooden walls of the sauna, while I writhed around between them, giving little cries—almost ashamedly cries of pleasure and wantonness—while the stranger pulled hard on my cock and fucked me hard like he was the only one inside me.

15

Slap, slap, slap, the sound of his balls thumping against my butt cheeks, was synchronized with the thrusting of his cock. I moaned and arched my shoulders back deeper into the Indian's chest, rolling my pelvis up to the stranger, wanting him deeper inside me.

"Harder, deeper," I cried out in a moan-tormented voice, wantonly wanting there to be no question what I wanted from the man. My reaction inflamed him to renewed vigor.

But he wasn't the only one inside me. The Indian's cock came to life too, and he was counterstroking me and sucking and biting me on the ear and singsonging to me how good I was doing and how sweet my ass was.

I came first and then the stranger and only later, as the stranger pulled out of me and wiped himself with the towel while standing there and watching the Indian lapping me again, did the Indian doctor come. Then he just gently moved me aside, off his cock, with me exhausted and filled with the cream of two men, turning over on my side on the sauna bench. The two of them left the sauna arm and arm then, speaking in low tones. I wanted them to be remarking what a good double lay I was, but I had no inkling what they were discussing.

I hadn't seen the tall stranger in the men's gym since that evening, although it wasn't the last time the Indian used me to double or turned me over to one or a group of men, as he fancied.

That night, the evening of the meeting on Chopin societies in the ambassador's residence, I was approached by a young Thai man dressed in a chauffeur's uniform. It was after the meeting dispersed, and while I was walking across the compound to the gate, where I'd parked my car out on the street.

Whereas many Thai men were small and thin, although being well muscled, this man was tall and bulky and heavily muscled. "Compliments of the ambassador," he said to me in a low voice, as he drew near to me and other people who had been in the meeting drifted by toward the compound gate. "If you have a moment, the ambassador would like to have a word with you in the garden."

It was more than a word Ambassador Bacher had. He—
and the chauffeur—fucked me, together, in a garden pavilion
beyond a swimming pool in a back corner of the compound.

Both were thick, and I gasped and huffed at taking them
both, with the ambassador lying on his back on a lounge bed, his
thick, long cock pointing straight up at the ceiling of the
pavilion, while the hulking chauffeur lifted me as if I weighed
nothing and settled me down on the cock. Immediately
afterward, he was straddling the ambassador's thighs, grabbing
and spreading my butt cheeks, and rolling my buttocks up to his
own thick, deep thrust inside me.

They pumped me hard and deep—both pistoning me—
there in the dark, the ambassador worrying my nipples and cock,
while the chauffeur held my waist with one hand and pulled my
head back to his shoulder with the other, his hand covering my
mouth and nose to muffle the cries I was making at the much
rougher and more brutal double fucking I was getting than I had
received from the ambassador and the Indian doctor in the
men's gym sauna.

I would complain about the brutality of it, except that I
thoroughly enjoyed it. Yes, there was more pain—at least until
the emotional pleasure swept over me that there were two men
working me, wanting me, enjoying me together. I couldn't get
past the thrill of this sensation of desirability. I'd always want
more of it; it would block out any pain involved. And I had been
trained well to take it. The only thrill that approached it was
being on a chain—we called it being on a string in Bangkok in
those days—with men standing in line to fuck me, all of them
watching me being fucked, all of them wanting to be inside me
too, all of them getting their turn. But in those circumstances,
the men weren't having intimate sex with each other at the same
time. Nothing served this fetish as doubling did. My only guilty
thought was what my employers would think about it. I would
have to tell them. They couldn't learn that I was keeping
anything back from them.

I protested that my car was there outside the compound
when the chauffeur was pulling me toward the embassy
limousine, saying he would drive me home. But he paid no
attention to me and could—and did—manhandle me at will.

The ambassador was sitting, naked, in the center of the backseat when I entered the limousine, and I sat in his lap, facing him, and fucked myself on his tool during the ride back to my own compound. The chauffeur stopped short of my compound, on a dark cul-de-sac where the buildings were still under construction, and joined us in the backseat, crouching over my buttocks and thrusting up inside me for a second double fuck.

In the morning my car was parked in my spot in the embassy apartment compound parking garage. I remarked on this mystery to the chief of station when I got into the embassy and had told him about my nocturnal encounter with the ambassador—and his Thai chauffeur.

"We drove your car back for you," was all he said.

"What now?" I asked, trying not to think of just how much my own people knew about the encounter and, perhaps, how much of it they were responsible for. "How do I get out of this Chopin Society business and avoid this situation?"

"You don't," was the reply. "We want you to cultivate the ambassador. We think he's ready to defect, and we want him to defect to us. You just have to fuck him. We will pitch him. You are the candy for the deal. Blackmail, if necessary."

Oh. That was my first operation for the station to this effect. I was to become less naïve about these matters later— much less naïve.

* * * *

My "affair" with Ambassador Jacek Bacher, if it could be called an affair, went on for two more months before he disappeared from my life altogether. I attended two more meetings, hosted by his wife, Lidka, during this time, but the ambassador didn't appear to me there again. Instead, I would periodically receive notes in my mailbox at my apartment compound from the chauffeur that just listed an event happening somewhere in the city. He would say no more in the notes or sign them, but if he thought he was fooling anyone, he was the fool. I certainly wasn't fooled. I knew that someone from the station was reading them before I received them—and I turned every one that I received over to the station chief, as well. I was holding no secrets while still being amazed that the Agency could have a stringent policy on sexual activity and still use me in this way.

Without exception, the station chief directed me to make every assignation.

Most of the notes were about sporting venues. I played tennis on the embassy circuit. So did Ambassador Bacher. And I went to the horse races at the Bangkok Sports Club near the corner of Wireless and Ploenchit roads, as did many of the rest of the diplomatic community. So did Ambassador Bacher. The ambassador's car would pick me up at a bar near my apartment compound on Soi 51 an hour before the event. Sometimes the ambassador and the chauffeur would fuck me somewhere private at the event. More often than not, though, it would be the ambassador lapping me himself on the way to the event and the limousine being parked somewhere hidden on the way back and rocking on its springs as both Bacher and the chauffeur took me together in the backseat. At the actual event, my seat wasn't anywhere close to the ambassador's. Apparently he thought we were being discreet. It didn't take me long to notice that we were being watched by agents from the station.

Bacher said he couldn't get enough of me, and he started to talk of me coming back to Warsaw with him. And I believe he had become that infatuated with me; it came across in his lovemaking, which was becoming less frenetically rough and more attentive and sensual. When I told the station chief this, his eyebrows raised, and, with that simple gesture, I "got" that we would move on to a new phase.

Less than a week later, the Indian doctor summoned me to his apartment. Ambassador Bacher was there. But so was another man, a man I knew in passing but who I had no idea was interested in other men. He was of German ancestry but was an expatriate American, Gerhard Kemp by name. And he owned and operated a well-regarded architectural firm in Bangkok. He was on Lidka Bacher's Chopin Society committee as well as I was and was a big financial backer of the expatriate arts community in the city. He was married to a Thai princess and moved in circles of Bangkok society even above that of the diplomatic community.

He also had a thick, if not long cock. He was on the beefy side, but not quite what I'd call fat yet. And he was quite athletic and vigorous. It wasn't until he was plowing me from between my thighs, as Bacher leaned back on the edge of the Indian doctor's examining table and held me in front him with his cock deep inside me and his hands on my waist, that I realized that I had seen him around the men's gym I went to. He had always been absorbed in a vigorous workout so I hadn't connected him to the underbelly side of the gym.

Until now. He was stubby enough that it was Bacher who had to hold deep inside me and let the architect, buried only shallowly in my channel, make hard jabs into me and, periodically, revolve his thick cock near my entrance to make the most of his size. The cock could reach my prostate, though, so I could pant and moan—and spout—for him as well as the next man.

The Indian doctor brought the three of us together a few times after that. After the sex, I'd be sent on my way. The doctor would see me to the door, sometimes even coming out of the apartment with me and only separating when we were down on the street, leaving the other two men in his examination room. I could see, in passing, that two glasses and a vodka bottle had been set out on the dining room table each time. I didn't know at the time who they were for—and only later did the significance of them hit me.

But that was only for one more month, until the evening of the Chopin piano concert I went to at the Bangkok Opera hall. As president of the local society, I had been invited to sit in Ambassador Bacher's box. His wife, Lidka, was the honorary sponsor of the concert, so we were in the king's box. Kemp and his wife were there too. And, to my consternation, a political officer from the American embassy was in the box as well.

Nothing untoward happened until the interval, although I could feel the heat coming off the ambassador as he took occasional glances in my direction. There was no pretense, I knew, in how much he wanted me, how hooked he was on me. The Indian doctor was still lending me out to his friends during this period, and I was finding that I melted more to a rough thug than to someone as elegant and refined as the ambassador. So, although I liked him well enough and enjoyed being doubled by him, in particular, he did not hold me in thrall. Certainly not as much as the Indian doctor did with his variety and his mesmerizing voice—and with perhaps the longest cock I'd had in Bangkok, a cock that was like a snake and could kiss my channel walls from any direction with its rubbing bulb and almost seemed to be able to suck on my prostrate until I came in prodigious flow.

At the interval, the men in the box were separated from the women. The women were sent down to the lobby to mingle with the other high rollers in the audience. The men withdrew to a nearby parlor for, the ambassador said, a smoke. As we were ushered toward that room, I realized that the ushers were all station assets from the embassy. I knew then that something was coming down, something important.

We had all been wearing tuxedos, and all, I knew, looked very good in them—as good, I had to say, as we looked out of them. The ambassador and Kemp started taking theirs off as soon as we entered the small parlor. The political officer from the American embassy stood at the closed door to the corridor and motioned for me to disrobe too. I knew then that he was from the station as well.

Bacher and Kemp fucked me, standing, with me suspended between them, my knees hooked on Bacher's hips and Kemp's dick pressed shallowly inside me from the rear. This time, Bacher was urged to take the lead in the fucking, and he did so, with gusto, coming first and then withdrawing as Kemp bent me over the arm of an upholstered chair and finished with his ejaculation. Bacher was invited to take me again, and did so in the same position.

Only afterward, while we were toweling off with wet cloths and dry towels provided, did Bacher begin to "get" what had transpired and why. He'd never asked about the political officer at the door, watching the double fuck intensely. But when he was putting his tux back on and murmuring that it probably was well past the time we returned to the opera hall, Kemp gently placed a hand on his chest and said that Bacher's evening at the concert was over, that they had something to discuss.

Kemp motioned me to dress and leave, saying I would be driven home from there. He was taking charge, and now the assignations at the Indian doctor's apartment and the two glasses and bottle of vodka on the doctor's dining room table each time, and my leaving and the two men staying all came together. Kemp wasn't just a highly placed German-origin American businessman in Bangkok. He was one of us—and probably the senior agent here. This was his defection operation.

As I headed for the door, I looked back at Bacher, who looked sheepish and somewhat confused and lost even as Kemp was pointing out the cameras attached high on the walls of the room, their lenses pointed down to where the two men had stood and shared me.

I was surprised—but in later years wouldn't have been—to find that the chauffeur who drove me home from the opera hall was Bacher's own chauffeur, who obviously had been embedded on Bacher's staff and was part of the operation. He stopped in the familiar quiet cul-de-sac short of my apartment compound and pounded my ass hard in the backseat. He was thug and rough enough for me, and I continued to see him and writhe under him for the rest of my tour in Bangkok.

Weeks later, I read in the newspaper that Ambassador Bacher had defected to the British in Singapore—everything well away from Bangkok. His family had been sent to London ahead of him. All neat and tidy.

"Regardless," the station chief said to me, looking down at me over the rim of his glasses, as we "discussed"—with him not sharing all that much—this matter in his office later that morning, "I don't think it would be wise now for you to accept that invitation to the Chopin competitions in Warsaw this year. You should arrange for your vice president to go. She's a classical pianist and you play show tunes, so I think you should manage to rationalize the switch."

"Oh, also," he said, as I was leaving his office. "There's a Russian freighter captain in town whose ship, we think, is carrying Russian arms to Vietnam. He's a rough thug, but we know that he likes your type. Rodney will brief you and arrange the encounter."

"Yes, sir, I understand," I said, as I turned and left the office. Not a preferred double, but the "rough thug" aspect was intriguing.

"And he has a first mate he likes to include in the play," the station chief called after me. "We have an officer in place on board who might be included too."

Even better, I thought, as my smile broadened. I was beginning to get a handle on my job here.

Chain Gangbanged

I was only in for thirty days, and then not because of something I'd actually done. My buddy Phil had left drugs in my car, and the cops found them when they stopped me because I was driving a little too fast when I pulled away from a country beer hall they were staking out. I should have known better. I was only nineteen, and I shouldn't have been in that beer hall at all, let alone drinking. But I'd just finished my first year up north at Yale, and I was on the top of the world.

Thirty days in a county lockup had been my sentence. And not a lockup in a suburban county like the one I lived in but in a county back in the hills, where life is a lot rougher than where I came from.

I stopped going to the workout room because of the tough-acting guys hanging out there, but the inaction was making me so jumpy that I volunteered to go out on work details. This proved to be a big mistake.

On my seventh day, my first work detail came up. We were going out to a rural spot to clear brush from the side of a road running through a heavily forested and hilly area. It was with great dismay that when I jumped up into the back of the van, I saw both Bobby Joe and Maurice among those who were going out on the detail—two men I'd been avoiding by not going to the workout room. Maurice was a guard; Bobby Joe was a trustee who was "in" with Maurice.

It was a hot day and the work was hard. We had small saws and machetes and were clearing brush and saplings back some twenty yards from the road. There were six inmates and three guards. Maurice clearly was in charge and everyone there, including the two other guards, was afraid of him. Everyone, of course, except Bobby Joe, who was a special friend of Maurice's.

Bobby Joe was probably the best and fastest worker among us. It wasn't long until he was so heated up that he stripped off his shirt and undershirt and was swinging away, covered with sweat that matted the thick, black hair on his chest and arms into swirls and made his undulating muscles gleam in the sunlight. The other inmates quickly followed suit in stripping down to their waists--all except for me.

"Take off that shirt," Maurice called out to me in a booming voice. "Can't you see it's too hot to work in?"

I pretended that I hadn't heard him.

"Take off the shirt, I said," Maurice boomed again.

"I'm okay the way I am," I answered in the most pleasant voice I could muster. "But thanks, anyway."

Maurice stomped over to me, and all of the inmates stopped to watch us.

"I said for you to take off that shirt, son, and I meant what I said."

"Sure thing, sir," I said and I stripped my shirt and undershirt off. My eyes flicked over to Bobby Joe, and I could see a wide smile of appreciation on his face.

"And because you didn't do what I asked, you can go ahead and strip all your other clothes off too and work that way for a while."

I was dumbfounded. "But, sir, this is a public road."

"Good point," Maurice said with a big smile. "You can go on into the woods there a bit and clear brush over by the picnic area. We'll see that no one goes in there, but not much of a chance they will. Not many want to picnic next to where a chain gang is working."

I started to argue, but I could see that this would just get me into more trouble, so I started to move off toward the picnic area.

"No. You can strip here," Maurice said. "The clothes will still be here when you get back."

So, I stripped all the way down to my work boots and could see that this gave both Maurice and Bobby Joe a little thrill. I had stopped at the briefs, but Maurice had barked for me to strip those off too. So, with a shrug, I did. I was in very good shape and was better hung than the average.

"Okay, now go on over into the picnic area and start working," Maurice said. "You can't go there alone, and if a guard goes, that will leave too few guards here, so . . . Bobby Joe, you come on over there with us. The rest of you go back to what you're doing here."

"Oh, god," I thought, as I stumbled off into the brush, trailed by Maurice and Bobby Joe. The very worst situation I could think of.

Maurice and Bobby Joe watched me work for a while, and the first thing I knew they both had their dongs out of their pants and were working them. Bobby Joe had one of those championship dicks in length and Maurice's was regular sized but was extra thick, and his balls hung low out of his fly.

I tried to make a break for it then and run back to the road, where maybe I could get some help from the other guards. But Bobby Joe lashed out with a hand and caught me as I ran past him and slammed me up against a tree. The blow caused me to sink to my knees, my back to the tree, and Bobby Joe was standing up against me, his pelvis pushed into my face.

"Suck me," Bobby Joe commanded in a husky voice.

"Maurice," I called out plaintively, begging for help.

"Maurice ain't going to help you none, pretty college boy. Open those lips and suck my dick. And don't do nothin' funny while you're about it."

He grabbed my hair with one hand and his dick with the other and forced his tool into my mouth. I gagged as he filled my mouth cavity.

"Ain't done this before, have you, pretty boy? Well, you're going to get real good at it in days to come. Open wider and get your teeth out of the way and your tongue runnin' under my dick. There, that's good. Now let it slide in and out. There, yes, like that. Ahhh, such a sweet, soft mouth."

I felt tears coming to my eyes, and I was having trouble not gagging. His dick was getting bigger and harder as he slowly worked it back and forth in my mouth.

"Now, I'm going to pull out," Bobby Joe said, "and I want you to suck on the head like a lollipop and to work your tongue around it. Ahh, yes, I like that. You're going to be a good bitch."

His dick head was big and the piss hole was leaking precum. It tasted salty. The sweat of his groin was giving off a strong musky smell. These were entirely new sensations for me, and were not all that unpleasant. I admit that when I was being propositioned in high school, I let my imagination play with the possibilities, and I could feel my own tool coming to life under these new sensations. I also admit that being forced took much of the guilt away and was also turning me on.

"There, that's good," Bobby was saying after he'd pushed his dick back in and had pumped my mouth for a couple of more minutes. "Stand up."

I did so, and he pulled away from me a bit. I was trembling there, close to him. He held my head between his hands and came in for a kiss. I struggled with him, holding my lips together hard, straining to create a solid barrier to him. My arms went between us, and I tried to elbow him away from me. He brought his chest in hard against mine and lashed out with one of his hands, backhanding me hard across the mouth. Then he brutally kissed me again, this time working his tongue into my mouth and causing me to gag as his dick had already done. My jaw came unhinged and I just let him have his way.

The next thing I knew, Maurice was next to us and was digging my arms out and swinging them up and around the tree, where he used handcuffs swung over a branch above my head on the other side of the tree to suspend my arms over my head.

Bobby Joe continued his long kiss, as his hands flew over my naked torso and explored my balls and cock, which started to engorge at his touch.

"Whooie!" Bobby Joe exclaimed, as he broke away from my lips and started to wander down my body with his lips. "You're one fine bitch. Candy, candy. How sweet."

My lips now free, I started to yell, trying to get help from anywhere it might come. The ever-helpful and well-equipped Maurice whipped a dirty handkerchief and a roll of duct tape out of his pocket and had me quickly gagged.

All I could do was tear up in frustration and make muffled sounds of objection as Bobby Joe tongued and teethed my nipples and continued working his mouth down across my belly and taking possession of my dick, which responded to his attention, and my balls. In no time, he had his strong hands under my thighs and jackknifed my legs up and off the ground and swung my ass up to his waiting lips and tongue.

I was being penetrated and wetted with his tongue, which dug ever deeper, widening and lubricating my hole.

"Ah, a really tight ass," Bobby Joe was saying as he dropped my legs and stood and turned toward Maurice. "We got ourselves a virgin, Maurice. Young meat. Yum, yum. Can I have him? Can I get firsties on a fuck?"

"Yeah, fine," Maurice answered. "But then you gotta do me, Bobby Joe. I'm dying here. And you gotta go easy with the kid. You've got a real club. The damage can't show when we get back."

So this was how it was between the two of them.

"Thanks, Maurice. You got a condom and some lube? He's gotta be open a lot more if I'm goin' get up in there."

Maurice, the walking supply closet, produced a small tube of lubricant and a condom in a packet.

"Now, let's get him turned around and hangin' on a lower branch," Bobby Joe said.

The two of them manhandled me while Maurice released the handcuffs and got me turned facing the tree. Then he handcuffed my arms again around the tree on a somewhat lower branch than before. Bobby Joe pulled my legs away from the tree by the hips and his lips went to my asshole again. Maurice slipped up between my legs and hunched in front of me, with his back to the base of the tree. He proceeded to take my cock in his mouth and give me head, while Bobby Joe was lubricating my ass, first with his tongue again and then with his fingers, heavily laced with lubricant.

I grunted in pain as he worked first one finger, and eventually three, into my ass, probing ever deeper and opening me up.

"You gonna need to be opened real good," he grunted, as he worked. "Believe me, you'll thank me."

The pad of a finger found my prostate, and, under the spell of circular rubbings on that, I ejaculated down Maurice's throat.

Then both Bobby Joe and Maurice rose and stood near me, where I could clearly watch, as Maurice opened the condom packet and rolled a condom onto Bobby Joe's huge tool. The two of them hugged and kissed deeply and worked each other's tools until both were fully hard again. Then Maurice stood in front of me, his eyes glued on mine, his hands wrapped around his dick, as Bobby Joe got behind me, pulled my hips back again, positioned his dick head at the entrance of my asshole, and slowly worked the head in.

I was screaming in pain and shock behind my gag, and my eyes were tearing up again. Bobby Joe pushed in a couple of more inches and then his hands went to my butt cheeks, encasing them and squeezing them and pulling them apart, giving him a bigger opening. I lifted my hips as best I could and arched my back, trying myself to widen the opening, knowing that all was lost now and no fight was going to get me out of this..

At the same time, a little guilty thrill ran through me. All of that dick was going to be inside me. I was turning this dude on. I was being forced, raped, and none of this was my fault. I was both in control of being the object of his lust and being controlled by a hot stud. All of my "what if" fantasies were being brought to life, and no one could blame me for what was happening.

I gulped for breath, pulling as much air as I could through my nose. Maurice saw that I was in distress and said that he'd pull the gag out if I promised to be quiet. I nodded my head in assent, and he ripped the gag off. My mouth now free, I couldn't help but grunt and whimper at the four inches of dick pulsating inside me. Bobby Joe was going slow. When he sensed my canal opening to him, he pushed in another couple of inches.

Six inches in now, and he went into a slow pump, two inches out and then back in two inches. After a couple of minutes of this, though, he came in another inch when he pushed back in; seven inches up my ass now. I yelped when he did this, and his hands went to my pecs.

He stroked my nipples, and I began to tremble and sigh for him, not wanting to do so, but my anger at being violated was being overcome with a new sense of pleasure mixed with the pain. He took his dick in one hand and revolved it in my ass. My ass walls responded by widening to him, and he pushed in another inch. I flinched, but I was managing him now.

"That's so nice," he whispered as he brought his mouth to the side of my neck and nuzzled me there. "Don't you feel it? Don't you feel yourself opening to me?"

"Yes," I whimpered softly. "But please, please stop." But I grunted in vain, as he went in another inch; nine inches now. But of course I didn't know how far he was in me. All I knew is that I felt totally stuffed and stretched, and my ass walls began to tremble under the strain. I also didn't know how long that was in relation to what any normal person could take until he whispered it to me. "God, I'm almost all the way in, son. Do you know there aren't many that can take this much of me even after a long time of trying? You're one sweet bitch."

I was panting and giving little yelps and grunts with the progress of the last inch he had to give. He had his chest pushed into my back now, and I could feel the wet hairs of his pelt on my shoulder blades. He was giving off a sweaty, musky scent that I found heady.

When I felt his curly pubic hairs tickling my butt cheeks, I knew he was in all the way and assumed that this torture was close to the end. But the ordeal had just begun. He started to stroke me deep then, pulling the head of his cock back to where it rubbed across my prostate and then, slowly at first, and then ever quicker, stroking back into me to the hilt.

No more gentleness now, and Bobby Joe himself was no longer in control. Instinct took over, and he went into a primordial fuck, no longer being sensitive to how new I was to this. But by now, my body had adjusted to him, and the pain was tolerable. At length, I felt him tense and the bulb of the condom fill up, and he just more or less collapsed against me.

After Bobby Joe had fucked me up against a tree, he and Maurice went over to a picnic table, and I just watched as Maurice rolled another condom on Bobby Joe's rising cock and they slowly aroused each other to the point where Bobby Joe laid Maurice on his back on the picnic table and held his legs up and out from his body, as he pumped away inside the guard's ass.

Maurice laid there on the picnic table, his arms stretched out and his eyes hooded, swimming in Bobby Joe's semen, and holding my own eyes by the intensity of his gaze, his desire palpable. His thick cock bounced around on his flat belly, maintaining its erection.

When they were done, Maurice handed Bobby Joe a third condom, and this time Bobby Joe rolled it on Maurice's thick cock. Maurice waltzed back to me and before I had a chance to even figure out what was happening, he lifted my legs off the ground and crouched under me and plunged that big, thick sausage of a cock up into me. My ass walls complained at the new challenge to their capacities, but Maurice was quicker at jacking off than Bobby Joe had been and couldn't go nearly as deep. By this time, though, I was too worn out and defeated to struggle.

Bobby Joe and Maurice dressed and I was freed and we returned to the van and the inmate crew, which had worked its way several hundred yards up the road by now. I quickly and silently dressed and just laid there on the ground as the others finished up what they were doing.

Only Bobby Joe and Maurice could keep their eyes on me while the van jostled us back to the jail, searing pain jabbing my ass with every jolt in the road. There was no question, though, that the other inmates and guards knew what had happened to me. I still had three weeks to go on my sentence, however, so everyone, including me, knew that I was going to keep quiet about this.

The next day was a rest day, and I managed to stay in my cell and to rest my body as well as to try to avoid Bobby Joe and the rest of the inmates. The following day, I went out on work detail with an entirely different set of men, and I began to build hope that my sexual abusing had been a one-time event and that I'd manage to serve the rest of my time without incident.

But late that night, my hopes were dashed. I was sleeping in the lower bunk of my cell. That morning, the other inmate they'd had in my cell disappeared and he wasn't replaced. At the time, I'd thought that was a stroke of luck. I was skittish now about being locked up with anyone else. But, of course, luck had had nothing to do with me now being alone in my cell. Deep in the night, I was rudely awakened by two figures grabbing my wrists and spinning me around in my bed and handcuffing my hands to the middle of the inner side of the rails of the bunk above me.

Bobby Joe and Maurice were in the cell with me, and Maurice stood beside the closed door as Bobby Joe tore off my clothes and roughly lifted my legs out and above me, with my feet wedged in the springs of the upper bunk. He lifted my hips and plunged his dick inside me and pumped me for several minutes, swinging my body back and forth on his pulsing skewer. Then he stood, and Maurice was inside me, forcing that thick cock in where Bobby Joe had just been. Bobby Joe moved in behind Maurice and fucked him while Maurice was fucking me. After they were done, Bobby Joe kissed me on the mouth and offered to protect me if I'd be his bitch for the rest of the time I was there. I refused, saying I wouldn't willingly submit to anyone. And Bobby Joe just laughed and said to let him know when I'd changed my mind, while Maurice uncuffed me and let me collapse on my bed.

Two nights after that, I woke as the door to my cell opened. A hulking blond guy loomed in the doorway for a second and then came barreling into the room, as the door clanged shut. I rose off my bed, groggily stumbling into him as he reached me. I threw a punch that went wild, while he connected with my chin with one fist, followed by a blow to my midsection. I reeled around and he got me with an upper cut to the eye.

I dropped to the floor of the cell on my belly like a rock, and he was sitting on my back, pulling my shorts down. His arms went around my armpits and neck in a full nelson, and I screamed in pain and surprise as his engorged dick found my asshole and pushed into me. He pumped me there relentlessly, and I tried my best to relax and accommodate him. He pulled me up to my knees and got up on his feet, crouching behind me, and pushed deeper into me.

He was barebacking me, and I had the fleeting thought that I hoped he was clean, as I felt the new sensation of unsheathed cock inside me. He must have been uncut, because his skin seemed loose, and I'm ashamed to say that my ass walls were intrigued by this loose friction. He spun me around and pushed me on my back, and I tried to rise again. He backhanded me across the face and wishboned my legs and pushed in to the hilt of his dick again. His mouth and teeth went to my nipples, and I grabbed his shoulders and tried to push him off me, but he was too strong for me, and the beating he had given me had weakened me. I dug my fingernails into his shoulders and he grunted and caught me in the chin again with his fist.

I must have blacked out then, because when I woke, he was under me, the full length of my body running along his, his strong arms wrapped around my chest and his cock still buried in me from the rear. We were hit with a square of light, as the door opened, and another man entered. He was tall and thin and was pulling off his clothes as the door shut. His cock was thin, but it was unusually long, and it was pointed out from his body, hard and ready to go.

He gave me a big grin as he dropped to his knees, pushing my legs out so that his legs were between mine and those of the blond below me. He then lifted and wishboned my legs, and I watched in horror as he moved up toward us, his long thin cock pushing into me and on top of the blond's cock that was inside me. I was being double fucked. The blond underneath me came to life in pleasure, as he felt the cock sliding in alongside his, and the two of them began to play me like a calliope. The door opened again, and Bobby Joe and Maurice entered, closed it behind them, and watched as I was being double boned.

I passed out again.

The following night, one of the guards took a turn. He pulled me out of my sleep, stripped me down, and handcuffed me to the bars of the window, facing them. He pushed a gag into my mouth, which filled my mouth with a hard, rubber plug. He stripped down to where he was wearing only a studded leather harness, a studded leather cock sheath, and shiny black boots. He was completely hairless, all bullet head, muscle, and bulging cock and balls. He had a leather riding crop at the end of a billy club, and he used both ends on me, first flicking the leather whip across my shoulders, on my back and legs, and against my butt cheeks.

And then, when those were red and slightly welted, he invaded my ass with the billy end of the club. The club was replaced with his studded cock, which caused my ass passage walls to scream with dueling pain and pleasure as they were rubbed back and forth with his relentless pumping. The studs on his chest harness dragged back and forth on the welts on my back, heightening both my pain and the sensations inside me. He sank his teeth into my shoulders, neck, and back as he fucked me, and he pinched my nipples and raked my chest and belly with sharp fingernails.

When he was finished, spurting semen deep inside me in several thrusting fountains, he ripped off my gag and released my hands, and I just sank to the floor of the cell in sobs of pain as he slipped outside the door. I looked around, as he left, to see that, once again, Bobby Joe and Maurice had observed my ordeal.

For two days after that, I received no visitors. But I also was left alone in my cell, with my meals deliver in a slot at the bottom of the door.

Then on the next night, the door opened, and the biggest and fattest of the guards was standing in the opening. I shrank back into the corner of my bed. The guard moved aside and Bobby Joe entered the room. The door clanged shut behind him. He came over and sat down on the bed beside me.

We just sat there for several moments, staring at each other. And then he spoke. "There's no need for you to have to go through all this, you know. All you have to do is to say that you'll be my bitch and the others will leave you alone."

I just sat there rocking back and forth, not knowing what to say.

35

"I'm here to fuck you either way," Bobby Joe said with a slow smile. "I can do it brutally, or we can become lovers for the rest of the time you're here, and I can make the others leave you alone. Even Maurice."

I mulled that one over, my arms embracing my chest tightly.

"Ten inches. I'm going to give you ten inches again. You came to like it last time. I could tell. It can be even better than that, or you can keep fighting me, and be visited by friends of mine every night. Which is it to be?"

I let my arms fall beside me in defeat, but I didn't look up.

"Here, give us a kiss," he said gently, and he lifted my chin with his hand.

He brought his mouth to mine and gave me a kiss. I didn't respond.

"You can do better than that," he said. "I know you can. Should I call Chad in? You know, the one who used you as a punching bag before double fucking you."

This time when he approached me, I opened my mouth to him in resignation, and we entered into a long, tonguing kiss.

"There. That's better," he said. "Here, stand up."

I rose from the bed and he undressed me and then guided me in undressing him and we stood there, belly to belly, his hands exploring my body and, at his urging, my hands exploring him as well. His cock was already fully engorged and mine was coming to life as well. His mouth went down to my nipples and I arched my back away from him, while he played there with his lips and teeth. He pulled me back up so that we were chest to chest. He wasn't sweaty now, and his curly chest hair tingled on my smooth skin. His hands went to my butt cheeks, and then a finger of each of his hands entered my asshole and opened me.

We rocked back and forth in a close embrace, me panting, as he fingered deeper into me. I melted to him as he found my prostate and brought my cock to life. I was sighing and groaning as he laid me on the bed and then stretched his body along mine, head to toe.

"Follow my lead," he said. "Do what I'm doing." Then he took my cock in his mouth and sucked me off. I did the same to him. But I came after several minutes and he was able to hold off. He turned me on my back with him above me, still head to toe, and he then reached down and brought a condom packet and a tube of lube from his pants pocket. He went up on his knees above me. His dong was brushing against my face.

"Here," he said, as he handed me the condom. "Sheath me with this and then find something else other than my cock to play with while I'm busy down here."

I got the packet open and was rolling the condom on his cock while he rotated my hips until he could get his lips on my asshole, which he gave considerable attention to it with a wet, long tongue. Meanwhile, I sucked on his heavy balls. I lurched as the cold lubricant was spread around on my asshole, but it quickly warmed as he worked it into me with his fingers.

Then he turned me back around so that my back was nuzzled into his front along the bed. I felt his cock running up the small of my back and felt a guilty pleasure at the thought of all that length inside me. I was laying on my right side, and he lifted my left leg above us and slowly but relentless side split me with that battering ram of his and ran his cock up inside me, reaching for the very core of me.

I didn't fight him but matched my rhythm to his, and the pleasure of this fuck far overshadowed the pain. He turned my head, and we kissed, this time with a far more enthusiastic response from me than I had managed before. He ran his fingers on the hand of the arm that was wrapped around me around a nipple and slowly pumped me off to a second ejaculation with his other hand encasing my cock.

"Ah, that's my sweet little bitch," he murmured in my ear after we had ended our kiss. "How much longer are you going to be in here?"

"Two weeks," I whispered back.

"Sweet," he said. "By the time you leave here, you are going to be begging for this cock."

I didn't believe him yet that night. But by the time my sentence was up, he proved to be right. I was hooked—even when it turned out he'd lied about keeping Maurice away from me. By the time I was released, I was taking them both at one time.

Club Doblar

I was panting and straining and Grady was whispering to me, "Stay with it; you can take it. You are taking it. Doesn't that make you want to shoot higher than ever before?"

He was crouched between my spread legs, holding one up and away from our bodies, my other leg running up his torso, the ankle hooked on his shoulder. His forehead was plastered to mine, his eyes looking intensely into mine. His dick was inside me, to the hilt, not plowing. Pulsing, throbbing. The head of the dildo in his free hand was pressing into the entrance of my hole, above his buried cock. The head of the dildo had breached my ring. It was inside me.

I strained and whimpered. "Please, Grady. It's too . . .Oh, shit, Oh, fuck!" With a jerk, I arched my back and gave a little cry. He dropped my leg and wrapped his arm around my neck, holding me close to him, as I felt the shaft of the dildo moving deeper inside me.

"Shush," he whispered in my ear, "You'll be fine. You're doing fine. The head's in; the shafts not as thick. You're doing just fine."

"Please, Grady. Take it out. Oh, shit!"

He had withdrawn it a bit but then pushed it in again, farther in. His own dick, hard and pulsating, held steady inside me. Out and then further in. Out and . . . He laughed a low, guttural laugh.

"You love it."

Withdrawing to just inside the rim, rotating the bulb of the dildo. Panting, panting, begging him with my eyes, pleading with him. Wanting his cock, just his cock fucking me. Not both. "Holy crap!" I howled as the dildo plunged back into me, deep. Again the laugh and the repeated, "You love it, I know you do. I can tell you've never had this done before, that you love it. Opens you right up for all sorts of fun shit. Drive a truck in there when we're done."

Short pumping it. I'm moaning. Feel myself getting harder. I can't deny it, it was just so, so arousing. Feel like I'm going to spout. Bringing it back so close to the prostate. If he hits that, I'm gonna blow.

He wasn't going to stop. I did what I could to relax. And it seemed to help. But he pressed it in farther, almost as deep as his own cock.

"Please, Grady."

"Shush, Jeff, you're doing fine. More than fine. You told me you'd do anything for me for a fuck, didn't you?"

"Yes, but . . ." I had told him I'd do anything to be lying under him. Ever since college I'd wanted him—even more so when I found out he fucked guys. But he'd never fucked me before. Others had. He knew they had. But never him in college. Told me I was special; that he'd been saving me.

Afterward, when he was starting up a line of men's wear and selling it successfully, he'd come to me. For a model he'd said. Hired me to his permanent staff. And then he was willing to fuck me. But not until I pledged to let him do whatever he wanted with me.

This was what he was doing to me. Stretching me. Not just with his own huge cock, but also with a dildo at the same time.

He was working the dildo more rapidly now, in and twist, out. The long plunge, with me moaning and groaning and writhing under him, trapped in his strong arms. Emotionally trapped in wanting him, wanting him inside me, fucking me.

"Oh, god, Grady. Pleeazzzz!"

"Not till you come for me, Jeff. You come first and then I'll give you the real fucking cock. My cock. But you want to be able to take two men. I know you do. You took men on a string in college."

Yes, I thought, but not at once, not two in the hole at the same time.

"Come for me, Jeff. Show me you want it."

I was so close to coming anyway that I didn't really need any encouragement or see anything useful in pleading that I wanted his cock working in me more than this. My mouth flew open and I jerked and came with a long sigh.

"There, that was nice. I liked that. You liked that too despite what you were saying. Now the real thing"

I moaned as the dildo was drawn out of me—most of the way. But then he plunged it in again and I was fairly lifted off the surface of the bed in surprise and shock. He laughed and pulled it all the way out. Then he grabbed my hips in his strong hands, lifted my pelvis off the surface of the bed toward his, and fucked me hard and fast and completely with his own monster cock, not coming until I'd done so for a second time, exhausted but exhilarated and completely satisfied.

Without withdrawing, he covered me close with his heavily muscled torso and kissed my neck and my eyelids and then my mouth. A deep kiss. I felt him starting to go flaccid inside me, but not withdrawing, still reaching deep into me. I crossed my ankles on the small of his back, holding him close to me, wanting the afterglow of him going soft inside me.

"You can do it. You *did* do it," he murmured. "You will do it for me again."

Oh, shit, not again—now? Does he want me gaping permanently? I didn't ask him what he meant by what he said. In retrospect, I probably should have.

But I was occupied with other sensations. He wasn't completely flaccid and he was getting harder. He was kissing all over my face again, and down into the hollow of my neck. His lips and then his teeth were on my nipples, one after the other. He was hardening inside me. Young, virile, athletic. A short recuperation time. Very short. Nothing short about the cock, though. His lips devouring mine again, hunger in his kiss. Hunger in his reengorging cock.

41

I massaged his butt cheeks with the heels of my feet and clutched at his shoulder blades with my hands, trying to pull him as close to me as possible. "Yes, yes," I murmured. Too low for him to hear, though, I thought.

"I'm going to fuck you again," he whispered in my ear.

"Obviously," I murmured back. "Be good to me, Grady."

"You know it."

Lost in the fuck, slow, easy, a long glide and retraction this time. "Oh, shit. Oh, fuck!"

"You are mine," he murmured. "You'll do anything for me."

"Oh fuck. Yessss!"

* * * *

"Dress nice—take something from the Hamptons' line—and clean yourself out good. I'll pick you up at your apartment at eight."

I gave Grady a quizzical look.

"We've signed an important deal we need to seal," he said, sounding a bit exasperated, as if I shouldn't have felt the need to ask—even though I hadn't asked. "You're part of the deal signing. You're going to be fucked."

"Fucked?" I asked. Simply that. I didn't really say no or anything.

He flared up a bit. "You said you'd do anything if I cocked you regularly. Anything includes doing it with anyone else I say you do it with. Understand?"

"Yes, Grady. I didn't object. You were just a bit short on information."

"Eight in front of your apartment."

He picked me up in a chauffeur-driven limo. Business had gotten a lot better for him. It wasn't a stretch limo, but he was young and ambitious—intense and ambitious. There was time for that.

He also was a real hunk. I was lost to him. If he'd laid me in the backseat of the limo as we crossed LA and he'd told the limo driver he could watch and then have seconds, I wouldn't have let out a peep. But that didn't happen.

We rolled into a derelict part of Watts, much of which was still showing signs of having been burnt out in race riots. I was nervous, but Grady didn't seem to be, so I tried to show I wasn't. The block the limo stopped at the curb in was deserted and lined with litter. The vehicle had come to a stop in front of a one-story, windowless building hunkered between a sleazy-looking liquor store and a parking lot. The only hint of activity was a blinking sign over the door of a half basement walk down that read "Club Doblar" in green neon lights, with the light out on the "B."

With the light out, I read the name as "Dolar" on my way in and it had me thinking of money. It was only on the way out that I reread the sign and thought, "oh, yeah."

"This is it," Grady said. "Get out of the limo." For a minute I thought he meant to leave me here alone, but he climbed out of the car behind me.

The light inside the room—some sort of meet and greet room—we entered from the door to the street was dim, the furnishings something out of a 1950s burlesque house—the clientele sitting or standing around and looking at each other was a mixed bag of young and middle-aged; hulky, pudgy, and skinny; and white, black, Oriental, and Hispanic. What they all were, however, was that they all were very, very male. Some standing in pairs and whispering to each other. Others, younger guys, moving around the room, trying to look wanted. And they all were cruising with their eyes. I felt all eyes on Grady and me as we were led from the room into a club room and guided to a table near a small stage with a curtain in back of it. The table faced the stage but on the other sides it was surrounded by six-foot-high screens. All of the other tables running up a couple of tiers toward the back of the room on either side of the area were similarly screened from the sides and backs. Near total privacy from the rest of the room.

There already were two men sitting at the table, across from each other, with empty chairs between them. The waiter pulled one of the chairs between the men out from the table, the chair directly facing the stage, and motioned for me to sit, which

I did. Grady took the chair across from me, his back to the stage. The two men on either side of me were sitting very close to me.

He greeted the two men, letting me know that he knew them—that these were the men he was signing the deal with. That one—or maybe both of them—was going to fuck me as part of the deal signing. I took a look at them, in turn, trying not to be too obvious with my curiosity. But as both were grinning at me when I turned my face to them, this seemed not to be an issue.

"These are the Smith brothers, Jeff," Grade said. "Bill and John." He'd already told me that he wouldn't be using their real names, so I didn't snigger. They certainly didn't look like brothers. They were both older—at least older from the perspective of mid-twenties guys like Grady and me. Pushing forty-five, shall we say. And not at all looking like brothers. One was thin and rather bookish looking. Expensive clothes that were tailored for him. Not bad looking in the face. The other was puggish and thuggish, reminding me of a bulldog. Bullet head and practically no neck. I presumed guy number one was probably noticeably taller than guy number two. The bulldog was expensively dressed too, though, his clothes also obviously tailored to fit.

It made sense. Grady had told me that they were opening up a string of expensive men's boutiques in Midwestern upscale shopping malls. Consigning our clothing lines to them would double our business, and there promised to be a further expansion of our business with them if the initial deal worked out. Grady had told me that it was very, very important that I impress them.

We only had a few minutes for chit chat until the lights went down even lower than they had been in the hall before—except for the spots on the curtain—and then the curtain drew back and I gasped in shock and surprise—and rising understanding.

A young white guy was lying on a chaise lounge on the stage—completely naked. And as my eyes focused, I saw that there was a naked black guy under him, working his ass with a black cock, and another naked black guy saddled up over his spread legs, and the audience was getting a clear shot—to the accompaniment of bump and grind music, of a dance of double penetration by the black guys in the white guy's ass.

This was that kind of club. I should have thought something about it. The men in the first room we entered did seem to be in pairs and were ogling single men and whispering to each other. And here, in this room, as we were escorted down the tiers to our table, I should have noticed that the men all were in threes—and some sitting nearly—perhaps directly—on top of each other.

I felt the hands on my knees on either side of me, and the hand of the thinner guy, Bill, cupping my chin and turning my face toward his for a long kiss. The hand of the other one was unbuckling my belt, unzipping my pants. Grady must have gone under the table to flip my loafers off and to tug the trousers off my legs.

I was nearly naked, my trousers and briefs off, my jacket gone, my shirt unbuttoned and flared open, my tie still around my neck, but being used as a leash to move me as they wanted rather than for anything else. The two of them remained dressed in their suits, only their flies flared open to release their hard cocks. I wondered for days if their expensive clothes had been ruined, knowing, though, that Grady would just clothe them again in suits from our expensive line, if that's what they wanted.

Surprisingly, it was the thuggish one who was built smallish—but not too smallish to be able to hold it inside me as he sat under me, having raised me and settled me in his lap on my own chair so that I still could watch the double fucking going on on the stage—which I'll admit did help with my arousal and hardening and enjoyment of the fuck. He had his thick arms laced under mine and was stretching my arms over my head, making them useless for any sort of defense unless I really struggled. Not that there was any defense to be mounted. I was to give them anything they wanted. Grady had made my role quite clear—if I wanted to continue being cocked by him. And that's what I wanted. More than anything else. More than trying to have two cocks inside me for a brief time.

He just hadn't bothered to tell me that it would be two cocks at once. He hadn't told me he had been preparing me to double. He had just said as he continued with the cock and dildo routine that he liked me loose—loose enough to drive a truck in he'd kept saying.

All three of us were breathing heavily, but it was me doing all of the panting and most of the moaning.

The thinnish guy, John, who was the long and thick one, was doing most of the work and a lot of the grunting and groaning. He was the one crouched between my legs. He was the one stroking me deep and hard with his cock—sliding his cock over Bill's, the two of them sighing and groaning in unison, making love to each other—probably long-time lovers—while they made sex inside me. It was John who teased my nipples with his fingers and his lips and teeth as he fucked me. It was John who grasped my cock and worked it until I had ejaculated up the belly of his expensive silk shirt.

When John dipped his face to my chest, it was Grady's face I had to look past to see the double fucking performance on the stage. I didn't think they were doing any better at it on stage than these three men were doing to me—but then I was so much more intimately involved with what John and Bill . . . and Grady were doing.

Grady was hunched over the table, his hands grasping and holding my legs up and out over the table as John worked between my spread thighs. Grady's eyes were boring into mine, and he was whispering to me throughout the whole servicing of the two men, assuring me that I was doing great and that I loved every stroke of it—telling me not to screw this up.

John and Bill came almost together and collapsed into a deep shared kiss over my shoulder. Long-experienced lovers. Needing this to bring out the most in a fuck.

They hadn't moved, still inside me—they'd lasted longer than the guys on the stage had—when Bill murmured, "That was very nice. Can we take him to our hotel for the night?"

"Of course," I heard Grady answer from the other side of the table as he let my legs down, one after the other. My socked feet found the floor, but I had to maintain a wide stance as both men were still inside me. Grady's voice had a twinge of relief to it, as if he hadn't been sure that the deal would go through and now was.

I tried to think about that rather than about what I'd just done for him—or how quickly he had told them that they could take me away and do it again.

"And when you come out to St. Louis for the meetings next month, you'll bring him with you?" This asked by John, who, I was somewhat concerned to realize, was still hard inside me. Or maybe hardening again?

There was applause from the stage as the next set of three came out and started their routine standing up, with, this time, a little Thai guy between two Hispanic bruisers. Would the Smith brothers want an encore here as well? If they did, I had no doubt it would happen.

"No problem," Grady said. "Would you like me to send him out a couple of days in advance."

"That would be great," the "Smith brothers" said almost in unison.

"Do you want to double him again right now?"

The two looked at each other. No, John wasn't hardening. It had been an illusion. They both were flaccid now.

"No, thank you," Bill answered, somewhat regrettably, I thought. "I think we'd be more comfortable in the hotel room."

"Whatever you want."

Whatever they wanted. I couldn't say he hadn't warned me. But it was just for the night—this time. Tomorrow, it would just be Grady fucking me. And grateful for what I'd done for him. Surely he'd be grateful. I couldn't wait for Grady to be inside me again.

Congo Drums

The riverboat hit a log, or something, on the hull right at my head, and I woke with a start. The first sensation in the soft, wavering light of a single lantern hung by the doorway was the sound of drums and low chanting from somewhere above. The driver and cook at it again. The sound was monotonous and comforting all at the same time. It also seemed to be richer than before, almost stereophonic, and the second sensation to reach my senses was the dull thumping against the cabin wall above my head, which was what was providing the stereophonic effect of the drums. The Millers were copulating again to the rhythm of the drums. Who would have known the old man had it in him to fuck so often and so long?

Heavy breathing, inside the cabin, reached me on a third level of sensation. I rolled over. Ethan was slouched, naked, in the chair, legs spread, a shock of salt-and-pepper hair hanging down over one eye, the other eye boring into me. He was slowly masturbating himself—also to the rhythm of the drums. He had a trim and scarred, but hard, body, well built even though he was pushing fifty. He'd had an active life and it showed.

A chill went down my spine. This was Africa. Raw, primeval, and sensual. Instantly feeling the mood and the need of the drums, I turned toward Ethan; stretched my body out, unwinding every bunched muscle like a jungle cat waking from a nap; arched my back; and moved my hand down to my own hardening cock. I lay there on the lower bunk and Ethan slouched in his chair, each of us silently and intently staring at the other, both working our cocks up, panting. Knowing we were going to fuck. Already fucking each other even though we weren't touching. The drums picked up their beat, as did the thumping on the wall above the bunk. In a separate dimension, the cry of a native woman from the deck overhead cut through the rhythmic sounds followed by the growl, in his distinctive South Afrikaaner dialect, of the guide, Bull. "Spread 'em wider, you native doxy, and stop your yowling. Stop acting like you've never been fucked before."

Bull had broken the spell in the cabin.

"Come. And bring a condom," Ethan commanded in a hoarse whisper. I knelt between his spread thighs and opened my mouth over the bulb of his cock, being rewarded with a long sigh and the feel of his long, sensuous fingers gliding through my hair, holding my head into his crotch.

Ethan enjoyed the exotic, picked up from his extensive world travels. He fucked me without leaving his slouched position in the chair, my body swanned out from his torso and over his thighs, my feet hooked on his shoulders, him grasping my wrists and, bowing my arms back, my torso arched out over his thighs. With his cock throbbing and making slow and shallow strokes deep inside me, he maintained the rhythm of the drums, slowing in the wake of the sharp cry of release by the native woman overhead and the sudden ceasing, with a jolt, of the cabin wall thumping. With a tightening of Ethan's body, a jerk, and the sound of a gasp and a sigh, I felt him fill the bulb of the condom, and he slowly lowered my chest on his thighs without extracting his cock from my channel. We both held there, panting heavily. I knew he'd fuck me again once he had regained his breath and the hardness of his cock.

That's why we went together so well. He could fuck forever and I wanted it that way. Had we brought enough condoms on this journey?

Stretched out on the bunk, me on my back on top of him, his cock inside me, Ethan slowly masturbated me to my own ejaculation and nibbled on my ear, whispering endearments to me. Then we both slept, sensitive to whatever scant breeze invaded the cracks in the hull of the Congo river steamer to cool the sweat on our bodies.

I woke up in the darkest of the night to silence other than Ethan's heavy breathing and his hissing through chattering teeth. The lantern had sputtered out, the boat was gently rocking from side to side, and, although there were sounds of low muttering in a foreign—to me—tongue coming from overhead, the drums and chanting had stopped.

Ethan and I were both bathed in sweat—his—as were the sheets. He was mumbling and shaking. I felt his forehead, which was burning even though his teeth were chattering. I scrambled out of the bunk and pulled the blanket down from the bunk above, which was supposed to be mine but which Ethan hadn't allowed me to occupy in the six days of our river journey. It had been nearly a year of absence since we'd met up on this safari, and he insisted on going to sleep with his cock inside me every night. This was fine with me.

I bundled him up in the blanket and, not knowing what else to do, went looking for Bull, even though I felt intimidated by the man.

Bull, bulky, but not fat, all muscle and power, seemingly took up all of the space in the cabin as he squatted and peered at Ethan's trembling body.

"Yep, malaria. For sure. Where's he been?"

"Everywhere," I answered. "He does TV documentaries from the ends of the earth. He's been doing a film on lingering insurgency in Angola."

"Yep. Probably got it there. Could have got it here too, but it wouldn't show up this bad in six days if he got it here. We'll have to have him sent back to Kinshasa when we reach Lokutu Mombongo later this morning."

Bull was giving me an appraising look as he said that. I only then realized that I was naked.

* * * *

"The question, I suppose, is whether we press on or call this off for now." Although this was on everyone's mind, it was Sondra Miller who asked it. Of all the people here, she was the one most out of place—and well aware of that. A statuesque blonde who looked every lovely inch the runway model that she was, she would look good in any setting—but a lot better in most every one other than the upper Congo, where we now were. Her voice sounded just slightly bored when she'd said it, but everyone was aware of the hope behind her words.

"Of course not. We've come this far," her husband, Charles, answered, an edge to his voice. "Ethan said he already had enough notes to begin the documentary as long as I was still in. Jim here can take notes for the rest of the journey. What say you, Sean?" he asked turning to me. "You are the editor on this and have talked with Ethan on his vision. Can we do the rest of the research without him? We'll have to come back to do more filming when the script is together anyway."

"Probably so," I answered, not looking at Sondra directly to see if she'd mar her pretty face with a scowl but looking, rather, at Charles's young, black secretary, Jim Jackson, to see how closely he was watching Sondra. Very closely. A pity, I thought. With Ethan gone, Jim Jackson was looking very good to me. And I needed almost constant attention.

I wondered why Sondra had come on the safari at all. Probably didn't want to let Charles Miller's money out of her sight for very long. He was a good thirty years older than she was and definitely of the florid-faced, slightly pudgy aspect. He was the money behind this documentary film and Ethan had told me to treat the man right. Thus far I hadn't had many dealings with him, but he seemed the all right sort. He certainly didn't flaunt his wealth—not like his wife did. She was wearing diamonds even though we were sitting on the banks of the Congo at Lokutu Mombongo in a primitive tent camp. The guide had said that it was best to camp in tents in the open under mosquito-repellent lamps whenever we could, as the boat cabins would be harder to protect against the mosquito.

If Ethan was any evidence of this, Bull was right.

Ethan had been bundled off in a floatplane by noon and the others had gone on to their daily excursion to the Lokutu Oil Palm plantation. Sondra had shown more interest in this outing than in the ones of previous days, probably because the plantation owner was a Frenchman with a roving eye, a good physique, and randy banter. Sondra very much gave the impression that she needed to be bedded constantly. I didn't fault her; it was my sin as well.

"The safari is already paid for," Bull interjected. "We can take you back now, but there won't be a refund."

"We won't be going back," Charles Miller decreed. "I've already sunk too much money into this documentary to abandon it now."

"Good," Bull said, the palm of his hand going to the buttocks of the young Congolese woman laying the place settings at the camp table. "We leave on the boat at daybreak tomorrow. We'll reach where the Congo is at its widest, where you will see a vast field of hyacinths on the water and visit the Bafoto pygmies."

"Ethan told me about the hyacinths," Charles said, turning to his secretary, Jim. "Be sure and have your video camera for those, Jim. Ethan will want coverage of them. You'll have to do the photography now, if Sean doesn't want to do it."

Miller had turned to me. "Sorry," I answered. "I'm terrible at it. Ethan asked me to begin on the script."

"I suggest an early night," Bull said, as he stood up and put a hand on the small of the Congolese woman's back.

I chose to take in the twilight and sunset over the Congo River before turning into my solitary tent—the first time I would be sleeping alone on this trip. Ethan and I had met in Bangkok when we both were covering a coup there, me for the Associated Press as a journalist and editor and he as director of a documentary. We each retreated into a bar on Soi Cowboy off Sukhumvit, near the international enclave, to escape the teargas of a spontaneous clash between the police and university students. It proved to be a gay bar, and after several drinks, Ethan fucked me in a small room beyond the beaded curtain at the back of the bar. After the teargas cleared, he took me back to his hotel room and fucked me repeatedly there. He was nearly fifteen years older than I was, but I liked older men, and he was hard bodied and fully capable. We had met sporadically, as on this safari, and worked together and fucked periodically over the past seven years. If anything, he got better at it with age.

Now he had deserted me near the end of the earth, up the Congo. The sex the last seven days had been as good, if not better, than it ever had been, and we were reaching a shared rhythm that raised possibilities of a more permanent living arrangement. But now he had malaria and was probably in a hospital in Kinshasa awaiting medical evacuation back to the States. I wasn't even sure how to contact him in the States. Charles would know, though. I'd have to ask him.

It was dark enough that night was stealing into the clearing between the tents and the central fire was dying down to embers. The driver and the cook were starting up the drums. The cook was an old man, but the driver was young and heavily muscled and quite handsome. He also moved with an assurance and with sensual grace. I had stolen glances at him with possibilities in mind during the first six days, even when I was being possessed fully by Ethan. I wondered if he . . .

I found my hand wandering down to my crotch, not even thinking if I was safe from observation. The clearing seemed deserted other than the low sound of the drums and of the soft chanting by the two Congolese men. As the darkness drifted in, though, the glow of the lights in the tents almost made their walls transparent, and the shadows from inside them caught my attention.

Bull's idea of turning in early was fucking the young Congolese woman in his tent. I could clearly see their silhouettes against the tent walls. A lantern was burning inside. He was standing up and taking her, with her bent over in front of him. I watched for nearly an hour as he turned her and she just flopped back, her arms dangling down to the floor and her head thrown back, while he clutched her buttocks and fucked on. I wondered if she was still conscious. And more than that, I wondered what it would be like to be in her place. There was similar activity in the Miller's tent, where the copulating couple was more reclined and he was stretched on top of her, his buttocks rising and falling, again to the rhythm of the drums.

I almost resented the others getting what I wasn't getting—and now wouldn't get until the safari was over.

Charles Miller walked into the light of the clearing from the direction of the boat. He had a bottle of scotch under his arm and was holding two glasses with his fingers. As I watched him approach, flabbergasted and letting my eyes dart to his tent and what was obviously happening therein, I couldn't help but gasp my surprise that it wasn't him in the tent. The woman there most certainly was Sondra. He calmly sat down beside me where we could both watch his tent and said, "Share a scotch with me and enjoy the show together? Sondra gives a good fuck. Better for others than for me, truth be known."

While we were both on our second glass, with the fucking still going on in both tents, he turned to me, laid a hand on my thigh, and said, "I'll give you fifty dollars if you'll let me suck your cock. Ethan said you'd be good to me if I asked."

I didn't need the fifty dollars, but after the silhouette shows I'd been watching, I certainly needed the attention to my cock.

So that was what Ethan meant about treating the angel for his documentary well. I unzipped my shorts and he crouched between my spread thighs, fished my cock out, grasped it at the root, and closed his mouth over it. He gave expert head and welcomed the facial I gave him. I wasn't quite as melancholy at Ethan's absence anymore.

All melancholy was dissipated in the night when I felt a body stretch on top of mine as I lay on my belly on my cot in the tent I shared with no one. In the dimness of the glow of the pulsating mosquito repellent lanterns I could tell that the heavily muscled arms lying on either side of mine were black as ebony. Outside the tent, a drum beat softly started—and a low chant— but it was the sound of only one drummer, one chanter.

A whispered question in my ear, the accent more French than English, but very polite under the circumstances. "Please, may I. Will you receive me? I was told you would want me. I fuck good. You been watchin' me from beginning. I seen you . . . have wanted to fuck you."

"Yes," I whispered back, aching for the sex that was being denied me in Ethan's absence and thrilled at the feel of the size and insistence of this man's phallus at the small of my back. I turned my face to his and opened my mouth to him, and he pulled my tongue into his mouth and sucked on it as he moved his lithe, hard body on mine, showing me what French kissing was all about.

"Oh, shit. Fuck me," I whimpered when coming up momentarily for air, as, by instinct, I raised my buttocks to him and opened my legs, permitting his cock to move into the crack. He rubbed the upper side of the hard phallus on my hole, again and again, dry fucking me already as I gasped and writhed under him. He grasped my wrists and held my arms above my head. I recognized the signaling that he would fully possess me, and as we came out of the kiss, I took a deep breath and murmured, "Yes, yes, fuck me hard."

He laughed, a low guttural laugh, and, murmured, "It is good with you? You want me fuck you, yes?"

"Yes, yes, I want you to fuck me good," I answered with a gasp. "Don't ask for anything; just do it. All of it."

The weight of his body came off me and he was licking and kissing down my back. But that wasn't what had my attention. He already had a moistened finger exploring my asshole. He was on his knees between my spread thighs, and as I lifted my buttocks higher in the air, his mouth went to my ass, a hand grasped my cock through my thighs, and he was stroking it.

"Please, please," I groaned. "Fuck me. Don't make me wait." I was clutching hard at the thin foam mattress and rubbing my cheek against the rough cotton sheet.

I groaned when his lips left my hole to be replaced by a thumb, and his mouth swallowed my cock. I moaned and writhed under him, until he immobilized me more by moving a knee up next to my waist, holding my chest down with a fist between my shoulder blades and began roughly working my hole with three and four fingers.

"Please, please," I whimpered.

And then he was straddling my hips, crouched over my pelvis, and feeding his cock inside me. When he was deep inside, he encircled my chest with his arms and brought me up on my knees in front of him, closely plastered against his chest. One strong, muscled arm extended up my chest and he held my head close into his shoulder with a grasp on my chin. He was stroking my cock with the other hand. Then he began to plow up into me in earnest in long, strong jabs, making little grunting noises, while I egged him on with continuous babbling that he probably didn't understand a word of. He was longer and thicker than Ethan was, and more vigorous in his stroking and longer lasting. I came long before he did, and then again when he flipped me over, wishboned my legs, and took me from the front, with me glorying in palming his hard, glistening, ebony-black chest and thrumming his quarter-sized aureoles with the pricks of blue tattooing circling them.

When Bull came to rouse me near dawn, I was flat on my belly on the cot, my arms hanging down, with my knuckles dragging on the earth of Africa, and burbling my appreciation for the night.

Bull gave me a quizzical look, and I was trying to think of something to tell him to explain how exhausted and fully satiated I was, when he obviated that. "Was it OK with you?" he asked tentatively. "When we were putting Ethan Woodsmall on the plane, he was begging me to arrange for someone to take care of you. The driver has been—"

"Yes, that's fine. It was more than fine," I answered.

"Do you want him again? I can always cut it—"

"Yes, he's fine. Send him every night."

"Also, If you're interested, one of the boat men. The young one who wears the orange and red dhoti—"

"Yes," I murmured. "I know who you mean. Yes, him too."

"Separately or together?"

"Whatever."

I was hoping he was going to mention himself. But he didn't. He just smiled and whistled. Then with a, "Breakfast in ten, and then it's steaming on to Lisala," he was gone from the tent.

Groaning, I struggled out of my cot, my mind going to the young Congolese boat man who wore the orange and red dhoti, the scarf-like long skirt, leaving the chest bare, that men of his ethnic origin wore—tall and rangy, not a black man, but an ethnic Indian. But I'd gotten a peek at his cock. Very, very long. Long and thin, like a snake.

I found how very long later that morning as we steamed up the Congo en route to the town of Lisala, where we were to have our afternoon outing and camp for the night and which the Congolese safari staff twittered excitedly about as the highlight of our trip. Such morning boat trips had become somewhat of a monotonous glide up the river, staring desultorily off into the jungle in continual search for a view of exotic plants and animals that we had seen hundreds of times before on lower stretches of the river.

The chief boat man was standing at the wheel, with one of his subordinates kneeling at the bow and watching the water for possible dangers to the boat's hull floating in the approaching stream. I didn't know where the other boatman was at the moment, the tall Indian with the orange and red dhoti. When we'd first boarded that morning, he'd been there near me, helping me aboard and then touching me and smiling, paying particular attention to me. And then as we were settling on the benches and the boat was pulling back into the midstream, coming back close to me, leaning down and whispering, "The guide, he said—"

"Yes, that will be fine. I wish it," I broke in, not wanting him to complete whatever he was going to say. It was a weakness of mine, wanting men's cocks—and as many and in as much variety as I could get them. I had gone exclusively with Ethan for the first seven days. After being plowed by the driver the previous night, I realized that if Ethan hadn't been taken away, I might by now be feeling the frustration of just his cock. It wasn't what I was used to, and, upon reflection, I realized I had been eyeing not just the driver, but the Indian boat man and Bull, and even the secretary, Jim Jackson, for days before Ethan left us. They probably noticed that I had. I'm sure the driver and the Indian wouldn't have been as forward with their intentions if I hadn't been unconsciously signaling them.

"It is very long," he whispered. "Some men don't—"

"I've seen it. I want it."

The Indian smiled, touched me on the hip, and melted away.

Jim Jackson was at the stern, where the Congolese woman was washing out some clothes. Despite the language barrier between them, I expected to see them disappear below at any moment. The biggest wrinkle was that the young driver was there too, probably trying to cajole Jim to give him the same thing Jim was trying to get from the woman. Neither Bull nor Sondra Miller were in evidence on deck. I knew where Charles Miller was, though. He was sitting close beside me on a padded bench, set where we could watch the southern bank of the river glide by. He had an arm around my shoulder, and he had my cock out of my shorts and was slowly masturbating me. He was purring like a kitten and was kissing and licking the side of my neck.

"Would you like me to go below with you?" I asked. Ethan had told me that Miller was a necessary evil to getting this documentary in the can, and I didn't have any other prospects for projects at the moment—and the driver had cocked me so well that I was feeling generous and not too picky.

"No, dear boy, thank you," Miller murmured. "This is quite nice as is. Just get nice and big and come for me, and I'll be satisfied."

That's when I realized that he couldn't get it up and that this was the next best thing. That's why he was so calm with his secretary, Jim, fucking his wife. Sondra probably hadn't agreed to come on the safari at all without a boy toy. I felt sorry for Miller, and when he pulled my head back and put his lips on mine, I gave him a kiss to remember. I also ejaculated for him, and although he dipped his face down to my lap to clean me up, I stood afterward and said I would go down to my cabin to clean up better.

Jim Jackson had the Congolese woman bent over a crate and was fucking her from behind when I reached the top of the stairs down into the cabin area. The driver was sitting on another crate and watching.

I heard them as I was coming down the steps into the lower corridor. The door to the Millers' cabin was slightly open and I looked in as I passed. Bull was naked and on his back on the double bed in the cabin, and Sondra, also naked, was straddling his pelvis and riding his cock. Before I moved on, I saw her dip her face down to his and him run his hand into her luxuriant cascade of blonde hair and take her lips in his. He brutally attacked her lips and, with a tug of her hair and a thrust of his hips, turned her in the bed and was mounting her to take over the driving. She threw her head back and laughed a hoarse, lusty laugh and then cried out as he thrust hard up into her.

I ached to be so lustfully and roughly handled.

Knowing now that Miller couldn't perform for Sondra, I felt much more forgiving of—and a kindred spirit with—her. I passed on to my own cabin door. The Indian, sans his dhoti, was waiting patiently for me in there. If one can say they were fucked gently, this would have been that fuck. I sat in the chair that Ethan had slouched in just a couple of nights previously, while the Indian gave me the most sensual blow job I think I've ever had. I tried to return the favor with him standing and me kneeling in front of him, but I doubt I succeeded all that well. He was just too long for me to come anywhere close to deep-throating him as he had done for me.

He then amazed me with his strength. He appeared so tall and thin that I could not imagine that he had the strength to lift me and stand, a bit crouched, in the center of the cabin, while I wrapped my arms around his neck and my legs around his waist and he entered and entered and entered me with that long, snake-like cock of his and rotated it around inside my channel and stroked it in long glides in and out until I was yodeling to the ceiling, and no doubt announcing my very satisfactory taking to all aboard the boat.

Later he took me even more slowly and sensually, face on, atop the bunk, with me looking down the length of our torsos and watching how impossibly all of that was slowly sliding up inside me and, though going in rock hard, seemed to have the flexibility of a hose inside me, finding every nook and cranny of my channel and caressing it with the bulb of the cock.

The Millers, Jackson, and I all had to contain our mirth later in the day when we were shown what the Congolese considered the highlight of the safari, which was a tree commemorating the birthplace of their former leader, Mobutu Sese Seko, founder of Zaire. The members of the party, each giving looks to the other, properly praised the event, though, not wanting to be on the bad side of any of the Congolese this far up the remote river. Charles made a great to do of directing Jim to take multiple photographs of the site, but, in sotto voce assured him that they didn't need to be good photographs.

I felt a chill in the air that evening after we had finished our dinner at the campsite in Lisala. No one else claimed to feel it, though, so I put it out of my mind. Once again Bull suggested that we make an early night of it, as we were pressing on to what he called a "beautiful fishing village" at Laté. The rest of us interpreted that to mean that we had to stop somewhere for the night before going on to something we really wanted to see, so it might as well be at the collection of mean little huts at Laté. We had come for the excitement of the national animal preserves, and it was taking us considerable time to find them.

With a smile Bull told us that we would be crossing the equator in merely five days. We all suppressed groans. We wanted the experience of crossing the equator, but we weren't wild about the idea of having to wait for five days to get it done, in what had become one monotonous day after another, if you didn't take the good sex into account. I was willing to take the good sex into account.

No, not the good sex—the great sex.

At dark that night, Charles Miller appeared from the direction of the boat with another full bottle of scotch under his arm, causing me to wonder just how many bottles he had brought on the journey and if he was thinking of the need to ration them for the return trip. The driver and cook were on the drums again, and, again, Miller and I sat parallel to the Miller's tent so that, while he was slowly and expertly sucking me off, we could watch the show in his tent. Tonight it was a spectacular silhouette show, with Jim and Bull standing, facing each other, and Sondra suspended between them and taking cocks in both entrances.

I wondered how Miller could so calmly take this until, as if he could read my mind, he said, "I can no longer give Sondra what will keep her with me. And I enjoy watching those who can, servicing her. That alone is worth what she costs me in jewelry."

I had to agree that that was simple enough. Thanks to their performance, I was quite randy when I went back to my tent. Thanks to the driver and the Indian boat man, my randiness was fully serviced. I had watched Sondra get double

61

plowed one way. The driver and the Indian showed me there was more than one way to double plow.

I was quite content riding the driver's cock, facing him, as he lay on his back on my cot. I lost my contentment and gained a half hour of "Holy Fuck!" when the Indian slid in behind me, encircled my chest with his arms, pitched me forward, and entered me with his snaking cock on top of the driver's thick one. They played me like a calliope and left me just a few hours before dawn, exhausted, sweating profusely, and with my tongue hanging out.

The sweat turned out not to be from the sex. By the time Bull entered my tent at dawn to rouse me, I was wrapped in a blanket alternating between chills and hot flushes, sweating like a pig, and chattering my teeth.

Bull pronounced the dreaded word: malaria.

As I was being bundled aboard the float plane, I heard the drums playing. It seemed to me that they were a bit more loose in rhythm and had a lighter beat than before the driver fucked me. I hoped I'd had a good influence on the driver's music. Bull was helping to tuck me in on the plane and was regretting that I hadn't been able to stick it out to cross the equator later in the week. My regret was that I had to leave before I had experienced Bull's cock—and Jim Jackson's, for that matter. The medic was looking really good to me, and I wondered what might be possible on the way back to Kinshasa. Would the plane fly high enough to qualify for the mile-high club? I wondered.

Dancer for Hire

(Excerpt from the novella *Gotta Keep Trying*)

The Web site was on the air when they got to the precinct. The captain raised an eyebrow as Hardesty, pulling Freddie along with a hand on the dancer's arm, slid into the semicircle of detectives looking at the film.

It obviously was already near the end of the film clip. One naked, balaclava-helmeted bruiser was on his back on the bed. Todd was draped on top of his chest, looking up at the camera. The man's cock was inside Todd, and Todd was moaning and looking dopey at the camera. The man's legs laced through Todd's and lifted his out and up. A second man, with a balaclava on, a little more pudgy and older than the first, came down on the bed on his knees, he walked on his knees to between Todd's spread leg. A side-angle shot showed him entering Todd's ass with his cock—on top of the cock already there.

The man on top was whispering something lost to the camera, and Todd answered in a thick voice, "Yes, it's OK . . . I can . . . oh, shit."

The man on top was beginning to stroke inside Todd. He's taken Todd's ankles in his hands and was holding the young blond's legs up high and spread well apart.

"Say it. Tell the viewers you want it. That we take care of you. That we're good to you." An off-camera voice with a German accent.

"Yes," Todd conceded in a slurred voice, "You're all good to me. You're my friends."

"And you want other friends from out there, beyond the camera, too. Invite them to join the bid to share you."

"Yes, I want it again," Todd murmured.

But then his eyes snapped wide open and he grabbed out for the shoulders of the man on top. He began to writhe between the two men and to cry out, "Yes, yes. Fuck me. Both. Harder! Getitgetitgetit, Give it, Give it . . . Oh, God, YES!"

Hardesty had seen where the guy on the bottom had moved a hand to Todd's gecko tattoo and was rubbing it.

He knew what that did to the dancer's arousal. He knew from very personal experience. Todd began fairly dancing on the two cocks, writhing and moaning, screaming for them to pound harder, deeper. Laughing, the two men complied.

"Turn it off. Turn the fucking thing off," Hardesty said.

Double Attention in a Cairo Hashish Den

(Excerpt from the novella *Gilded Cage*)

As the opera was coming to a conclusion, Rushdy leaned over and kissed me gently on the lips again and whispered in my ear how sexy I looked in my tuxedo and how much a "good stick" I was to be a help to him.

I nearly flared up, but then I could see the danger in his eyes, the flash of dominance. "David tells me that this is little different from your life in New York. Was he lying to me?"

Embarrassed—because David didn't really lie, although he had no right to make such decisions for me—I lowered my eyes without answering. Then he whispered something about how beautiful and alluring I was, and I immediately was lost to him again.

I was walking on air as we left the opera house. I assumed the Rolls coupe would be brought around and we'd go back to Giza to fuck and fantasize over the lush sets and powerful music of the opera. But once again Rushdy surprised me.

"Let us walk the streets for a bit and come back for the car when the crowds have dissipated."

We did walk, into dark streets that narrowed into almost alleys, but it didn't seem like Rushdy was just rambling; it seemed like he knew where he was going.

In the middle of one narrow street, he stopped, turned abruptly to his right, and rapped on a wooden door on the ground floor of a building next to stone stairs that led up to what seemed to be the building's formal entrance. A window shutter in the door was pulled open and then the door was flung wide and a portly middle-aged Egyptian in a galabiyah, the traditional, long robe worn by Egyptian men, and a turban was all bows and welcomes, ushering Rushdy through the door.

The man leered at me as we passed and I shrank against Rushdy.

As the man was shutting and locking the door, Rushdy leaned down and whispered to me, "And now we are at the other end of the political spectrum. This is considered a hotbed of revolutionary fervor. I must play to the English tune, but this is where my heart is, with my people. But if the British ever—"

He broke off there as we were being ushered down a darkened corridor toward a beaded curtain covering a door, beyond which was dim light, a cloud of smoke, and a low hubbub of sound. As we passed, hands reached out from the shadows and caressed the silk of my tuxedo. They reached out from so many directions and retreated so quickly that I found myself weaving back and forth rather than walking a straight line.

The room we entered was directly out of the Arabian Nights: layers of Oriental carpeting on the floor, low tables in mother-of-pearl inlay, a mass of silk throw pillows, and draperies on the wall providing a tent-like effect. The room was full of bubbling hookahs, which helped explain the smoke. Scattered about the room were men, many of them middle-aged, some of them very young and paired with middle-aged men. Few were sitting alone, not being touched by someone else.

Most were stretched out in various degrees of embrace, puffing on the hookahs, and many in some stage of sexual intercourse. Most of the young men in any form of dress at all only wore billowy diaphanous pants and turbans. A few wore spangled-decorated short vests over bare chests.

Rushdy and I were escorted to a hookah in a pillow-strewn area of the room that wasn't already occupied and bade to settle down. As soon as we had, though, four men, two fairly young, two older, all beefy, appeared and sat, cross-legged, arrayed before us. All had their eyes on us—mostly on me.

"These men are among the revolutionary leadership, very important to the new Egypt. Strip down to your under linen," Rushdy said to me. "You'll be more comfortable."

"You?" I asked.

"Later," he answered. "Have you smoked hashish before?"

"Never," I answered.

Rushdy turned to the Egyptian who had admitted us, who had slipped his galabiyah over his head and was sitting, facing me, in a loincloth and his turban, and stoking up the hookah. Rushdy said something to the man in Arabic, which I hoped was an instruction to keep the hashish content in the pipe mild. The man had a pot belly and slightly drooping breasts like a woman, but he seemed well muscled as well and had strong hands with long, sensuous fingers, which I watched, mesmerized, as he manipulated the parts of the hookah.

The pasha bade me to lay back in the pillows and relax and he stretched out beside me, putting an arm under my neck and gently stroking my nipples and belly with the fingers of his free hand. I thought back to his statement of thinking of fucking me in the box at the opera during the performance and wondered if I was less inclined to let him do so here, with these half-naked Egyptian men staring at us. I decided it wouldn't inconvenience me a bit.

The Egyptian moved between my legs, dragging the hookah toward me, and I spread my legs, raised my knees, and placed my feet flat on the carpeting.

He leaned over my bare torso, drawing the long cylinder of the pipe toward my face and looking down into my face with an expression that was half smile and half leer. I took a short pull on the pipe and a sense of lightness and well-being flowed through my body. I took a longer pull and felt the smoke flow through my body, moving me to the sensation of floating above the earth. Rushdy was stroking my chest and belly, and I felt his

67

touch with heighted, sensuous sensation. It then seemed like more hands than just his were gliding over my body and touching me intimately. Another long drag on the pipe.

My underdrawers were being pulled down my legs and off and I raised my knees, my legs together, toes pointed so that the underdrawers could easily be stripped off. But then hands were palming my knees. Long, sensuous fingers, coaxing my knees apart, knees bent, bare feet flat on the carpet. Another long drag on the pipe, and I felt my legs spreading, moving apart, flowing away from me. I was floating on the clouds, above the tree tops. Looking down at the trees. Seeing every individual leaf.

Long, sensuous fingers cupping my buttocks, raising my pelvis a bit from the pillows. Moistness coming down over my cock. Slick fingers entering my passage. I was engorging, my hips rising and falling gently, listening to a slight sucking sound above the bubbling of the hookah. And the murmurs of voices, in a language I couldn't understand. All of my sensations were gathering at my center; I heard myself sigh at the pleasure washing over me from the moist, rhythmic pressure on my rock-hard cock.

"Another pull on the hookah," I heard a voice say. Low, rich tones. Rushdy?

I did as bade. A tight, warm feeling came over me and I felt my seed release in a gentle flow. The moist pressure moving down my perineum, searching for, and as I dug my heels in the carpet, rising to it, finding the entrance to my channel with something thicker than the fingers.

"Again," Rushdy's voice whispered, and I took another drag on the hookah.

A body was crouched over me, between my legs, I arched my back and gave a long, low moan that went on forever as the throbbing shaft entered me, and slid and slid and slid up into my passage. Interminable stroking inside me and the feel of the flow along the walls of the channel.

"Another pull," the voice said.

We were riding above the clouds, me facing up into the heavens. He on top of me, embracing me, his cock, not feeling the same as before, the bulb rubbing in different places on the walls inside me, pumping slow and deep inside me as we floated through the air. I was sighing and holding him close to me, wanting him inside me. We began turning in the air, his cock thickening and lengthening inside me. And stroking, stroking, stroking. Releasing.

Rushdy at last, I thought. At last taking me. Again and again. Thicker than before, reaching deeper than before. I gave a little cry and a lurch as he released inside me, held, throbbing, for a moment, and then withdrew. Thinner now on reentry as he started stroking again. I was facing down toward the earth now and the cock was stroking up into me. My eyes picked out each individual leaf on the trees passing below and followed the intricate veining—on each individual leaf. Milky white cum flowing over the leaves.

Ah, Rushdy. Who would have known he would be so gentle and so filling and so big? So varied in his touch. And so fecund, releasing inside me again and again, always with a different feel of the cock.

"Inhale again."

Laying stretched out on top of him, in his embrace, him inside me, probing deep, his bulb kissing the walls on my channel deep up inside me. And then him also on top of me, under and above at the same time. And entering me again from on top. While still inside me from underneath. Panting to stretch to two cylinders rubbing against my walls and each other inside, the bulb of one deep and that of the other pressed against my prostate, rubbing, rubbing. Two shafts in countermovement, as I pant and stretch, working hard to encase them both. A peaceful flow, deep, interrupted by a forceful spouting closer to the entrance, my body tossed about in the last seconds of frenetic thrusting both from above and below.

"Very good. Breathe normally. Take another pull on the hookah."

Hunched in the corner of the Rolls, the cool night breeze flowing around the windshield and blowing into my face, bringing me back into the world, I began to question whether it had been Rushdy at all. I was still naked other than my underdrawers. My tuxedo apparel was neatly folded at my feet. Rushdy was wearing his tuxedo.

69

He turned and smiled at me. And he was saying something, but, though I could see his lips move, I couldn't hear a word he said. But we'd had all-out sex at last. Hadn't we? My ears were buzzing, everything around me outside of the car was a swirling blur.

Out in the desert again, beyond the pyramids. In the backseat of the Rolls, rising and falling on the cock. This time I was sure it was Rushdy.

When I woke in the late morning, naked, on my bed, Egyptian sun streaming into the chamber, it was to the realization that much of what had happened earlier in the hashish den hadn't been Rushdy at all. And it hadn't been just one man. Not even one at a time.

Double Black New Year's Present

(Excerpt from the novel *Brambleton*)

When Matt had arrived earlier that afternoon from Brambleton, the judge had met him on the staircase and almost breathlessly and, with great excitement, had taken Matt's arm and pulled him up the stairs, leaving Emmet standing in the foyer holding Matt's suitcase.

"You can take that to the north bedroom, second door on the left, Emmet. Matthew will be coming with me for the moment."

Atherton nearly dragged Matt into a large bedroom on the back of the house, overlooking a long formal garden. He pushed Matt down on the end of the bed in a sitting position and then started pacing back and forth along the foot of the bed, undoing his tie and his shirt and moving on to removing his trousers as he spoke in an excited voice.

"She's gone."

"She?" Matt repeated.

"She. The witch. Ding dong, the witch is dead. My wife is gone—at long last. She's filing for divorce. Has flown out to Nevada. I'm not contesting it, of course."

"You and your wife are getting a divorce?"

"Yes, Matthew. She's got a young man. Isn't that rich? Well, so do I. That's why she wanted just the family here to Christmas, to tell us all. That she was leaving me. She sounded like I should be mortified. She acted like I would balk at being the one filed against, but I told her I'd do anything she wanted. I did try to act the part of someone just wanting her to be happy, even though what I really want is the bitch gone for good. But I'm free to do as I like now. I waited . . ."

He was rambling on. He also was down to his socks. And he had a hard-on—or at least what passed for a hard with him. Matt knew what he'd want now. Matt wasn't listening. What was the judge free to do now that he hadn't already been doing? As far as Matt could tell, the judge pretty much did as he liked as it was.

Atherton sat down on the bed beside Matt, put an arm around his shoulders, cupping the back of Matt's head and turning his face to where they could kiss. With his other hand he started to undress Matt. Matt knew better than to help him with that. This part seemed to be what aroused the judge the most, and it did seem to be helping his cock to stand up straighter. At least Matt didn't have to wear women's clothes for this ritual, which the judge had made him do twice in the last week they had been together.

When this was done, the judge leaned over and took Matt's cock in his mouth and gave him suck. This was the time that Matt could reach around and take the judge's cock in his hand and slow stroke him. Atherton had brought packets of condoms and a bottle of lube to the bed when he'd sat down. His lubed fingers went under Matt's balls and between his legs. This was Matt's cue to slit open the condom packet, extract the disk, and crown Atherton's cock. It wouldn't be hard long, and he'd fire off fast—and a bit weakly. So there wouldn't be much in the way of preliminaries. Although during their first time Atherton had been strong, it had been with the help of pills, and he had noticeably less vigor as the weeks went on.

He hadn't lost interest, though. And it was Matt's job to see that he had a good time. Matt would be taken care of afterward—to the extent that the judge took care of him at all.

"Now," the judge murmured, and Matt raised his hips over the judge's lap and Atherton held his cock erect, its bulb at Matt's entrance, while Matt lowered his channel on the cock. He didn't put his full weight on the older man. He leaned forward and grabbed his ankles with his hands and put weight on the balls of his feet, rocking back and forth on the cock as the judge, holding him by the waist, also rocked back and forth, groaning, giving sounds of sexual pleasure.

When Atherton had come in the exclamation of an "Oh, shit, fuck yes"—virtually the only swear words Matt ever heard the man utter—Matt carefully moved off the cock and to the side. Atherton embraced him again and turned his face, finding the same position where they started. They kissed, while the judge took Matt's cock in his lube-slicked hand and began to stroke him off.

This was when the judge was at his strongest. He held Matt in a vice-hold embrace, while Matt started to breathe heavily and to pant and to writhe under the relentless stroking of his cock—until, with a gasp, he came.

To some extent it was an act. But the old man did know how to bring Matt to an ejaculation with his hand, sometimes rhythmically pressing and releasing on his piss slit with a thumb and other times working his pinky inside the slit. And Atherton seemed to enjoy the ritual encounters immensely, as when they weren't kissing, he was telling Matt how beautiful his body was and how much the judge enjoyed being with him.

Thus, later in the evening when Matt joined the family for dinner at the table with the missing chair at one end, the younger children—perhaps with the exceptions of the teenaged grandson, who looked from his grandfather to this young, blond stranger with a bit of question and speculation showing in his face—were just happy that their grandfather appeared so happy, even if no one but him was speaking, and then only occasionally and in short statements. Two of the adults looked less than happy. The daughter, Miriam, was so smitten with the handsome young man who was the architect restoring the burned-out wing of Brambleton that she didn't notice the worry on the other adults' faces. And her husband, Rick, was looking at Matt with the same slitted-eye interest that the judge did.

As they rose from the table—not before 10:00 p.m., as, of course, they dined at the formal hour, and the children were arguing about which, if any of them, were going to be permitted to stay up and watch the new year ushered in on the television,

Atherton leaned over and whispered to Matt, "We'll go ahead and go upstairs. I want to ring in the New Year inside you."

Matt would be surprised if the judge could get it up again today, but he was calling the shots, so Matt just climbed the stairs with Atherton as the children buzzed around, headed toward the basement recreation room, exuberant that they all had been given permission to stay up, while the four adults, each with a different expression on his or her face, watched the judge and his young architect climb the stairs together.

Atherton bade Matt to shower first. When he came out of the master bath, with a towel around him, the judge, in a robe, stopped in passing and embraced him and kissed him.

"We celebrate tonight," he whispered. He showered with the door to the bathroom open, and Matt lay in the center of the bed and watched him. He was still a handsome man. And he was trim and well-muscled for a man his age. And hung. He must have filled out eight and a half or nine when he was younger, Matt thought.

Matt had seen the judge open a medicine chest and take some pills before he went into the shower. And he did a double take when the man stepped out of the shower. More like nine hard, Matt thought as the man walked toward him, naked and toweling off. Matt then knew what the pills the judge had selected had been for, and he worried whether the judge's heart could take what was coming.

But it wasn't his call. He had been bought and paid for, and he fully understood where he fit into the scheme of things— all because of his love of a house.

Matt looked around for the condoms and lube, but, although Atherton produced the lube, he said, "Tonight will be the way I like it. It's just going to be you and me now. Flesh on flesh, nothing between us except ecstasy."

A murmur of "Perhaps we shouldn't . . ." didn't have any effect on him. And, in any event, Matt was busy trying to process the "just you and me" now statement. Was this about the divorce and what he meant about being free to do as he liked?

They fucked in the center of the bed, with two pillows under the small of Matt's back, his legs spread wide, and the judge crouched between Matt's thighs and fucking him missionary style. Matt didn't have to act challenged to the limit this time. The cock was huge and hard as a rock, and it punished his channel as it hadn't done since that first time. And it throbbed. With nothing between it and Matt's channel walls, Matt could feel the throbbing vein. And there was no give; it was rock hard.

The judge fired off fairly quickly. But he didn't lose the hard on. Matt pushed him over on his back. He was panting hard, but he was prodding Matt to reverse on him and when he did, Atherton took Matt's cock in his mouth. Matt sucked on the judge's still-hard cock. Atherton's sound of enjoyment encouraged Matt to continue sucking. At length Matt came.

He was ready to call it quits then, but Atherton was pulling at him again. "Ride me. Like a cowboy. I want to come again."

And he was still hard and gigantic. Matt was worried for him, but he was the boss. Matt was as gentle as he could be as he straddled the judge's hips, facing his head and slowly rode the cock. At length he felt the weak flow of a second ejaculation inside him. He rolled off to the other side of the judge's body as they heard fireworks going off outside of the mansion's walls to mark the advent of the new year.

The judge turned on his side and pulled Matt's butt into his belly and entered him again with a cock that would not go soft. "Stay with me a few hours," Atherton whispered. "This is what I've been looking forward to. You are so sweet and young and yielding. Just what an old man needs. I want to be inside you as long as I'm hard."

Even it if doesn't go down for a week? Matt wondered.

He lay there in the old man's arms, listening for the steady breathing, waiting for him to be deep in sleep. He was still hard and buried deep up in Matt's channel. At last, the breathing was steady—raspy but regular enough that Matt knew he was asleep.

He slowly pulled away from him and silently climbed out of the bed. He redressed and left the room, shutting the door slowly behind him, trying to click home the mechanism as quietly as possible. He turned to pad down the hall to his own room at the far side of the house, barefoot and carrying his shoes under his arm.

The son-in-law, Miriam's husband, Rick, who Matt remembered having been introduced to and told was also the family lawyer, was standing half in and half out of a doorway down the hall, between where Matt stood and where he had to go. He was wearing just sleeping shorts, and was a muscular, hairy, dark-haired man in his late thirties or early forties. Matt had first seen him because of the gleam of the gold medallion on a chain that was nestled in bulging pecs and reflecting the ceiling light in the hall. He was frowning, but he also was hard. Matt could clearly see the line of his cock inside his sleeping shorts. Matt took his breath in. Under other circumstances, this could be a man for him, not least because there was an aspect of cruelty about him.

The son-in-law said nothing. Having seen Matt leaving the judge's bedroom, he just gave Matt a hard look and withdrew into his own bedroom and shut the door.

Back in his room, Matt didn't bother to turn on the light. He stripped, leaving his clothes on the floor inside the door; went straight to the private bath, turning on the light there; and entered the shower. No sooner did he have the water on than he was being crowded from behind and shoved into the back, tiled wall of the shower. Muscular black arms encircled him and a voice hissed at his ear.

"You were with the old man a long time."

"I had to wait until he went to sleep. Oh, shit. Oh shit," Matt moaned as he felt the fingers digging up into his channel.

"You're as loose as a ten-dollar whore down there," Emmet growled.

Matt's first instinct was to say that he had become no better than a ten-dollar whore, but what he answered, with a groan, was, "The judge took Viagra or something. He was rock hard and the size of a horse. I'm sure he reamed me well."

"Just as well," Emmet muttered. He lifted and turned Matt to where Matt's back was against the tiles. "Straddle my hips," Emmet commanded. Matt did so, and Emmet thrust his big, black dick up into Matt's channel and began immediately to pump. Matt buried his face in the black man's chest, finding one of Emmet's nipples with his lips and moaned at the taking by a cock as naturally thick and long as the judge had produced earlier that night and even more vigorous in the stroke.

Matt felt himself being pulled away from the wall, though, and another black man was pushing in between him and the shower wall. Another muscular, hard-bodied man, although taller and thinner than Emmet. Uglier than Emmet, a black of the American south in contrast to Emmet's Caribbean origin. But none of that mattered. His height was matched to the cock. Another hung black man, although the cock wasn't thick. It was, however, probably a good ten inches long and curved up in its full erection.

"His name's Lamont," Emmet muttered. "Works in the kitchen. Said he'd love to do you together with me. I told you I'd put you on a string, because I knew you wanted it. But you're such a slut that I knew you'd like this best."

Matt threw his head back against the stranger's chest and cried out in surprise and ecstasy as the man started working his cock up inside him on top of Emmet's.

"Happy New Year, fucker," Emmet growled.

Matt would have answered, but he was taxed enough just to maintain his breathing. Atherton's pills hadn't opened him up nearly enough for this double working of his channel. He panted hard, every bit of his attention focusing on those two black cocks sliding against each other inside his undulating walls.

* * * *

Matt swam up from a deep, erotic dream, reaching over to feel the hardness of the dark chocolate skin of Emmet, only to find no one was there. The smell of the man—no, the men, he remembered now—remained. Similar to that of his first black lover, Dashad. A musky scent of honest sweat and cum. Closing his eyes again, imagining himself not alone, Matt luxuriated in the knowledge that both the sweat and the cum had been for him—repeatedly—in the night. Emmet had laid on the bed watching Matt writhing on top of Lamont for a while, with Lamont on his back and Matt moving on top of him, trying to take in as much of that long cock as he could, and staring up at

77

the canopy of the bed. But then Emmet was below them, straddling Lamont's closed legs and lifting and spreading Matt's legs and working his cock in on top of Lamont's this time—doubling him again. Matt opened his mouth wide in a silent scream, silent because Emmet was stuffing a good part of his fist in Matt's mouth so that he wouldn't awaken the rest of the household.

"This is the New Year's present you want, I know," Emmet growled. "Two black cocks inside you at once."

Matt began to work his hips, working with the two men who themselves had just set into a rhythm of their own. After he'd ejaculated, Matt drifted off, exhausted from his long evening, both of the black men still working him like a calliope. When he next woke, he was alone in the bed.

Double Trouble

I knew where this was going.

I was sitting in Kamrod Tikka's lap, both of us naked, me facing him, and with my heels resting on the headrests of the adjacent seats in his business jet high over India en route to Bangkok.

He already had his fat cock up inside me and I felt his hands go under my buttocks from each side, and my buttocks spread and a finger from each hand enter me as well. I was grabbing the headrest on both sides of his head for dear life to stay in place as his hands no longer were encircling my waist.

I moaned as a second finger from each hand penetrated me as well.

"You liked the copilot, didn't you?" he murmured to me. "I can have him back here in a minute. I know he'd like it."

"No, Kam, not now, please. Maybe someday, but . . . oh god, oh god!"

A third finger from each hand had entered me, and he had grasped his shaft with his fingers and was moving it back and forth inside me.

I panted and gasped . . . and came up his hard, dark belly in the rivulet of black, curly hair that descended from his chest into his pubes.

Kamrod wasn't done, though. He was only beginning. He had superb control. The fingers came out of my channel and he was grasping my buttocks and pulling them apart, and with

79

the strength of his strong arm muscles, raising and lowering me on his shaft too, until, finally, as the jet started its descent into Bangkok and I nuzzled my face into the hollow of his neck and gasped and moaned, he gave me his seed in three prodigious jerky bursts.

I lay against him, panting, while he ran his hands up and down my back and went flaccid inside me. I whimpered for him, letting him know he had mastered me. I knew it was what he wanted. India putting America in its place.

I even asked him to do it again in a low whisper of longing, knowing there wasn't time before we landed, but also knowing it excited him to have that control over me and that well into his fifties, he could still have a twenty-two-year old blond beg for it from him. I felt him stiffening again at the thought, but then there was a ding, the red light went on over our bank of chairs, and he muttered with regret that I'd just have to wait—that we were descending into the Thai capital.

I took his face in my hands, kissed him, and wiggled my butt on his shrinking cock, as if I wouldn't listen to reason. And I knew that this excited him as well. I needed to keep him excited.

I knew he wanted to double me. He'd been building up to it for some time. But I had fended that off. I didn't know how much longer I could do that. If I truly didn't want to give in to it, I'd have to find another daddy. And it would be hard to find another man in Mumbai as hard bodied, hard cocked, and rich as the international entrepreneur, Kamrod Tikka. And not having my passport in my possession, Mumbai was pretty much my selection pool.

He had picked me up in a male bordello in Mumbai after I'd been there less than a week, abandoned by the American businessman who had brought me there and suddenly decided he preferred dark-skinned Indian boys to American beach bum blonds.

I had gone with Kamrod willingly, because after a week in the bordello, and discovering that young blond men were in high demand in India, I didn't know if I could survive another week in that place. On the whole, I'd found Indian men small cocked, but they had some peculiar notions of what to do with their cocks and they had fuck positions that were very taxing. The Western businessmen who visited the brothel wanted their money's worth and generally wanted rough sex that they didn't think they could get away with in their home environments.

Kamrod had been both the hunkiest and most refined of technique of the Indian men who had bought my time, and he took his time with me. I found the fingers plus cock routine he liked painful at first, but I'd been with him a full month now, and one night I'd even managed most of his hand buried and gripping and rotating his cock inside me. He took it slow and gave me plenty of time to adjust.

He was tall and burly for an Indian. A handsome face and an assured manner. He was dark skinned, telling me that he was from south India, where that was normal. And I liked the black, curly body hair he had on his forearms and thighs and cascading down from his Adam's apple to his cock.

His mouth was sweet and persistent on my cock, and he could play me for nearly an hour at a time, bringing me to the brink and then holding me off. Then suddenly entering my channel with three or four fingers and spreading them and making me come in a flood as the pad of a thumb thumbed on my prostate. Sometimes that was the end, but more often, he'd move between my legs then, and I'd feel his thick cock entering me between the fingers and he'd work me for another eternity, showing that he knew how to control himself as well.

And, as I said, he took his time and made love to me with his voice as he fucked me. He had a mesmerizing tone to his voice and he could speak in the rhythm of the fuck.

I was never quite sure how long he would want me. He seemed the type who could keep in thrall a young man of his own choosing from his own business world and who didn't need to go to a brothel.

I actually saw that in the first week I was with him in his home. A young German man, who obviously didn't like Indians and who visibly pulled away from them and showed distaste at their touching manner, came—reluctantly, I'm sure—to Kamrod's house for a business meeting and no more than two hours later was coming on a toilet stool, his ankles on Kamrod's shoulders, and melting at the love Kamrod was making with his voice in the young man's ear and with his cock in the German's channel.

I asked, apprehensively, why he had brought me from the brothel—and then not just discarded me when he'd done all he wanted to do to me. He told me that he had heard about me from a colleague and that I was just the kind who turned him on. He also smiled and said he hadn't done everything he wanted to do with me yet, causing me to shudder as much from the way he'd said it as from the touch of the backs of his fingers gliding up the inside of my thighs.

He more than hinted that he liked threesomes and double penetrations, but I didn't hop on that suggestion. Increasingly, though, I figured I'd either have to show interest in that or find another way home from India.

I was in India illegally now. I had no papers. Whatever man I was with could pretty much do anything he wanted with me as long as he was able to keep me out of contact with the authorities—or had the clout to make the authorities turn a blind eye. I felt lucky that Kamrod, hunky, not too old—maybe early fifties—refined, and filthy rich was the man who had me.

When he said he had to go to Bangkok on business and he wanted me to go with him, there wasn't much I could—or wanted to—say other than yes. I started to mention the problem of leaving the country, but he produced my passport, which he somehow had managed to acquire.

He didn't give it to me, though, and I didn't ask him to.

We were booked at the Oriental Hotel, Bangkok's most prestigious hotel.

That night, in a tenth-floor suite, Kamrod was all about my needs rather than his. Although he was a good lover, everything we'd done before was because he wanted to do it. On this night, though, he wanted to know what I wanted. He said we could just sleep too, if that was my wish.

I would have liked the "just sleep" suggestion—Kamrod was quite virile and had fucked me at least once a day since he had, essentially, bought me from the bordello. But knowing his appetites, I didn't want to do anything that lessened his ardor for me.

So, I asked him to take me out onto the balcony overlooking the Chao Phya river, with the Wat Arun temple lit up across the water, and lay back on the chaise lounge out there, while I mounted him and fucked him slowly and gazed out over the exotic river scene, the water still alive with small long-tail boats even in the night.

He seemed pleased with my choice and came twice for me.

The next day, he was in meetings until the evening. I sat by the pool, where I got several propositions—from men and women alike. But it was nice not to have to say yes.

Except for a young, small Thai pool boy, who assured me that he was in his twenties and who I fucked down in a patch of bougainvillea near the river's edge, happy to be the top for once in a very long while, I politely turned aside all other offers.

Near sunset, Kamrod came back to the room and told me we'd be dressing formally for dinner and that we'd be eating with the Belgium businessman he had come to Bangkok to strike a deal with. I didn't ask what sort of businesses Kamrod was in—and he didn't tell me. I surmised there was more than one business, though, and I could tell they were lucrative.

As we were leaving our suite for the hotel's Le Normandie restaurant, Kamrod leaned in to me and said, "I believe I have the deal I wanted, but he has expressed an interest in you. I need for you to be pleasant to him—despite whatever impression he makes."

Of course, I thought. Why wouldn't I be pleasant? But then I met the man. Kamrod introduced him as Hugo Jaguerman. I would have thought that Pig would be a more fitting name.

He was a massive man, even bulkier than Kamrod. But I could tell by the way that he filled out his tux shirt that it was mostly muscle, not fat. His jacket must have been specially tailored for him to accommodate the girth of his upper arms. His head, a pig's head, complete with snout, seemed to lay directly on his shoulders. What little I could see of his neck was as thick as his head.

He was bald, with folds of fat at the base of his neck, and his ears looked like those of a pig too. His eyes were small, buried in puffy cheeks, but as he squinted at me, I could see the same expression of lust that I'd seen in men's eyes most of my adult life.

He ate like a pig too, his eyes rarely leaving mine, as he chewed noisily on all of the artistically prepared dishes that were wasted on him.

He and Kamrod talked—although Jaguerman looked at me rather than Kamrod. But they spoke in French, which I didn't understand. I was disgusted with how the pig would stuff his mouth and then talk. He left the impression of a coarse man with huge appetites that were almost impossible to satiate. I shuddered at the thought of what I assumed I was there for.

Hearing French coming out of such a hoggish face was a surprise. But he was Belgian, so I suppose it was natural that he'd speak French. It was more of a surprise that Kamrod spoke it—and when he spoke it, it sounded like music. A little chill went up my spine at the thought of him speaking soft French in his mesmerizing voice while he fucked me.

When the coffee was served, Kamrod stood up from the table and walked away without a word to me, although he leaned down and spoke softly in Jaguerman's ear, which was answered by a leer.

And Kamrod didn't come back to the table.

"We go now," Jaguerman said in heavily accented English when he'd finished his coffee.

"Mr. Tikka?" I answered in a surprised voice.

"We will meet him at apartment."

I started to object, but a burly man in a black suit was at the side of our table. He had a chauffeur's hat tucked under his arm and seemed to be well known to Jaguerman. I got that he was Jaguerman's driver and that I indeed was going someplace with Jaguerman. The Belgian alone was muscle enough to manage that even if I didn't want to, but here in the best restaurant in Thailand, his bulky chauffeur made clear that I shouldn't make a scene.

I knew for sure now what Kamrod meant by being pleasant to the Belgian businessman. And I probably knew exactly why I'd been brought along for the jet ride. I would not be surprised to find out that the Belgian had specified what type of young man he wanted Kamrod to bring with him from Mumbai and that this was what prompted Kamrod to take me from the brothel.

The thought struck me that I would not be flying back to India with Kamrod. But this was quickly replaced with the fear that I would not be leaving wherever I was going now alive.

In the back of the Mercedes limousine, where I half assumed I would be thoroughly fucked, I wasn't.

I sat in the middle of the backseat, and Jaguerman, taking up much of the width of the seat, sat across from me and stared at me and picked at his teeth with a toothpick.

"Let me see it," he said in a low growl.

"See it? See what? Oh." He was motioning with his hands what he wanted to see.

I spread my legs and unzipped my trousers and fished my cock out.

I cupped my balls in the palm of my hand, and we sat there for several moments, Jaguerman picking his teeth with a toothpick with one hand, his legs now spread too, and his other hand holding himself through the fabric of his tux trousers.

I assumed this was the start of rough sex. But it wasn't.

"Enough," he said, and I folded my goods back into my trousers and zipped up. He kept his hand on his crotch, though, and it was obvious he was aroused.

We didn't have long to drive after that—to yet another high-rise building on the banks of the Chao Phya.

Jaguerman lived in the penthouse, which, although large, was surrounded on all four sides by terracing that dwarfed the apartment.

I held back a gasp when we entered the apartment and he flipped on the light switch.

The lounge room we entered, with an S-shaped sofa winding its way through the center of the room, lit up in a soft glow—but not from any lights overhead or on floors or tables. Instead, track lighting in the ceiling spotlighted onto paintings on the walls.

My almost gasp was caused by seeing that all of the paintings were male nudes—or, more precisely, male torsos. An impossibly muscled—almost cartoonish in its muscle definition—highly erotic torso and legs, bringing to mind that of a muscle-bound satyr.

"Sit on couch. You want drink?"

"Umm, yes," I answered. "A beer is fine, if you have it."

"Bottle or can?"

"A bottle's fine, thanks."

He laughed. "You choose wisely. But, then again, maybe not."

On that strange note, he left the room and went into another one overlooking the terrace, which looked like it was a bar.

When he came back, he was swinging four bottles of beer—two in each hand—but I hardly noticed them, as shocked as I was.

He was naked. And what immediately dawned on me was that he obviously was the model for the paintings lit up on the walls. And the paintings no longer looked like exaggeration. His body was horrible and magnificent all in one sweeping impression. All of the muscles were where they should be, but they were almost grotesquely overbuilt. His waist was thick, but with plates of muscle rather than fat—his abs looked like those of a Roman breastplate. His chest muscles overpowered his torso so that his waist looked tiny in contrast. And his arms were as thick as telephone poles, with bulging muscles.

And his cock was as thick as a telephone pole too, with two baseball-sized balls hanging behind it. He was already in full arousal.

I moaned as he set three of the beer bottles down and, sitting down close beside me, took a big swallow from the bottle still in his hand. Then, encasing me in one arm, he pulled me to him and took my mouth in his.

I almost gagged as the beer swished into my mouth, and then I did gag as his tongue followed.

I closed my eyes, not able to look at his piggish face, and let him hold my mouth captive with his as his hands moved across my body, unbuttoning, unzipping, pulling clothes off my arms and legs.

I was trapped in the embrace of one of his arms while the hand of the other encased my cock and he started a slow pump.

My nerves were standing on end. His technique of tease in the car leading directly into this no-preliminary assault had me on edge and confused. It would have been useless to resist him anyway, but I was completely disarmed, yielding to him. The reflex was involuntary, but my hips were going with the motion of his hand on my cock. He loosened the grip, while keeping my cock encased, and I found myself slow-fucking his fist.

He released my mouth and then, thankfully, all I could see of his head was the bald top as his mouth was going down onto my chest.

The hand on my cock was crushing now and was beginning a faster, more demanding cadence.

My eyes went to the paintings on the wall. His body really was a wonder. And none of the paintings showed his face. I could take the body. I looked back down at him and could see—and appreciate—the bulge of the shoulder and muscles on either side of his shiny, billiard-ball-smooth head. He was pulling me over into his lap, and I could feel his hard cock at the small of my back and those thunderous thighs under my naked ones.

I panted hard to the rhythm of his jacking, and I cried out in little huffs of breath in response to what he was doing with his mouth on my nipples.

I shouldn't just be giving it to him. He was a gross pig. I should let him know I didn't want it—or that I'd give it to him but not because I wanted it. Because I didn't have any other choice. Make him demand it and take it by force and then not be able to fully enjoy it, as I couldn't enjoy sex from a beast like this.

If I just didn't have to . . . look . . . at his face.

I brought my hands up to glide over the lines of his fantastically defined muscles.

It was OK, in the almost dark, with the lights just highlighting the paintings. I could let him have it and enjoy it.

I wanted to reach back and grab his cock—to get the measure of it. Both thrilling and moaning to the thought of it inside me. Had I ever taken something that thick and long? Would I have a sense of triumph when I had?

God, I wanted it. I moaned and involuntarily whined, "Please . . . please."

I heard him laugh, a low, rumbling chuckle. I couldn't be doing this. I couldn't want it. Not from a coarse pig. As if in evidence, he bit my nipple and I cried out and stiffened.

Fight him, fight him, I screamed inside to myself. Stay stiff. Make him take it. Don't let him know . . . God, I wanted it. I relaxed, all of my senses going to the rising seed in my cock. My butt twitching. My channel crying out for attention.

Fuck me, fuck me, fuck me. I was surprised that I wasn't saying it—that I was only thinking it. It was the fear of the size of him, though—and the fear of having to look into his piggish face while he plowed me that held back what my aroused body wanted me to cry out to him.

That cock. How much of it could I take? Oh, god, give me that cock. Once more I tried reaching around him for it—but his waist was just too thick.

"Come for me," he said in a low, guttural voice. "Come for me."

I realized that I was on the brink of doing just that. And, shockingly I was overcome with a sense of loss and disappointment. No, fuck me, fuck me, fuck me, my mind was screaming.

And then I came for him.

He laughed and released me. He pushed me over to the side, and I just toppled over on my side on the curving sofa.

He stood over me, in magnificent erection. If my eyes just rose up his body as far as his nipples, I could remain in full arousal myself. I knew I could. Just don't look into the face.

He picked one of the beer bottles up from the coffee table set a couple of feet in front of the sofa and handed it to me.

"Drink," he said. "Drink. Then we fuck. No, I fuck; you scream."

He laughed at his little joke. I shuddered. A few seconds before—before I'd exploded—I'd wanted the cock. Not now.

Now I was scared of it again. I could see his evil, piggish face again.

He had already finished off one of the other bottles. I took the bottle, keeping my eyes at the level of his navel, although they kept moving down to his cock and balls and causing little shivers to go up my spine.

I took several swigs, and so did he.

But then he took the bottle from me and put it back on the coffee table.

He turned and sat on the sofa and ran an arm under me and lifted me up and pulled me over to his lap, facing him. I turned my eyes to one of the paintings on the wall.

Here we go, I said to myself. Remember not to hold your breath. Breathe easily, don't tense your channel, be loose, very loose. Eyes on the paintings. It's the body. You're being taken by that magnificent body. That monstrous cock. Not the face.

But then, rather than setting me down on his cock, he pushed my head toward the carpet in front of the sofa. I felt his thighs go over mine on each side as my shoulders and neck hit the carpet. My thighs were trapped between his and the edge of the sofa. My legs were spread in the air. His feet were on my shoulders at the arm pits, holding my shoulders to the floor.

I shuddered as I saw his face above mine and then, again, when he reached over and took the fourth bottle of beer from the coffee table.

I lurched and gasped and he laughed as I felt the cold beer stream into my channel. And then the neck of the beer bottle.

"Good choice, maybe, the bottle not the can. But when I fuck you will wish you had been prepared by the can."

I whimpered and moaned as he fucked me with the beer bottle, my channel sloshing with beer.

He took my dick in both hands and started to work it again. "You come for me."

I was overcome for several moments, but then I got angry. No, you come for me god dammit. Fuck me. Fuck me.

Again it was an internal cry.

But I managed to reach up with both of my hands and grasp his cock and start driving him as hard as he was driving me.

He let out an animalistic yell, and the first thing I knew, I was dangling from his side with his arm around my waist and we were moving across the room.

Into another room we went, dark, but for only a brief moment. When the lights went on, it was another room with lighting spotting on paintings. Three of them. The same grotesquely gorgeous torso. But fucking a small, dark-skinned youth—a Thai I presumed—in three different positions.

It was a bedroom, with a gigantic king-sized bed in the center of it.

I was dumped on the bed, on my belly. The hand under me, palming my waist, pulled me up onto my knees, while the fist of Jaguerman's other hand grabbed me by the back of my neck and smashed my face into the thick material of the bedspread.

I managed to turn my head and found myself facing a painting of just this fuck position. The cock of the top in the painting was gigantic.

I cried out as Jaguerman's cock head fought for entry in my channel. But only with the bulb of the cock. Pressing in but holding there.

Again the tease, the hint of preliminaries as briefly the bulb moved back and forth just inside my entrance—and then the long plunge, with no further preliminaries.

Yes, fuck me, fuck me. Don't hold your breath, reach back and pull your buttocks apart, relax, relax, relax your channel, relax your . . . oh god, oh GOD. Oh, Holy SHIT! Oh, yesss!

Fuck me, fuck me, fuuccckk me. Moooannn.

Oh, shit, I've got it all. Can feel his pubes on my buttocks. Breathe, breathe. Oh, holy shit. But I've done it. I could do it.

And then, as I felt his balls begin to slap on the tender skin of my inner thighs, the screaming started. It was mine. Giving me no quarter, he was pistoning me to beat the band.

The second painting had me lapped, facing away from him and making love to his cock with my channel. Slower, more sensuous this time. Lovers finding each other's arousal points.

Now he had lost control too. Now he was moaning and groaning.

And it was OK. No, it was great—as long as I wasn't facing him.

But in the third painting position, I *was* facing him. Laying on my back on the bed, with him standing between my legs.

But I was beyond caring what he looked like. Every fiber of my senses was concentrated on the gigantic staff inside me. Deeper, deeper, thicker. Moan. Faster, deeper, deeper. Oh god, oh shit!

He didn't come. I came. He said, "You come for me," and I came. But then he stopped.

I looked up into his face. Just barely being able to do so now. Any man who could fuck me like that deserved to be looked in the face.

With him stopped, inside me, like that, I could get the measure of him as never before. No, I'd never had it like that before. Never as deep, never as thick. And it was pulsating inside me.

I was mewing and sighing and groaning. "Fuck me, fuck me. Don't stop."

It wasn't spoken internally now. I'd said it. I looked him in his piggish face and I was all desire, no disgust.

"Fuck me," I whined. "Finish it. And then fuck me again."

He was smiling. It was an evil, mischievous smile.

He held there, inside me. I half expected a sudden flow, a gut-wrenching drenching to rival that of the beer.

But he was withdrawing from me. And I wanted to cry. I clutched for his buttocks, trying to hold him inside me.

But he laughed and pushed my hands aside.

I was exhausted. I had just realized that. When he was inside me, everything had been focused on that monster shaft and begging it to reach further, to stretch wider. To throb and to flood me.

But now that was gone, I felt the loss of it. I whimpered.

He laughed. And then he reached down for me and lifted me off the bed and slung me over his shoulder.

He padded across the room and out into the hall. Down the hall to another closed door. He opened the door to darkness. He flipped on the light switch.

Again, spotlights on paintings on three walls, the fourth wall a solid sheet of glass overlooking the terrace and the sultry Bangkok night, the noise of a city that never slept spiraling up into the room.

I whimpered again as my eyes focused on the paintings. Three men now. One of them my Belgian satyr. The other another burly Westerner. Again a small Oriental youth between them. Three fuck positions. All doubles. Two cocks, fighting for dominance, within the small youth's channel.

On the bed, waiting for us. Naked and in full erection. Kamrod Tikka. Smiling. Hand encasing erect phallus.

"There," the Belgian boomed out, "I told you Mr. Tikka would meet us at the apartment."

"Oh god, oh god," I murmured. Not able to respond in any other way in my utter exhaustion.

As Kamrod held his rod stiff and licked his lips in anticipation, the Belgian turned me away from Kamrod and lowered my channel on his cock.

Kamrod encircled my waist with his arms and took my cock in one of his fists. He kissed me in the hollow of my neck.

I watched Jaguerman full in the face as he fisted my ankles, spread my legs up and wide and began working his cock inside my channel above Kamrod's already fully encased staff.

"Oh, god, oh, god, Oh shit." But it was barely a whimper.

Free Pottery

I needed to get away from Avis. I normally hadn't gone with her on her buying sprees for the boutique gift shop we owned and she ran in the well-heeled Buckhead suburb of Atlanta. I tried to keep busy managing the tennis program at Georgia Tech. I'd been a top twenty professional once and still played doubles in tournaments when I could get a partner willing to chase the balls down. At nearly thirty-five I wasn't up to that anymore. I had to rely on a power backhand and placement.

That's what I taught at Georgia Tech. Power backhand and placement, and I always had a student or two willing to show me power and placement of another kind when Avis was off on her buying sprees.

For some reason I'd lost my reason and agreed to go to Greece with her in search of exotic pottery for the store. A week of her yapping and arguing with Greek merchants had given me a headache. I volunteered to canvas the northern, Turkish coast of Cyprus, alone. Getting into that enclave was such a hassle and required such a convoluted travel schedule, which required traveling via Turkey, that Avis let me go by myself.

What Avis didn't know, though, was that I had been given some very good recommendations on where to stay and what to do in Turkish Cyprus—and that ever since that Turkish exchange student, Erdiz, had shown me that masterful backstroke of his the previous summer, I had been dying to have another young Turkish man between my thighs.

I arrived in Turkish Cyprus on a plane from Istanbul, having already made reservations at a gay boutique hotel east of Kyrenia on the northern coast. I hadn't given Avis anything but a name and a number and she was so wrapped up in herself that I knew she wouldn't check the hotel out—in fact that she wouldn't try calling me at all. The hotel consisted of six separate villa-style suites cascading down the Kyrenia mountainside below the artists' enclave of Bellapais and toward the Mediterranean coast. The rooms of the hotel clustered around a series of terraces and a swimming pool.

The man at the desk when I checked in, a heavily tanned, solidly built, muscular man in his fifties with a white-toothed smile, wavy gray hair on his head, and salt and pepper hair curling at the neckline and armpits of his athletic T-shirt, asked me if I was in Cyprus on business or for pleasure. I answered, "Both, I hope."

"I assume you know what sort of hotel this is," he asked, with a guarded smile this time.

I answered that I did, that it had been recommended to me by a previous pleased guest, and that I hoped that would be the pleasure part of my trip. I added, though, that I was here to buy pottery in bulk for a boutique in the states.

He gave me a big smile, a wink, and a second, lingering look.

He had a slight, young Turkish man lead me to one of the small villas, which was one large room, with full plate glass at the end pointed to the sea and a bath on one side and small kitchenette on the other side at the opposite end, with the entrance foyer between them.

The young man walked with mincing steps in front of me. He was close to being beautiful rather than handsome. Somewhat androgynous, but arousingly so, I'm sure, for anyone aroused by such a type. This didn't really include me, though; I preferred muscle men who would use me. He was wearing a white cotton shirt and trousers that were almost transparent. He had thong briefs on underneath. And he was barefoot.

When we arrived at the villa and he'd done the obligatory instructions on what was what and how it worked, he asked me if there would be anything else he could do for me—anything at all. It was quite obvious that he was offering himself to me.

I told him that he was quite handsome, but that he wasn't really what I was looking for.

He took it well. He asked me what I *was* interested in, and I saw no reason not to tell him directly and in detail. I was to find that all Turkish men took it well. I was also to find that if they saw something they liked, they took it—and they usually took it well.

My first experience of that came not more than two hours later. The invitation of the swimming pool and the dark-blue sea beyond were too enticing, and I changed into a Speedo and took my sunglasses, a book, and towels out to the pool and claimed a lounge bed.

I was the only one there, except for an older man across the pool and one terrace down who was availing himself of the hospitality of the young bellhop who had offered himself to me, without luck. They were entwined on a lounge bed, with the guest—who was probably northern European and whose body was going to fat—huffing and puffing as he fucked the young Turk.

I tried to ignore them and to get interested in my book and taking the sun's rays. I hadn't been there very long, though, before the man who had checked me in—who I was to learn was the owner of the hotel—put me in the shadows by standing between me and the sun.

He was a fine figure of a man. In fact, other than age, he was very much like what I had told the bellhop I was interested in. He now was without his T-shirt. He was muscular, with a barrel chest, and his torso and arms were quite hairy. My tennis player, Erdiz, had been hairy too. It was part of what I enjoyed about him. Erdiz was much younger and trimmer than the man standing before me. He was also much more handsome of face. But this man had a rugged charm about him. And that ready smile. And his hands were big and his fingers long and thick. And I looked down at his toes in his open-toed sandals. They were thick and long too, and hair covered. I had always let such attributes guide me on the man's equipment, and I'd rarely been wrong.

95

"I am Karamat," he said. "We met at the reception desk."

"Yes we did," I answered

"I own the hotel. I sent Musa with you to your room, but he said you were not interested—at least not in him."

"Musa is very nice," I answered. "But, no, he is not what interests me. He seems to be busy now. And from the position he's in, I don't think the two of us could have done each other much good."

We both looked over at the other lounge bed. Musa was on his chest, with his midsection and legs in the air. The northern European was holding Musa's legs at his side and fucking the young man like he was fucking a wheelbarrow.

"I'm not sure I've ever seen that position," I remarked, keeping my tone amused. "I certainly haven't tried it."

"Ah, so, you do not think you could make much use of Musa because of position. You must like men inside you too then," he said rather matter-of-factly. "And it's a fine position. You *should* try it."

"Yes, I do like men inside me—just as Musa obviously prefers. And maybe someday I will try that position," I answered in the same vein.

He sat down on the lounge bed beside my thigh then, leaning over me, with his hand down beside my opposite side. "Would you like me to suck and fuck you, then? I assure you that I do it very well. Do you like Turkish men? Not boys, men."

"Yes," I said. "I like Turkish men very much. And before you ask, I like hairy men. But I've only had younger men."

"Bah. What do younger men know about fucking other men? You need to be at least fifty to do it well, to make men beg for it again."

"I've always thought that the second fuck was nicer than the first," I said. "You have your hand on my cock." And he did; he was lightly massaging my basket.

"Do you mind?"

"No. It feels good."

"Do you want to see what I fuck with?"

"Sure. Why not?"

Karamat stood and dropped his shorts to the ground. I gasped at the size of him. He was in half erection. And the hair on his dark brown body was salt and pepper everywhere but on his head, which was gray, and his pubes, which were still black.

"See, my head is old, but my cock is young," he said. "The hair tells you." And then he laughed. "The best for you. My head knows what to do; my cock can still do it."

"That's nice to know."

"I suck and fuck you now, yes? I make your trip worthwhile."

I smiled and lifted my hips off the surface of the lounge bed. He leaned down and pulled my Speedo down my legs.

"Very nice," he said, giving what Turks must use for a wolf whistle, making a popping sound from his mouth with his plump thumb. "Many men fuck you? Your hole tight or slack?"

"Not many—and usually with weeks or months between one and the next. Tight, I would guess. Does it make a difference?"

"If slack, I have ways to tighten it up. Tight is good. You feel it good. You not afraid?" he asked. He was holding his cock and waving it at me.

"Yes, of course I'm afraid of what you're waving at me. But that's part of the enjoyment, isn't it?"

"I like you. You're not shy. I give you good fuck, I think. It's always better to take it with joy," he said, with a broad smile on his face.

He fished around in the pocket of his shorts and brought out a tube of lubricant and three condom packets.

"Three?" I asked in mock shock.

"You said the second is better than the first, so we see what three is like." He was smiling again.

"We'll see about that," I said, with a laugh.

He sat back down on the lounge bed, opened the lubricant, and took some in his hand. Then he leaned his face over my groin, took the bulb of my cock in his mouth, and started to suck. I moaned and ran the fingers of both of my hands into his hair. I had every intention to get as much enjoyment out of this as he would give me. One of his hands went under my thighs, and I felt his lubricated fingers at my hole. He licked up and down my shaft and then took it all in—once, twice, three times. I shuddered and lifted my hips off the lounge bed. He had moved a finger deep inside me.

I moaned deeply. It was obvious that he could give me much enjoyment.

He came up for air and said, "Yes, very tight. I like tight. Like taking a virgin. But we loosen it up a little, I think. You enjoy it more." He took one of my legs and lifted my ankle to his shoulder and then went back to sucking the bulb of my cock and worrying my hole with his lubed finger. Then two fingers, and he was moving them in and out, finger fucking me. His tongue was flicking my piss hole, and I was groaning and writhing under him.

"Young men do this to you?" he asked when he came up for air.

"No," I answered. "They are more direct and more insistent. They focus on themselves, their own needs."

"Ah, older men like me—and soon you—know how to savor it. How to have more pleasure; but more, how to give pleasure. And you are a guest here. We work to your pleasure."

Three fingers and I was grunting and groaning. His mouth was pumping down on my shaft. Quicker and quicker. I came in a flood into his mouth.

"Sorry," I whispered. "It was too good."

"Just one," he said with a laugh. "I make you come four times. Each one better than the one before."

He lifted the hand that he'd been fingering my hole with and flashed four fingers. He slowly and with a wink inserted each finger in his mouth, in turn, and sucked them.

"Oh, god," I croaked.

"Now me. First one very businesslike. You like second, so first one just to put us both in the mood." He stood up from me, straddling the lounge bed and my thighs and made a show of rolling a condom on his cock and lathering it up with lube.

"First time is for conquering," he said. "Once you are mine, we make love. Or maybe you don't—"

"Stop talking and fuck me," I said. "Yes, hard and deep. Take no prisoners. Make me feel it. Use me." I spoke in a low growl that I didn't recognize as my voice.

He gave me an intense look, grabbed my ankles and spread and raised my legs, pulling my pelvis up off the lounge bed as well. I rolled it up. He positioned the bulb of his cock at my entrance. I grunted and groaned as he worked the bulb inside.

And then he stopped, leaving his bulb inside the entrance, while I adjusted to it and tried my best to pull it further in with the muscles of my sphincter. This was working; he slowly was moving inside.

"Ah, good. You are good at this. I think we both will take our pleasure from this," he murmured. "But you are too anxious. More pleasure if you know your need for it enough to beg for it."

I began to pant, to beg for it. I scrabbled for his nipples through the matting of hair on his chest, trying to provoke him to plunge into me. He was smiling more cruelly now.

"Shit. Fuck! Give it to me!"

"We will see if a young man can do this for you."

I cried out as he plunged down, down, down. Out and then plunge, again. I cried out again and raised my pelvis to him. When he'd bottomed this time, he held deep inside. I plaintively begged him to fuck, pulling at his body hair, raising my mouth to his nipples and sucking hard, getting my hands around on his buttocks and squeezing the meaty globes and trying to pull him deeper inside me. I beat on his chest with my fists.

God, I wanted him to fuck me hard—more than I'd ever wanted in a fuck before.

He pulled away from me, and slipped out. Then he rose up on his feet, his legs straddling the lounge bed, and flipped me over. He grabbed my legs, pulling me up to where only my chest and cheek were on the surface of the bed. With a laugh, he plunged back into me with his cock, and began wheelbarrow fucking me like I had remarked on about the fat guy and androgynous bell boy across the pool. I grabbed the upper legs of the lounge bed, hanging on for dear life, and cried out my passion while he pumped me hard and deep, not stopping until I had come again.

Karamat let me collapse on my belly on the bed, and he came down, full length, on top of me. He had come too. I was so absorbed in my own ejaculation that I don't know if we came together or he came first or after.

I felt him go soft inside me while he ran his hands over my body and nibbled at the hollow of my neck. He moved down my body, kissing as he went, until he was crouched behind me. He tongued and nibbled at my buttocks, and then I felt him pulling my dick and balls through my legs. I moaned, widened the stance of my legs, and came up slightly on my knees, presenting my ass to his attentions.

When he swallowed my ball sack and began to roll my balls inside his mouth, I rewarded him with another deep moan. He was holding and slow-stroking my cock with a hand.

"Do your young men give you this attention? Has anyone else done this to you after a first fuck?" he asked.

"No," I answered with a groan. He moved his mouth to my cock and then my hole. Back to my cock and then my hole. And I ejaculated for the third time.

I heard him fiddling with a condom packet, and then he was straddling my hips and riding me in long, deep, slow strokes. He had his fists pushed into my shoulder blades, bearing the weight of his body, but then he slipped them around under my chest and arched my back up to him. I turned my face toward his and we kissed for the first time. He tasted of tobacco and brandy. He was palming my chest, rubbing both nipples between thumb and forefinger, and rocking my body back and forth on his cock.

This time I felt him ejaculate into the balloon of the condom inside me, and I sighed and murmured, "Thank you. The second time was even better."

"You are a sweet fuck," he muttered back in a matter-of-fact voice. "I leave you now for a while. I have to build up again after two and there is work to be done. If you want me to finish you, stay here and I'll be back."

"Finish me?" I murmured. "How could there be more?"

"Stay around and you'll find out," he answered. "I am Turk; there's always more."

I laughed at that—at the inference that I was some sort of project that needed to be finished well. But I stayed, on my belly, luxuriating in the pleasure I had gotten out of his mature, experienced body. And from his bull's cock.

I looked out over the pool. Musa, the small bell boy was riding the prone figure of the Northern European now. And nearby, two men were entwined on a lounger. I couldn't tell who was fucking whom. They were both Europeans and were young and thin. I decided they must be a couple, retreating here to do what they couldn't so openly do at home.

A young man was cleaning the pool. He had a gorgeously well-developed body and was wearing a skimpy black bathing suit. His body was a nutty brown, and he had a full head of black, curly hair and a Fu Man Chu mustache. He wasn't nearly as hairy as Karamat was, but there was a trace of matting under his pecs and a thin line running down to the waistband of his swim suit, which dipped down in front, permitting pubic hair to rim the waistband. When he raised his arms, though, there was a good bit of hair in his pits. His torso was tightly sculpted, and the veins popped out on his powerful arms.

I dozed, thinking of him. When I woke, not knowing why I had done so, Karamat was sitting beside me again, massaging my body with his strong hands. The Northern European and Musa were gone, as was the pool man. The young European couple were in the pool, one belly up to the side of the pool with his arms splayed out over the pool deck tiles. His partner was embracing him from behind and they were kissing— and, I presume, fucking.

"You are awake."

"Yes."

"You have not run from me."

"No."

"We know each other well now. Two fucks and we are friends. Now we will be lovers, yes?"

"Yes, please."

"I fuck you now like a Turk fucks his lover."

He stood and I watched him roll on a condom—the third one. He turned me on my side on the lounge bed, away from him, and then stretched out behind me. He pulled my body into his, and I turned my face to his, and we kissed, as we both explored each other's bodies to the extent that we could reach.

101

He pulled my pelvis into his groin and reached down and pulled my calf up so that my leg was bent. I felt the knee of his leg cover my other leg and pull it back a bit.

And then he was slowly entering me—and entering, entering, entering. One of his hands went to my cock and encased it and he slow fucked and slow stroked me to my promised fourth coming, his third, and to, indeed, what was the most sensual fuck of the three.

When he was done and still inside me, I brought myself back into the present, looking around at who else was at the pool now. Just the pool boy, standing at the other side of the pool, a long rod to skim the water in his hands. He wasn't skimming the water with it, though. He was looking at Karamat and me lying on the lounge bed. Karamat saw that I was looking at the young man.

"Not all young men fuck badly. You like the young man across the pool?"

"Yes."

"A experienced man like me and a young man like him together can give good fuck. You ever have the cocks of two men inside you at once?"

"Perhaps."

"You must lock your door tonight," he whispered in my ear.

"Why? I've heard that Cyprus is perfectly safe."

"If you do not lock your door, you may be attacked and raped."

I didn't lock my door that night.

In the darkest of night, I felt the weight of a body on my chest. And hands encasing my head. And a hard cock presented at my mouth. As I sucked, I ran my hands up onto his chest. Nearly hairless, trim but heavily muscled. Young, virile. The cock sweet in my mouth. Rock hard, but not especially long or thick. It wasn't Karamat.

He kneed my legs spread and pushed his knees underneath my buttocks. As he entered me, he leaned down over me, and we kissed. The silky smoothness of a mustache. I tongued his chest as he pumped me and ran my tongue up into

102

his hairy pits, sniffing and appreciating the maleness of him, his musky scent.

He came inside me and I realized he wasn't crowned. I didn't care. I wanted all of him. I regretted he had come so fast. But surprisingly he didn't soften. Young and virile. He turned me on my belly and rode my ass until we came together—me for the first time, he for the second.

Laying full length on me, he spoke for the first time, in a whisper. "Sorry. I saw you at the pool—with Karamat. I wanted you too. You did not lock your door. I begged Karamat, and he said I could have you. He told me that I was his gift to you, that he fuck you tomorrow again."

"He didn't ask me. You must be punished, I think," I whispered back. "Lay on your back, or I will complain to Karamat."

"You may do so now if you wish. He standing there, by the door."

And, indeed, Karamat had come in with the pool boy and had been watching us. He wasn't standing by the door after he heard his name, though. He was approaching the bed, erect cock in hand. He lifted me as the young man turned and lay on his back, his cock standing straight up from his groin. Karamat lowered me on the cock of the younger man who reached around and gripped and spread my buttocks to help Karamat work his own cock in on top in my channel, as he straddled the thighs of the younger man and pushed my torso over onto the younger man's chest. I cried out in ecstasy as Karamat's cock forced its way in and he began to pump my channel in a double penetration.

Karamat and I both came quickly, with me writhing about and Karamat thrusting hard, but the young man remained hard until after Karamat had withdrawn—from my ass and from the room. I rode the pool boy's cock into the dawn, as he gripped and spread my buttocks with strong, pool man hands—to open me for the repeated invasion of my spread hole with his ramrod cock.

* * * *

"Pottery? You want pottery? And you want to know if I know where this piece was made?" Karamat turned the coffee mug I'd given him over and over in his hands. He was smiling a funny sort of smile. "Sure, I know this pottery. It's from Kemal's. On the coast, west of Kyrenia. I'll call and have them send a man to drive you there, if pottery is what you want."

"You know what I want, Karamat, but pottery is what is paying for this stay at your hotel. It isn't really necessary for you to get me a driver. I can get a taxi."

"No problem; they want to send a car for you," Karamat said. He couldn't seem to lose that lopsided grin. "I'm sure they will enjoy serving you."

He went into the office of the hotel to make a telephone call, and I went back to my villa to rest until the driver came for me.

It had been a tiring day. I hadn't gotten much sleep and was gloriously sore, but walking down in the castle harbor town of Kyrenia had helped me exercise muscles back into shape and deaden any pain I had experienced. I just wasn't used to so much sex of that intensity—and from two different men—in that short a period.

In Kyrenia I had moved from one souvenir or gift shop to another, seeking local-made pottery Avis would like. There were some vividly painted scenes of ancient Turkish warriors done on large display plates that I found were made in mainland Turkey, and I managed, with the help of the shop here, to order a shipment of those by telephone to be shipped directly to Atlanta.

But other than that, there was disappointingly little. That was with the exception of the unusual coffee mug I had found. It was of a tan earth color, rough pottery on the outside, with geometric designs etched into it while the pottery was still wet— obviously by hand or a stencil roller but by a deft hand. Only the inside and lip of the cup were glazed before firing. I had found a few bowls of this and a set of wine glasses and a water pitcher, as well. I'd only bought the cup, though, so that I could show it to Karamat. The shopkeepers I'd asked concerning the origin of the pottery were only willing to obtain it for me. But I didn't want a middleman on the payroll or I wouldn't have come here directly.

I was dozing in my room when the telephone buzzed and Karamat was summoning me to take my ride to the Kemal pottery.

As I walked up to the hotel office, I saw that Karamat was talking with a young Turk, who, it seemed like all of the Turkish men here, was handsome, dark and sultry, and built like an athlete. He had a slightly thuggish look to him, like anyone who went with him would be used roughly, which gave me chills. He also cast on me the same speculative smile I'd seen others do since I came to Cyprus.

"This is Rafat," Karamat said. "He will take you to the pottery." They had been speaking with their heads close together as I approached. They both looked up and gave me brilliant smiles when they sensed I was there. They both were in shorts and droopy athletic Ts, with deep cuts in the armholes, showing thick matting of black hair in their pits, and curly hair cascading out of the dip in the neck hole. Such revealing wear seemed to be the casual apparel of choice in Turkish Cyprus. They both filled their clothes out very well—the mature, Zeus-like Karamat and the young, Apollo-like man talking with him.

Rafat and I were soon scuttling along the coastline on a bad road in an old Holden with so many knocks and squeals that I had to concentrate hard on what the young man was saying. I was watching his hands on the wheel, although his hands didn't spend much time on the wheel. He was being very expressive with them. They were good, sensual hands. The fingers were long, with curls of dark hair above the knuckles. He touched me a few times while we were driving and he was gesturing and even ran his hand down my chest once when he had flung his hand out, protectively, when we had taken a curve in the road hard.

"You stay at Karamat's hotel, yes?"

He damn well knew I was staying there. "Yes."

"Karamat, he treats you well, yes?"

"Yes, he's very hospitable." I knew what he meant by that. He'd put his hand on my thigh and squeezed as he shot me a brilliant, knowing smile. "And he's a master at what he does. I think Turkish Cypriot men are very sexy." I wanted Rafat inside

105

me, and I wasn't going to be in Cyprus long enough to beat around the bush about it. He'd left no question about what he wanted from me.

"Many Turkish men are hairy, like me. You like hairy men?"

"Yes, very much so. And I like men who take what they want."

"Good," he said, flashing a big smile at me. "Karamat said you were very enjoyable. Karamat takes what he wants. I do too. Karamat likes to share. He said you liked that too."

I just grunted. Karamat apparently had told him everything, and I needn't drop any more hints. It remained to be seen what he might do about it. He was a real hunk. I would let him do me in a flash. And if he had a friend as good-looking as him, I'd probably let them both do me. I had found sex on this island to be so free and easy that it made me horny rather than satiated.

Rafat let me off at the front door of a squat stuccoed building with picture windows on either side of the entry. Bars covered these windows. It had the look of an old, disused army barracks about it. Rafat urged me to go on in and look around in their showroom while he parked the Holden behind the building.

I entered the showroom to find, standing behind a counter—Rafat. Although he was quick to point out that he wasn't Rafat, but Selat, the identical twin of Rafat.

"Please, please. Look around. Uncle Karamat told us what you were interested in—and what you were looking for in pottery wholesale. He say you like the half glaze ware."

"Yes, that intrigues me. I don't think I've ever seen any pottery like that. It's just glazed on the inside." "Uncle" Karamat, I was thinking. He hadn't told me they were related. Perhaps that was why he'd given me such a sloppy grin when I'd shown him the coffee mug.

"Yes. That makes it cheaper. But we find many tourists like it—even better than our more artistic, full-glazed pottery. But, please, look around. We make you a very nice deal. Yes, very nice indeed. Uncle Karamat tell us what you like."

I knew he wasn't talking about pottery any more, not really. I felt myself going hard—especially as Rafat had just entered the showroom. Seeing the two of them together was very arousing.

As the two talked to each other in whispers and indulged at furtive looks at me, I wandered around the store. The half-glazed pottery, indeed, was very enticing—as were many of their fully glazed and decorated pottery pieces. They had pottery with vine leaves either etched into the raw clay or painted on the surface that would, I believed, sell very, very well in Buckhead—and at high prices. One of the ironies of such handicrafts is that Americans valued the handmade as superior to machine-made goods, whereas most of the world made things by hand because they couldn't afford the machinery to make them with. Yes, very enticing. I looked at the twins, standing there and smiling at me, proud of their work and hopeful of its sale. They were very enticing too.

"Are these all the samples?" I asked. "Any more somewhere?" I couldn't hide that I was looking for some place more private than the showroom.

"Yes," Selat said, with a broad grin. "We have more. And a very special collection in the back. You come back and see?"

"Yes, please," I said. Selat ushered me toward a doorway covered with a beaded curtain. I saw that Rafat was at the shop door, locking it and turning the sign to "Closed."

The room Selat led me into was not large. Three sides were lined with shelves containing pottery. A double bed was set against the fourth wall, between two shuttered windows.

My eyes went to the double bed and lingered there.

"Selat and I take turns sleeping here at night," Rafat said. "For protection of the shop. We also fuck here."

I turned my gaze toward Selat, being only slightly embarrassed that the young men were so openly hitting on me and were so assured. I had given them every reason to be assured.

"Perhaps this pottery will interest you," Selat said, as he led me over to one wall.

Arranged on the shelves, using the half-glazed technique were a dozen or more cups, bowls, and pitchers.

"Pick one up," Selat said. "Examine it closely. I think that you'll like it." Rafat was standing close behind me. As I picked a cup up—and then almost dropped it as I saw the images etched into it—I felt his hands go to my hips.

I shuddered. The cup was covered with homoerotic art. Like ancient Greek urns, men straddling men on couches. Fondling, sucking, fucking. Examples of double penetration too.

I picked several pieces up, all the same, plus some of stylized hard penises.

"You find them interesting?" Selat asked. He was very close to me now too.

"Very interesting, yes," I replied. "Especially this one."

He looked at the one I held in my hand. It depicted a double fuck of what was probably a young, naked slave by two men in disheveled togas.

He gave me a sexy, hooded-eye gaze and smiled.

"But not really what I can sell in Atlanta—at least not in my shop," I continued. "You have much more—out in the showroom—that I could use, though."

"But perhaps we have something you would want, could use, more privately," Selat said in a low voice. "We can give you a very good deal—a very good deal for someone who was a good friend of Uncle Karamat's—and, we hope, of Rafat and me too."

Rafat had his hands running up under my T-shirt, to my pecs.

"Let's see what kind of deal we can make," Selat said. He took the bowl I was looking at out of my hand and gently returned it to the shelf. Rafat was pulling me over into the center of the room.

"We fuck you now, yes?"

"Yes," I answered breathlessly.

"Both together? We give very, very good double fuck."

"If you want."

They sandwiched me, Selat in front and Rafat in back. They had already shucked their own Ts. Rafat pulled mine over my head as Selat unbuckled my belt, unzipped me, and let my shorts hit the floor. Rafat was embracing me from behind and moved a hand to cup my chin and turn my face to his for a deep kiss. Selat pulled my briefs down off my legs and he followed them down, going down on his knees and taking my cock in his mouth. Rafat went down on his knees too and he was working between my crack with his mouth and fingers.

I had to grab their heads, Selat's with one hand, and Rafat's with the other, to maintain my balance.

But I didn't have to do that long. The two stood, stripped off their own shorts and briefs, and began working me between them. I could feel both of their cocks between my thighs. For a brief moment, I thought they were going to take me, together, standing there. I had given permission for that, but I'd thought it would be something we'd work up to, if it happened. Selat had already raised one of my legs against his thigh with a hand under my knee. I felt he was on the cusp of pulling the other one up and settling my channel on his cock—with Rafat's right there as well. I moaned, scared, but half wanting it. But when I was sure that was going to happen, they were moving me, toward the bed.

They had me on my back at the end of the bed and were tag-teaming me. Taking turns holding my legs spread and fucking me and feeding me their cocks while kneeling above my head. Every five minutes or so they would switch positions. They occasionally showed concern that maybe I had had enough. They didn't volunteer to stop altogether, but they assured me that they could finish me if I was growing weary. Fascinated by being taken by hunky twins, though, I encouraged them to fuck on.

One of them pulled out of me—I no longer remembered which was which—but rather than switching, the one at my head started working underneath me, until I was fully on top of him and his hard cock was pushing up under my ball sack. The brothers worked together to get his cock inside me and then he crossed his arms tightly across my chest, right under my pits, which drew my arms up to where they were effectively trapped.

Then what I had both feared and hoped for before was happening. The other twin was working his cock inside me on top of his brother's. I panted and whimpered, surprised that I could take them as big as they'd both gotten.

"Can you manage?" a voice in my ear whispered. "I can tell Rafat—"

"No, please. Don't stop. I've never . . . but I want . . ." So the one on top was Rafat. The one under Selat.

And then Rafat began to pump, and I zipped right to heaven. I was spouting in no time and Rafat pulled out of me long enough to lean down and clean my cock with his mouth. And then he was inside me, pumping again. Selat was moaning now as well and the brothers kissed over my shoulder and then each, in turn, kissed me.

When I opened my eyes, there was another man in the room. A near duplicate of Karamat. He pulled his T over his head. The same hairy barrel chest.

"Our father, Kemal," Rafat said. "This is his shop. He can give you really, really good deal."

"Yes," I answered. I knew what he was asking.

Rafat's face and cock disappeared and now it was Kemal staring down in my eyes, Kemal entering me, Kemal—thicker than Rafat—pumping me on top of Selat's buried cock.

"Kemal says you are A number one good fuck," Selat said afterward, sitting beside me on the bed I was still laying on, panting and recovering. Selat was smiling broadly.

"The three of you were great too."

"Kemal, he doesn't speak English. So I ask for him. He says you can have two boxes—like that one over there—full of the pottery of your pick, for free—you just pay shipping and handling."

"That sounds good," I said. My mind was contemplating how much I had made on that marvelous fuck. I felt the need to close the deal before these guys figured out that I should be paying them for the cocking.

"You might want better deal—three boxes," Selat said rather haltingly.

"For what?" I asked.

"If you stay here, the night, with Kemal. And let him do whatever he wants with you."

Kemal was standing inside the door with the beaded curtain. His body was still beautiful to me. His smile was too. He was holding several lengths of nylon rope in one hand.

110

Ah, Avis, I thought, the deals I must make to keep your boutique shop profitable.

Handed On

"I really do worry about you. When did you eat last?"

"Please, please, don't stop," Marc whimpered between pants. "Finish me, please. Don't make me wait."

"Now you want it," the dance master laughed. "We'll see how badly you want it."

The two young men were lying on a pile of old costumes in the dark corner of the back of the stage behind the wings. The dance master, Patrick Moran, only a couple of years older than Marc, was mostly on his back, although listing to the left, and underneath. Marc was stretched out on top of his body, Patrick's cock up his ass, and Patrick grasping Marc's cock. Patrick held the back of Marc's head so that their faces were close together, the eyes of each staring into those of the other. He said he wanted to watch the expression in Marc's face as he was being fucked, even though the dimness of the light in the back corner of the stage made this difficult.

Patrick's tights were rolled down to his knees, keeping his legs close together. Marc's tights had been stripped off him as, overtaken by lust in their practice on the darkened stage, Patrick had lifted and carried Marc into the shadows, and the tights were now laying to the side of the pile of clothes, legs suggestively spread as wide as Marc's were to accommodate the cock inside him. Very theatrical, Patrick thought. And he laughed. It was working out well, and right on schedule.

"You weren't so eager for the fuck two weeks ago. It was murder seducing you." Patrick was holding Marc's cock but had stopped stroking it, holding it steady despite Marc's efforts to move his hips in rhythm against it. Similarly, Patrick's cock was buried, but he wasn't stroking with it.

"Please, please fuck me," Marc plaintively moaned. "Finish me. Please."

It indeed had been quite a campaign to get Marc into the male dancer's ensemble of the recently founded Metropolitan Opera, established in 1883 and now only in its third season—and third production.

Patrick had been on the prowl with the impresario chosen for that season's production of Gounod's *Faust*, John McManus, when they had come across Marc doing acrobatics in a Vaudeville skit and showing grace of movement and flexibility that made him stand out on stage and assure Patrick that the handsome young man had received classical training. The production of *Faust* required a team of male acrobat dancers, and Patrick's team was lacking a man who could perform as well as they found Marc doing in an inferior skit.

Patrick would have worked to recruit Marc just for the needs of the troupe and didn't think he'd have any trouble doing that—why would any male classically trained in ballet, as this young man obviously was, not want to work in ballet and opera rather than Vaudeville? But John McManus had thickened the brew. McManus, who had brought Patrick in as the dance master for his Met production as much because Patrick was his procurer as for Patrick's unquestioned dance talent, had declared, wetting his lips and slitting his eyes as he watched Marc glide across the stage, that he wanted to fuck Marc too—and not just once. And not just by himself. John McManus had a fetish, one that he wasn't able to feed nearly as much as he wanted to.

As Patrick worked at seducing Marc to his sexual charms—seducing him to come to work at the Met was, as he figured, no problem—he decided that Marc had been fucked before but that, quite possibly he'd been in a relationship that had gone bad and was skittish about involving himself in another.

114

It was only after Patrick had first successfully spiked Marc—on this same pile of costumes after Marc's addition for the Met troupe, when he was euphoric over being able to find a classical dance job in New York—that Marc told him that he had been brought to New York by a rich, older man, who had abandoned him here after a couple of months, with no safety net, and gone back to his wife and children. Marc had convinced himself that the man would take care of him forever—financially as well as sexually—and he'd been hit very hard by reality. He'd had a rough time picking himself up and getting enough work to barely live on in New York. He'd planned on going back to western Pennsylvania but hadn't saved enough for the fare yet.

Thus, Marc was happy to have sex with another young man like Patrick just for the enjoyment of it. But he was skittish of becoming mixed up with an older man again. This presented a problem for Patrick in conditioning and handing him over to John McManus, but Patrick was up to the challenge.

Patrick had held Marc close and kissed him. And he'd assured the younger man that someone would take care of him now. And then he'd turned Marc on his belly and fucked him again. He didn't tell Marc that it would be John McManus who would take care of him and he was already calculating how little to pay Marc to keep him on the edge of starvation and prepare him for willingly going with the impresario.

"Tell me, was this man of yours—the one who brought you to New York—a big man?"

"A bit heavy, yes, and tall," Marc had answered.

"That's not what I meant by big," Patrick said.

"I don't . . . oh, you mean his staff?"

"Yes. His dick, his cock, Marc. We must loosen you up, take any guilt in this away from you. His cock. Thick? Very thick?"

"Umm. Very thick, I guess."

"Thicker than mine?"

"Do you really want to know?"

"Yes. Tell me."

"Please, Patrick. Give it to me. Stroke me. Make me come. Don't hold me off any longer."

"Tell me, for true, and I'll give it to you again. You won't get the cock until you tell me."

"Yes, then. Yes, he was thicker than you. But you're—"

"Good. Good that you've had it thick," Patrick had said and then he embraced Marc close and began stroking hard inside him.

Through the moans and groans of Patrick's fucking, Marc had been confused. Why had he asked that? Patrick wasn't all that thick, but Marc hadn't mentioned it; hadn't complained.

Patrick's reason for asking that started to become apparent weeks later, when Marc found himself being fucked again as an extension of his one-on-one practice session in preparing for the soon-to-open *Faust* production. They once more were on the pile of costumes in the back corner of the stage area. And once more Patrick was fucking Marc. One difference between this time and when he'd done it to cap Marc's successful audition with the Met troupe, was that this time Marc had begged for the fuck. This was the second time, Marc had begged for it—and had whined for it to continue when Patrick had put it into suspension.

Another difference this time was that more than just Patrick's cock was inside him. Patrick had three fingers running down the sides of his cock inside Marc too, and, as Mark huffed and puffed, was stretching the channel wider than needed just by his cock.

This was also the time that Patrick had told the impresario, John McManus, the scheme they had concocted could proceed. That Marc was ready, in more ways than just emotionally.

"And what is this we have here?" McManus said gruffly from the edge of the light on the stage. Patrick had told him to come no farther—to be enough in the light for Marc to instantly recognize who had "caught" them fucking.

"Mr. McManus!" Patrick called out, and he rolled over on top of Marc as if he intended to hide Marc's identity.

"Patrick? And is that young Marc you are fucking?"

McManus said no more; he just stood there in the light under the stage light after he'd uttered that expression. By design then, he turned and jumped off the stage and marched up the aisle to the theater lobby.

"Oh, god, we're undone," Marc wailed. "We'll lose our jobs. I'll lose my job."

"There, there, little one," Patrick said, embracing Marc, smoothing out his blond curls, and kissing his teary cheeks. "I think it will be OK."

"OK? How could it be OK?" Marc answered through snuffles.

"I think it could work out because Mr. McManus likes young men, small, lithe, flexible men—in the same way I do—and I've heard him admire you."

"Admire me?" Marc asked.

"Yes," Patrick answered, the exasperation clear in his voice. "McManus fucks young men. I'm sure he'd fuck you given the chance. If you are willing to cultivate his attraction to you, I think we might manage this. You wouldn't lose your job here. Neither would I. If you aren't willing for yourself to make the sacrifice and to try to get him to want you and to keep you in the production, could you consider doing it for me? I would have almost as much trouble finding another position this good as you would—and the sacrifice would be for everyone in the production. *Faust* is too close to opening to replace us."

Marc sniffled, but didn't answer. Patrick thought perhaps that he was resisting the proposal in his mind, but Marc was actually thinking about McManus and assuring himself that the man had his attractions. He was big and gruff—a bit on the heavy side—but he was a handsome and commanding man. And he obviously was rich and important in Marc's chosen world. Marc had already thought about being fucked by the impresario. He looked on all well-heeled middle-aged men in a "what if?" way since he'd let one bring him to New York.

"You mean if I get him to fuck me," Marc said.

"Right. I think he already wants to fuck you, and I fuck you, so we both know you'll let a man do it. Do it for him and you'll solve a lot of problems. If you could get the man to want you, it might even be better for your life," Patrick said. "You said an older man brought you to New York and said he'd keep you. I'll bet if you work hard to please Mr. McManus, he might set you up somewhere too and improve your life's lot. Young men like you and I have to make our opportunities where we can. What do you say?"

Marc couldn't say much of anything at the moment, because Patrick had been working his body back up to a need. Patrick took the sighing and moaning—and lack of an objection—as victory. As well he should. To seal the deal, he turned Marc on his stomach and fucked him again.

An hour later, Marc was in the back of McManus's closed carriage riding out of the city toward Long Island, where McManus said he had a country house. Patrick had cajoled Marc to go with him to the front of the theater to find McManus in the theater's offices so that they could both beg to keep their jobs.

Without telling them what he'd had in mind, McManus granted them the opportunity to talk more to him about it, but he said that he was late for driving to his home. He gruffly told them to ride in his carriage with him. Chastened and Marc visibly worried, the two young men climbed into the back of the carriage with him. There were facing seats in the carriage and Patrick went to the one behind the driver, facing the rear, while McManus and Marc sat on the forward-facing seat.

With Patrick's help, Marc threw himself on the mercy of the glowering impresario and did what he could to make McManus know that he was available to him.

As the carriage rolled out onto Long Island and out of the city, McManus fucked Marc, with Marc sitting on his cock in his lap and facing him. McManus's cock was thick, but not overly so. But, when McManus put his hands under Marc's thighs and lifted and spread them and rolled them up and, upon McManus's command, Patrick crouched behind and started to work his own cock in on top of McManus's, Marc suddenly could understand why Patrick might have asked him about how thick a cock he'd taken from his previous patron. It wasn't being able to handle the thickness of one cock that was in question—it was the ability to take two at the same time.

"Patrick!" Marc declared as the dance master's bulb breached his hole.

"Shush," Patrick whispered in his ear. "This is what he likes best. This will assure the success of our plan. You can take both. Just relax and breathe. Breathe and relax."

Thus revealed was John McManus's special fetish that he had such difficulty fulfilling and that he had enlisted Patrick to serve.

Marc had started to make a ruckus of being violated as he panted and wailed at Patrick's grunting efforts to enter him on top of where the older man already was buried deep in his channel, but passersby didn't hear or care and neither did McManus's driver. The carriage never wavered in its journey and, four inches sheathed along with McManus, Patrick leaned into Marc's ear with his mouth and whispered, "There, it is done; the rest you can handle well enough," and begged Marc to think of their need to keep their jobs—not just for Marc or even Mark and Patrick but for the entire production. McManus had it in his power to dismiss them both immediately.

And it *had* been McManus who had barked for Patrick to join in the fuck. It hadn't been any more Patrick's idea, as far as Marc knew, than it was his. They were both just trying to save their jobs. It had been McManus who had demanded this.

By this time, they were both in to the root and Marc realized that he *could* handle them both—even when the two, grunting and groaning above his moans and whimpers, settled into a rhythmic counterpistoning. It was dark in the cab, and if Marc relaxed and stopped tensing up and flopping about between them, he could manage this. The longer it went on, too, the more pleasure filtered in to counter the subsiding pain. Two men wanted him, both men who had power over him. Both desirable and powerful enough themselves to have anyone they wanted. And they both wanted him. Together.

This must have been McManus's idea—his demand—Marc thought. And the older man obviously was enjoying it. And maybe wouldn't fire either Marc or Patrick. Might even make Marc's life better if he stopped fighting this and started making McManus believe he wanted it—which, to some extent—a growing extent—he did, he realized. His own hardened cock and approaching ejaculation assured him of this. And that he took pleasure from it wasn't hidden from the other two men either. They could feel him hard. They could hear the moans and sighs and the involuntary expressions of pleasure he was giving as the cocks worked him inside—the pleasure of realizing he *could* take two cocks and that two men wanted him together.

And he could feel that Patrick melted to it too. He had been party to Patrick almost losing his job. Patrick, who had been such a good friend in giving him this job, and then such a good lover. If Patrick enjoyed it too . . .

With a cry, he came up the belly of the impresario's silk waistcoat. With a grunt of his own, McManus came as well. Patrick came last, and what was it to Marc, if McManus and Patrick kissed each other over his shoulder before they disengaged? Patrick had told him that they both had to do what they could to get into the good graces of McManus.

Nearly tossed into the corner of the seat by McManus when they were done and Patrick had fallen back into his own seat and was buttoning up the fly to his trousers, Marc lay in a heap of soreness and exhaustion as McManus barked for the driver to stop and to hail a cabbie.

Marc was able to see street lights from the side windows of the carriage, so he knew they hadn't gotten completely out of the city yet. He looked on dully and a bit confused as McManus and Patrick put their heads together between the seats and conversed in low tones. McManus took out his purse and gave Patrick some money, and Patrick exited the carriage, which started up again almost immediately.

As they were wheeled out into the darkness of the estate areas of Long Island, McManus pulled Marc back onto his lap and fucked him roughly again.

For the next four weeks, covering the last week of preparation of *Faust* and the three weeks the opera ran, McManus kept Marc at his country house—and in his bed when Marc wasn't at the theater performing in the opera. McManus would fuck him in a big four-poster bed in the late morning when they both woke up. Frequently the young carriage driver, who obviously did much more for McManus than drive his carriage, would join them in the bed, and Marc would gain more experience in the double-penetration fuck. It seemed to be a favorite fetish of McManus's—he murmured at one time that he was in a secret club cultivating the practice—and Marc himself increasingly became accustomed to it. Patrick had slowly trained Marc to beg for the fuck. Even Marc realized that McManus was having him on the way to begging for the double fuck.

To his surprise, McManus and the chauffeur showed Marc that there was more than one position—the bottom man sitting, the middle one in his lap and facing away, and the top coming in facing the middle one, as performed in McManus's carriage—of the double fuck. They took him with them facing each other, legs overlapping and cocks held together, with Marc lowering himself on the cocks, either facing McManus or facing the chauffer. They took him standing, with Marc's legs hooked on the hips of the crouching McManus, and the chauffeur fucking him on top of McManus's cock from the rear. And when they had gotten Marc's hole well stretched, they even took him with McManus on his back at the end of the bed, his legs stretching to the floor, and Marc reversed on his body, his head toward the floor and McManus's ankles hooked behind his neck, and the chauffer sitting on McManus's belly and stroking inside Marc's stretched channel.

McManus would take Marc into the theater with him in his carriage in the late afternoon and Marc would remain there, dining out with McManus and the other dancers seeing that Marc was in special favor—with Marc not being able to complain about how McManus took care of his personal needs while he was with the impresario. And then, after the running of the *Faust* performance and another after-the-theater meal, McManus would fuck Marc again in the carriage on the way back out to the Long Island house, all the time whispering to Marc what form of the double they later would be using.

Patrick didn't fuck Marc again. He no longer told Marc that Marc needed any private sessions to brush up his dancing, and Patrick's attention now went to another dancer. Marc was disappointed, but he thought no thoughts that perhaps Patrick's work with him was done—and McManus more than kept his sexual life occupied. Marc was not particularly the contemplative kind of a young man. As long as his personal needs were met, he

121

was allowed to dance, and he was in the minimum of pain, life for him was fine. He did miss Patrick's fucking, though.

He wasn't sure, however, if he got off more on being fucked by a single man than by two. He had enjoyed Patrick, better than he enjoyed McManus alone. But he wasn't really sure anymore that he preferred Patrick alone to Patrick and McManus or McManus and the carriage driver together. When he was being doubled, he had two men wanting him—and after his channel had been conditioned to open to two at once, a double stroking was maybe more arousing than having a single cock inside him. He wasn't sure and was half afraid of thinking about it. But he thought that just maybe . . .

And he enjoyed having an older man, a rich man, taking care of all of his needs. He hadn't been the least happy starving and living in hovels waiting for something good to happen to him in New York. Patrick had been something good. McManus was something even better. McManus plus his carriage driver or Patrick . . .

He sometimes wondered how he'd react to two muscle-bound hunks, not just one beautiful body like Patrick's or the carriage driver's plus a middle-aged man like McManus.

* * * *

Life was good to Marc—even with the heavy-demand fucking and the snide, jealous comments behind his back in the Met troupe that he almost was able to hear. But life didn't stay all that good. As good as *Faust* was as a production, it was an extremely expensive production to put on stage, and New York society in the mid 1880s was prepared to take only so much of it. The seats could only be filled to break-even capacity for two weeks. The production went on for a third week before McManus realized that production costs were bleeding him far more than he could manage.

He needed a financial angel. And he needed the angel just to stop the hemorrhaging of costs and to cover accumulated debts. The show would have to close anyway.

He went to Henry Powl, a manufacturer with money to burn, and a colleague in the secret "doubles" society he belonged to.

"If you help me get out of this production in the black, you could be an equal investor in my next production without putting any money in," John McManus said.

"I'm not sure New York is ready yet to make any opera of high-quality production profitable. I don't know what would be in it for me to make it worth my while."

"I've seen you at the theater, Henry," McManus said. "I've seen the way you look at one of the male dancers."

"So?"

"He takes doubles," McManus said. "I've trained him to take the double in several different positions."

* * * *

McManus told Marc they were having dinner with a friend of his who also had an estate out on Long Island. This was the night after *Faust* closed. Marc was worried about work, but McManus said that, if Marc trusted him, McManus would take care of him.

The two were met at the door of Henry Powl's country mansion by Henry, who was wearing a cloth robe.

"I thought we'd take a swim before dinner," he said.

Marc's first thought was that the weather was much too cold to be taking a swim, but Powl anticipated that.

"I have an indoor pool in the conservatory."

Of course you do, Marc thought. What he then said, though, was. "I didn't bring a bathing suit."

"Neither did I," Powl said, with a smile. He opened his robe to reveal that he was naked underneath. And in erection. And better equipped, younger, more handsome, and with better body definition than McManus had. Longer even that McManus's chauffeur.

"I didn't bring a suit either," McManus said. But Marc didn't hear what he said. His attention was focused on the beautiful—if older than his—body of the financier and manufacturer.

McManus was sitting on the side of the pool, and Marc was in his lap, sitting on his fully sheathed cock. When Powl moved through the water toward them and said, "I want to fuck you too," Marc merely smiled, opened his legs, leaned back into McManus's chest so that his hips rolled up, and opened his mouth to Powl's kiss, as the manufacturer fisted and spread and raised his legs, and started working his cock inside Marc's channel above McManus's.

Powl was long and thick. This was the thickest combined taking Marc had received, but after the initial difficulty opening to it, he reveled in the fuck. Powl was more of a man than either McManus or Patrick were. And he did all of the stroking. McManus remained hard, but dormant, as Powl stroked hard and deep, his kisses, the touch of his hands on Marc's body, and the endearments he whispered in Marc's ears sending Marc over the moon. Not just once. Twice. The man had stamina and each man came twice before he was finished.

As they were dressing for dinner, McManus told Marc that this was the way he was taking care of Marc, unless Marc wanted to just go out into the city on his own. That the production was dead and McManus couldn't support Marc anymore, but that Powl would take care of him, if Marc didn't put up a fuss and just stayed here.

Marc didn't put up a fuss. And the tears he shed when McManus left him there with Powl were mainly to be polite and to show his gratefulness.

* * * *

They were in a latticework pavilion in the extensive, well-manicured Italian-style garden of Henry Powl's estate. Marc was bent over the side of a chaise lounge and Henry, his hands gripping Marc's waist and moving him back and forth, was fucking him from behind.

The man had been insatiable, fucking Marc constantly and on every surface of the mansion for more than a week. Marc's needs were being met—all of them. He missed dancing, but all of his other needs were being met. Slowly but surely he was forgetting his need for independence and to dance—dance on anything but one, or two, cocks.

If only Henry had the prowess of a McManus and the youth of Patrick, he thought. Or if Henry had a well-built friend.

As he was being fucked, Marc was looking beyond the pavilion, through the latticework. A gardener was working in a nearby bed. He was older than Henry, but even more heavily muscled. He moved with the grace of a dancer. He was stripped to the waist, and his flimsy-material shorts were pulled down in front to just below the line of curly hair, black, flecked with gray, of his pubes. They were held up in back by bulbous cheeks. When he stood and turned, Marc could see that the gigantic bulge of his basket was what pulled the shorts down in front.

He was a god. Not young, but Zeus-like, with perfectly defined bulging musculature and curly hair on his chest running down into his shorts and on the backs of his forearms and cascading out of his armpits. All virile man.

He was watching the fucking now that he'd seen Marc and Powl in the pavilion. There was a little smile on his face. He stripped off his shorts and Marc gasped at the size of his cock and his low-hanging balls.

Powl saw him too. "Tony. You want a piece of this too? He does doubles."

Marc felt a whisper at his ear. "You want Tony too?"

"Oh, yes. God, yes," Marc whimpered. "But, he's so big. And you are too. I don't know . . ."

Powl was lying flat on his back on the chaise lounge, Marc mounted on his cock, facing him. Tony pushed Marc down onto Powl's chest with a strong fist in the middle of the back. Marc cried out and begged for mercy as the horse-hung Italian gardener, straddling the chaise lounge and Powl's thighs with his legs, worked his cock inside Marc's channel above Powl's shaft.

Marc was panting and howling. Powl solicitously whispered in his ear, asking him if it was too much.

"Yes, it's too much," Marc cried out. "But don't stop, please. Fuck me, fuck me, fuck me!"

And Tony did. Once saddled, he began to stroke hard and deep and his arms embraced Marc's chest, his hands covering Marc's pecs, thumbs thrumming Marc's nipples, while Powl fisted Marc's cock and stroked him in rhythm to what, first, Tony was doing inside him. And then, when Marc had settled down and moans and panting and begging for the fuck replaced all of his fears and objections, Powl started stroking him in counter rhythm.

Marc no longer thought of being taken care of or when his next opportunity to dance on stage would be. He only thought about this double fuck—and the next one.

He thought he'd never have it as good as Henry and Tony, but when Henry handed him off to Tony to take home and they were met at the garden cottage door by Tony's young, handsome, muscled, horse-hung, and smiling son, and the two men put Marc on the cocks right there, standing, with him sandwiched between them, his legs hooked on the young son's hips, and the two men competing with each other on stamina and hard-stroking ability, Marc knew there were always new heights to reach in being double fucked.

Hanging Out Hangover

(Excerpt from the Clint Folsom series mystery novel *Death in the Rockies* in *Clint Folsom Compendium 2*)

I was coming up from a fog; I could hear the buzzing, but I couldn't quite figure out what it was and was struggling with whether I should even care. Where was I and what was I doing when I drifted off? It was dark in the room, but the curtains weren't drawn over the window, so the blue and yellow alternating flashing of the neon sign across the canyon of a street was bathing the room in pulsing, if soft-focus, light, and the noise of not-yet-dead-of-the-night traffic was drifting up from several stories below. I forced my eyes open and saw the bullet head, with the buzz cut, the nose that probably had been broken several times and indifferently set, the scar running from lower eyelid and over the cheek toward the cauliflower ear. Much too close though, and the breath smelled like a beer hall on the morning after. Pulling my head back, I was now staring into a blue-and-black-ink tattoo of a grinning skull on the side of his neck.

Looking down along his body, I saw that he was virtually nude, had the musculature of a body builder, and was breathing deeply and snoring slightly in repose. My own body, stretched along his, was turned slightly toward him as we lay full out on the bed, and I could see that I had my forearm running across his belly and was holding his generous-sized genitals. He had black leather cuffs at his wrists and was wearing heavy hob-nail boots.

In bed. In my bed. Ah, I was remembering at least that much. The room did have a familiarity now that I thought of it. My own bedroom. I hadn't had the small apartment near the village in New York City for long, though, so I forgave myself the slow uptake.

My head was throbbing, and I was still in a half haze. I'd either drunk too much or not quite enough. I couldn't figure out which. I had the notion that I would have been better off going one way or the other.

I was, however, beginning to remember bits and pieces of the earlier hours of the evening. I was on my way somewhere, but I was out of sorts and stopped in at Benny's on my way for some fortification.

I wondered briefly why'd I'd been out of sorts. The buzzing had stopped but now had started again and I wondered about that. The guy lying next to me snorted in his sleep, and I pulled my hand way from his balls, but I didn't wonder about what he was doing here. I felt that was strange even as I wasn't wondering—I didn't recognize him as anyone I knew. But I felt the pressure to think of something else—and maybe more than one something else—as being more important to think about just then. Somehow I knew that figuring out who this guy was and what he was doing in my bed wasn't my highest priority. Fundamentally, I knew I was the champion of the one night stand. And I wasn't at all surprised this guy was in my bed. He had a monster cock, muscles—and tattoos. Those were almost always enough reason for me—all together or individually.

About all a guy had to do was unzip and pull out something that size and tell me he wanted me, and I was good to go. I think they call guys like me satyriasis. I didn't make excuses for it; it was what it was. So, for the most part, I just enjoyed it. Sometimes I concerned myself a bit about not being able to be steady with one guy—and I almost got there once, with Brad. but think about that made my head pound so I willed it away.

How had this motorcycle guy type gotten here, though, I wondered. And why did I feel pangs of guilt about that? It had some time years since I'd felt guilty about bringing guys home and letting them fuck me. Even guys I didn't know—especially guys I didn't know. But somehow my mind was telling me I should be someplace else.

But en route to someplace else I'd stopped at Benny's, one of the rougher clientele bars near police headquarters. And I'd been in a deep funk. Yeah, right, now I remembered. It was that thought of not feeling guilty for some time. There was a time when I would have felt guilty, when life was more steady and I was monogamous.

This was Brad's birthday. Brad had been my partner—in more ways than one. This had been in the years when I'd cared enough to live someplace that wasn't a six-floor walkup bathed in blue and yellow pulsing neon lighting from the building across the street. Brad had been murdered two years ago, and I'd been on a downward spiral ever sense. Cleaned up his murder, I had, but I was his partner and hadn't been on the ball in our case. If I had been, maybe we would have gotten the guy before he got Brad.

Today was Brad's birthday. I was suppose to go someplace where they were celebrating—not Brad's birthday, but something else I couldn't help being bitter about. And maybe if it wasn't supposed to be a happy time—a beginning—on Brad's birthday, I wouldn't have concentrated on it being an ending—or at least a "never can be again." Maybe I wouldn't have felt so sorry for myself. And maybe I wouldn't have stopped at Benny's for some fortitude.

Obviously I'd had too much of the fortitude. I did remember now the drinking and the boasting and the challenge to dance the pole at Benny's and how well that exercise in pushing the thoughts of Brad and how I'd failed him out of my mind had gone over. Guys—rough-looking guys, when I was feeling like being handled roughly—were working my vanity and playing a yelled-out guessing game of what movie star I looked like while I danced and stripped for them—with a few actually coming up with the name of the matinee idol of years gone by who was, in fact, my father.

I'd obviously made an impression on their libido and they on mine, because here I was, in my bed, next to a lightly snoring biker type with a nice fat dick. I almost regretted that I didn't remember what we'd did here that tired him out so much that he was sleeping in my bed. It couldn't be much beyond 11:00 p.m., I didn't think, gauging from the noises that were coming up from the street.

That part had amazed me when I moved in here—discovering that it didn't take me more than two weeks for my internal clock to set to the differences in the types and volume of sound coming up from the canyon-like New York street. That I didn't need any other clock.

And thinking about the time told me why I was hearing the buzzing off and on.

"Shit," I muttered and turned over toward my nightstand to where I was sitting on the edge of the bed, feet on the cold, dusty tiled floor. A new cell phone. I wasn't used to the ringtone I'd set it to.

I picked the cell phone up and hit the talk button. Didn't even have the chance to say anything.

"Clint, where the hell are you? I've been ringing for an hour."

"Uh, sorry, Chief. Not feeling well; decided to give it pass, but forgot to call before I hit the sack."

I nearly added a yelp. My answering the cell had awakened the giant, and he had rolled over toward me and had an arm around me. One hand was on my cock and the other one was running under me, snaking between my butt cheeks, a finger pressing up into my hole. I slapped at the hand encasing my cock, and I felt the bed shift as he snorted and rolled over on his back again. The other hand stayed where it was, though, and I felt a second finger pushing into my channel. Visions of memory hit me of earlier—mostly the vague sensation of feeling, though. He had been good with his cock, very good. The memory was almost of more than just his cock into there, a counterpistoning. I didn't wonder why we'd both been exhausted enough to doze off.

"Danny told me that would be the case." Burton was saying into my ear. "He isn't surprised and sore. He said you could catch him on his bachelor's party for the next marriage. Reminded me it's Brad's birthday."

"Thanks. Tell Danny thanks—and that I'll toast him alone some day this week. And sorry, Chief. You're right. I guess I just couldn't party today."

I felt guilty about that, about giving the chief the impression I was alone and just in a funk I wanted to handle in solitary. Obviously, I could party. A vision of the guy on my bed on his back and me straddling him and riding his shaft hard blew through my mind. I was hardening right up and knew what I'd be doing when I clicked the phone off. I was partying. But not in the "new beginnings" way the guys from the squad were partying. I was doing it my own way, my own self-pitying way, I had to acknowledge. But it was my way. And I was hooked into it, even though some of my friends, meaning the best, told me it was self-destructive behavior.

"Won't be toasting him this week," the chief of NYPD Homicide said. "Got a call after you left. You might pack your bags tonight. You'll be going out West tomorrow night. A special assignment. Your specialty. I'll tell you about it when you come to headquarters tomorrow."

"Right, Chief." I didn't need to ask what my specialty was. Whenever they had anything involved with guys doing guys or needed someone who could get close to that, they called on me—not just in New York, but also farther afield. I didn't mind. I guess I knew it was an ideal job for me. I loved being a cop. But I also loved being cocked. And as long as they needed the specialty and knew they needed it, I was safe from the normal rules of serving in the NYPD and didn't have to hide my wants. Because my wants were my wants; as much as I liked being a cop, I couldn't deny my wants.

As I placed the cell phone back on my nightstand, I looked up at hearing an unexpected sound and from suddenly being bathed in light. The door to my bathroom was opening and another guy not unlike the one on my bed, but hairier, scarier, with bigger muscles and hanging even lower than the guy on the bed was standing there, grinning and naked. In the light, I picked out the residue of white powder at his nose and could see beyond him to the glass shelf over the sink, where he'd been cutting his stuff.

131

Oh fuck, I thought. Not in my own apartment. But then that sort of crime wasn't my look see.

He had a raging hard-on, which I figured now would last for hours. I didn't like the idea of the drugs in my place, but the hard-on was just fine.

In two strides, he had reached me and pushed me down on my back with a beefy hand pressing on my sternum. I went down with my head on the belly of the other guy on the bed, who gave a grunt, but his belly was so rock hard that I knew I hadn't done any damage there.

I didn't know the druggy from Adam, but I knew I was having a personal pity party, and I knew I liked what I saw between his legs—not just the flesh, but the thick cock ring piercing the bulb of his cock. I gave him a big smile as he roughly grabbed my legs by the meat of my calves, spread-eagled them with a splitting jerk, and thrust his dick inside my channel, splitting me with a thickness that had me arching my back and yelping to the ceiling and him shouting out with pleasure. As he began to pump and I thrilled at the feel of the metal of the ring rubbing on me inside, my hips began to counterpunch as if they had a mind of their own. My channel grabbed the digging monster tool and pulled it deeper inside me, the other guy took my head in his hand and turned it southward on his body, where I saw that he had something rising there for me to work on with my mouth. I moaned and sighed and steeped my senses in the best drug I knew of to remember and then try to forget that it was my Brad's birthday.

But the funk wasn't only because it was Brad's birthday. And I was only beginning to acknowledge that, as I felt the guy who had been stretched out on the bed pull his cock out of my mouth. He changed positions, close behind me now, his chin on my shoulder, his hard nipples pushing at my shoulder blades, the leather wrist cuffs rubbing roughly on the small of my back as his hands moved to and grabbed my waist, working his way under me from the back. The guy crouched between my legs with his bludgeon up my channel was lifting me off the edge of the bed, his meaty hands cupping my butt cheeks, enabling the other guy to move his thighs under my butt, lapping me. I moaned and began to breath in big gulps as I remembered now that it wasn't just him counterpistoning me earlier in the evening.

The biker in front of me whispered something.

"What?" I murmured. In a daze, steeling myself, pumped up with fear and exhilaration. A hill to climb, a challenge to take on, something to transport my mind, focus it on managing a challenge, while knowing it wasn't impossible, because I'd already scaled that height once this night.

"A snort? You want something . . . to help?"

"Nooo," I moaned. "I want it all. I want to feel it . . . working together."

"You're gonna feel mine for sure," he muttered, "'Cause the snort really made me into a horse. You're gonna feel them this time, pretty movie star boy. You're going to squeal." And then he laughed.

I was trembling, shuddering, groaning as I felt the bulb at my entrance, there rubbing the underside of the cock of the biker crouched between my legs. Begging entrance, demanding entrance, gaining an inch, as I panted hard and groaned. Yes, this was what I wanted—what I'd gone to Benny's for. It wasn't just because it was Brad's birthday. It was very much as well because it was Danny's bachelor's party. It was the two, together, pushing me over this edge—seeking this punishment.

Danny's impending wedding. Danny, the young, black stud macho cop, just up for from the beat and learning the ropes in Homicide. Strutting around boasting of how much cunt he got—often and from whatever woman he fancied. His tales maddening, because of his hunkiness and the chip on his shoulder and mostly because of what he didn't boast about— that I opened my legs for him on demand too. And had heard him whisper that he loved me—and only me. Danny, who I'd wanted every inch as much as I'd wanted Brad.

I panicked, having second thoughts, even while knowing I'd gone beyond the stage of refusal, both bikers now grunting and straining, not to be denied—knowing they could have it because they'd had it before. But the druggy was right. He'd become a horse. I didn't think . . . I . . . . could. And then I had. "Oh, god," I cried out—squealed just as the biker said I would—as the second splitter worked up into me and the bikers went into a counterpumping sharing. "Oh, god, Yesssss!"

They danced their cocks in my channel. I writhed between their heaving, sweating chests and worked my legs in the air in a bicycle movement in a vain, instinctive movement to master and diminishing the filling of their cocks—and, with a cry, shoot my load up a sweaty belly. The bikers laughed and pumped on toward their own ejaculations.

So much to forget. Sometimes depression is too much for just one cock in the channel at once.

Horrid Bliss

Had he really drunk enough to be this woozy? His head was swimming, the sound of his ears being the rushing of water—real or imagined?—and he was having difficulty distinguishing teak walls from sienna brown curtains on the portholes and from separating his tremors from the slow bobbing of the yacht. Why, in this state of confusion, could he feel every luscious sensation of his dick sliding up and down in the channel of the Thai cabin boy? Or rather, the Thai cabin boy rising and falling on his dick, now that he thought further on it.

Samit was doing all of the work. Thane was lying on his back on the bed that took up most of the cabin, and the small Thai was straddling his hips, the heels of his hands dug into Thane's nipples as he arched his back and licked his lips in apparently deep pleasure, while slowly rising and falling on the dick. Samit's channel was tight and his muscles were rippling over Thane's cock in a most arousing way. Thane couldn't think when his cock had been this hard or the channel had been this tight, even as slicked up as it was. The sliding was easy and gave off a slight slurping sound—a sound that harmonized with the lapping of the water on the ship's hull. Did that mean the ship was moving?

How and when had Thane lost control and become so woozy?

The slickness of the channel, his ability to feel the sensation of the muscles undulating on his cock? Protection.

135

Had there been a condom? Why couldn't he remember how this had come to pass? Had Samit offered himself or had Thane, drunken, forced him? Not likely forced him, if Samit was on top and doing the stroking—and seeming to be getting so much pleasure out of the fuck.

Why couldn't he think straighter? Why was he so confused? And why could he feel every crease and knob inside Samit's channel and the slickness of him? Surely if there was a rubber . . .

Leaving Macau for Bangkok. The thought shot across his brain, a brief, clear thought. Why weren't there more? Why couldn't he put two thoughts together? Where was the Greek? They had been sitting in the fantail, looking at the lit-up bulk of the Venetian Macau Casino and hotel complex, and drinking scotch. Drinking scotch.

The Greek was his ride . . . he had agreed to take him to Bangkok in his yacht, hadn't he? Did the Greek know Thane was fucking his Thai cabin boy? And how did Thane even know Samit was the Greek's cabin boy? Or even that his name was Samit?

Samit had been serving them the drinks. And as he had been doing so had been smiling shyly at Thane. What was that the Greek had asked? Something about whether Thane liked the Thai cabin boy. And in what way? And telling Thane to drink his scotch.

Cabin boy. Oh shit. Was this merely a boy? Were they in international waters, or still in Macau, or, worse, in Chinese waters? But, no. That was clear. He'd been told that Samit was small bodied, the way that many Thai were small. That he was, in fact the same age as Thane. Old enough. Was that before or after the Greek had asked him if he wanted to fuck the cabin boy? Had the Greek really asked him that? Not a boy . . . or so he was told. Had he asked or had the information been volunteered to him—as part of the question of whether he wanted to fuck the Thai. A man. But the body of a boy. The channel of a Hoover vacuum cleaner, though.

Thane heard himself laughing. He didn't feel the laugh, but he heard it. Briefly he checked his memory banks on whether there were any hysterics in the laugh. There didn't seem to have been. But the laugh seemed so disembodied. Entirely unlike the sensation in his cock—such sensual pleasure there that every focus of his body was racing to center on it, to make the most of it. Strange.

And the laugh hadn't only been disembodied, it had been in stereo—but his laugh higher range than the echo.

"A Hoover vacuum cleaner. Very funny."

Had he said that? Surely not. The voice was from across the room. A lower register than his. The Greek's. Cosmo Eracules. The ugly, almost simian, but, at the same time, sensual Greek who had clucked at Thane's loss and volunteered to give him a ride from Macau to Bangkok for fucking privileges en route. That much was clear to Thane. But how had that translated to Thane lying on his back and the Thai cabin boy riding his cock?

The Greek had smiled up at Samit and asked if he wanted to be fucked by Thane. That memory clearly scanned across Thane's brain. But what had the Thai cabin boy's response been? Is this what he really wanted? The scotch—the Greek had kept pressing him to drink the scotch. And his world had begun to spin.

The bother of the difference between the tactile sensation of the Thai's channel sliding on his cock and his inability to "feel" his facile muscles returned. And not being able to stop this rushing of water in his ears or feel himself laugh or know that he had spoken?—because surely the Greek had gotten the Hoover image from him. The tight, hard feeling in his cock. Building up to something big. The cloud-stepping pleasure of the sliding of the slick, tight channel on his cock. And now . . . now . . . Oh, shit! The Thai had moved a hand behind Thane's bare butt and was fisting and squeezing and rolling his balls.

"Oh, fuck. Oh, Shit! I'm gonna . . ."

The explosion of the ejaculation. Thane lifting his torso off the surface of the bed. Grabbing Samit's thick, black hair and pulling him into a kiss . . . as . . . once, twice, and again . . . Thane fired off. The gush of cum. Cum everywhere inside the tight ass. Dribbling down Thane's still-hard cock, as he jerked. Once, twice. More eruptions.

No condom. No way there had been a condom. Who gave a shit? That was . . . spectacular.

Moaning, lying his shoulder blades back on the bed. Samit grinning down at him. Squeezing the cock with his channel—rhythmically. Pulling three last little spurts of cum out of him as his body jerked with each release.

Two heads. Samit had two heads. One so ugly it was arousing, though. The Greek. Peering, leering over Samit's shoulder. Samit leaning his torso down toward Thane's chest, but not actually touching it. Samit turning his face to the Greek's for a deep kiss. The Thai cabin boy moaning and groaning through the kiss.

A new sensation. Something else. Oh, shit, the bulb of another cock. Pressing at the root of Thane's cock, buried still in the Thai's channel. Not as hard as before he'd jacked off, but not flaccid either.

What in the fuck? Another cock, forcing itself into the Thai's channel, on top of Thane's cock.

No way. No way can the Thai's tight channel take it.

But it was taking it. Opening right up as the Greek slid inside, along the top of Thane's cock, making Thane moan too and arch his torso—and, involuntarily—bend and raise his legs and dig the heels of his bare feet into the tops of the meaty, naked mounds of the Greek's ass. Rubbing the small of the Greek's back with the heels of his feet—in rhythm with the moving of his pelvis, the ever-so-slight stroking of his cock inside the channel of the sensually groaning Thai while the Greek's cock began a stroking of its own, sliding in and out on the upper side of Thane's cock.

The Greek moving his cock, fucking the Thai cabin boy, but also fucking Thane's cock. No other way of describing it—stroking in the Thai's channel, still tight, but stretched to accommodate them both, and also stroking along the top of Thane's cock.

Thane hardening up again. Stroking too. Joining in with this horrid . . . fantastic double fuck. Groaning and moaning—in three registers, the Thai's voice even higher than Thane's. Writhing and bucking, all three against each other. And the

Greek pistoning, with Thane, hard as a rock again, balls aching, stroking too.

Grunting expletives in English, Greek, and Thai, as the three worked as one toward a combined goal—exploding as one. Together. Kisses and exclamations of satisfaction and release all around.

* * * *

Thane woke up with a headache, having no question, by the rocking sensation, that the yacht now was under way. He was spread-eagled on his back on the bed, the sheets rumpled so wildly that he had no trouble remembering what he had done the previous night.

But all of it? Was all of it true, not just partly a wild dream? What the fuck? That would be horrible. He hadn't even thought of doing that before. Surely he hadn't. He'd have to think about that. What if he had been the one in the middle? He shuddered at the thought. But he also felt himself hardening up at the thought. Nope, it was nothing he'd ever do. He wasn't sure he could think straight even now. What the fuck had he been given the previous night? It couldn't have all been liquor. The scotch tasted fine. Of course what did he know about fine scotch?

It was horrid—just the thought of doing that, the double fuck, Thane thought as he increasingly accepted that the double fuck had happened. His hand involuntarily went to his hard cock. In the back of his mind, a radically different thought was tugging at him—it had been totally arousing. He'd gone with it—in a big way. He'd never been so hard. He'd never ejaculated so profusely. It was exhilarating. It was bliss. After they'd finished and the Thai and Greek had drawn away from him, he'd had a feeling of loss. He had wanted to do it again. Then, not now, of course. Not when he was sober.

He would never, ever do it again.

"Good morning, sir."

Thane looked up. The cabin boy, Samit, dressed smartly in black pants and a white shirt, was standing, grinning, in the cabin doorway. He had towels draped over his arm.

139

A vision of the Thai, his lithe little brown body naked, straddling Thane's pelvis—the Greek grinning over his shoulder—raced through Thane's mind. With every effort he could manage, he slammed the door on that image.

"You will want to shower before breakfast," Samit was saying. "As you shower, I'll lay clothes out for you. It's a balmy day on the sea. You have many tennis clothes. I will lay a set of those out for you."

Thane lifted his head and peered at the Thai cabin boy standing in the cabin doorway. To do so, he had to look down the full length of his naked body. For some reason looking at Samit was making his dick twitch. It already was hard.

Oh, yeah, He'd fucked the little guy last night all right. And Samit had been really, really good. But it just wasn't him. Thane groaned. The Greek appeared in the doorway behind Samit.

The image that had been in his brain knocked on the closed door again.

Thane's impression of the Greek, Cosmos Eracules, who had identified himself as a Greek shipping fleet entrepreneur when he had put his arm around Thane at the baccarat table to console him and to offer his help, had changed from that night. Hooded eyes that were almost Oriental but that bored right into a man. A squat, graying, middle-age bulkiness that was as much packed with muscle as fat, and a hairiness that was more hinted at then observed at the Venetian Macau Casino on the peninsula's Cotai Strip, but that had been fully revealed to Thane the previous night.

A sense of power and privilege and command.

"Thank you, Samit," the Greek said from behind the Thai. "Mr. Carlin will be showering and taking his breakfast later. He has his passage to start working off now—using his passage." Thane heard the dry, deep laugh that he'd heard several times cutting through the fog of the previous night.

"Yes, Mr. Eracules," Samit said, lowering his eyes, a half smile on his face and backing into the passageway as Eracules pushed past him, already untying his velour robe and opening it to reveal his squat, hairy body in full, thick erection. The Thai clicked the door shut behind him.

Thane had no more time than to contemplate just how hairy the man was, and how thick and up-curved his erection was, and how big and low-hanging his ball sac was before, robe flopping open, the Greek was at the foot of the bed, grabbing Thane's ankles and pulling Thane to the foot of the bed, splitting and raising Thane's legs, thrusting inside him, and pounding, pounding, pounding, while Thane arched his back and writhed under the onslaught.

"Oh, shit. Oh fuck YES!"

* * * *

Thane had been served his breakfast in his room and given time to contemplate what was happening here. He had been active with men, both fucking them and being fucked by them. He certainly hadn't doubled before, though. And he hadn't done anything much that approached that kinkiness.

Still he had come onto the yacht eyes wide open. The Greek had made him acknowledge that his ass was the Greek's for anything he wanted to do between Macau and Bangkok. Eracules said that the rough fuck before breakfast was to make a statement of what Thane had agreed to and to voice pleasure that Thane had so willingly given in to it.

"You have known many men, yes?"

"Not that many."

"But when you have needed to use your body, you have done so—and taken pleasure rather than resentment out of it, yes?"

"I guess that's true. All I really want to do is play competitive tennis. But until you make it into the top one-fifty at least, you have to do what you have to do to continue to be able to make the second week."

"And you make it into the second week often, with this tennis of yours?"

"Not often. Not yet. Actually, not at all yet. But I'm getting close."

"You know that you are very good with the sex, don't you? A beautiful body. A very nice cock. You could do far more than just make it into the second week giving pleasure to men. You realize this, don't you?"

Thane didn't respond.

"Well, it's something to think about," the Greek said, as he slapped Thane on the rump and stood up from the bed. "And if you are interested, I can help you. You can do much better for yourself in a partnership arrangement." Having said that, Eracules turned and left Thane alone in the cabin to shower and dress.

Thane didn't want to give what the Greek had said much thought. He knew he was sexy, yes, but that would pass. So would tennis-playing years on the pro circuit. But tennis was his passion. He had needed the transportation—badly. At twenty, he was at a place in his tennis career that he needed either to start going up the ranks in tournaments or go into the family business. And the trash disposal business, no matter that his father was known as the trash king of San Diego, just didn't match Thane's view of his future.

As far as tournaments, though, he was still in the minor ATP leagues, barely winning enough to keep him going. He'd gotten to the third round in the Tokyo tournament, which had been enough to get him invited to the PTT Thailand Open in Bangkok in late September—and had come with enough prize money to fly him there, although he'd have to live on a string during the tournament if he spent the money on air fare. The Bangkok tournament had a prize purse that wasn't astronomical, but just by showing up, he could pick up enough to get him to his pro job at the San Diego tennis club he worked at while living with his parents and waiting for the season to start up again. But he'd been greedy. He wanted to live well the week or two he'd be in Bangkok.

A Japanese businessman who had attended the Tokyo tournament and who had sniffed around Thane there and had exchanged a good restaurant dinner for a fumbled fuck and comfortable night in a snazzy apartment, had offered to take him to Bangkok by way of the gambling tables in Macau for free— well, for occupying the businessman's bed. And the thought of the air money Thane would save muddled his mind. Taking the Japanese guy was no sweat either. He was all foreplay that required little from Thane other than to open his legs to receive a weak, fast-shot fuck from a tiny cock after the man had sucked Thane off.

The Japanese businessman was fickle and had a roving eye. He picked up a swishy young blond who was cruising the tables at the Venetian Macau, the world's largest casino—an upscale of the Venetian in Las Vegas—and had left Thane high and dry at the Chemin de Fer baccarat table in the Red Dragon area of the casino. Thane fed his anger at being abandoned less than half way to Bangkok with unwise decisions at the baccarat table.

The Greek had been at the table, a hulking bodyguard standing behind him.

"Your friend seems to have deserted you—along with your luck, young man," the Greek said. He folded his hands in front of him, leaned over the baccarat table, and peered at Thane with those piercing, all-knowing eyes of his that Thane had already seen trained on him while the Japanese businessman was still present and bankrolling Thane's play. Thane had the sensation of being undressed. And he knew that look, although most didn't exude the power and command that the Greek did when they cast their eyes on him.

Thane's attention was on the man's folded hands. The hands were massive, the fingers thick. The backs of the hands were hairy, curly jet-black hair sprinkled with gray, and Thane felt the fuzz on his own back chafe on the starched white shirt of his tux as he looked at them. He melted to hairy men—and the size of the hands and fingers had a promise in them. The man had a massive signet ring on the middle finger of his right hand. Thane's imagination was running wild at what the man might be capable of doing with that ring. It may have made a difference that the Japanese businessman had been so small, so lackluster and prissy in his lovemaking. Thane was in the mood for rough sex from a manhandler.

"No problem," Thane had answered. "I don't need him anyway."

"His dick too small for you? He isn't enough man for you?"

Thane's head snapped up. "You are very direct."

143

"I am good at assessing people, and bad about expecting to get everything I want. Was the Jap's dick too small for you?"

"Yes, if you must know."

"Mine isn't. What was the Jap going to do for you? He looks too old and frail for you to be with him by preference. You are a professional male prostitute, are you not?"

"No, I am not." Thane bristled at the assertion, his flash of defensiveness occasioned by how many times in the past week he'd asked himself the same question—was he just a male prostitute? "I'm a professional tennis player. There's a tournament I'm signed up for in Bangkok next week. He was going to pay for my flight there."

"Ah. It so happens that I leave for Bangkok tonight myself. And I have a yacht in the harbor here. I might be willing to give you a lift."

"Might?" Thane asked after a brief pause.

"Yes, might. I feel the need to go to the men's room. You do too, I think."

"I do?"

The Greek just looked at Thane and then stood up from the table. He signaled for his winnings—which were impressive—to be taken away for him, and a floor manager stepped up to the table and respectfully brushed the winnings up. He didn't ask the Greek's name. That was enough for Thane to know how important he was.

The bodyguard followed them as the Greek moved off toward the back of the casino room.

"I think the men's room is up by the entrance," Thane said.

"Not the one we're going to."

The bodyguard stood guard on the door while the Greek pushed Thane into a stall and onto the back of a toilet tank. He had Thane's trousers unbuckled and those and his briefs off his legs in short order and, crouching, straddled the toilet bowl with his own thighs, pressing his crotch into Thane's.

So commanding and strong was he that Thane made no move to resist. And although he couldn't see it, Thane could tell that the man's cock was massively thick.

Placing his forehead against Thane's and holding Thane's gaze with his piercing eyes, the Greek held Thane's chin firm with one hand—his left—and Thane felt a thick finger of the right hand—one topped by a huge signet ring, penetrating his ass.

Thane shuddered and whimpered, his eyes held by the Greek's, while the Greek finger fucked him and worried his rim with the signet ring.

"You aren't playacting with me? Men fuck you? More than just that Jap's feeble attempts."

"Yes, men fuck me," Thane answered in a horse voice.

"I am going to fuck you. Here. Now."

"Yes." The man was overpowering. He got whatever he wanted. Because of the inadequate Japanese businessman, this was what Thane wanted too. The Greek seemed to know just how Thane wanted it. By surprise, little warning, hard, fast, brutal.

When the ring was replaced with an unseen, but very, very thick, hard cock, Thane gasped, his eyes watered, and, fully saddled, he hooked his knees on the Greek's hips. The Greek wasn't wearing a condom and gave Thane a full load—taking his time but not sparing the thrusts.

"Yes, I think I will offer you a ride to Bangkok," the Greek muttered in a low voice when he'd ejaculated. "If you will pay for your passage with more of this—anything I want—and can leave tonight."

* * * *

The luncheon on the fantail had been so civilized that Thane was nervously twitching, wondering how Eracules could be so calm and polite to him as roughly as he had fucked him in the night and then again in the morning. Of course, they weren't alone. The body guard was there, for one. Omar. The Greek had introduced him as Omar. He looked Turkish to Thane. And monstrously big. It was disconcerting to think that he might be Turkish—and Eracules undoubtedly was a Greek. The two men shouldn't get along. Greeks and Turks didn't mix. But Omar obviously was prepared to do whatever the Greek wanted.

145

Thane wondered whether it was money, personal loyalty, or sex that bound Omar to the Greek—or a combination of the three—and he shuddered at the thought of it being primarily sex, as he viewed the bulge at the bodyguard's crotch. The man was in a Speedo. The bodyguard, the Greek, and Thane all were in Speedos, a swim off the boat having been dictated by Eracules before lunch.

Thane was able to think all these thoughts, his nerves sending him fleeing from one thought to another, unrelated one, because Thane wasn't the only guest. There also was a tall, thin Chinese man, who spoke broken English but who was conversing with the Greek in some dialect of Chinese, and whose gaze frequently and disconcertingly fell on Thane. The man was middle aged, not bad looking—for a Chinese, Thane thought—was elegantly dressed in a silk robe such as Thane could imagine a wealthy Mandarin of years gone by would wear. He moved with graceful elegant sweeps of his arms as well.

Since Thane didn't speak any dialect of Chinese, he was left pretty much to his own devices. And part of his devices were to look at the other bodyguard. Standing to port, while Omar stood to starboard, both intently watching the luncheon table, the Chinese bodyguard was a bruiser to match Omar. Quite the thug, Thane thought. Thane hadn't seen him before and he was Chinese and standing behind the Chinese gentlemen, so Thane assumed they were a pair.

Thane rather liked the bulky thug type.

He found himself wondering whether he'd prefer being fucked by Omar or the Chinese bodyguard, and hadn't made up his mind by the time Samit and another Thai male servant were out and clearing away the luncheon table.

The Chinese man and Eracules had seemed to be haggling over something at the end of the meal, but right before the Greek clapped his hands and the Thai servants were clearing away the table, they had both stopped. And they were both smiling, so whatever they had been discussing—transportation of drugs, Thane was willing to bet—had ended with both satisfied.

Then, to Thane's surprise, The Chinese man was settling in a chair facing the chair the Greek was in and the Greek was tugging on his Speedo and telling Thane to strip his off.

The Greek fucked Thane sitting in his chair and Thane in his lap, facing away from Eracules. The Greek held Thane at his waist on either side and guided the rhythm of the fuck as Thane raised and lowered his channel on the thick cock by leveraging off the soles of his feet on the teak deck. Embarrassed, of course, but Thane knew he had promised to do whatever in the way of sex that the Greek wanted. And, since he was facing the Chinese man who was watching the fucking closely with hooded eyes and a little smile on his face, Thane realized this was some sort of show for the Chinese.

He wasn't that worried until the Greek spoke to Omar, telling him to strip and to join them. Thane started to whimper and hyperventilate as Omar approached and Eracules reached around and lifted and spread Thane's thighs, rolling his pelvis up in the same motion.

This was last night again, but this time it was Thane, not the Thai cabin boy, sandwiched between two big-dicked bruisers. Thane writhed and cried out—first in pain, and eventually, as he accommodated the two dicks—being full of wonder that he could do that—in ecstasy. He was taking two cocks. Again, horrid and bliss at the same time. His spirit soared across the sky at the wonder of being able to manage them and at the deeply sensual feeling of two cocks, these two working in a rhythm of thrust and counterthrust, plowing inside him and the two men moaning in lust and arousal as much as he was.

He . . . had . . . no idea how extraordinary this could feel. He cried out and ejaculated onto the hard abdominal plate of the bodyguard as the two men fired, one after the other, and caused him to gasp and moan just as Samit had done the night before at the feel of the double load of cum bathing his channel.

Omar pulled out of him, backed up, picked his Speedo off the deck, pulled it back up his legs, and stood there, at attention, just as if nothing had happened.

Thane remained collapsed against the Greek's chest, with the Greek's arms around him, gliding over Thane's chest and dick and balls. His right hand cupped and lifted Thane's cock.

The underside of the signet ring was rubbing against the underside of the root of Thane's cock, and Thane was hardening again—and breathing a little hard.

The Chinese man said something, and Thane lifted his head and looked at him through dreamy eyes. The Greek answered back. Thane, in the throes of the exhilarating sex, had forgotten that the Chinese man and his bodyguard had been sitting there, watching. It occurred to Thane that Eracules was purposely putting his privates on display for the Chinese man.

"He says he thoroughly enjoyed it and that he's willing to buy," the Greek told Thane in English.

"Enjoyed? Buy? Buy what?"

"Buy you."

Thane laughed.

"I'm serious," the Greek said. "Perhaps it would have been different if I had sensed this morning that we could work together—that you weren't so wrapped up in tennis and getting to Bangkok."

Thane gasped and started to try to struggle, but the Greek held him fast. Omar took a step toward them, but the Greek barked something and Omar backed away. Obviously he had told the bodyguard that he could control Thane. And obviously he could, as Thane gave up the struggle.

"I don't understand. You can't sell me."

"The Chinese gentleman certainly thinks I can. And I can if I do."

"No, you can't."

"Did you see the name on my yacht when you came aboard?"

"Yeah, but it was Greek to me."

"It's Greek to everyone. This yacht is named *Apyko*—which means procurer in Greek. Pimp. I'm a high-stakes procurer. I sail around the world, picking up abandoned and luscious men like you, and selling them to the highest bidder. Hsieng here was the only bidder, but he bid high, and I'm happy with a quick turnover."

"You can't," Thane said, with a moan. "I'm going to a tennis tournament in Bangkok."

"As it turns out, you're not. I'm dropping you and this gentleman off at his home. Which is in Shanghai. Which is north of Macau, not south, the direction of Bangkok."

"No, we can't be . . ." Thane started to say, but then he took the time to look at the sun's angle. The sun was off the port side—west. They indeed were sailing north, not south.

"No, you can't," Thane exclaimed. But this time it was no more than a whisper. Because he realized that, indeed, the Greek could. No one even knew where Thane was headed. When the tournament started in Bangkok, they would just scratch his name and some lucky qualifier would be given his spot.

The Chinese gentleman was standing, and pulling his robe over his head. He was naked under the robe. He was tall and thin and sinewy, and his dick was rather thin, to match. But it was extraordinarily long. The Chinese bodyguard, though, who was also pulling his robe over his head and also was naked underneath, was as thick as Thane would want if only one man was fucking him.

They fucked first on the bed in Hsieng's cabin, Hsieng wanted the experience of being double fucked. As horrified as Thane was with the whole scenario, he enjoyed the fuck, being more turned on by the Chinese bodyguard hovering over Hsieng and between his thighs as Thane lay underneath him than he was with Hsieng—which made it more palatable that both men were fucking him. If it had only been Hsieng . . .

By the time the Chinese bodyguard was standing in the middle of the cabin, holding Thane in front of his heavily muscled body with his beefy hands gripped under Thane's thighs and parting them and Thane arching his torso and gripping his fists behind the bodyguard's neck, Thane was lost to the fuck. And he was no less lost to the fuck when Hsieng approached him from the front and the bodyguard tilted up Thane's pelvis, and Hsieng started to work his cock inside Thane's channel on top of the bodyguards.

Thane knew he'd have to figure out a way to escape this situation—and he had every confidence that he would find a way. But not right now. Right now he was acknowledging that he was lost to the glories—the horrid bliss . . . again—of the double fuck.

New Master at Riverbend

Jerome stood just inside the doorway at the shadowed end of the room. He should have just turned and gone down the stairs and out to the carriage to tell Thomas that Master John wasn't ready to go yet. That's all Thomas, Master John's carriage driver, had told him to do. But the shock of what he'd found when he'd entered the house on Decatur Street and been waved to the second door down the hall on the second floor held him plastered to his shadowy vigil spot long enough to engage his curiosity.

He was old enough to understand this between a man and a woman—he'd been fucking cook's daughter, Macey, long enough in the smoke house himself that she was waddling around supporting her belly with both her hands and with a big smile on her face. And he did the field hand Lottie regularly out in the cotton field too. She was too old to bear, he thought, but she knew what to do with a young man's cock. She'd been riding his since he became a grown man, old enough to go to the fields. These things Jerome already understood in his nineteenth year on this earth. But this. This was not something he had considered possible.

When Jerome had quietly pushed open the door and stolen in, he was suspecting something like this was going on. Everyone knew what went on in the Decatur Street house. But he didn't expect this. He didn't expect this at all.

A small black man of not more than Jerome's age was lying on his side on the bed—naked. He was up on one elbow and his back was turned to Jerome. Young Master John, also naked except for the billowing white cotton shirt with the flounces on it, open so that Jerome could see his hard-bodied chest, had the fingers of one hand buried in the black, wooly hair of the black man's head, holding the head to his groin. The black man was moving his mouth down and up on Master John's cock. The white man's other hand was reaching down and gripping the black man's cock and was stroking it.

Jerome hadn't ever seen anything like this before. He should have turned and run out, but this was something entirely new to him, and Jerome was the curious type, especially where it came to sexual activity. And not knowing any better, the old master not having pushed the Riverbend plantation slaves to attend church, Jerome had no internal prejudices set on things such as this. Slave row at Riverbend was an earthy place. As soon as he had become aware of his sexual nature, Lottie was showing him how it could give him pleasures that transported him from the hardships of plantation life. She didn't tell him that it was only something that men and women did.

Still, it had not occurred to him that there were other couplings possible such as this one.

Before Jerome could get the notion to leave and go tell Thomas that their new master, John, didn't appear to need the carriage any time soon, the tableau on the bed was changing. Master John was standing on the floor on the other side of the bed and had turned the black man on his side and lifted the man's left leg to rest his ankle on John's shoulder. The black man's plump buttocks were plastered to the white man's pelvis, and the white man was fucking the black man's ass with long deep strokes. Master John was still fisting and stroking the black man's cock, and the black man was moaning and writhing against the deep stroking inside him. He had his left arm raised and a black hand palmed on the white chest, whether to try to push the white man away or to establish a connection to the man fucking him, Jerome couldn't tell. His other hand was stretched out across the bed and he was clutching the bed cloth in a fist. It seemed to Jerome that he was bunching and releasing the material in the same rhythm that Master John was stroking him with his cock. Whether or not that was so, Jerome saw it as so— and it aroused him.

The black man's face was turned toward Jerome, set in an expression of almost pleading. Jerome wondered if the man could see him there in the shadows. Possibly so. There was little danger that Master John could see him, though. White slaveholders rarely saw their slaves even in broad daylight; they looked right through them as if they weren't even there. The black man's eyes were opened wide, glittering, and his mouth was slack. He was moaning and groaning.

Master John turned him again to his back, his buttocks at the edge of the bed. The white man grabbed the black man's ankles with his fist and brutally jerked them wide. He was leaning over the black man's chest, growling and grunting. His hips were pistoning fast and hard. The black man was clutching at the bed cloth with both of his fists and writhing under the white man and babbling incoherently and crying out at each deep, rapid thrust.

Master John tensed, abruptly stopping the thrusts. His body jerked and his head turned up toward the ceiling. Jerome saw in his face the same ecstasy he saw in Macey's when he released his seed in her. One, two, three more pumps and Master John let out a long sigh and collapsed on top of the black man, who just lay there, moaning.

Jerome realized that he had wet himself with his own sticky manseed. He hoped that Thomas wouldn't notice that when he returned to the carriage. Master John's ejaculation, though, broke the spell, and Jerome realized that he had been away from Thomas too long. He withdrew quietly and then clattered out onto the street.

"I do believe Massa John be ready soon," he said breathlessly to Thomas when he arrived back at the carriage. "But he ain't ready now."

"Why you be so long in findin' that out?" Thomas asked suspiciously. "You find some pussy to poke for yerself while you in there?"

"No, no. They's not want to tell me where he was. Took me a time to get them to check on him. You know I can't 'ford the pussy they got in there."

"You such a handsome stud, I figure they give it to you for free just so they can watch. Nice big cock like yours and fine body."

Jerome blushed—if a black man can blush. Thomas had been talking to him like this for some months. It was only now that Jerome could come to the point of considering what Thomas might be meaning about that. True that often when he was sluicing himself down, having come for the fields, Thomas was there to jabber with him while he was naked. Jerome would need to give that some thought now. Now that he knew that men did it with men too.

Fifteen minutes later, Thomas gave Jerome the evil eye. "Thought you said the massa was about done."

"That's what they tell me in the house," Jerome answered defensively.

"Best I go check, I guess," Thomas said, moving to get down from the driving box.

"No, I'll go," Jerome answered.

He went quietly back upstairs. Although patrons and servants of the house were moving about, no one saw him or challenged him. There were advantages to being invisible to the whites, Jerome thought as he approached the second door down the hall.

The black man was on all fours in the center of the bed and Master John was crouched over his pelvis, fucking him in long, fast strokes. He was cupping the black man's throat from behind and arching his back up. The black man had a wild-eyed look in his eyes and his tongue was lolling out of his mouth. That's how Jerome liked to fuck Macey. Lottie liked that position too, but she preferred Jerome fucking her in the ass when he took her this way. He never realized that it could look so arousing. Master John was leaning well forward on the black man's buttocks so that Jerome could clearly see the thick white cock burying itself in the black asshole and then sliding out and then in again. He focused his attention on that action and felt chills running up his spine. He envisioned himself as poking a white man like that—maybe even Master John, although that gave him a start and a jolt of fear—and maybe even being poked like that.

He was surprised at the thought—but he was even more surprised that he didn't shrink from the thought.

He did, however, step out of the room and down the stairs and out to the carriage.

"I reckon Massa John won't be ready for a time yet," he told Thomas.

Thomas didn't bother to ask why. It wasn't the lot of a slave in the plantation world to ask why, just to stand by, invisible, until some white person told them what, where, and when.

Later that night, when Jerome left his hut to take a piss, he heard moaning and men whispering to each other in the shed where they housed the mules. He went to investigate and found Thomas and one of the overseers doing the same thing to one of the young field hands Master John had brought with him from his own plantation on a bale of hay that Jerome had seen Master John doing to the male prostitute in the brothel. Not quite the same thing, though. Thomas and the overseer had the young black man between them and they were both fucking him together, both moving their cocks in and out of the man's hole at the same time. He was collapsed between them like a rag doll, not struggling or even working with them, just resting his ankles on the overseer's shoulders and moaning, his arms dangling down at his sides.

Wadya know 'bout that? Jerome thought as he pulled away. Tain't seen nothin' like that before. It registered with him, though, that Thomas fucked men, something Jerome thought might be useful to know one of these days.

* * * *

The various strata of the Riverbend plantation community had been living carefully and on the edge of concern for several months now, since even before young Master John came to take up residence. The Rembeaus, the family that had owned and lived at Riverbend for generations, were almost all

155

gone now. Master John was the last of the lot, and he was just a cousin to Master Edward, the patriarch of the family last in residence here. But Master Edward's family had, to a member, been taken by the fever while visiting a plantation farther down the Mississippi, and Master John had inherited.

The big concern was what Master John was going to do with Riverbend. There were rumors that he would break up the place—sell the land and sell the slaves too. Neither the slaves nor the next strata up, the overseers, liked this thought one little bit. For the slaves, it inevitably meant a breakup of a community that had lived here for some hundred and fifty years, including, probably, family units. To the overseers it meant new, quite possibly less-desirable, employment needing to be found.

Nothing had transpired yet, but everyone was living in fear. Some, the customary leaders of the slave community, a small network of the older women who were house or kitchen slaves, were not content with sitting and waiting.

"How long has your Adelle been housemaiding at the big house, Naddie?"

"Ever since the young massa arrived. She done everthin' I told her to do—leastwise she claims so—and still he not taken her to his bed."

"Ever thing?" Zumma Mae said, with astonishment. "She a right tempting morsel. I can't see no white man not wanting inside that if she be shashaying around his bed already."

"I don' know what else to try, Zumma Mae. We always have someone in the massa's bed to give us some voice in how things run around here. We gotta do somethin'. I can't live with the thought of being parted with any of my kin. Thas happenin' elsewhere, but we don' wan' it happenin' here."

Jerome, who was standing in the kitchen doorway and watching Macey move around, putting pots she cleaned away and moving things back and forth into and from the larder room, muttered under his breath, "Usin' wrong bait, I'se supposin'."

"What's that you say, Jerome?" Naddie asked, turning to him. "And wha ya doin' sniffin' around here for, anyhow? Don't think like I don' know what you after. Well, you already seeded up Macey here. You can just take it on out to the field. I think I hear Lottie a'callin' you."

The women sitting around the table cackled and Macey looked embarrassed and went into the larder room and didn't come right back out. Jerome didn't budge from the doorway.

"Nothin'. I was saying nothin'." But he sure was thinking about it.

"Might not be nuff on this problem anyhow," Zumma Mae picked up the discussion. "The man could plow Adelle from sundown to sunup and still come away and sell her momma on the auction block. Thas just the way white man do it."

"I suppose," Naddie said, but she added with a determined voice, "But someone gotta do somethin' about it."

The women were deep in conversation, so Jerome took his chance and slipped by them and into the larder. He came up behind Macey, who was facing a shelf, and embraced her, putting both arms around her and cupping one full, ample breast with one hand and her bulging belly with the other. Macey gave a low cry, but nuzzled back into him like she'd both expected and wanted this.

"What you doin' here sniffin' round me, Jerome? You already did your bizness here. You don' want no fat woman."

"I always want this woman," Jerome whispered. He sniffed at her hair, "You always smell so fresh and flowery."

"Flowery, eh? You can't even pick out a flower and bring it to me if you gonna try that silliness on me?"

"It don' matter. I figure you like my dick as well as the next man's. A hard dick is as much flower as I need bring you, I figure."

"More. You know that. You my master. You know that. You git that dick up inside me and move it and you know you my master. That I do anything for you. Oh, Jerome. You shouldn't . . . not in here. They's busybodies just in the other room."

Jerome had hiked up her gunnysack dress, finding, as he expected, no clothing underneath, and was cupping her triangle and working a finger inside her, looking for the spot that made her moan.

She moaned.

"Let them find their own dick," Jerome murmured. "If you promise not to make no noise, I'll promise not to either."

"You stop that now, boy. You know this tain't the time nor place."

"With you any time or place is right."

She moaned again as, having bunched the dress up around her waist, Jerome unbuttoned and released himself. He covered her mouth and nose with his hand to muffle her cry as he pushed up into her and started to pump slowly.

When he felt she could control herself, he dropped the hand back to her breast. "You still think we shouldn't be doin' this, sugar?"

"Jus' be good to me, Jerome. I tole you already. You get that dick of yours up there and I'll do anythin' you want."

He proceeded to be good to her.

A voice floated in from the kitchen. Naddie's voice. "Don' ya all think I don' know what ya all doin' in there, Jerome." The voice wasn't angry though; it had a tinge of laughter to it.

Jerome wasn't just fucking, though. He was also thinking. What had she said—twice? Get that dick up in her and he could do anything he wanted with her. There was something to think about in that. And what Jerome was thinking was that just maybe Naddie had the right idea but was looking at it from the wrong direction. When he thought of "the wrong direction," he gave a little laugh.

"What you find so funny?" Jerome, Macey asked in a breathy voice.

"Not a thing, sugah. You just keep pushin' back on it like that, and we do just fine."

* * * *

Jerome stood inside a two-walled isolated area set off behind a shed near the end of the Riverbend slave row, sluiced the first bucket of water over his body, and followed the rivulets of water down his torso and on to his thighs with his hands. He sensed that Thomas was nearby, watching him, and he smiled.

This was working as he meant it to. He turned three-quarters sideways toward where he presumed Thomas was standing and moved a hand down to his basket, first cupping his balls and the underside of his cock and then moving his hand to his cock and giving it a few languid strokes.

He lifted his eyes and looked into Thomas's eyes. Yes, there is want there, he thought. Now that he knew that men did it with men as well as with women, he could clearly see the want in Thomas's eyes. It wasn't any different, really, than the want he'd seen in Macey and Lottie's eyes—indeed, in the eyes of most of the slave women. He just hadn't looked for it in the eyes of a man before. He smiled at Thomas, and Thomas gave an embarrassed start.

"You wanna lift the other bucket over me, Thomas?" Thomas, dressed only in his breeches, came slowly forward. He was trembling as he lifted the bucket of water over Jerome's head and let the liquid roll down his body. Thomas was a massive man, standing a good head taller than Jerome and with bulging arm, chest, and thigh muscles. Jerome felt diminished in his presence, needing to act carefully, because if he gave too much too soon, the man would overpower him and just take what he wanted and walk away. Jerome needed him to want him so badly that the massive man would follow his lead.

"Umm, feelin' good," Jerome whispered, running his hands down his torso to his thighs again. He could hear the catch in Thomas's breath, and before the man could move away from him, Jerome reached back and took Thomas's hands, bringing his arms around his body. He held one hand to his breast and moved the other one down to cover his genitals. Thomas was trembling. He asserted some control, however, pulling his hands away and running them over Jerome's body as he wished, but when the hands stopped roaming, they were back where Jerome had put them. Jerome was fighting hard the moan his throat wanted to give in response to the feel of the massive cock running up from his waistline. If the man wasn't so much taller than Jerome, Jerome was afraid that the cock would be in place already and that Thomas would just hold Jerome in a tight embrace and enter and take him right there.

159

"Me bein' wrong, Thomas? Does you not want to fuck with me?"

"Yes, I want to fuck you. Very much. But you only lie with women."

"I was thinkin' that to. But do you know what Massa John was doin' in that Decatur Street house?"

"Yes, I know well."

"And that he was doin' a man?"

"Yes, I know that too. White massas do what white massas want to do—with who they want to do it to."

"I watched. I be gone so long because I watched."

"Ah. And you be curious now, be you? How it feels to have a man inside you? Or you inside him?"

Thomas wasn't trembling as much. He was holding Jerome closer to him, with a stronger embrace, and he was starting to work Jerome's cock. It was dawning on him that perhaps this really was an opportunity. Jerome could feel the hardness of the man in the small of his back. And now he was the one trembling a bit.

"Yes, I be curious. Havin' another man inside me. But I be also a little afraid. How can I tell it will give me pleasure?"

"There is a way I see that tells," Thomas whisper. "I always find that if a man can suck a cock, he can enjoy it up his ass."

"So, you think . . . ?"

Thomas was already gently turning Jerome's body and pushing the young man down onto his knees closely in front of him. His hardened cock was now pressing into Jerome's cheek, and Jerome just opened his mouth and took the bulb of it inside. Thomas sighed and shuddered, and Jerome showed that he needed little instruction to do what came naturally.

Lifting him back up, Thomas placed his lips on Jerome's and, though it surprised him, Jerome went with the kiss.

"Kissin' be as good a buildup to a fuck as anything else—as with a woman," Thomas said. He went in for another kiss, and while they were engaged in this, Thomas took both of their cocks together and stroked. Jerome was trembling again and released a moan.

"You can suck the cock and you can moan to a kiss," Thomas whispered. "I think you can moan to a cock inside you too. Is it what you want to try?"

"Yay, it is," Jerome murmured. He wasn't fully convinced himself, but he wanted to try it with Thomas first to see if he could endure it—at least whether or not he could convince another man he wanted it and then could take it with a smile.

Thomas gently turned Jerome around, facing away from him. "Bend over. Bend over and spread them legs," he said. And as Jerome did so, Thomas knelt down behind him, snaked a hand between his thighs, and grabbed Jerome's cock. Then Thomas's mouth went to Jerome's ass.

"What?" Jerome asked in surprise and half shock as he felt the wetness of the tongue at his channel entrance.

"Hold still. You be unused and I be big. We need to get you more open or you not bein' enjoyin' this much."

Jerome found himself sighing and moaning again as new sensations of pleasure rolled in waves over his body. The stroking of his cock didn't hurt either.

At length Thomas stood, bidding Jerome to stay as he was but to spread his legs even further, and Thomas was slowly working his cock inside Jerome's ass, as the young man panted and grunted and groaned and tried his best not to scream out or try to escape.

"Let your body go limp and breath regular. I be in now. We rest and then I take you to glory. Your doin' good. The hurt will go in a bit. You need to be stretched to fit."

Jerome whimpered, "Be good to me," and then almost laughed, as that was what Macey had said to him right before he had fucked her good and hard in that laundry room. And hard had seemed good enough for her to hear her comment on it while it was happening.

"You be liken this and maybe you like two men inside you," Thomas murmured.

No liken that, I don' think, Jerome thought. But he said nothing, not wanting to put Thomas off from what he was learning from him.

Then Thomas fucked Jerome good and hard and took him to glory, and by the time he was finished, Jerome was feeling more pleasure than pain. Half way through the fuck, Thomas pulled Jerome's shoulders up into his chest, and Jerome turned his head and they kissed deeply and shared in whispers how good the fuck was going. And Jerome proved he could take sex this way by shooting off into one of the buckets.

"You done good," Thomas said. "I knew you liked it when we kissed and you began fuckin' me back with your hips. You be made for this. You maybe made for two men."

Jerome didn't love it yet, but he liked it well enough to continue with his plan.

"I think you all the man I need, Thomas," he said. But then he continued. "I been tole if I take a cock and love it, the man is my master."

"I been tole that too," Thomas answered. "I'd like to fuck you nuff to master you, but I'se not sure you'd be letting me."

"How can the man tell he is accepted as master?"

"If a man will fuck hisself on the cock is a clue."

"Fuck hisself? I don't understand."

"I can show you."

Thomas sat on a bench, holding Jerome's waist, as Jerome sat in his lap, facing him, and on the cock and, at Thomas's direction fucked himself on the hard shaft by leveraging off the soles of his feet.

Jerome thought he had gotten the idea by the time they both had come again—and he now thought he had enough understanding and preparation to work out his plan.

While Jerome absentmindedly worked a plan in his mind, he remained sitting on Thomas's cock, and Thomas glided his hands over Jerome's body, kissed his neck, and moved a hand around to play with the his balls and cock. Jerome barely discerned when Thomas's cock was getting big inside him again. It was a jolt when he realized it and he moved as if to rise.

"Go down on your all fours on the grass," Thomas growled.

Jerome did as he was told and Thomas crouched over his hips, grabbed his waist in his hands, and began the fuck again. It was only later that it dawned on Jerome that Thomas had commanded and Jerome had simply complied. Thomas hadn't even asked if he could fuck him again, and Jerome had no idea what he would have answered if Thomas had asked. Was this, he wondered, what being mastered meant? If so, it was a powerful weapon.

Thomas settled that. He laughed and said, "See it works. You fucked yourself on me and then jus' did what I told you to do afterward. So's I's master of you in the fuck now. You gonna let me fuck you again when I wants to?"

"I guess so," Jerome answered.

"I guess so too," Thomas said. "Maybe even me and 'nother man too. If you be mastered right." Then he laughed again.

Jerome didn't laugh, but he didn't contradict Thomas either.

* * * *

"Did you feel what your muscles down there were doin' this time?"

Thomas had become more inventive with Jerome over the past two weeks. Jerome had confided part of his plan to the carriage driver. Naddie's plan of Master John bedding the housemaid Adelle and then Adelle having some sway over the master couldn't work because, as Jerome and Thomas knew and Naddie didn't, Master John preferred lying with men. Thus, part of Jerome's plan was to seduce Master John so that he could carry on with Naddie's plan. Thomas had told Jerome that Master John would be a sophisticated and demanding lover, so that Jerome should gain more experience and more knowledge of the various positions himself.

Jerome half expected that Thomas's main purpose in that was to continue fucking Jerome, but it fit in with Jerome's plans, and he had to admit he was increasingly falling under the mastery of the carriage driver and was becoming increasingly interested in being fucked by men—and by Thomas, in particular. That didn't mean he was any less interested in fucking women too. And as a reaction to all of this, he was broadening

163

his own pursuits of the young slave women of the plantation and was almost always well received because of his good looks and well-built body. Slaves could not help but think of themselves as breeding stock, because their masters certainly did, and Jerome was seen as a prime breeding stud. Even the overseer would look the other way and forgive both Jerome's unfulfilled work and that of the young Negress when he saw Jerome's rump between two chocolate thighs in the cotton field. Jerome was producing slave babies, which added to the wealth of the plantation.

Jerome's dalliances with Thomas hadn't turned Jerome from interest in women. Far from it. It had heightened his awareness of the pleasure of sex. There were three young slave women walking around the plantation with a smile on their faces and a hand on their belly now. And Jerome even was giving some thought to two men sharing another man. He'd already shared one of the slave women with another strapping field hand and all three had seemed to like that just fine.

This had been a new position. Thomas had been sitting on the grass, legs stretched out, and Jerome had been skewered on the cock facing away from Thomas with his legs stretched back past Thomas's hips and his torso careened out over Thomas's legs. Thomas had held Jerome tight by the wrists, bowing the young field hand's chest out. It was hard for Thomas to stroke in this position, so he had instructed Jerome to fuck himself. Frustrated with getting enough leverage on his knees and toes to create the desired friction on the cock, Jerome's channel had improvised its own solution. The muscles of the channel walls had made love with their undulations on Thomas's cock all by themselves. Both men had enjoyed that.

"Yay, I felt that," Jerome answered.

"Well, keep a doin' that. A man will go wild with your shaft makin' love to his dick like that."

It was after that, as they lay in each other's arms and Thomas was talking of exotic positions they had not tried yet that he brought up in more detail and as more of a possibility the special act that the truly jaded man who was fucked by men got excited about and sometimes dared. Jerome's breathing became labored at the mere thought of it, but he he'd already given it a lot of thought and was sure he could never go to that extreme. And he said so. Thomas's reaction to his response seemed one of disappointment, and Jerome became afraid that maybe Thomas was proposing such an arrangement. But he didn't bring it up again.

While Jerome trained in male seduction and the satisfaction of a male partner with Thomas, he was biding his time. He needed something to happen. And then it did.

The house waiter's arm was scalded in the kitchen one day, and it was clear that it would have to remain dressed and the waiter resting for days, if not weeks.

"I don' know what is to do," Naddie spoke in concern. She was merely the head cook, but in reality, at least on this plantation, that also made her responsible for the serving slaves. "He will not have a woman serve him his dinner."

"Let me do it," Jerome piped up to say. He had just fucked one of the laundresses behind the hanging sheets and Macey had heard of it and was giving him the cold shoulder in the kitchen. He had come here, though, to jolly her out of her funk. She was too far along for him to be fucking her, and, when she thought about it, she would realize that he had to be fucking and impregnating some Negress—that the economy of the plantation dictated that. And he continued to show Macey in many small ways that he was truly most fond of her.

"You?" Naddie said as if she had never heard such a preposterous thing. "You is jus' a field hand."

"Yay, but I be workin' with Thomas on the carriages long time now too, and I be picking up the ways of the house. Somebody got to do it. No reason it not be me."

He knew he was the favorite of all her sons and he gave her his best smile. If need be, he'd tell her how important this was for his plan—for all of their futures—but only if he had too. He didn't know how she would react to a man lying under another man.

The look worked. That evening, dressed in a white, billowy cotton shirt, a black velvet vest, and very tight black velvet breeches, Jerome was serving at table.

There were no guests. Master John was supping alone. There was only Jerome in the dining room. Master John insisted

165

on only having one servant serving the table when he dined alone.

Jerome moved as gracefully as he could about the room. He had cleaned himself well and been given a musky cologne to use by Thomas, who said it was a particularly popular one used in the male brothels of New Orleans. And Jerome looked as shy and docile as he could and did what he could to leave the impression that he was in awe of the master of the plantation and was attracted to Master John. He smiled a shy smile and took demure looks at Master John whenever it would seem that he didn't want the master seeing him do that—when it was exactly the impression he wanted to leave.

He was standing close beside Master John's chair at the table, serving dish in hand, when it happened. His crotch—on purpose—was on the level of John's face and close to it. John suddenly could not take any more of the dance of enticement. He turned his head toward Jerome's crotch, took in a heady, deep breath—undoubtedly breathing in the musky scent of the handsome, perpetually in heat young black buck—and put his open mouth on the bulge in Jerome's basket. At the same time he snaked an arm around Jerome's hips and clutched at a butt cheek, pulling Jerome in closer to him.

"You all don't fight me now," he muttered. "Remember who I am."

When he heard no opposition from Jerome, Master John turned his head up to Jerome's face and Jerome smiled down at him what he hoped would be a smile of acceptance. The master-slave relationship being what it was, John wouldn't have expected rejection, but he might have expected a moment of surprise and some form of reluctance. Not receiving that caused John to shudder in pleasure. Jerome leaned over and placed the serving dish on the table and then he moved his hand down to his waistband and unbuttoned the top two buttons on his fly.

Master John unbuttoned the rest and pulled out Jerome's cock, swallowed it almost down to the root, and began to stroke it with his mouth.

Victory one, Jerome thought. He remembered the theory that Thomas had told him: that if a man will suck another man's cock, he also will take that cock in the ass.

A bit later Jerome was kneeling on the floor in front of John's chair and between the man's legs and sucking on the master of Riverbend's cock.

And later still, Jerome, sans breeches, was sitting in the dining chair himself, his legs hooked over the arms and a pillow at the small of his back rolling his hips up, and Master John was crouched over him, his hands on the back of the chair and his cock jackhammering Jerome's ass channel, while Jerome moaned and groaned and held John's waist in his hands.

Jerome was flat on his stomach, stretched out on the carpet next to the dining table and John was riding his ass, when Master John leaned down, putting his mouth close to Jerome's ear, and whispered, "You cannot be an innocent. No innocent knows how to do that with his channel muscles. You will be in my bed tonight."

"Yes, Massa. Whatever Massa wants," Jerome purred. And then he gave a big smile. Victory in phase two.

God, the man could fuck, Jerome was thinking as Master John mounted him for the third time in his bed that night. But then Jerome knew that was the case already, having had to wait for Master John for a couple of hours at the Decatur Street brothel not many days earlier. Master John was on his knees on the bed, with Jerome's buttocks resting on his thighs, Jerome's legs bent, and his feet flat on the bed next to Master John's hips. John was clutching Jerome's waist and pulling his channel on and off the cock, having tired of keeping his own hip action in motion to help him ram the cock home repeatedly.

He had been explicit in telling Jerome how much he liked the young black slave's body and that Jerome would be sleeping with him for the foreseeable future—all good portents for the success of Jerome's plans.

But the key thing was that the man seemed to be tiring, and Jerome wasn't, having made the man do most of the work. At the point of Master John's ejaculation and as he was allowing his body to relax and fall onto Jerome, the black slave took his chance. As John came down, Jerome turned both of their bodies so that Master John was still on his knees, but Jerome was on top of him, pressing his chest down on the surface of the bed and rubbing his own cock up and down in the crease between

John's buttocks. Weak from the night's exertion, John hunched there, panting. He was saying something, but Jerome wasn't listening to him. He grabbed John's wrists to help keep him immobile and moved his mouth to the puckered hole between the butt cheeks.

John squeaked and moaned as Jerome's tongue did its magic of opening the hole and lathering it up. Satisfied he could get in and just a bit surprised at how quickly it opened up and that Master John wasn't fighting him hard enough, Jerome mounted the man's hips and worked his cock into the channel.

The white man bucked and writhed and cried out within Jerome's grip. Jerome started stroking, running the thought over and over again in his mind that a man who will suck the cock will take the cock in the ass. And the master is the one with the cock in the other man's ass.

He fucked fast and hard, reasoning that if he was going to master John, it couldn't be a tentative matter.

Somewhat to his surprise, when he starting listening to what Master John was sounding off about, it turned out to be exclamations of passion. "God yes, fuck me! Deeper! Harder! Faster!"

The man was happy to be fucked. It was a revelation to Jerome and one that immediately endangered his plan. How easy would it be to master a man by the cocking if he was well used to being cocked. And a further revelation to Jerome was that he was enjoying fucking the man. So, there were men who could genuinely enjoy both fucking another man and being fucked by another man. Jerome marveled at all there was about the mysteries of life and fucking that he had never known.

Still, he fucked on, and Master John encouraged him to do so.

The next afternoon Jerome appeared in the kitchen house decked out in the white shirt, velvet vest, and tight black breeches he'd spent several hours putting back into order. At first the laundress he'd been fucking, who already was beginning to show the evidence of another of his children, was helping him. But she also wanted him to take time to give her a fuck, and he was much too spent to do that, so she'd deserted him to finish his own repairs.

"Ya can take those right off," Naddie spat at him when he entered the kitchen.

"I be serving Massa at supper," he said. "I have to wear these."

"No ya don' have to serve Massa at supper. He sent word you to be excused. That you got other duties. That you gotta rest. I'm using Nathan."

"Nathan be an old man, Naddie," Jerome said.

"Right. Thas right," Naddie retorted. "Seems only an old man is goin' be able to serve twice in the dining room when Massa sups alone. Don't try to hide from me what ya doin' with that man. Sound gets outta that dining room just fine."

"I'se a plan, Naddie. Now you know why Adelle didn't work. Now you know a man's got to do it. We has to try to keep the fambly together here. I'se jus' doin' what I has to do. The man don' fuck women, Naddie. He done like ta fuck men. I'se just tryin' to do what Adelle can't do. You be ready for Adelle to do this for the fambly, you need ta be ready to let me do it when she can't."

"It just tain't natural." Naddie began to cry. She collapsed in a chair and Jerome went over and stroked her hair.

"It be nec'sary, Naddie. You tell me to stop and I'll stop, Naddie. But it's for the fambly. Should I stop?"

Naddie didn't answer, but when Jerome reached the door, she mumbled. "Jus ya all be careful. Them white men is mean bastards."

Jerome would take whatever blessing he could get. So, this was enough for him. He wouldn't tell her all of it. He wouldn't tell her that he enjoyed both fucking men and being fucked by them. That didn't mean he enjoyed fucking women any less. And Naddie hadn't said all that much about the big stomachs being seen on the young Negresses of the plantation. Naddie liked her grandbabies well enough.

That night was the test of the next strategic phase of Jerome's plan. Master John fucked him just as he had observed John fucking the male prostitute at the Decatur Street house. First sidesplitting him and stroking his cock and then fucking him like a dog, crouched over Jerome as he was on all fours on the bed. But then Master John asked for the fuck himself.

This was the most dangerous point of all of this.

"I be tired. I don' think I can fuck you as long as you want."

"It's what I want. You were supposed to get rest today. I heard you were in the field. I don't want you using your energy in the field anymore."

I be in the field fucking Berta, Jerome thought, and almost laughed. Making more babies for your wealth. But that's not what he said. He had been building up to this moment.

"I be tired, but my cock still be strong. If you want it, you can ride it."

Make them fuck themselves and then you are master, Jerome heard Thomas saying to him.

"Lie on your back," Master John said.

Exhilarated, Jerome turned onto his back. Just as he had promised, his cock was hard and erect. John straddled his hips, facing him, and slowly descended on the cock. He rode the cock hard and wild like he was a ship being tossed on a stormy sea. Jerome came first and then John moved up to straddle his chest, and Jerome sucked him to an ejaculation.

They settled down, stretched along each other's bodies, and dozed. Jerome awoke with the sensation of Master John stroking his cock. This was the next danger point. Would John want to fuck him or be fucked.

"I want your cock again," John murmured.

"I still be tired."

"I want the cock." It was almost a whine.

"You be havin' to ride it yourself."

This time John rode the cock in the opposite direction, facing Master Jerome's feet. He asked the young black man to raise his knees, and he clutched them in his arms and pushed them out and in to match the rhythm of his rise and fall on the cock.

After several minutes, deciding that he had made his point and that he could acknowledge he was rested enough, Master Jerome rose and pulled John over to the side of the bed, with Master Jerome standing on the flour between John's thighs and pounded John's ass, while the white man writhed and cried out in ecstasy and clutched the bedspread in his claws.

Jerome sensed victory, but he didn't feel he could risk yet making the demand he was building up to. That John let men fuck him—and therefore at least partially master him—before Jerome had was disturbing. Perhaps the fucking didn't completely subjugate him.

But then Jerome remembered what Thomas had said some days before about the special act—that if a man experienced that and was one of the few men who loved having it done, that it was the ultimate leverage over a man who wanted to be fucked by men. It might be too much. It might destroy all of the work Jerome had already done. But if Jerome could think of one man who would melt to that act, it would be this man, John Rembeau.

The next night he had Thomas waiting in the shadows of the bedroom, just another invisible slave, when he entered the bedroom. John was there before him as well. He was wearing just a robe, open to reveal the well-muscled line of his body and a half-erect cock. He was standing in the center of the room, reflected in the dim, dancing light from the fireplace and holding a snifter of brandy. He had already been drinking heavily.

"Strip down and come here," he commanded, and Jerome did so, a bit worried that the man was going to reassert control. Perhaps even send him away as a threat to the man's authority. He put the snifter down on a table as Jerome approached. Jerome, like all of the slaves, wore a leather collar. That was all he was wearing now, but it clearly marked him as the slave. As he reached John, the white man grabbed the collar from behind and pulled Jerome's lips up to his—Jerome being shorter and trimmer than John—and took him in a brutal kiss. As they were kissing, he reached down and grabbed Jerome's balls and squeezed them until Jerome's eyes watered. He refused to cry out, though.

There was an ottoman right behind where Jerome was standing, and John pushed Jerome down in a sitting position on that. He reached over, picked up the snifter, took another deep drink, and then put it back on the table. He moved his legs between Jerome's thighs and Jerome reached out and cupped John's balls and brought the cock to his mouth and sucked it. John picked up the snifter again, while moving his hips in a face

171

fuck of Jerome's mouth. Nothing was being said by either man. All that could be heard was heavy breathing. John didn't seem to notice, though, that three men, not two were breathing heavily in the room.

The brandy finished, John pulled his cock out of Jerome's mouth and went down on his knees between Jerome's thighs. He took Jerome's cock in his mouth, while he fingered Jerome's balls and rimmed and invaded Jerome's ass with his fingers when he got tired of the ball work. Jerome laid back on the ottoman, his head dangling off the other end and his arms dangling off the sides.

Moments later John was fucking Jerome's ass and Jerome was giving appropriate moaning and groaning sounds. But this didn't last long. This wasn't what John seemed mainly to be interested in, although he thrust to an ejaculation that Jerome felt flow deep inside him. Withdrawing his cock and moving his legs over Jerome's hips, John descended on Jerome's cock and started fucking himself, leveraging his rises and falls off the soles of his feet. Now he was the one moaning and groaning.

Master Jerome was smiling an inner smile. What John wanted most from him was his cock, and he was willing to fuck himself to get it. Jerome was the master. But there was one last act to try to drive this home.

Thomas was stealing across the room. Big, hulking Thomas. Thomas of the monster cock. When he reached the ottoman, he grabbed John by the hips and pulled him off Jerome's cock. Surprised, John let out a shriek and went pale in terror as he turned his head and saw the other, giant black man.

Wasting no time, and standing right there, crouching a bit down, to give him a good center of gravity, Thomas just lifted John up and set him down on his erect, upturned cock. John's cries of violation and fear quickly turned into those of passion and ecstasy as Thomas began to pump John's channel up and down on the massive cock. As John settled down, Thomas turned him around so that they were facing each other, and John locked his fists behind Thomas's neck and began to move his own pelvis in counterthrusts to take as much of the big cock inside him as possible.

The time of reckoning, Jerome thought, as he rose from the ottoman and approached the two men. Thomas, seeing Jerome coming and knowing what the plan was, slowly bent backward, shifting weight here and there to maintain his balance. Jerome came up behind them, pulled John's butt cheeks wider, and positioned his cock head at the place where John's rim stopped and the top of Thomas's embedded cock began.

There was no room there to squeeze anything in, but, slowly, to the tune of John's cries, Jerome made room for his cock to slide in on top of Thomas's cock. And then, Thomas holding his cock still, Jerome started to pump. John was writhing and clutching as Thomas's biceps and bulging pecs and flopping around and crying out.

The first time Jerome heard the man screaming "Fuck, yes. Plow me. Fuck me. Harder. Deeper!" he knew that he'd guessed right.

Thomas laid John's body on the bed. The man was sobbing. But it was a well-fucked sob, and he was babbling. "The . . . best . . . damn . . . fuck . . . I've ever . . ." He looked up at Jerome and whispered, "Thank you."

"It's just the first of two," Jerome said.

John whimpered and began to pant.

The second time, Jerome laid on his back on the bed for a while and let John fuck himself on the cock, facing Thomas who was kneeling over Jerome's legs and feeding his cock into John's mouth. After a while, Jerome pulled John's back down into his chest and Thomas grabbed the white man's legs behind the knees and spread him and worked his cock in above Jerome's. And this time it was Thomas slow pumping his cock. Both Jerome and Thomas managed to come together inside the stretched channel and John seemed quite pleased.

Later in the night, in the darkness, with John and Jerome stretched out together and in an embrace that was marked by brief dozes and short sessions of kissing, John spoke for the first time since Thomas had left them.

"He was magnificent. Where did you find him?"

"He Thomas, your carriage driver," Jerome answered. He tried to keep the sarcasm out of his voice, although he was thinking, he's driven your carriage since you came here and he's just another invisible black slave to you?

His restraint apparently worked, as, oblivious to the insensitivity he'd shown, John whispered, "Please bring him back from time to time. I have never been as satisfied as I was with what the two of you did. Not every night, but every so often."

"As long as I be in service to you. Yes, I be your slave. I do whatever you want, of course."

"My slave? No, you are my master. I want you here with me forever."

Jerome's heart leaped. Was he on the brink of the ultimate victory?

"I can't be here forever if you might sell the plantation and break up the slave community. I be but a slave. You own me."

"No, as I said, you own me now. And I will never sell you—and I won't sell this plantation either."

"The slaves, though. They all be my fambly."

"And they will all stay."

Master Jerome sighed a sigh of victory and happiness and moved slave John onto his side and slowly entered his channel with his commanding cock.

There was a new master at Riverbend plantation.

Play time

(Excerpt from the Clint Folsom mystery series novel *Death to Blonds: Stolen Judgment*)

What, again? Clint thought as he rolled over in the bed and encountered warm, hard flesh. His head was pounding. His ass was tingling too. Felt like a Mac truck had rammed itself up in there. He liked that feeling; seemed he spent half his life trying to open himself wide—with help, of course. He liked it better when the truck was still parked, though. And when it did a little rocking and forward and reversing in there. He rolled back toward the edge of the bed, ready to continue out onto the floor and stagger to the bathroom. A headache you wouldn't believe. But his eyes couldn't find the bathroom door where it should be. No, he didn't have to piss. Must have done that in the night. So there must be a bathroom somewhere. Smelt like lust, like heavy sex. Sweat. Cum. Needed the shower.

Shit. This wasn't even his own bedroom. Where had he gone after leaving the precinct last night? All he knew was that he'd gathered another grief yesterday to add to those he wanted to forget. It was another guilt-laden one. He'd pumped Garrison for information—using a goddam lie—and then pumped him and left him. Not long after that Garrison was dead. Was that in any part his fault? Was any part of that not his fault?

What bar had he wound up in? What sleazy hotel room? Shit, he hoped this wasn't the Christopher Hotel. But, no, what he'd seen of the Christopher recently had been refurbished. This one obviously hadn't been refurbished since the Hoover administration. How did they get those stains on the ceiling? Guy must have been a real gusher.

Well, it must have a bathroom. He sure hoped it did. Needed to get under a shower—and find some Tylenol. There had to be a bathroom here somewhere. First things first. Get out of the bed first.

He moved closer to the edge and began to swing his legs over the side. But a light brown arm—colored tattoos from here to there, a full sleeve of riotous color—reached over him and pulled him back into the center of the bed. No problem doing it at all either. Much bigger guy than Clint.

An Hispanic, Clint thought. Tattoos. Bulging muscles. Where was there a bar featuring Hispanic motorcycle gangs? Had the fuck been good? Important questions first. Did the size of the cock go with the size of the body? Hard. Young. Prime.

"Good morning, blondie. We fuck good. We fuck again." The voice heavily accented. Guttural. Commanding.

Without even getting a good look at him, Clint felt himself being pulled over on top of a prone, hard body, facing a pair of gigantic feet. Big hands at his waist settled him on the cock.

"Beautiful bod. You could be a star. Done porn? You fuck like you done porn."

Yep, big body, big cock. God, he's long, Young and hard bodied, Clint thought as he felt the cock slide up into him. No problem on the fit. How long ago since we did it? How many times? God, I wish I'd been there for it. I haven't gotten a good look at him. Who cares, with a cock like this?

Clint's knees were on either side of the big Hispanic's torso, folding his thighs down to his calves. He arched his torso back, digging his fists into the mattress on either side of bulging biceps.

Well, maybe just one good-morning fuck, he thought. The cock was in deep. He knew he'd enjoy it. He began counterthrusting, moving with the thrusting of man's cock. Groaning and grunting. Panting for it. Let's do this!

"Knew you wanted it. Couldn't get enough of it last night."

Condoms. Had they done it with condoms? Were they doing it now with condoms? Were they . . . ? "Oh fuck, yes. Oh, shit! Getitgetitgetit!"

The Hispanic hunk folded Clint back flat against his chest, one tattooed arm across his chest, a hand cupping his chin, holding the back of Clint's head into the hollow of his neck. The other hand went to encircling Clint's cock and stroking it to the rhythm of the churning of the cock inside Clint's channel.

The hand on Clint's cock. "Yesss! Fuck me. Fuck me hard!" Once that hand is on my cock, we gogogogo.

A hand pulling on Clint's right calf, pulling his leg out and unfolding it. Another hand doing the same with the other leg. How many hands?

Clint's eyes flew open. His eyes could hardly see the second man, holding his legs up and out with fists on his ankles. Hovering over Clint and the man under him. Moving his knees up on the bed on either side of the Hispanic's closed legs and between Clint's spread-eagled ones.

Another Hispanic. Chest a riot of colored tattoos. Black hair down to his shoulders. A bodybuilder's torso. Young. hard bodied. Prime.

"Oh, shit, no." Two of them. There are two of them! And the second one isn't going to wait for a solo turn. But, god he's got a beautiful body. It was coming back to Clint now. Big Mike's bar. The challenge. A double. Begging to be punished with a double.

He felt the bulb of the second guy at his entrance, above the already-sunk cock of the guy under him. Strong hands on his ankles, pushing his legs up and out. The muscle man under him gripping his buttocks and squeezing and spreading them, creating as much room for the relentlessly invading second cock as possible.

"Yes. Fuck me!" Clint cried out. "Get it in there! Both of you. Do it. Now! Shiiit Yessss."

The young Hispanic above him, giving a cruel smile, thrusting hard, inside him and sliding along the top of the

177

already-embedded cock. Clint panting, willing his channel to spread, fully focused now on the new cock beginning to plow him.

"Oh Fuck YES!"

The ultimate barrier against remembering what you don't want to remember.

Prince's Punishment

(Excerpt from the novella *The Indian Prince*)

The Rawal couldn't have been more pleased that I was going to let him fly the photorecon plane. I'd told him he'd need at least one more day as copilot, and although he hadn't been happy, he had acceded to my declaration. It was interesting that in all things but military duties, the Rawal was a spoiled, stubborn man, but that when it came to operating a piece of military equipment, he followed the rules explicitly. It's probably what had kept him alive through many years of training in on exotic military systems—this most likely being a bit chagrining to some factions within the Balrampur palace cliques.

Bhadur Khan returned to demanding and driving after we'd landed and I was told, once again, to step into the backseat of his limo. I rolled and sucked his balls as he sat in the center of the backseat, his head arched back on the headrest and moaning quietly and working his cock himself. This time rather than coming when I tugged on and squeezed his balls, he lifted me with strong hands at my waist before I could do that and sat me on his cock. He growled when I placed my palms on his chest, and I immediately raised my hands to grasp handles in the ceiling of the limo. He still didn't want me to touch him. I leveraged the soles of my feet off the floor of the car to rise and fall on his cock as he did his part, controlling the rhythm, by lifting and lowering me at my waist and thrusting up into me at a counter rhythm pace.

After he came, he held me there, motionless for a moment, and whispered, "I have been told that you have been seen in the corridors of Vimala's, the Rawalina's, wing. You haven't been attending her have you?"

"The Rawalina lives in the palace?" I asked, feigning surprise. "I would have thought she would be someplace else."

"What are we to do to make you remember what is wanted from you, what your place is?"

I realized that this was a rhetorical question, because although he'd had me suck his balls in the limo and left me on the tarmac the first time, this time, we had had our sex while the limousine was on the move. When he'd asked that question, we had arrived in the motor court of the palace, and the two burly guards that opened the doors on either side of the vehicle when the limousine stopped . . . were naked.

"Remember who you are here for," the Rawal said in a calm voice as he was handed out of the limo. And as he emerged, the two guards entered from either side. They both had condoms on erect cocks, so no time was wasted in one taking up the center-seat position the Rawal had vacated and pulling me into his lap and onto his cock. The other guard went between my legs and grabbed my ankles. He spread and raised my legs until my feet were leveraging off the ceiling of the vehicle, while the guard under me tipped my body back and the one crouched between my legs and grunted as he worked his cock inside my hole on top of that of the other guard.

It was a rough fuck, as I'm sure they were told to do. And I could tell that they had worked together in this way before. They were good, able quickly to reach a pattern of stretching to the max and counter sliding. I could tell from their heavy breathing that they were enjoying themselves.

I did all of the begging and sobbing and pleading and yelling that I thought was appropriate for the occasion, but the truth of the matter was that I'd been doubled before—and by guys better equipped than this. I sort of enjoyed it. But I certainly didn't let the guards know that. They were young, handsome, toned brutes, which seemed to be a requirement to be in the palace guard.

And they had stamina and good timing. Pushed over the top by the rhythm of their counterpistoning, I came up the hard belly of the one in front, collapsing then into a low moan as they continued to pump me for interminable more minutes to their individual ejaculations. It was all good until, both grinning, the one who had been on top punched me in the stomach, doubling me over onto the floor of the vehicle, as, duty done, they exited the limo.

Porn War

The song "Kisses Sweeter than Wine" sprang to my mind, because that was what his kisses were. As far as I could tell in the dimly lit Blue Moon resort hotel room in Las Vegas, he was a young hunk, no older than I was. Most of the men in the room were older, a few probably twice or more my age. None were complete throwaways, but he was prime among them. And he had latched on to me as soon as I'd entered the room, probably the last to arrive of eight or nine or twelve. It was that murky in the room. The rest of them already naked. Most of them already humping.

We stood, rocking together against each other in instant high heat, and kissing—those sweeter-than-wine kisses—as he pulled my clothes off me. We all wore face masks, which, along with the dimness in the room, supposedly would make it difficult to identify each other during the meetings of the conclave the next day when we were clothed—but surely not impossible.

He certainly couldn't hide his mop of blond hair or his magnificent build or his extra-long cock completely even in clothes in the light of day in a Las Vegas hotel meeting room. And if he touched or kissed me again, I'm sure I would know it was him.

I could recognize Marty Doans without any trouble. Muscle solid, but a bit squat, nearly bald, and bordering on pudgy—and very, very hairy. I could identify him primarily, even with a face mask, because he obviously was holding court. I'd

183

never seen him naked before, and although I'd heard about him having a super-thick cock, I couldn't see this now. He was sitting on the side of a bed, one of two queen-sized beds in the room, with another man kneeling between his knees and servicing his cock. Which is why I couldn't see it. Two men were on the bed behind him, fucking, and Marty had a cigar in one hand and three or four fingers of his other hand up the ass of the man doing the fucking behind him.

Marty was the organizer of the conclave and a big-name publisher of pornographic e-books. You got your books under his gay male imprint and you could quit your day job.

My books were under his imprint, and I'd never had to have a day job.

So, yes, I knew Marty, of all the guys in this room, even with the mask on. And I also knew the squirrelly little guy who came with Marty, Peter Knoles, who, though obviously wanting some of what others were getting, was nervously flitting around the room from coupling to coupling, but pulling back almost immediately because Marty wanted something or Peter was afraid Marty would want something and someone other than Peter would supply it. Last I saw of him on this night, he was standing at the wall trying to adjust the temperature because Marty complained about it being too hot in here.

Of course it was hot in here with a dozen or so guys in high heat.

I didn't know whose room this was. Probably either Marty's or Peter's. The invitation delivered under my door shortly after I checked in earlier that afternoon just said, "If you're really a player, and we're not talking cards, there will be more of this in Room 103 at 11:00 p.m." The invitation had included a fifty-dollar bill.

The sweeter-than-wine hunk had me straddling him on the bed Marty wasn't using himself. The hunk was on his back, my knees were buried in his pits, and I was arched back, grabbing an ankle with one hand and his cock with my fist, while he sucked me and I slowly face-fucked him. He lifted my torso to vertical after a period of good moaning and servicing, raised my hips a bit more, and brought them forward so that his mouth and tongue could get to my asshole. The underside of my cock was thumping on his forehead and he was bringing me to a boil so fast I hoped I wasn't going to be leaving anything sticky in his wavy blond hair.

He'd already asked me if I took cock or gave it, and my answer of "both, but more of the taking," had pleased him immensely. I knew then that I was going to be fucked by a long cock. In truth, from the atmosphere of the room, I knew I was going to be fucked by more than one. By Marty, for sure, if this was his party. He'd asked me for it before, in New York, but I'd never given it. I'd always managed to fend him off with a plausible excuse. I sure was going to be giving it tonight.

Didn't matter to me tonight. I was walking along the edge on a vodka high already, and I didn't mind doing research for my books and being gifted with new plotlines.

I went to arch my back again, but couldn't, because I realized that there was a chest behind me, a chest obviously sporting a studded leather harness. And two beefy, hairy arms encircling me, one holding me in place and the other possessing my cock, slick from the attentions of the sweeter-than-wine hunk. The new arrival had leather bands with studs on them on his wrists, and his arms were tattooed. The hard cock at the small of my back wasn't anything to sniff at.

Between the hunk working my ass with his tongue and the leatherman working my cock with his fist, it wasn't long before I gave the hunk a facial. Sorry about the hair, I thought. A protein shampoo. My ejaculation signaled the leatherman to move me back and set me on the hunk's long, curved cock—it took an eternity for me to slide down that pole—and then he moved around to kneel over the hunk's face and receive attention for his own ass and for me to bend down and suck his cock. He didn't take that position for very long, though. He moved back to behind me, embraced me with one arm, and stuck a popper under my nose with his other hand.

"Inhale this good," a growly voice whispered in my ear. "You're gonna want it. We're gonna go for a DP here."

I moaned and inhaled. I kept right on inhaling—and moaning and groaning—as the leatherman slowly worked his cock in on top of the one the hunk already had buried inside me.

The hunk held still with his while the leatherman began to slow pump me. They came almost simultaneously inside me.

My world was spinning from the popper, so I didn't much care or feel very much pain. I did do a lot of groaning and grunting, though.

I think I was only semiconscious, but I was awake enough to realize when the leatherman was pulling me off the hunk and carrying me over and setting me in Marty Doan's lap, facing him, and on what I found was a very thick cock indeed. I just let my shoulder blades fall back onto the tops of his feet and my arms dangle on the carpeting beside me, as Marty began pulling me on and off his cock. The leatherman knelt down and gave me another pull on the popper before sliding his cock down my throat.

I woke I have no idea how much later to the flush of a toilet in the bathroom off the hotel room. The lights were off in the room, but a weak glow of sun was coming in from around the edges of the curtains on the windows and the light was on in the bathroom. The bathroom door was open. I saw a naked, fat, hairy rump standing in front of the toilet. I heard a second flush.

No one else was in the room. My arms were pulled above my head, my wrists bound to the headboard with restraints. My legs also were spread and restrained at the ankles, with leather leads running down to the bottom corners of the bed. The leads on the legs weren't pulled tight. There were a couple of pillows under the small of my back, elevating my hips. And I saw a small collection of toys—dildos and beads—laid out on the bed beside me. I had no idea if these had already been used or were waiting to be used.

It all seemed familiar. I wondered if I'd written this scene before. My predecessor under my pen name, Brent, certainly had.

As Marty walked out of the bathroom and toward me, he was adjusting a wide, studded leather band around the base of his cock. He also was stroking himself to an erection.

"Hey, what're you doing?" I asked.

"Wrong question," he muttered. "It should be what have we been doing? Good of you to join the party again. There for a while it was like fucking Raggedy Andy. Too bad you weren't more awake. The part of you that was awake was enjoying it."

Without further ado, he hopped up on the bed, crouched in a half stand between my spread legs, and reached down and grasped my waist in strong hands. He pulled my pelvis up to his, shifting my weight onto my shoulder blades with my torso arcing down to the head of the bed. He thrust his thick, studded cock inside me and began to pump. Feeling no pain or even difficulty in taking his cock with added studs, I realized that my channel had been reamed well open, with no opportunity to tighten up again for however long I'd been in this room.

Whatever.

I turned my cheek to the side and moaned. He was fucking me good. I just wouldn't look directly at the gnome he appeared to be in this stance. He was fucking me really, really good, in fact.

But the restraints and the toys had me a bit worried.

"Um, Mr. Doans . . . Marty . . . just because I write gay male BDSM doesn't mean I practice it."

"You do now," was his response. "Do you want me to stop?"

"No, not particularly."

"You need another shot of the poppers?"

"Depends on what else you're planning on doing."

"I'll take that as a yes. Before I do it, I'll give you another shot or two. You'll want it."

At the front of my mind was the knowledge that Marty Doans could either make or break a gay male porn novelist.

Before he untied me and sent me back to my room, with another $100 in my jeans pocket, to shower, breakfast, and show up at the conclave only an hour late, I discovered that, no, he hadn't used all of those toys already.

* * * *

Before facing the first session of the conclave, an annual meeting of gay male porn writers, held pretty much in secret wherever Marty Doans's Bent Stallions Publications made arrangements, I felt I needed a real drink. It wasn't that far from noon. I saddled up to the bar of Las Vegas' Blue Moon resort hotel, a gay guy's only place, and asked for a Bloody Mary double. I'd met Marty before, face to face, in his New York offices when my lover, Brent Davenport, the original Jasper of the Jasper rough sex novels fame, died and I had to establish that I had written Brent's last three manuscripts—his highest-return best-sellers—myself. But I'd never been to one of Marty's conclaves, although I'd been invited before.

The main reason I'd never come was that Brent had been in a war of traded barbs with one of Doans's other best-selling authors, the gay male Romance novelist going by the pen name Niles James. The bitterness was such between them that, if they had ever met at a venue like this, the fur would fly.

I had only come to this conclave because I had been asked to come as a paid speaker—and was assured that Niles James would not be attending. Once here, though, I saw his name on the attendees' list. Well, I would just have to do my best to avoid him. I had half a notion to take off my "Jasper" name tag and go in as someone else—but I was a paid speaker in that name, so I guess I'd just have to find out who the old codger was—he had to be old if he was a contemporary of Brent's—and stay clear of him.

When I went to put the Bloody Mary on my room tab, the bartender checked his computer and said, "Your account has been linked to the Room 103 account, Mr. Jasper. You may just cite that room for charges from now on."

Marty, I thought. This was beginning to look like a setup, like I was lured here for Marty to use. He'd made clear before that he wanted me, and I'd only barely been able to outrun him—until now, well, until last night, of course. I'd thought that last night would do it for him, but now he was slowly owning me. I downed the Bloody Mary, ordered another one, and, that one in hand, soared into the meeting room.

A panel session on the difference between erotica and porn—an argument I had no time for; what I wrote was what I wrote—was in full cry. I took a seat toward the back and looked around. There were maybe seventy people there. I wasn't a bit surprised to see that well more than half of them were women. Brent had had a major burr under his saddle about the false genre of women writing "just pretend" or "how we'd like to fantasize our man" stories read mostly by other women. I had come to share his disdain for this quite large share of the gay male porn market, but like him, not too vocally because many women buying and reading that fake stuff were also buying ours, even though we thought of ourselves as writing for the actually actively gay male.

Over half of the men present were well into their fifties and sixties. Although I felt a bit sorry for them writing what most of them weren't actively engaged in now, I respected that most of them—probably all who dared come to a conclave such as this—had once been active and were now writing from memories they wished to remain captured and arousing them for as long as possible.

Only a few of the men present were young, as I was, or not much beyond forty, and probably writing from active experience. Not that I could say that much of what I wrote was from active experience myself—or was before Marty started taking me under his jaded wing the previous night. I had enough gay sex, just not that much that could be classified as BDSM. I now certainly could write BDSM stories better, the specialty Brent had known best and written most—with the knowledge of experience. At least light BDSM. I was willing to bet that it was from this core group of younger men here that Marty had chosen his invitation list for last evening's party in his hotel room. And I wondered if more active and intimate sessions were in store during the three-day event. I wouldn't be surprised if they were the only reason Marty even held these conclaves.

I scanned the room several times, trying to pick out who Niles James might be. I couldn't very well avoid him if I couldn't identify him. At the next break I asked the older man I'd been sitting beside if he knew who Niles James was and could point him out to me. He did and could and pointed over to where a pudgy cross between Orson Wells and Truman Capote older man was talking with a well-built young blond guy.

"That's him," the man said. "Writes great Romances. The best-selling author in the Bent Stallions stable."

I bristled at that claim, but I remained polite. I had marked James's looks so that I'd remember to stay away from him, but my attention had already gone to the young blond he was talking to. I was sure just from watching him move and assessing his build that he was the sweeter-than-wine lover I had started with last night—and would have been more than pleased to continue with. Now him I would make no effort at all to stay away from.

I turned to ask the man if he knew who the blond was, but he was gone, and Marty was bearing down on me. I was to have the privilege of lunching at his table, at which he had gathered a bevy of twittering women authors of gay male Romance. It was not lost on me that Marty was introducing me to many disparate forms of sadism.

* * * *

The porn war between Jasper—as initiated by Brent Davenport—and Niles James was of the most bitter sort. It was born from a love-hate relationship. Brent and Niles had been lovers. They met as writers, with Brent writing mainstream sci-fi short stories for a pulp magazine and Niles already writing his gay male Romances for another publication of the same pulp magazine conglomerate. This, of course, was light years before the advent of the computer, let alone the e-book, which had caused the porn novel industry to burgeon because a buyer didn't have to worry about what to do with the book after he'd read it—or that much while we was reading it. Although Niles wrote Romances, he practiced BDSM and introduced Brent to the practice before Brent ever thought of writing that genre. It was Marty Doans, a young BDSM adherent of Niles's, who both encouraged Brent to switch to writing gay male BDSM for his startup Bent Stallions publishing effort and came between Brent and Niles sexually.

And it was Marty who tore Brent away from Niles and who egged on the two in competition with each other as writers and who, gleefully, started and nurtured the porn war between the two. He touted and promoted them both as *the* best-seller in his stable and encouraged and exaggerated the professional animosity between the two. It didn't take the two long to buy into the hype themselves.

This manufactured animosity was a palpable source of energy in this conclave, I clearly could see from the first session I attended. Nearly every side conversation I heard concerned the porn war between Marty's two standards and the fact that this was the first time that anyone had seen both Jasper and Niles James on the list of speakers. That neither name was applied yet in the schedule of sessions and the key concluding session time slot was not filled in yet only added fuel to the fire of anticipation.

If this was Marty's doing, I'd have to give him props as a consummate showman. Even I didn't know for sure what session I was to be impaneled on. The invitation to speak had suggested that I talk about the rules of BDSM in writing, which I found to be laughable. There were no definitive rules for BDSM in either doing it or writing about it, I believed, after having picked up writing it upon Brent's demise. There were, of course, clubs of it with rules of their own, but I had found that there was a whole range of application of the genre in both practice and stories and that a varying readership could be counted on for falling into this range.

My own BDSM writing thus far had been a toned-down version of Brent's and more heavily geared to bondage and milder toys and full enjoyment by all concerned. I would be the first to admit that I had little personal experience in the heavier BDSM arena and would be writing Romance myself—which only added to my resentment of Niles James dominating that aspect of the gay male market—if given the choice. I did enjoy a rough kind of sex, though, and I had been taking Jasper's work more in that direction. The fans of Jasper hadn't seemed to be complaining about that, at least yet—that I knew of.

Brent had not practiced BDSM techniques with me— well, beyond some of the tying-up practices. By the time we met, he had softened and was actually quite romantic with me in our lovemaking.

I had accepted the invitation and the topic and had proceeded to put together a talk on the various techniques, equipment, and toys of BDSM in the gay male world and on how they could be—were being in Jasper's writings—applied to pornographic writing. I would just ignore the word "rules" altogether unless it came up in the question period. And if it did, I knew there would be a knock-down-drag-out fight in the room no matter what I said I believed about it.

As we went into the afternoon session, still without a topic for that last session or a mention of either me or Niles James as session speakers, I became increasingly convinced that I had been given a fake topic and wouldn't be speaking on the rules of BDSM at all, but rather would be paired with Niles in some sort of cat fight to conclude the conclave.

In this I was proved to be quite right.

My eyes kept going to the puckered-lipped, obviously self-satisfied pile of blubber who had been identified to me as Niles James and who sat simpering in the front row of the other section of chairs in the meeting room in the middle of a harem of equally simpering female writers. And as my eyes bored into him, I was aware that others were looking at me too, apparently having zeroed in on my "Jasper" nametag and already in delicious anticipation of what Marty obviously was planning.

When I couldn't take any more of this, I rose and slipped out of the room—I had sat as far back as I could find a seat—and went to the hotel reception desk.

"Is there an appropriate bar I can go to around here?" I asked. "Not in this hotel." I already was taking my name tag off as I asked. I wanted to be away from all of this for a while.

"The Men's Paradise bar is just a couple of blocks west on Western Sahara. Kind of a dive, but there's a play area in back, if that's what you're interested in. A little early, though. They just opened at 4:00."

"Sounds fine, thanks," I said. I was just looking for a drink or two away from here, but I wasn't bothered if it was the kind of place that had action in the back. If it was on the rough side, it was close to where I had been in my early days.

* * * *

I saw him as soon as I entered the dimly lit, nearly deserted bar—my sweeter-than-wine blond hunk from the previous night of sex in Marty's room.

I saddled up to the bar beside him, ordered a beer, and turned to him. He was looking down into the bar top rather than at me, although I had seen him glance up when I entered and then look away quickly.

"Hi, my name is Tim," I said. "I think we've already had a bit of sex. Maybe more than a bit."

He looked up at me, his expression a mix of embarrassment, interest, and amusement. His smile was much too glorious to have been partially hidden behind a face mask. He didn't deny we'd had sex.

"For real? Your real name is Tim?"

"Yep. That I cannot deny."

"In that case, I'm Julian. I admit that I've been looking for you today, but didn't see you at the conclave. Both of those sessions were insufferable, though, and not finding what I was looking for, I came out of that gaseous balloon to soak up my disappointment."

"Anyone tell you your kisses are sweeter than wine?" I asked. "Not to mention that you have a terrific body and a great cock."

"So that would make us twins?" he asked, with a laugh. "Gotta admit I was thoroughly enjoying you before that leather guy pulled you away. Nothing half that good again before Marty shooed us all out of there to have you alone to himself. You weren't looking all that conscious when I left. I was a little worried for you, especially when I couldn't pick you out in the crowd today."

"No, I slept through most of Marty," I answered. "Sure would like to take up where you and I left off, though. I'm told they have accommodation for that beyond that doorway over there covered with a beaded curtain."

The room was small and pretty grungy, but it had a quite adequate six-foot-square vinyl ottoman in the center of it that the bartender who took Julian's money wiped down when he'd shown us to the room. It was Julian's money, because he insisted on being dominant and calling the shots, which was just peachy with me.

When we'd been left alone, Julian got right to business, and I let him work, as I had enjoyed letting him take the lead the previous night. We did the sweeter-than-wine kiss thing, rocking against each other, as we stood beside the ottoman, stripped off each other's shirts, and unbuckled and unzipped each other. Julian retrieved both of our dicks and worked them against each other, while he slowly arched me back, bending me over the ottoman. I let him do as he wanted, holding his head between my hands, keeping him in the honeyed kiss.

When he'd bent me to where my shoulder blades felt vinyl, he pushed me up onto the ottoman until my head flopped over the end. He moved around to the head of the ottoman, and I found myself opening my throat to the slow stroke of his cock while he leaned over me and ran his hands over my torso as far down as running his fingers into my pubes and tantalizing the root of my cock. I went right hard for him, which was a good sign to me that he was what I wanted and would scratch my itch. He eventually returned his hands to cover my pecs and worry my nipples.

When he felt the time was right, he pulled out of my mouth, turned me onto my belly, my head still flopping over the end of the ottoman and my arms dangling off the sides, and lay full on top of me, moving his body slowly on top of mine, listening to me moaning softly. He took his time. I spread my thighs a bit and his cock fell into the crack and I felt his cock slide down along my entrance. He lifted his hips, sliding back up to my entrance. Then down and then up and repeating until he felt me shudder in his embrace. If I could have trained my rim to catch his bulb as it passed and suck it into me, he'd already be fucking me.

"Yes, yes, fuck me," I murmured, as I raised my hips to him, presenting for him. But he was taking his time. After a bit of pressure work on my rim with the bulb, he started moving down my body, kissing me on the back as he moved. He had an arm around my waist and he pulled my rump up even more into the air than I had raised it, wanting him to enter me.

His tongue and mouth went to my hole, and I groaned my pleasure and need. He pulled my cock and balls through my legs, having nudged my thighs to spread their stance further. He sucked the cock and balls, giving equal time to those and my hole, as I writhed under his attention and whispered the mantra of "fuck me, fuck me, stick it in, please fuck me, now, please."

And then he did just that after I heard the snap of the condom he'd rolled onto his cock, going into a crouch over my hips and folding his body over mine, and slowly, but relentlessly, entering and entering and entering me. I shuddered and trembled as I felt him throbbing and moving inside me, fully possessing me. Not terribly thick, but terribly, terribly long—reaching for my tonsils. Fucking deep. Then shallow; then deep again.

His arms were wrapped around my chest and he rose up on his knees, bringing me with him. One of his arms lay diagonally up my chest. The hand of the other one was stroking my cock in rhythm to his stroking inside me, a stroke that paused and then picked up in a different rhythm and speed whenever I felt I had the measure of it, making me gasp and gulp and beg for more, deeper, faster, harder.

He cupped my chin with a hand and turned my face to his for a sweeter-than-wine kiss that went on almost forever . . . until, with a lurch and a muffled cry, I shot out over the vinyl. I felt his encasing arm pull back from me then and I fell forward on my chest on the cum-slickened vinyl. He crouched closer over my hips, grabbed my waist with his hands, and pumped me harder, faster, deeper to his own ejaculation.

We returned to the Blue Moon separately, after paying extra to use the bar's shower, Julian showering before me, me still lying in a pool of cum and moaning when he was finished. The supper had already started before I reached the resort hotel. Marty's table was fully seated—thank god, I thought. But it was somewhat disconcerting to see that Julian was seated there, and looking fresh and somewhat disinterested. Who would have guess that just a half hour earlier he had his long cock up my ass? Also seated at the table was the pudgy Niles James. A bevy of old maidish women were fawning over him. Understandable, I thought. He did write that insipid Romance. But then I admonished myself. I rather enjoyed his Romances, I'd have to admit, especially the ones of recent years. I never admitted to Brent that I read them, of course.

I didn't realize before I sat down at one of the few empty seats at another table, though, that it put me right next to who quite evidently had been the leatherman who DP'd me the previous night. I wouldn't have known him from Adam—at least until I zeroed in on the studded wrist bands he was wearing and got a peek at the leather harness under his half-open shirt—but he certainly remembered me. I spent half the meal removing his hand from my thigh and even my basket and listening to him whisper in my ear what he wanted to do to my body. Some of that sounded rather enticing, though, and I didn't have much to say when he pointed out that the last time he groped my crotch, I was hard.

Sometime during the meal I discovered that he wrote leather and biker books, which came as no surprise, but also that he read my—or, more correctly, Brent's—BDSM and rough sex books and was dying to take me for a solo ride, test out positions and tie ups Jasper wrote about, and compare research notes. He even told me, in hushed tones, that he had a whip he'd named Jasper.

He followed me back to my room after dinner, which I didn't realize until I already was trapped in a dead-end hall. The only thing that saved me from a research session, which I'll have to admit I was half tempted by, was that I found my pass card wouldn't work on my hotel room door. I turned and breezed by him, with the explanation that the key didn't work, and he was so nonplused by that, only half believing me, I'm sure, that he didn't impede my passage.

"You are no longer in that room," the hotel desk clerk cheerily told me. "You've been moved to Room 103, and your luggage has already been transferred. Just a minute and I'll prepare you a new pass key."

"Marty Doans again," I exclaimed. I said it loud enough that the leather guy, who had followed me in disbelief out to the reception desk, overheard and immediately vanished. I smiled at the thought that he probably was one of Marty's authors too and knew better than to mess with someone Marty was being possessive with.

I seethed through the two evening sessions, paying little attention to what was being said and looking over at the leatherman occasionally and frowning my "I'm not in the mood anymore" warning. Although he continued to eye me, all it took was for me to look annoyed at him, and he turned his eyes elsewhere.

That night I was reminded that the Blue Moon was a full-service gay male resort. When I entered Room 103, I immediately noticed the sling suspended in the middle of the room from four chains attached to a strong hook screwed securely into a ceiling beam. The sling hadn't been there the previous night and the room had been too dimly lit and filled with teeming naked bodies for me to have noticed special amenities like strong ceiling hooks.

I was contemplating the why of the plastic cover—more of a kid's swimming pool effect because of the lip around the sides—that was under the sling, when a naked Marty emerged from the bathroom and had me undressed and in the sling, with my arms and legs running up and bound to the four corner chains, before I could think of a reason why he shouldn't do it. My attention was riveted on the impossible thickness of his cock. Brent's cock had been impossibly thick. I actually liked impossibly thick cocks.

I told him something of this after I'd finished screaming at the tit clamps he applied to my nipples.

"We don't have to do it this way, Marty. You've got a thick cock. That's enough for me to give you a good time in a fuck."

"I'm startin' to get complaints on your writing, Jasper," he said. He always used my pen name. To him, I *was* Jasper. "Buyers are beginning to notice that Jasper doesn't have the BDSM zing he used to have—rough sex, yes, but you need a refresher in some of the finer techniques and toys, I think."

Refresher? I thought. Heavy BDSM was Brent's bag, not mine. There was a reason I wasn't writing heavy BDSM. But then, as Marty, already inside me and pounding to beat the band, started jerking on the leads to the tit clamps and I resumed some minor screaming again. I recognized that I certainly was getting experience in what he wanted me to write. I wouldn't have trouble writing how pinched and pulled nipples felt like from now on—or how, mysteriously enough, they were, in fact,

197

connected to the arousal of my cock and to my enjoyment of a thick dick working my channel.

I spouted for him. And it wasn't long before I learned what the plastic cloth with the rim under the sling was all about either—when he came inside me, pulled out of me, fisted his cock, and lifted it over my belly.

I'd never actually included water sports in anything I'd written before. But I guess the point was that Brent, as Jasper, had. And that Marty wanted this sort of stuff to be included in Jaspers books again.

I got the message.

* * * *

Peter Knoles, Marty Doans's flighty assistant, was hopping from one foot to the other in front of me the next morning as he handed me the final schedule for the day's sessions, the last day of the conclave. As he got me to accept it, he skipped back a few extra paces from me and almost went into a fetal position, as if I was going to swat him like a fly.

After I looked at the schedule, I certainly felt like doing so—but only because Marty wasn't there himself. Just as I feared, the last session was now titled "Porn War," and Jasper and Niles James were the sole listed panelists.

I could have spit bricks and was building up the effort to do so, when I heard a surprised exclamation of "Shit!"

I looked up and into the wide-open eyes of Julian, who had just appeared in front of me. He was staring at the nametag on my shirt.

"You. You're Jasper!?" he both exclaimed and quizzed.

I looked at the nametag on his shirt. It said "Niles James."

"Shit!" I said.

"But . . . but . . . you aren't old enough," he said, being the first to recover.

"Neither are you . . . to be Niles James," I retorted.

"The original Niles died. Marty wanted to keep the franchise going and he liked my Romance writing, so I took over as Niles James."

"And the original Brent died and Marty had me take over Jasper," I said. I didn't reveal that Brent had been my lover as well. When you're shopping for a new lover, you don't necessarily tell the prospects about the earlier ones—beyond telling them enough to know what you could do. Julian definitely already knew what I could do—and what I would do for him, which was anything he wanted me to do.

"Well, you do Romance just as well as you write it," I said, maneuvering from the sticky situation to more amenable ground.

"You know we're supposed to be sworn enemies," Julian said.

"Yeah, I know. That's pretty much what the schedule of this afternoon's session says. So, what do we do? Cut out again? Leave 'em hanging?"

"I can't afford to do that," Julian said. "I need this gig."

"Me too," I answered.

"Then let's give them what Marty wants. Let's tear into each other in the conclave session and then go off and hide and fuck while they think we're in mortal combat somewhere."

"Sounds good to me," I was quick to agree. "But it'll have to be your room. Marty had me moved in with him."

"He's giving a press interview now. Switch your luggage to my room while he's tied up with that. He'll never find you there. Tomorrow we'll duck out when no one's looking and figure out how we can be together more. I live in New York."

"So do I."

"Sweet."

I smiled, thinking of wine and his kisses.

When I got to Marty's room and opened the door, I shuddered at what I found. The sling was gone, but chains with wrist restraints now hung from the hook in the ceiling. And on the bed was a flogging whip and a chain ending on each end in tit clamps. I gave brief thought to whether Marty had named the whip. I loaded my suitcase and got out of there as soon as possible.

But I had to admit that Marty was right. If I was going to continue to be Jasper, I was gonna need more experience in what Jasper wrote about. Marty lived in New York too. Guess I just wouldn't avoid him and his research sessions. It could only make my writing better.

And he did have a very thick cock.

Sailors and Flyboys

Flyboys

Pete swung into the gym with a big grin on his face. "Fleet's in and I've already talked with Javier. His ship will be in early, on Thursday. Says he can get a three-day shore pass. Time for a special weekend."

"I'm game," Todd answered, but he was looking up at the man spotting him on the bench press and asked, "How about you, Dan?"

"Every weekend's special with you, babe," Dan answered. His idea of spotting was to have his hands on the inside of Todd's bare thighs and stroking them.

Pete was standing in the middle of the gym room at the Air Force base near San Diego, one of several workout rooms scattered around the base for airmen's use, this one being one of the most remotely located ones. He was toweling himself off after his run to the gym. He, like the other three men, Todd, Dan, and Bill, was wearing only a jockstrap, gym shorts, and athletic shoes. All four men, all Air Force officer pilots, were cut superbly. Pete was black; the others were white.

"I'll arrange the BOQ room at the officers' club," Pete said. "But I guess Bill better be the one to go down to the harbor to meet up with Javier and do the hunt. He's the prettiest of the bunch."

Bill grunted his assent at the assignment without losing count in the leg lifts he was doing on another apparatus. Bill indeed was the best looking of the four, although all of them looked great, especially the way they'd developed their bodies. Bill was tall and sultry dark, with some intriguing curling body hair on his forearms, pecs, and in a trail down his sternum, across his belly, and into the waistband of his gym shorts. Broad shoulders and slim waist. Big biceps, washboard abs. The face of a movie star, with a perpetual five o'clock shadow. Bedroom eyes.

"Money for the meals, liquor, and condoms and for Javier's tip go to Todd as usual," Pete said. "Five hundred each should do it, but if it's not enough we all agree to kick in more, right?"

Grunts of agreement were heard all around.

"Make sure you have a good supply of rubbers," Bill said, turning to Todd. "We almost ran out last time."

Todd was doing his own count of his bar lifts, but he stopped in mid cadence. "Dan! You'll make me lose count."

All he heard in answer was a slurping sound, as Dan had pulled Todd's gym shorts off his legs, pulled his cock out from the jock pouch, and was giving him head.

Todd and Dan could almost be twins—Siamese twins— hooked at the crotch. Both reddish blonds of medium height, and, though well muscled, both on the wiry side. Not an ounce of fat on either one. Both with buzz cuts. Todd was the younger and more handsome of face of the two. Dan, who usually took the lead, as he was doing here, was distinguished by the veins that stood out between his muscles and the skin on his arms and legs, the veins having no fat at all to sheath them. His facial features were more rugged than Todd's. He didn't smile much, and he was more demanding and a bit cruel and rough. He'd had his dick inside Todd most of the time since Todd had come on duty at the air base. Todd, preferably a top, accepted this from Dan but from no one else. What mostly the two had in common, though, was that they liked to share another guy between them—at the same time. They were continually on the look for a guy willing to take a double.

"Could you spot the door for us, Pete?" Dan growled.

Pete picked up two twenty-pound hand weights and moved to where he was standing in front of the door to the corridor, staring through the small window in the door.

"Oh shit, oh fuck," Todd exclaimed as, hunched over him, Dan worked his cock into Todd's hole. Todd's ankles were on Dan's shoulders and Dan was lifting Todd's buttocks with palms that spread the butt cheeks, opening the hole that now hungered for and fit his cock like a glove, and fingers that moved the jock straps out of the way. He revolved the cock head to remind Todd's channel who was boss and then dove deep and began immediately to pump as Todd, gripping the pillars of the weight rack with white-knuckled fists, began to groan and move his hips to the rhythm of the fuck. Dan was thick; Todd was long. Bill, the hunkiest of the four, stopping his leg lifts to pull out his cock, start stroking, and to watch, was both thick and long. The black Pete, the bulkiest and most muscle bound of the four, standing spot at the door and feeling himself going hard at the sound of the fucking, was thickest and longest of the four.

Although not watching, except by way of a faint reflection in the window in the door, Pete could hear the stroking as marked by Todd's groan and Dan's grunt with each thrust and by the sound of the slapping of Dan's big balls on Todd's inner thighs. Pete raised the hand weights to his shoulders. Thrust and groan, up with the right weight; thrust and grunt, lowering the right weight; thrust and groan, up with left weight; thrust and grunt, lowering the left weight. Thrust and . . .

The four Air Force officers were a close-knit group, having discovered their mutual interests in jockeying jets, keeping their bodies hard, and fucking young sailors.

Sailor Tim

Tim stroked down the front of his Navy whites and turned this way and that, looking at himself in the mirror on the back of the cabin door of the dorm-like space he shared with nine other sailors on his destroyer. The clothes were tight on his small frame, with a trim, but well-muscled, torso and legs, but they really looked good on him. The jerkin was tight, showing his definition and his small waist, and the white trousers were tight at the thighs and across the crotch and flared at the hem. It was the first time he'd worn them. His first shore leave on his first naval cruise. He was barely nineteen and fresh out of the Iowa cornfields, getting his first taste of the greater world.

His brother was a sailor too, but he'd done everything he could to deter Tim from joining up, saying that with his blond, pretty-boy looks and small stature, he'd be eaten alive on board a naval ship. That had titillated Tim more than scared him, although now that he actually was in the Navy and had just been on the sea on a tin can with mostly randy men, he better understood what his brother had meant.

The hedge on the men who had initially circled around him like sharks on the prowl, however, was sitting on a bunk beside him, watching him dress and admire himself in the mirror.

Big Ralph, named that for many reasons, including his bulk, his scare factor on board, and his seniority in the naval enlisted ranks, had become both Tim's oppressor and his protection. He was oppressing enough, though, that Tim was elated that he'd gotten a two-day shore pass in San Diego—and that Big Ralph hadn't.

It had been four weeks since Big Ralph had made good on his pledge to protect Tim from the sailors, including a senior ship's officer, who had been chumming ever closer around Tim as he moved around performing the deck duties of a bottom-of-the chain swabbie.

He just hadn't set up the protection the way that Tim had imagined he would. He'd done it by staking his own claim and staring down the competition. Big Ralph had managed to get Tim reassigned to a top bunk in his own cabin and in the darkest hour of one night, had climbed up into Tim's bunk, naked and already crowned and with a bottle of lube.

Tim woke up on his belly, with a heavy body on top of him, a hand smothering his mouth and nose, and thick, greased fingers inside his channel entrance. He had struggled, but to no avail, with the big man. He managed to bite the hand of his assailant in reaction to the surprise and pain of a hard cock entering him, and, when the hand was taken away, he screamed for help against the attack. But he writhed ineffectually, while

Big Ralph laughed and pumped his ass with increasing speed and depth. There was no indication that anyone heard him struggling or, if they did, that they cared—or, if deep down, they cared, that they had the nerve to go up against Big Ralph.

Tim, who had been curious about what it was all about before coming into the Navy, now knew exactly what it was about. No one came to his aid that night, because every other man in the cabin was under Big Ralph's protection as well. They had all had their first night with Big Ralph.

And Big Ralph, indeed, did protect them from others, as long as they were willing to put out for him.

After spending the night on top of Tim and fucking him again in the morning, with Tim realizing that resistance was both futile and a little late, Big Ralph whispered the rules of their relationship to him. Since then Big Ralph had fucked him as many as three times a week, and, as promised, had kept all other takers at bay.

Tim came to accept this as just another aspect of the routine of life aboard the destroyer. But he was looking forward to this two-day shore leave in San Diego for a change of pace.

Sailor Javier

"The USS *Halsey*. My second year aboard. And you?"

"I'm on the *Shoup*," Tim answered. He looked away and nudged in closer to the table as another older sailor drifted by close to him in the bar and smacked his lips suggestively. "Just four months, though."

"Ah, four months." The guys would be pleased, Javier knew, if he landed this one. The guy was perfect. Probably only eighteen by the looks of him and just the right bod. Javier was judging this on his own body; he'd obviously been just right for the four of them last year. And this guy and he were almost identical in size and body style. This one was a lot prettier than Javier had been, though, he had to acknowledge. The major differences between them were that this guy was a blond and Javier was Hispanic—and this guy seemed so shy and a little skittish of the attention he was getting in this bar loaded with sailors off the ships. There were sailors who would love this, the sense of innocence. Javier wondered if he'd been this shy last year at this time and decided that he'd never been that shy. He'd known the score for as long as he could remember. And the almost palpable fear of the sailors swimming about the guy—he said his name was Tim—could, Javier thought, be put to his advantage.

"That means you've gone through all the hazing on ship then, I guess."

"Yeah, I suppose so." Tim wasn't acting like he wanted to talk about it. Bingo, Javier thought. That means you've been nailed already, little buddy. That's helpful.

"As bad as mine, I guess. Mine included being turned. Sailors go right for the little guys. Which is OK now, I guess, but it was really something at the time. But I got myself a protector and then it was mostly OK. Guy with a face like yours, and your size and conditioning, I bet you've had a really rough time."

"Well . . . it's OK now."

"So, you got yourself a protector too."

"Yeah . . . I guess."

"Makes a lot of demands, does he? Cock too big to handle?"

"No, not really." This given with hesitation. "He's got several sailors he's protecting, and he isn't too big."

Well, baby, you're in for a real surprise then, Javier thought. But with an ass that's still tight, you'll be a hit with the guys. Dan and Todd will love sharing this one.

Tim was looking like he really wanted to change the subject—like he might even jump up from the table and bolt, so Javier changed the subject. He didn't want to lose this one. This pigeon looked like the mother lode as soon as he'd walked into the bar, all glassy eyed and looking like he was lost and might just back out again. The older sailors had seen him immediately and started jockeying for position. It had been Javier's luck that, to Tim, he looked like the most similar, familiar kind of guy and all Javier had to do was motion to him and pull out the chair next to him to get the pigeon roosting in his cage. He'd just come straight to him. Javier wouldn't tell the guys it had been this easy.

"So, this being your first shore leave, you bring enough cash for two days?"

"I've got $200." Tim said it as if he was rolling in cash.

"Well, shit, that ain't enough to get you through supper in a town like this."

"It isn't?"

"No. Did you ask anyone on the ship how much you needed? The prices get jacked up when the fleet's in. Two bills ain't even enough for an hour of pussy. And forget getting a room. You'll have to go back to the ship for the night."

"I will?" The prospect was crushing. Two days shore leave but he'd still be going back under Big Ralph's control for the night.

"'Course there's a way you can avoid that."

"There is? How?"

"I got a friend that would really go for someone like you. And he's an officer. I bet I could get him to feed you and take care of your room for the night. You could go back to the ship at the end of your leave with the two bills still in your pocket."

"For what?"

"He'd want to lay you, of course. But I'm telling you that he's a real hunk. You'd enjoy him. You've said you get fucked regularly on the ship."

"Not all that much," Tim answered. "And I don't know. I—"

"You go back to the ship tonight and your protector is going to fuck you, ain't he?"

"Well . . ."

"And is he a looker? I'm telling you that my friend is a real hunk. And he's an officer. An Air Force officer. He'd treat you right."

"I didn't really come on shore—"

"The hell you didn't. You sayin' you got all outfitted in those tight Navy whites and came into a sailors' bar at 11:00 in the morning just to have a couple of meals on shore and spend a night in a dirty hotel room all alone? You come out to get a little pussy from a dirty whore? You ever even had any pussy?"

He'd lost Tim half way through that. What *had* Tim come on shore looking for? It wasn't a woman. Javier had struck home there; Tim had never been attracted to women. It had always been men who had turned him on, although he hadn't done anything about it until it was forced on him. But why did he make such a fuss with his dress? And how *did* he plan to use his shore leave? Wasn't it more not to have to be on the ship and at Big Ralph's beck and call?

"Tell you what. Let me make the call. Maybe the guy's busy and won't even come. And if he does, you can scope him out for yourself. Think about it. A hunk who will pay for everything and all you gotta do is let him fuck you once. If you go back to the ship, you'll have the same old guy layin' you. At least you'd be tryin' out someone new. Have a little adventure on your shore leave; somethin' to remember it by. I've been laid by this guy. It was heaven. He treats guy right."

Javier didn't wait for Tim to reply and Tim wasn't moving real fast in providing a reply. Javier was already pressing the buttons on his cell phone. He winked at one of the sailors hovering around when Tim wasn't looking and the guy came in closer. Tim shuddered, which is exactly what Javier wanted him to do. Bill, who had been waiting for a call, picked it up on the first ring. Javier managed to convey through prearranged signaling that he had a hot prospect and that it would help if Bill came in like a knight on a white horse.

Javier pointed Bill out as he hit the door and let Tim see for himself that the man really was a hunk, and that he looked spiffy and commanding in his closely tailored Air Force officer khakis. Tim also saw that as Bill entered and strode straight to the table, all smiles and in-charge authority, that he gave side looks of staking his territory that had the sailors who had been hovering around Javier and Tim—and had been egged on a bit by Javier when Tim wasn't looking—backing off.

The guy was an officer. No one in that bar was going to challenge him.

The overall impression was of protection arriving, which placed Bill in a niche with Tim that was just what Javier wanted. Protector/fuck master. It was what Tim understood.

Bill, who liked the looks of Tim immediately, was all smiles and sultry sensuous looks, and touching Tim's arms and, once, his cheek, and, later, his thigh, while he guided a discussion about Tim's life up to this point and moved into everything they could be doing in the next two days other than fucking. No, Tim had never been to an officer's club. No, Tim didn't know they had bedrooms an officer could check out for a guest's use right in the club, something called a bachelor officer's quarters, a BOQ. And that Tim could sleep there in a real nice room if Bill reserved it. Yes, Tim was hungry enough for lunch. Yes, Tim had thought of touring the USS *Midway* Museum, a decommissioned aircraft carrier open to the public, while he was on shore leave. No, he didn't know that they had one of the world's best zoos right here in San Diego.

Tim was completely disarmed. Bill, indeed, was a hunk. Dark looks; black curly hair; an open, friendly smile; a magnificent physique in that Air Force shirt, with curly black hair peeking out of his neckline and on his forearms. Biceps that pushed his shirt sleeve up to his shoulders. A commanding demeanor that held back the sailors who had been zeroing in on the table. His conversation put Tim at ease. The occasional touch of his fingers on Tim's arms and hands sent chills right up the young sailor's spine. And the officer didn't once mention that going with him would require that Tim let him fuck him. Before long Tim was catching glimpses under the table of Bill's basket—and wondering.

Let the Games Begin

The air base was on a plateau above the city, and as they drove there, Bill told Tim how convenient the officers' club was. Everything was right there together. A dining room that served good, hearty food—all to be put on Bill's club tab, of course—a well-stocked bar, and the wing of bachelor officers' quarter rooms that were well used during the week but more or less deserted on the weekend. It would be no trouble putting Tim up in one of these. It wouldn't cost him a dime. Bill, who indeed loved using the officers' club for the purpose he had for Tim, didn't mention that the club officer was a good friend to Bill and his friends and that he ran a back bar as well as a front one— that the back bar was more for Bill's kind. Nor did he say that because of the nearness of the airstrip and the concern that visiting pilots get good sleep, all of the BOQ rooms were soundproof.

They had steak sandwiches and piles of French Fries and a couple of beers—to add to the two Tim had already had at the bar with Javier—for lunch in the club dining room.

Afterward, Bill suggested that he show Tim the BOQ room he'd booked.

Bill stood and so did Tim, but Javier remained sitting.

"You coming too?" Tim asked.

"No. I'll sit out here a while," Javier answered. And then in a lower voice that at least pretended that Bill couldn't hear, he said, "I think this is where you pay the rent."

Tim shuddered, but he turned and followed Bill back down the corridor leading into the BOQ wing.

He was sitting in Bill's lap on the end of the bed, feeling the hard cock under him through the material of the trousers they both still were wearing. They both were shirtless, though. They were kissing and Bill was working Tim's torso with a hand, while holding him in an embrace with the other arm. He was working slow. All of this was new to Tim. Big Ralph always just went for the fuck and he always did it in the dark. Bill was preparing him, making him moan and sigh. His kisses were making Tim breathless. What he was doing with his hands was driving Tim crazy. Tim felt the bulging of the biceps and also of the man's pecs. He ran his fingers through the man's chest hair. It was silky soft.

Bill unbuttoned Tim's fly, flared the opening, pulled Tim's cock out, and started to slow stroke it. This was attention Big Ralph had never given Tim. He quivered and felt his hips start to go into a motion that pushed his cock up through the encircling hand and then down again. Up and down. He was fucking himself in the cupped hands. Bill refused to let his lips go, pushing his tongue inside Tim's mouth and flicking it in and out. Tim began to writhe in ecstasy. Bill, much larger and meatier than Tim, just held him fast and continued kissing and stroking until Tim came with a shudder and a long sigh.

"Now me," Bill whispered, coming out of the kiss, and turning Tim and pushing him down on his knees on the carpet between his thighs. Tim moaned as Bill unbuckled himself, pulled down his zipper, and pulled out a half-erect cock.

It was bigger—both longer and thicker—than Big Ralph's was. Tim gasped and groaned at the sight of it—and then at the feel of it as Bill stroked his cheeks with it, always returning to pressing it at Tim's lips. Although he'd never done this before, it had been going on around him on board ship for weeks and Tim had seen several examples of it, so he opened his lips to the cock and did what came naturally in sucking and engorging.

Everything was new to him. He had no idea that sex with a man could be like this. Later he would go over all of it in his mind again—to consider what he liked and what he didn't like. For now he'd do whatever was demanded of him. He'd pay the rent and it would be over.

He was laying at the foot of the bed, with his butt on the edge. He was staring straight up at the ceiling and was arching his back and then releasing, arching and releasing, bunching up wads of the bed spread and releasing. Bunching and releasing. Gasping and groaning, every neuron of him concentrating on his cock and balls being sucked, on the tongue going to his channel entrance, on the lubricated fingers invading his ass.

Bill then was standing over him, between his thighs. Naked. A magnificent, slightly hairy body. Long, thick cock standing out and curved up from his black, curly bush. A smile on his face. Rolling a condom on his cock.

Tim trembled and began hiccupping deep in his throat, as Bill gripped and lifted and spread his thighs, rolled his pelvis up, and placed the bulb of his cock at the entrance.

"Oh, shit, oh fuck!" Tim cried out as the bulb pressed in a bit and revolved, seeking entrance.

"You've never had one this big, have you?" Bill asked.

Tim shook his head.

"But you have been fucked before?"

Tim nodded and covered his face with his arm.

"No don't do that," Bill said. "I want to watch your eyes while you take it. I'll go slow and be gentle, but don't deny me the view of you taking it."

Bill was slow and gentle—at least until he was in and Tim had opened to him and was moaning how good it felt, how filling it was, how he'd never had it this good before. And then

211

Bill started pumping and Tim started writhing and crying out a commentary on where the cock was—everywhere—and what it was doing to him—sending him over the moon.

"That was great. You're so sexy. A natural," Bill said after he'd withdrawn and rolled the condom off his cock. "Now, why don't you go get a shower and then I'll take you out and show you some of the sights of San Diego. We'll do something with your shore leave other than spend it here, fucking." He pulled Tim off the bed, turned him toward the connecting bathroom, and gave him a slap on the rump to get him going.

Tim spent the shower trying to decide whether he really wanted to see the sights of San Diego or just stay here and be fucked by Bill again. All thoughts of doing it once to pay the rent and that was it had floated out of his mind and desires. Javier had said he'd only need to do it once—or at least had strongly hinted that. Tim wasn't sure that he didn't want to do it constantly over his two-day pass. Where would Bill spend the night, he wondered. He lived here and had his own place, of course. But was this room for just Tim or for both of them? He now wanted it to be for both of them.

He walked out of the bathroom with just a towel around him and stopped dead in his tracks. Bill was sitting on the side of the bed, still naked, but, most tellingly, with another condom rolled on his erect cock.

"I decided there is plenty of time for sightseeing. Come here." He reached over and pulled the towel off Tim. "Unless you don't want to."

Tim quickly showed that he wanted to. Bill marked this as a done deal for his friends' plans for the weekend.

This time Bill fucked Tim on his lap. Tim was sitting in his lap, facing Bill. His torso was laying back, supported by Bill's long, strong arms, with Bill's hands hooked over Tim's shoulders. Tim's legs were stretched out on the bed behind Bill. Bill's long torso was hunched over Tim's chest. Bill pulled Tim's channel back and forth on his cock. Bill was looking down intently into Tim's eyes, watching them come alive and flash and burn as Bill increased the pushing and pulling. Faster and deeper, ever fast and deeper, until both men cried out, coming nearly together.

Two hours. Paying the rent had taken two hours. Or so Tim thought. They showered together then, Bill making a joke about conserving water in drought-ridden southern California, and Tim almost wanting to be taken again from the arousal of Bill soaping up and rinsing off his body.

Javier wasn't there when they came back to the main part of the club, so the two of them drove off in Bill's Mustang convertible. Bill drove Tim down from the plateau and through the old, historic part of the city to the docks, where they toured the USS *Midway* Museum. Tim was like a little kid in his need to explore everything, and the actual little kids present all wanted to ask Tim, dressed in his Navy whites, about ships and sailing— and he stood with many of them for the photos they wanted. More than one of them asked Tim if he was a museum guide, and Tim almost wished that he was. Standing by, Bill nearly laughed, at what the parents of these kids would think if they'd known that Tim had been riding his cock just an hour earlier.

From the ship, they checked out Balboa Park, and then Bill took Tim to the San Diego zoo and watched him revert to a young child again. Bill had to keep telling himself that Tim wasn't a child, that he was a delicious young man with a sweet ass that was going to be reamed beyond his wildest imagination over the next two days. The thought didn't make him apprehensive, though; it made him go hard. He wanted nothing more than to pull Tim behind the monkey house and bang him again right there. He settled with buying Tim a stuffed monkey toy, which Tim accepted with a big smile and held close to his chest as, in the gathering twilight, they drove back up onto the plateau and to the welcoming arms of the officers' club.

Dinner and Dance

Javier was at the dinner table when Bill and Tim entered the dining room. But he wasn't alone. Pete and Todd and Dan were there too. They were drinking, waiting for Bill and Tim to arrive. They were all smiles for Tim when he was introduced to them. He was everything they had hoped for. Their smiles broadened as Bill went around to his friends to whisper how much greater than they anticipated Tim's ass was and how much the innocent he played while he was being played. While Bill was

213

making the rounds, Tim was telling Javier what he'd seen that day and, with a blush now that he thought about how immature having the stuffed monkey was, still couldn't resist showing Javier the prize Bill had given him at the zoo. Javier beamed at the news, contemplating a bonus on his finder's tip.

Tim contemplated Bill's new friends while they were eating dinner. Dan and Todd didn't bother him. They obviously were into each other. He didn't see how they whispered to each other about him when he wasn't looking. Pete worried him. He was a hulk, and a black hulk at that. Tim didn't think of himself as prejudice, but there weren't all that many blacks in the Iowa town he came from, and he had learned to be wary of them since he'd entered the Navy. On ship they seemed to move in packs, and they'd give him the most worrying looks. He'd been warned about their interest in gangbanging sailors they could isolate in hidden compartments on ships. And in the shower room, he'd seen that, to a man, they were lower hung than the whites and Hispanics he saw. They both made him shudder and fascinated him. And this Pete was no different. He seemed to be the Alpha Dog of this gathering of friends. All of the other men deferred to him, and, although he didn't say much—just sat there with an inscrutable half smile on his face most of the time—when he did speak, everyone stopped what they were doing and listened. And when it came to developed bodies, although all four of these guys were built like tanks, he was the awesome one.

After dinner, Pete led the way toward the back of the club. There was activity in the front bar, but they found that there was even more going on in the back bar. One wouldn't have known it before opening the doors into the bar. Although they were met with raucous noise from a DJ sound system, they heard practically nothing before opening the doors. The building had really good soundproofing.

The back bar was all guys and most of them were shirtless—which all of Pete's crew, including Tim, were in short order. Guys were out on the floor dancing with each other. The DJ was up on a platform, at one end of it. In the middle of the platform was a pole going up to the ceiling. The guys all bellied up to the bar and Bill took possession of Tim. Bill perched against a stool, facing out into the room, and just pulled Tim's butt into his crotch and embraced him with his arms. He played Tim's bare chest with his hands, letting one glide down occasionally to cup and squeeze Tim's basket. When he did this, Tim would turn his head and they'd kiss deeply. Tim was getting the idea he wouldn't be sleeping in the BOQ room all by himself, and he had warmed up to that idea. Bill's fucking was nothing like Big Ralph's was.

A couple of more loud songs with a strong beat and Javier was on the platform, dancing on the pole, and slowly shedding parts of his Navy whites. Dan and Todd were at the end of the bar, on stools, and kissing and touching each other with their hands. They also, though, were watching Javier dance. Pete was sitting in the stool next to Bill and Tim. He was turned toward those two and was watching him. Again the little half smile. Every once in a while he'd take a swig of his drink, but Tim got the impression that he didn't look at the drink—that he continued watching Bill play Tim's nipples, suck on his ear lobe, and cup his basket with his hand.

Tim could feel how hard Bill was for him—and that aroused him too—and he was beginning to wonder if Bill was going to fuck him again right there on the bar stool—with the black bruiser, Pete, watching. It seemed possible. Some of the other guys in the room were fucking. The party was getting pretty wild.

Tim didn't know if he cared or not. This wasn't costing him anything. This certainly was different from life on the ship. And this certainly was some shore leave. Bill was such a hunk. Tim couldn't wait to be alone with him again.

They went into a long kiss, with Bill stuffing his hand under the waistband of Tim's Navy whites, which wasn't an easy thing to do as tight as the trousers were. Bill had had to unbutton Tim's fly to get his hand inside. Tim's balls were now being cupped flesh on flesh, and he'd gone hard. He was panting. If Bill stripped his trousers off and put him on the cock right here, right now, Tim would have been happy.

When they came out of the kiss, Tim looked at the platform. Javier had been down to his briefs when they had started the kiss. Now he was gone. Gone too were Dan and

Todd, and Tim assumed they had gone off to some corner to hump. They practically had been doing it there at the bar. He didn't know where Javier had gone off to, though.

Bill pressed another beer on Tim. This was, what? his eighth or tenth beer of the day? He'd lost count. Bill made him chug it, though. Then Bill moved his lips to Tim's ear so that Tim could hear what he said over the noise of the crowd and music, and growled. "It's time to go to the room."

As they were walking down the silent, dark corridor of the BOQ, seeming like a cemetery in contrast to the noise of the party room, with Bill guiding a somewhat dazed Tim with a hand on his buttocks, Tim was not unaware that Pete was following behind them.

* * * *

Fifteen minutes later, Tim was lying on one of the queen-sized beds in the room on his side, cupped into Bill's chest. Bill was holding Tim to him with an arm around his chest. He was lifting Tim's upper leg with a hand under his knee. And his cock was slow-pumping Tim's ass. Tim was moaning through a slack jawed mouth. His attention, through glassy eyes, was riveted on the other queen-sized bed.

Todd was lying on his back, his arms embracing Javier's chest. Javier was lying on top of him. Todd's thick cock was stuffed up Javier's ass. Todd's legs were laced through Javier's, holding them imprisoned and spread. Dan was kneeling between the spread legs, crouched over Javier's chest, his arms stiff-armed on either side of the chests of the men below him. His hips were cruelly punching at Javier's hole, pistoning his long cock inside Javier and on top of Todd's stretching and hard, but dormant, cock. Javier was squirming and breathing hard at the double invasion.

As Tim watched, Dan slowed down his thrusts, but Todd's movement came to life. Javier was crying out. Some of it was expressing unbounded pleasure. Some of it wasn't. But Javier was a trooper and knew what he was being paid by these men to take.

As if the atmosphere was turning up the lust dial, Bill started pistoning his cock inside Tim as well and Tim buried his face in the bedspread, groaned . . . and ejaculated.

Pete, naked, was sitting in a chair, watching, and pulling on his cock.

Twenty minutes later, Tim was lying back, cantilevered over the surface of the bed. Pete was kneeling, his knees pushed under Tim's buttocks and gripping his sides to hold his torso off the bed. Tim's legs were stretched out beyond Pete's hips. Tim's torso revealed that he already was spent—and, now, was overpowered, nearly overstretched. He was just lying back, his arms dangling at his side, his head flopped back, staring at the headboard, jerking just a bit at every long push of the channel off the monster cock and then a tired gasp at the long pull of his channel back onto the shaft. All of Tim's fears and anticipations were being realized. A black man's cock that was thicker and longer than anything Tim had ever seen hanging between any man's thighs, white or black. A fuck that was both horrendous and glorious. A filling that surely would split him, but somehow didn't.

Tim hadn't been asked if Pete could fuck him too. But Tim was no dummy. Six men in this room with two beds, two of them small, young sailors and four of them big, hulky Air Force officers. Tim knew that he'd found the gang bang that he'd been avoiding on board the ship.

On one side of the bed beside him, Javier was on all fours and Bill was crouching over his hips pistoning him hard. Next to them, pointed in the opposite direction, Dan was in the same position on top of Todd.

Alone but still moaning at Pete's taking, Tim was dozing. Bill was sitting next to him, stroking his cheek with his fingers. He lowered his mouth to Tim's ear. "You were really hot with Pete. If you can take Pete's cock, you can take any man's. It's good preparation."

Preparation for what? Tim wondered. He heard growling and grunting in the room, beyond the beds. The room reeked of musk and the smell of sweat and cum. Pete was stalking Javier on the other side of the room. Both were in a crouch and Javier was feinting this way and that, testing Pete's reactions, while Pete

217

was moving from one side to the other, trying to figure out the smaller man's pattern. Pete's gigantic cock was waving out in front of him. Freshly crowned. Tim knew it was a new condom, because he had felt Pete fill the one he was fucking Tim with. When he had pulled it off his cock, it was thick as a sea slug, filled with cum. It was a slight thrill to Tim that he had caused Pete to cum that much for him.

Bill moved Tim to his back and was sucking on his nipples and lacing fingers in his balls and tugging on them. Dan and Todd were lying on their backs next to each other on the other bed, resting. Tim dozed off.

He woke again to the feel of hands on his ankles, pulling him toward the foot of the bed. It was Todd's turn to fuck him. Tim groaned. Dan was still on his back on the other bed. Pete had caught Javier. Javier was suspended, horizontally in the air over the floor. He was gripping the arms of a chair in both hands. Pete was behind him, between Javier's legs with them spread out from his hips like Javier was a wheel barrow, and he was slow-fucking Javier's ass. Javier was sweating like a pig and groaning deeply.

The shower was going. Bill was missing, so Tim assumed he was the one in the shower. For some reason, Tim felt a loss of his protection, although he had a flash of anger in the realization that Bill hadn't protected him from anything and was unlikely to.

"No, please, enough," Tim murmured, but Todd wasn't listening to him. He gathered Tim up in his arms and turned him as Todd sat on the end of the bed. Tim heard a roar from the other side of the room. Pete had come again. Dan stirred and sat up in the other bed. Todd lowered Tim's channel on this thick cock, with Tim sitting in his lap, facing the room. Javier was on the floor in front of the chair, curled up, and Pete was standing over him, rolling the condom off his still-hard cock. Once again, the spent condom reminded Tim of a sea slug. Todd was raising and lowering Tim on his cock and murmuring in his ear how tight and sweet he was. Pete walked by the bed and dropped the spent condom in a waste basket and peeled another packet off a string of them on the bedside table. A tired Tim, eyes slitted and seeing everything as a blur, leaned his head back into Todd's

218

shoulder as Todd, his arms crossed under Tim's diaphragm continued to lift and lower his channel on the thick cock.

Tim opened his eyes to the feel of a hand on his shoulder. Dan was standing in front of him, holding his cock up in his other hand. Tim took the cock in his mouth and started sucking it hard.

"Lower and stretch him," Dan said, and Tim felt himself being lowered on the surface of the bed on top of Todd's chest. Todd's legs were pushing on Tim's, raising and spreading them. Dan was crouching between the spread legs and Tim felt the bulb of the long, now-rehardened cock at his rim above the root of Todd's buried cock.

"Noooo," he moaned weakly. They were moving in to trap him in a double penetration.

Pete voiced some sort of command, though, and was brushing Dan aside and reaching down and pulling Tim off Todd. He pulled Tim out into the center of the room. Tim was just about to voice some form of thanks when Pete bent him over at the waist and started entering him from the rear. Tim groaned weakly. When Pete started pumping him, Tim's legs went to jelly, and Pete put an arm around his waist, pulling his feet off the floor, and went into a balancing crouch. He continued pumping, faster and deeper. Tim ejaculated weakly, shortly before Pete did so more strongly. Then Pete just let Tim sink to the floor in a heap. Javier wasn't far from him, also still curled up on the floor.

Bill had come out of the bathroom and stretched out on the bed. Dan and Todd took their turn in the shower. Pete went and sat in the chair. When Dan and Todd had showered, he nudged Javier and told him to go clean himself. With a groan and a grunt, Javier slowly raised himself and went off to the shower. When he was done, Pete rose from the chair, picked Tim up, slung him over his shoulder, and took him into the bathroom. Tim just stood, weakly in the shower as Pete soaped both of them up roughly and let the shower rinse them off. He tossed a towel to Tim, who was on more sure legs now, and went into the bedroom with a towel to dry himself.

When Tim came out of the bathroom, the lights were off in the bedroom. In the light from the bathroom, Tim could see

219

that Dan and Todd were in the far bed, with Javier between them, being doubled by them for the second time. Pete was in a chair with his heels on the bed where Bill was stretched out. The level of snoring indicated that maybe they all were asleep.

His ordeal was over, he decided. Was this worth free room and board during his shore leave? Whatever it was, it was something he'd never forget. And it wasn't necessarily bad. Now that it was over, he could concentrate on the pleasure of it. What Big Ralph gave him wasn't fucking. This had been fucking. Lying under Big Ralph from now on would be no big deal.

He switched off the bathroom light and went and collapsed onto the edge of the bed Bill was on, seeking whatever privacy he could get. Bill's arm came over and pulled Tim into the curve of his body as he turned toward Tim.

In the middle of the night, Tim woke. Bill also was awake and saw that Tim's eyes were open. "Have you ever been fucked like that before?" he whispered.

"No," Tim answered honestly.

"We enjoyed you. Like Javier, we'd enjoy doing you any time you come in on shore leave. You won't find a cock like Pete's anywhere else. You're spoiled for it now."

"We'll see." Tim was suddenly mortified. He'd meant the "we'll see" to be finding any better fucking than Pete did. Bill probably took it as an answer that he wanted it again the next time he had shore leave. He was right in that.

"Good," Bill murmured. "When I take you back to the ship, I'll give you contact numbers. Next time, we'll pay you the same we pay Javier—$500 for the weekend for unlimited access."

Unlimited access, Tim thought. What a strange way to express it. He was on the verge of laughing about that, but his attention was arrested. Bill was moving him.

"It's late," Tim whispered. "We should be—"

Bill laughed. "We got you for the weekend, little buddy. You're going to be fucked all through the night."

Tim moaned. Bill was on his back, pulling Tim over on top of him on his back. Bill was getting his legs between Tim's and lifting and spreading Tim's legs. His cock was sliding into

220

Tim's channel and his arms were lacing through Tim's and stretching and trapping the young sailor's arms over his head.

Tim woke up laying on his belly diagonally in the bed. Dan was saddled over his hip and fucking down in him. Pete was doggy fucking Javier in the other bed. Tim's head was hanging over the side of the bed and he was staring down into a waste basket half full of spent condoms.

Todd and Bill were nowhere to be seen or heard.

Dan filled his condom and got off Tim and went to the shower. Tim was moving to get off the bed when strong, brown hands gripped his waist and pulled him down to the side of the bed, moving his feet to the floor. Tim was bent over on the bed on his belly. Pete entered him and began a strong stroke.

Javier got off the other bed and went into the bathroom, and, presumably into the shower. When both Dan and Javier came out of the bathroom, they stood there, toweling off, and watching Pete stroke on inside Tim.

Tim was moaning and panting and gasping. He had been a bit premature in thinking it was all over the previous night.

Dan and Javier continued watching as they dressed. Pete stroked on.

After the two had left the room, Pete shot his load, pulled out and went to the shower, tossing his sea slug of a spent condom in the waste basket on his way to the bathroom.

He hadn't said anything at all to Tim. Tim was just there for their special weekend.

It was nearly noon when Tim struggled into the dining room, so he ordered a hamburger and shake with fries. Pete and Javier were gone. Bill was there. He'd finished eating, but he said he would wait around and take Tim to see something else of San Diego after he'd eaten and then take him back to his ship.

Dan and Todd weren't there, but they came into the dining room as Tim was finished eating.

"Want you back in the bedroom after you're done here," Dan said. "We got interrupted doin' you together last night. We're not done." Then they walked on toward the corridor to the BOQ rooms.

"No," Tim said to their departing backs. "No," he said, turning to Bill. "Please, no. I've had enough. You guys have had enough of me."

"It's still the weekend," Bill said.

"No," Tim said, starting to rise from the table.

Bill stood, gathered him up, tossed him over his shoulder, and started walking down the corridor.

Dan and Todd took him the way they had started to do the previous evening. Todd was under Tim on his back, Tim's back on him, Todd's cock buried up Tim's channel. He was embracing Tim's chest with his arms and pushing Tim's legs up and out with his. Dan crouched between Tim's legs, forced his cock in over Todd's, and did most of the pumping.

Tim lay there, whimpering and trapped between them. It wasn't as bad as he had imagined it to be. Pete had reamed him well for it.

Back to the Sea

Before taking Tim back to the ship, Bill drove him up the coast in the Mustang to Sunset Cliffs Natural Park. They parked in a lot right next to the cliffs, and Bill pulled Tim over toward him, wrapping an arm around his neck and took him into a deep kiss. He moved the other hand under his jerkin and rubbed his nipples and glided his hand over Tim's chest. They were looking out over the Pacific on a beautiful, rugged section of the Pacific. He unbuttoned Tim's Navy white trousers—not that Navy white anymore—fished out his cock and slowly stroked him.

"You were terrific, baby," Bill murmured. "Can't get enough of you."

You and three others, Tim thought. But he was melting to the man. He was such a hunk and he had such a beautiful smile and a soothing voice. Tim could almost believe him.

"I'm sorry if it was a bit taxing . . ."

A bit!? Tim thought.

". . . but it's because your body is so beautiful and yielding. You are a natural. We must have you again."

Tim's hips were moving, thrusting up inside the hand encasing his cock. Was this what he wanted too. Would it be

222

pabulum with Big Ralph from now on? Maybe this was what he wanted after all.

Bill's tongue was inside Tim's mouth, swabbing it. He took Tim's tongue in his mouth and sucked on it. He was pulling on Tim's cock harder. His thumb was pressing into Tim's piss slit, slicking around the precum Tim was producing.

This was more than fucking. This was fully arousing, more attention being paid to Tim's needs than anyone had done the previous day. He could lay under Bill and fully enjoy him. Of them all Bill had done him best. And he was the best looking, the hunkiest, the best talker. The kindest.

Both of them were aware that Tim was tensing. Bill withdrew from the kiss and moved his mouth down to cover Tim's cock and to suck until Tim came.

No one in the previous day had cared when and how Tim had come. Just now, here with Bill. Only Bill cared. He'd been given a telephone number. Was it Bill's. He could call the next shore leave and meet him again if it was only Bill.

Bill came back up and went into another kiss on the mouth. He had been holding Tim's cum in his mouth and it rolled around between their mouths. Tim moaned deeply. This was a new sensation. Not all that unpleasant. The most intimate sharing he'd ever done with a man.

"Come let's walk," Bill said, rebuttoning Tim's fly.

They got out of the car and, arm and arm, walked alongside the cliff. A hundred yards along the cliff the foliage got to be denser, trees and bushes came closer to the pathway.

Suddenly Bill lifted Tim off the ground and dragged him into the bush. He was pawing at Tim like a wild man. Tim was struggling against him, but it was no use. Bill pulled off his trousers and briefs and forced him onto all fours in the scrub, thrust inside him, and pounded, pounded, pounded his ass.

Tim sobbed and writhed under Bill's thrusts, the most brutal that Tim had had all weekend. With a yell, Bill pulled out of him and shot off across the small of his back. Tim rolled over onto his side and Bill stood, crouching over him, panting.

"Get up."

Tim whimpered something neither one of them could understand.

"I said get up."

Tim didn't. Bill kicked him in the ribs. He still couldn't rise.

Bill reached down, pulled him up, slung him over his shoulder, marched back to the car, and dumped him over the side of the convertible into the passenger seat.

As they drove back into the city, with Tim curled up in a ball in the passenger seat as far away from Bill as possible, Bill spoke only once. "$500 for the weekend plus room and board. We don't make love; we fuck. It's good money. Think about it and call us your next shore leave. You're going to find that you don't want vanilla any more after us. So you'll call."

At the dockside, he stopped near the gangplank to the USS *Shoup*, reached over and opened the passenger door, and nudged Tim out onto the blacktop. He reached over and pulled the door closed and then drove off without giving another look.

A couple of sailors passed Tim as he was struggling to stand up. They'd seen drunks coming off of shore leave like this, though, so they just passed him by.

Tim was happy for three weeks. Big Ralph kept the other men off him and fucked him three times a week. Bill had been right, though. After Pete and his friends Big Ralph's fucking was bland. Tim started to let the occasional bruiser fuck him without letting Big Ralph know that he was doing it. He found two guys who wanted to fuck him together, but Tim discovered that what they had in mind was one after another, but at the same time. And it was pretty bland.

One twilight he arranged to be standing near the hatch doorway to a rope locker, apparently unaware of a group of black sailors moving around him, ever closer, but knowing they were there. When they fucked him on coils of rope in the dark, one after the other as several hands held him down, all big dicked and heavy pounders, Tim felt about as close to the thrill he now associated with his Air Force officer weekend as he'd ever gotten.

Three months later, the *Shoup* was pulling into San Diego again to let its sailors go on shore leave—and Tim was looking around in his kit bag for Bill's telephone number.

Sam, Sam, Sam

All the time I was standing out on the balcony of Colleen Addison's house fourteen miles south of Athens, in Voula, overlooking Greece's Miroon Sea, and engaging in chit chat with her and the man who was introduced to me merely as Sam from the Economic Section, I kept thinking that I knew him from someplace but couldn't place him. He, on the other hand, seemed to remember me well and was giving a knowing little smile while we talked that I found maddening. It was burning me up not to be able to place him. It evidently was from somewhere in my past, and I wasn't real anxious to dredge up some of my past.

I was on TDY—temporary duty assignment—at the U.S. embassy in Athens, where I was training the local employees of the American Cultural Center in the new computer programs that would enable them to churn out professional-looking publicity material at their desks without having to go to a printer. Colleen was the embassy's cultural affairs officer and was doing what she could to make my stay less dull than it usually was when I was on one of these swings around Europe. She wasn't holding this gathering of a smattering of embassy officers and Greek artists, writers, and actors for me, of course, but she had invited me to attend and had seen to it that a driver was available to bring me out to her place.

Colleen's Voula house was quite a place, high on a hill overlooking the Mediterranean, with a long terrace off the back and good entertainment space. She'd been assigned the house in keeping with what her job was—promoting U.S. culture while pretending to have interest in promoting the culture of Greece, as if Greek culture needed promoting.

Colleen, Sam, and I were in a tight group as the crowd was thinning out and had nearly run out of chit chat, especially as Sam seemed to be savoring something the other two of us weren't privy to, when we were joined by a Greek god. I could only call him that because, while many Greek men were handsome and exuded macho sensuality, he was a man among men—muscular, dark and sultry with what was probably a perpetual five-o'clock shadow, as he was hirsute. His curly black hair seemed to grow perceptibly as we stood there talking. I was lost in his startling blue eyes.

"Pirro," Colleen said, "You know Sam, I'm sure"—and the Greek god turned an indulgent smile on Sam, which was answered with one I perceived to be subservient, as if Pirro knew Sam intimately. The back of my mind was beginning to rumble toward a possible recognition of Sam from a previous life. "And this is Trent Townson from Washington, who is out here helping us tone up our publicity systems. Trent is a short story writer too. Pirro is the star of one of the most popular Greek soap operas."

I shook hands with the actor as we both juggled our cocktail glasses to another hand. His handshake was firm, I'd almost say possessing. My mind was beginning to stir possibilities with Pirro that went beyond conversation. The four of us spoke briefly before Colleen saw a Greek writer she wanted to introduce me to and then we walked off and left Sam and Pirro to entertain each other.

I felt a bit weak in the knees. I found the Greek actor beyond sexy. And it was while we were walking off that I at last placed Sam firmly in my mind—and blushed. I think it was the "knowing" look between the economic officer and the actor that eventually had done it.

I had only seen Sam once before, but it was under the most compromising of circumstances. We were on side-by-side twin beds in a bedroom of the Delta Tau Delta fraternity at Duke University in North Carolina, where we were both being fucked by members of Miami University's track and field team. I was being doubled by a shot putter and a long-distance runner. Sam, who was lying under a decathlon stud, was from the nearby University of North Carolina, also in Chapel Hill, and Duke was the venue of an all-conference track meet. Sam was still there when my second set of doubles took up positions, so he every reason to believe that it was a specialty of mine.

I was what was known as a "reliever" in my fraternity at Duke. It was a jock fraternity, and I was there by right of being on the swim team and highly ranked in the conference in that sport. But I also was there because I gave blow jobs and took cock on demand—and I was one of very few who took doubles on demand too. That was the reliever part. When one of the other fraternity brothers needed relief, I provided it. I rather thought that Sam did the same thing at his fraternity at UNC. The day I had seen Sam, we'd spent several hours on side-by-side beds in my fraternity room entertaining a procession of visiting field and track jocks.

This definitely was part of the past—nearly five years previously—that I was trying to keep in the past. It had just been that one year for me. I'd pulled out from underneath it, so to speak; gave up the fraternity; applied myself to my studies and to the swim team; did extremely well; and I'd like to say that it was all in the past.

I hadn't exactly turned to women, but I had kept my encounters with men to the bare minimum, and my current job with the government put me in danger for engaging in any homosexual activity. So, for the most part, I didn't. For the most part. Luckily the State Department wasn't as strict about that as other agencies were. That, I guess, was why Sam could be a foreign service officer. He was certainly more gay than I was. You couldn't talk to the man or watch him walk and not know that he was gay.

There was no chance I would be getting it on with Sam here, of course. We wanted the same thing from another man, so it wasn't anything close to a fit. We had kissed and fondled each other during that day in the frat house, but it was more of a sharing experience thing—we each had a macho guy between our thighs at the time, fucking us. Some of the time that day I

227

had two at once. We weren't having sex with each other—not really. The Greek actor—Pirro—was more what I went for in a lover than someone like Sam.

But Sam was a danger while I was here. And perhaps I was a danger to him, as well, although he had recognized me and he certainly hadn't acted like he was in any sort of danger. I resolved to stay away from him as much as possible—and hope that he wasn't a gossip. My suppressed sexual proclivities weren't something I thought needed to become part of this TDY.

Upon leaving the party, Colleen noted that later in the week she would be going to a beach to get out of the smog and bustle of Athens and figured I'd be ready for a break then too.

"Want to do a picnic at a Greek beach?" she asked. "I know of several that will be virtually deserted and where neither of us will have to deal with a crowd of boisterous Greek artists for a couple of hours."

"Sure," I answered. "Nice of you to include me." I momentarily hoped that she wasn't coming on to me. I'd go along, to a certain limit, of course, for appearances sake. But she was a bit too openly flirty even for my limited taste in women. She was quite good-looking, though.

As it turned out Pirro was included in the outing too. I about melted when I came out of the hotel to get into Colleen's Volvo convertible and Pirro was sitting in the front seat, all curly black hair—he was shirtless and had a magnificent, darkly tanned and hairy chest—blue eyes, and pearl-white smile.

I have no idea where the beach was that Colleen took us to—and don't even know what direction from Athens it was in. We walked down from the road through a picturesque field of red poppies, though, to a line of tall rocks split by a curving rock-walled passage that ended at the top of a secluded beach. A stretch of something short of a hundred feet of white sand in a cove protected at each end by high rocks went down to the sea, which was so translucent that I could see to the bottom a good distance out into the water. There were shapes of smooth-topped rocks in the bed of the sea, but most of what I could see was an extension of the sand under a slowly rolling surf.

We parked the basket and blanket near the top of the beach. Colleen, a willowy sunshine blonde in her early thirties, pulled the halter top of her bikini off while I was opening up and setting out the two beach blankets she'd brought. She had breasts, but they perked more than flopped. Still, I took my breath in at how cavalier she was with the gesture—and how good-looking she was. She wasn't exactly beautiful. It was more that she had accentuated her best attributes and seemed so free and uninhibited.

I gasped again when Pirro slipped off the shorts he was wearing and ran, naked, down to the water and dove into an approaching wave. I hadn't caught a glimpse of his goods, but from the back, as he ran to the water, nothing dispelled the original Greek god impression I'd gotten. It was clear that these two were comfortable with each other—most likely in a sexual way. I began to reassess what I had taken to be Pirro's sexual preferences.

Colleen nonchalantly busied herself in laying out what she'd brought in the hamper. She handed me a bottle of wine to open and then, with a smile, held a glass for me to pour it in. I was sitting cross-legged on one of the blankets. I'd slipped my T-shirt off. I thought the wine was for her, but she handed me the glass, stepped out of her bikini bottoms, and, giving me a smile, cantered toward the water.

As she entered the surf, Pirro, who had swum out to sea, careened up and out, like a dolphin, on an incoming wave, his arms spread wide, enveloping Colleen as their bodies collided, and they went down in a heap in the shallows of the water, Pirro on top of Colleen. They stayed there, laughing, him on top of her, for a long minute. I watched the transition as the moment dragged on. Her arms encircled his muscular back and her legs spread and knees bent, and they kissed. Coming out of the kiss, her head arched back and his face went to her breasts, and I could see the rise and fall of his bulbous buttocks. I knew he had entered her and that they were fucking.

I couldn't help but be disappointed at this declaration of his preferences, although I had to admit that they made a handsome couple. It was curious, though, that they had brought me along, and more curious that they felt comfortable being so cavalier in front of me.

At length he struggled up to his feet, bringing her up with him. He lifted her off his cock, which then I could see was thick and long, and I gasped again as I watched her roll her buttocks up to him, and, holding the root of his cock in one hand, he moved the cock to her asshole and slowly entered her there. He stood in the shallow surf, holding her body to his, palming and spreading her buttocks, as she hooked her legs on his hips, locked her hands behind his neck and cantilevered out from his chest so that he had to bend over—which he did--to get his mouth to her nipples. Using the strength of his hands he pulled her ass up and down on his cock.

I could tell the instant that he came, as she jerked and cried out and collapsed against him. He laid her on her back at the surf line and moved down her body, burying his face in her muff. She writhed under him and, again, I could tell the instant that she came.

I was hard and had drunk nearly half a bottle of wine without realizing I had done so. It wasn't Colleen I'd been watching.

Pirro rose off Colleen and slowly walked up the sand toward me, his now-flaccid, but still manly cock and balls hanging low. Colleen rose as well and walked out into the sea. I didn't follow where she was going. My eyes were on Pirro. He flopped down on the blanket beside me. He'd picked up a couple of strands of a wheat-like plant on his way up the beach and just reclined next to me, rather close, and propped his head, turned toward me, on an elbow. He couldn't help looking like a perfectly formed, black-pelted Greek god.

"Would you like some wine?" I asked, looking over toward the basket to see where the glasses were.

"Later, after we fuck, don't you think?" he answered in a nonchalant manner. "We'll have to wait a bit, but the sight of you will make me hard again."

"After we—?" I turned back sharply. I was both shocked and exhilarated at his open, knowing declaration.

"I know men fuck you. Sam told me they did. That is a good thing, because you are beautiful and I am beautiful, and beautiful people should fuck. Did you enjoy watching me fuck Colleen?"

Oh, fuck, I thought, and then almost laughed nervously at the transference of the spoken word into my thoughts. There went any resolve I might have. That damned Sam. But, no, I knew I wanted Pirro to fuck me. If I didn't know it before I'd watched him fuck Colleen, I certainly knew it now, when he was teasing me by moving that stalk of wheat around on my thighs. He dropped the stalk, though, and moved his hand into the leg hole of my bathing shorts and up to my cock. There was no keeping the secret from him that I was hard.

"I *am* going to fuck you, aren't I?" he asked, raising those beautiful blue eyes toward my face, a little puppy dog expression on his face.

"I'd say you are going to do anything you want with me," I answered in a low voice.

He laughed at that, and if his smile could be said to broaden, his did.

His arm moved away from propping his head up and encircled my neck. He leaned my torso back toward the sand and took my mouth in his in a deep, lingering kiss. His other hand was slow pumping my cock through the leg hole of my swim suit. I took his hardening cock in my hand. He rolled over on top of me and our bodies writhed against each other's in a dry fuck as the kiss continued.

He was moving fast, but I wanted him inside me now, so he could move as fast as he wanted. We were both hard enough to fuck. I hadn't done this in months. And then it wasn't with a Greek god. Full steam ahead. Consequences, if any, be damned. I spread my legs and bent my knees. I rolled my pelvis up and pressed down on his buttocks with both of my hands. I was still wearing my bathing shorts. If I hadn't been, he'd already be inside me. As it was, the material of the bathing suit didn't prevent his bulb from being inside me.

He came out of the kiss and moved slowly down my body, kissing and teething me as he went. The trunks slid off my hips as he moved down, and by the time he reached my cock, they were off my legs, and my cock was in his mouth. Colleen appeared beside us and settled down cross-legged above me and moved my head to her lap. She ran her fingers through my hair while he sucked my cock and my balls. From time to time, she

231

moved her finger to my nipples and scraped my nubs with her long fingernails.

But then she was reaching her arms down my torso and receiving my legs at the ankles as Pirro raised and spread them, rolled my pelvis up, and started working my asshole with his tongue and teeth.

I was writhing under him, my head in Colleen's naked lap, and murmuring, "Fuck me, fuck me, fuck me," under my breath. I didn't consider this a time to be more inventive with the words of what I wanted.

And then he was fucking me. He was crouched between my thighs and moving up inside me. The cock filled me and expertly kissed every inch of my channel. My ankles were hooked on his shoulders. He kissed Colleen on the lips as he started to pump me. This was no slow, languid fuck. He pistoned me hard and deep. I came before he did.

Without ceremony, we disentangled, and Colleen set out a lunch. Pirro opened another bottle of wine. Just another day at the beach to the two of them. I was humming and feeling in touch with every inch of my body that Pirro was gliding his hands on. Both Pirro and Colleen complimented me on how hard I was, how cut my body was.

It took me longer to eat than it took the other two. While I was eating desert—fruit and some sort of Greek pastry—Colleen was on her belly on the blanket beside me, half turned on her side, her torso turned up to Pirro, who was stretched behind and on top of her, one hand turning her chin toward his face, their foreheads touching, their eyes locked, while he pressed her thighs between his and pistoned her ass with his cock as vigorously as he had mine.

"Always fuck them in the ass if you're going to come inside them," he whispered at one point, as if he was giving me instruction. "No question of anything unwanted then."

Colleen was moaning and telling him never to stop.

At another time, he muttered, "I'm an ass man, yes I am."

I countered with a, "I noticed." All three of us laughed. A cheery, little uninhibited group we were. I almost wished there were more of us here with the same comfortable openness. I

232

don't know why I was so nervous about my past being known. It certainly had cut some corners here.

He stopped fucking Colleen eventually and then nonchalantly rolled off her, turned toward me, took up a wine glass, and talked art and politics as if we weren't doing anything unusual at all—and I suppose for Pirro and Colleen this wasn't unusual.

He invited me to go for a swim with him, but half way down the beach he decided to show me how strong he was, getting behind me, snaking an arm around my waist, lifting my feet off the sand, and setting me down on his cock. He fucked me bent over in front of him with my arms and head dangling toward the sand and my feet off the ground. I didn't care how he fucked me as long as he did.

We all swam and cavorted then until almost twilight. Pirro fucked me again in the backseat of the Volvo, with its top up, on the way back to Athens. I sat in his lap, facing him, my knees pressed into where the back of the seat met the seat cushion, raised a bit off him, and his buttocks thrust forward on the edge of the seat while he thrust up hard inside me. I didn't know while returning to the city what the orientation of the Greek capital was to the beach we'd visited any better than I had when leaving Athens earlier that day. I spent most of the ride with my face buried in the hollow of his neck and moaning.

It was all business at the cultural center the next couple of days. Colleen said nothing about the picnic, so I didn't either. Pirro didn't contact me—which was a bit of a disappointment. I didn't see Sam again, but if I had, I would have thanked him for blabbing about me.

Sunday was the next day and the cultural center was open but not for business like I had to perform there. I tried calling Colleen to see if she could put me in touch with Pirro. Sunday was going to be an awfully dull day for me, trapped in the hotel with nothing to do. I'd been to Athens so many times that I was beginning to think I'd been here before all the old buildings fell down. And Sunday was a madhouse on the Athens streets. I couldn't get Colleen on Saturday. I wasn't surprised. The weekend was a busy time for a cultural affairs officer.

I was interested in a different kind of affair, though. And Pirro taking me like he had was like turning on a spigot. I walked the streets around the hotel Saturday night, looking for any signs of a gay bar. I wanted to get laid. But it was no go. Several men I encountered were willing, even eager. One or two would have been insistent if I hadn't been careful to stay where many others were milling around. None were anything like Pirro was. I went to a regular bar and drank until I had a buzz on. In addition to men just looking to get laid where I had started drinking, I was hit on in these bars by three, maybe four—it got to be sort of a haze—prostitutes. But they were all women, although I couldn't be completely sure about that last one. In any event, they weren't what I was looking for.

I thought of trying to call Sam. Not to try to interest Sam in anything, but because he probably would know where I could get some action worth the risk. But I couldn't get him on the phone either. I laughed at the thought that it probably was because he was off getting action.

At last I went back to my hotel room and slept until I could hear the room maids out in the hall, jabbering in loud voices to each other. I would have wondered if they didn't know that the hallways echoed the sounds rather than deadened them and that they were disturbing a floor full of paying customers— but I knew better. It was their way to get the hotel guests up and out so that the maids could complete their daily work quickly.

It worked with me. I was up, showered quickly, and was dressed in shorts and a T-shirt and at the door in less than a half hour. The maids were swarming around the corridor like buzzards and were inside my room almost before I could get out of it. I thought it probably was just as well that I didn't bring a guy back to the hotel for the night. I couldn't have slipped him by them in the morning—and couldn't get anything going in the morning with them mouthing off in the hall. I'd probably also see the charge for an extra guest on the tab—the tab that had to be turned in to government accountants for recording and reimbursing.

The hotel had an outdoor café. I went down to it and saw him—or rather them—as I approached the tables. Pirro was sitting there and drinking coffee. Next to him was a thinner, more wiry guy, not hirsute like Pirro, but every inch yet another Greek god.

"You sleep late," Pirro said. "This is my fifth cup of coffee. Sit and order breakfast. You'll need your strength."

I stood there, looking meaningfully at the other man, who obviously wasn't Pirro but who hadn't been introduced to me yet.

"This is Theo. He's a cameraman on the set of my television program. He is interested in a double fuck of you, just as I am. Sam told us you let two men fuck you at once. Theo and I have often said we'd like to share. But it's so hard to find willing young men—especially ones as beautiful as you. Those we've asked have wanted to see our cocks first and then they go screaming out into the night."

Pirro laughed at that and Theo touched him on the arm and asked him a question in Greek. Pirro apparently repeated the joke for him and they both laughed.

I sighed. Sam, Sam, Sam. Sam of the big mouth.

"Sit, eat. Then you take us to your room and we fuck." Pirro was smiling. Theo was smiling. I couldn't tell whether Theo even spoke English, although he seemed to have understood Pirro's joke about the size of their cocks. I guess it didn't matter, though. He obviously knew why he and Pirro were here. He already was reaching out and running his fingers down the side of my thigh.

"You want to see Theo's cock first? They have a men's room here you could go to." Pirro asked. "You'd have to promise no fooling around without me, though."

I blushed, as the waiter was hovering nearby, waiting for me to sit so that I would order. Still, I found Pirro's directness and openness arousing, and Theo's hand on my thigh was heating me up too. The waiter, who wasn't bad looking himself, gave me a smile and a knowing look, but he waited a few steps away from the table. "No, thanks. That won't be necessary," I answered.

I sat and ordered a big breakfast. While I ate, Pirro and Theo jabbered in Greek, all smiles and some laughter, and Theo occasionally reached over and touched me—like he was checking out the Pillsbury Dough Boy or something. The waiter was being very attentive to our table.

I made the mistake of asking Pirro what they were talking about.

"We were discussing the ways of getting two dicks in one man," Pirro said. "Theo doesn't quite know how we'll do that. I told him we'll manage. He thinks you're a hot stud, by the way."

"That's nice to hear," I said, not fully believing we were having this conversation, or that they were letting the waiter enjoy it as well. "Does he think I'm done yet?" I asked, as Theo prodded me with a finger on a nipple that clearly was pushing out at my T-shirt now. I was in full arousal. I had no intention of not doing anything Pirro wanted to do to me. I'd been doubled before. Sam knew that. And obviously Pirro knew that too. Sam, Sam, Sam, I thought.

Pirro gave me a questioning look, and I realized he wouldn't have gotten the dough boy reference. I hadn't said anything about it. But then he smiled and said, "Don't worry, we'll do you real, real good."

I'll bet you will, I thought. And they did. And they didn't have any trouble with the doubling—twice, because I blabbed and told them a second position that could get greater penetration. I did worry a bit about the maids in the room when we went upstairs, but they were long gone. Breakfast had taken me a while to eat.

Just inside the door to the room, I was stripped and Theo was in front on his knees sucking my cock and Pirro was knelt at my rear door. The first time they doubled me they did it right there, standing up, with me sandwiched between them. Pirro told me to bend over at the waist and roll my buttocks up and then told Theo to run his long, thin cock up into me. That done, with me groaning at how deep the thin guy could dig in, Pirro, from in front, grabbed and wishboned my thighs. He told Theo to rock back a bit to lilt me up, which he did, and then Pirro worked his cock in on top of Theo's. Each of them had a leg to hold out and a butt cheek to squeeze and separate, and I locked my hands behind Pirro's neck.

Pirro doled out his time kissing me, kissing Theo over my shoulder, and calling out the cadence of which of them was to pump and which one was to remain dormant inside me—and just doing what he could to stay inside me.

I hadn't done this since my senior year in Delta Tau Delta. These men were beautiful, and they both were fucking me. I was at least in eighth heaven.

About the time it dawned on me that it didn't feel like either one of them was wearing a rubber, Theo came inside me. Then I came, just from the sensation of Theo's spouting. Pirro came last. He told Theo to pull out of me, which Theo did, and Pirro carried me over to the bed and laid me gently there. He kissed me on a nipple and murmured, "Thank you. You are beautiful. Rest now. We fuck you again later."

Again? I thought. Well, why the hell not? These Greek men were gorgeous. And I melted at how matter-of-factly they approached this. I wasn't home. This would just be a pleasant interlude for me to remember. No strings. This wasn't new. I'd done this in college.

That's when I told them about a position providing deeper penetration. They seemed happy to know that and tried it happily—and with success.

The two of them sat in straight chairs, the chairs reversed and the men folding their arms along the tops of the chair backs, smoking cigarettes, and watching me. All very macho. I'd never felt so naked. Or so aroused.

"Masturbate for us," Pirro directed. "Come for us." And I complied.

I watched as they both slowly went hard again, just sitting there watching me, and talking softly to each other in Greek. I knew they were talking about me.

The second time I began by riding Pirro's cock for a while. He was on his back on the bed and I was facing his face, straddling his hips. I was just getting into riding the cock hard, when Pirro called Theo over. Giving direction now, I told him to straddle his legs behind me. Pirro wrapped his arms around me and pulled my chest down to his. Theo entered me from behind and began to pump. Pirro held me and his cock steady and close. I felt my heart beating against his and heard myself moaning happily. The three of us came almost simultaneously.

"I'm thirsty," Pirro said, maneuvering deftly from underneath me and bouncing to his feet. "We shower and dress and go down to the bar now. Then we come back and fuck double again."

Sure, why not? I thought.

It was single standing fucks in the shower, Pirro the pitcher both times, taking first me and then Theo. Theo didn't seem to mind going both ways.

"You know how to double, standing up in the shower?" Pirro asked me.

"Yes, of course." And then I showed them how.

"You doing anything tonight?" Pirro asked me later in the bar.

Just lying there and moaning, I thought. But what I said was "No."

"Good," was all he said. He left the bar for a few minutes, pulling a cell phone out of his pocket as he moved.

For the fourth double, back in the hotel room, Theo sat at the end of the bed and I sat on his cock, facing away. When Pirro came in between our legs, Theo, under Pirro's direction, laced his legs in mine and spread and raised them, while, arms encasing my chest, he laid back on the bed. Pirro worked his cock in on top of Theo's, held my waist with his hands, and pumped me harder than they'd done before.

After all of us had come, Theo rolled me off his body and pushed me up onto the bed, and the two of them went back to their chairs and their cigarettes. They were talking quietly to each other in Greek and eying me, and I was wondering if Pirro was trying to come up with another position I hadn't told him about and was having a hard time doing so. I must admit that I knew at least one more way they both could get their cocks inside me, but I wasn't offering any more advice. This was their fantasy. I was just along for the riding. By now, though, I was so stretched that I didn't care what way they thought of.

We both looked up at the knock at the door. Pirro was the only one not surprised by it. He got up and opened the door. I could see bruisers four deep in the hallway.

Pirro turned to me. "From the Athens footballers. You want or you want me to send them away? Sam told me you took sportsmen one after the other at university."

Sam, Sam, Sam, I thought as I scooted down to where my butt was on the edge of the foot of the bed, bent my legs, widened my stance, dug my heels into the edge of the bed, and rolled my pelvis up. I smiled at Pirro. "Is this what you want, Pirro?"

He shrugged. "I like to watch a beautiful young man with many fit men."

"Then bring on the footballers."

The next morning, before I left for the airport, the waiter in the hotel's café had me for breakfast over a toilet in a stall in the café's men's room. I was already scheming on how I could include the need for more TDY work at the American Cultural Center in Athens in my work report.

One thing I knew for sure that I was taking from my TDY in Greece. Life was too short and you aren't young for very long. I wasn't going to hold off now like before. I was sure that there must be some Pirros in the States. And I was returning determined to find them.

Swimming Lessons

"I'd like to make an Australian Crawl." Stan gave a hearty laugh and acknowledged an empty glass up the bar. While he was gone, Keith, in turn, acknowledged that his own beer glass had miraculously filled on its own. He didn't have much doubt that Stan was trying to get him drunk so that Keith would go in the back room with him. The burly barkeep had been putting the moves on him for some time now. Keith had to admit, though, that he came back because he was getting a lot of free beer—and also because he was getting closer to giving in to Stan.

It wasn't that Stan was bad looking, in a big bruiser, boxed-a-bit-too-often way. And it wasn't because he was old. He probably wasn't older than about forty and obviously still went to the gym, although the bartender was putting a bit of a paunch on him. It was more because Keith had heard that Stan fucked a bit rough. Keith didn't mind getting fucked; he just didn't like to be manhandled all that much—or so he thought. He'd shied away from it enough to only know it as a concept.

"And I kinda like the touchy-feely sound of it," Stan said. He was back, looking straight in Keith's eyes to hold the younger man's attention, while he deftly topped off Keith's beer. "The back stroke. The breast stroke—particularly like that one. The side stroke. That's not bad either. And the butterfly. They got an interesting fuck position called the Butterfly in that artsy-fartsy Indian shit—the Camera Suitable, or somethin'. You ever

241

try that? Ever thought of tryin' that? Now the free style, that would really be something I could get in to; I've wrestled semi pro in my day—maybe with some diving. Get it?"

He laughed and was off again to serve another customer. But Keith knew he'd be back. This was how Stan moved toward a more direct proposition. And Keith knew Stan had been asking around about him and knew he took cock. So there wasn't much subtle about Stan's propositions when he got down to them.

They had been talking about swimming and who at the bar had and hadn't had swimming lessons. It turned out that only Keith had. And he'd also made the mistake of saying that he went to Larson's pond most Saturday afternoon's during the summer for a swim. Larson was a rich guy into both nudism and gay sex. He'd opened his pond to guy-only nude sunbathing and anything else guys might want to do during the summer months. All you had to do to get an invitation was to either let Larson fuck you or, if you were a top too, bring Larson someone he could fuck.

The latter was what had happened with Keith. Chris, who Keith had been shacking up with at the time but Keith didn't know liked fucking around a lot, had wanted access to Larson's beach. He had taken Keith to the beach and turned him over to Larson while he cruised the other guys. Larson had fucked Keith silly for nearly three hours straight. Keith resented being used by Chris like that and gave him the gate. But he had enjoyed Larson's cocking enough that he continued to come to the beach and let him do him when he wanted to. Larson liked fresh meat, though, and had ready access to it, so he didn't bother Keith much.

It was a good routine for Keith. It would be over at the end of summer, of course, as Larson closed down his beach house then and went back to the city. But summer was all about "what the hell." Keith would start worrying about what to do for swimming in September.

Stan was back, standing in front of Keith, and leaning into him. They could have easily kissed, if Keith wanted to—and he thought that's probably what Stan wanted. But Keith didn't take the hint, so Stan went back to talking. "Wouldn't mind getting some lessons like that down at Larson's pond. Especially if you was the one who was teaching me. What say when I get off work here, we trot on down there and you can teach me some strokes and I'll teach you the Butterfly—you know the Indian one?" He was leaning over the bar toward Keith and leering to beat the band.

"Uh, I don't teach swimming, Stan. I can barely remember which stroke I'm using when I'm swimming. And right now I have some place I need to be. Sorry, but—"

A beefy hand shot across the bar top and grabbed Keith's forearm. This was what Keith was a bit afraid of. Stan was quite a bruiser and Keith was wary of being alone with him and in his grip. The grip didn't quite hurt, but almost. Keith wondered if Stan realized when he was hurting a man. He looked down at the forearm. A colorful tattoo of some sort of dragon. Keith wondered if Stan had other tattoos—and where. Keith got a little extra aroused by a man with tats. And he couldn't say that Stan didn't arouse him. He just scared him a bit.

"Come on, man. You know you want it. And I know you put out. I don't know the names of the strokes I use either, but I can stroke real good. Right here in the back room right now, or I'll meet you down by the swimming pond. I'll teach you the Butterfly. I can dick you deep with that. Chris Tucker told me you go wild with the deep diving. And I got a cock ring. You ever been fucked with a cock ring?"

"I really do need to be someplace, Stan." Keith managed to pull himself off the bar stool and out of Stan's grip. What he was thinking mostly was that he'd like to beat Chris Tucker to a pulp.

"But you will let me do you sometime, won't you?" Stan asked. There was an intense gleam in his eye.

Keith was trembling a bit. He'd thought about it and had decided that, yes, under the right circumstances he'd go with Stan just to see what it was like. One of his friends one night at a party had regaled the guys he was talking to about that cock ring Stan had and how different that felt. That's when Keith had first come in the bar. So, he couldn't say he wasn't interested. He had been wondering for weeks how it felt with a cock ring.

"Yeah, sure, we can hook up sometime, Stan," Keith said as he backed away from the bar and acknowledged the good-bye waves of a few of the other patrons, some of whom had been campaigning to get in his ass almost as much as Stan had been. "Just that I have to be somewhere else now."

As he left the bar, he tried to review in his mind what he'd told Stan about his visits to Larson's pond. He hadn't actually told Stan when he usually was there swimming, had he?

* * * *

The sun was out strong on Saturday afternoon and Keith was out on a blanket by Larson's pond working on an all-over tan. He had his Kindle and a good stash of GM action/adventure e-novels he'd downloaded the previous evening, so he was good to go for a while.

He wasn't the only one there, and there wasn't the normal crowd for a Saturday, but there was activity enough for him to glance away from the Kindle occasionally to take in the action. Between the fiction on the Kindle and the reality of the action on the beach, he was managing to keep at least half hard. He was putting off doing anything about that. He'd usually rev up for a while, jerk off, and then take a dip in the pond. If there was time, he'd repeat the cycle. If he saw a guy he clicked with, he got fucked. He liked his Saturday summer afternoons at the pond.

The action, now that he thought about it, was actually very low for a Saturday. Off on the sand below Larson's vacation house, an area of the beach he reserved for himself, Keith could see Larson's bare rump between two bent brown legs. From the tightening and loosening and forward and backward movement of Larson's buttocks and the way the soles of the feet on the legs of the black guy were raising and lowering on the sand, Keith could tell that Larson was giving his usual good fuck. Keith didn't mind Larson fucking him, even though he took a lot of time doing it and left a guy wiped out; it was how Keith kept the welcome sign out for his own pond visits.

Larson fucked deep. Chris hadn't been wrong about that; Keith liked that.

Nearer, on the same side of the pond where Keith was staked out, two college-type hunks were playing a pass-the-beach ball type of slow-moving game out on the sand. Keith had seen these two out on the beach before. They usually played around like this until someone showed up they liked and then they shared him. And by shared, Keith meant that he had seen them do a guy together, two dicks in one hole, a couple of times. Keith had never done it that way, and although he thought about it, it scared him. He had been pretty standoffish with these guys and usually there were a lot more here on the beach when he saw them. He was usually just part of a crowd. If it looked like they were zeroing in on him, he'd look away or strike up a conversation with another guy. Today, other than Larson humping the guy on his own beach, it was just these guys and Keith here so far.

Keith actually thought about retreating for the day when he saw that no one else seemed to be showing up on the beach. He shuddered at the thought of these two working him over. They were both studs and appeared to be about the same age, twenty or something, like Keith himself, but they were quite different in their physical perfection. The guy Keith had named "Thick," was Nordic, blond and hairless. He was on the short side and compact, heavily muscular. Not fat, but solid and on the bulging side when it came to muscles. A ruggedly handsome face. A buzz cut for hair. He was the boisterous one, all smiles and laughter and jocularity. Keith had noticed that when they zeroed in on a guy, he was the one who took the lead in getting a guy interested. The name Thick came, naturally, from what was between his legs. Average in length, but thick.

He contrasted with the other guy, who Keith thought of as "Long." He was more the Mediterranean Mafioso type. Swarthy and brooding. Handsome in a dark, silent, sensuous, dangerous sort of way. He was hairy to Thick's smoothness, with intriguingly curling hair on his pecs and down his sternum to his bush. And on his forearms too and his legs. His head hair was curly and a lock fell almost over his eyes. He wore a permanent five-o'clock shadow, and Keith got the impression the guy probably had to shave three times a day to keep it cut back to the exact length. He was taller and thinner than Thick, but still well-muscled, and he, too, got Keith's name for him from what he was swinging. Not thick, but longer than average.

He often was the guy who honed in on the mark after Thick had already buried his cock in the guy's ass. He was the one who sweet talked the guy the first time until the guy realized that he already got his cock inside him and was past trying to do anything to prevent the double.

Keith thought arousing thoughts of being fucked by them individually, but he wasn't all that sure about this doubling stuff he'd seen them do.

And right about now, they were forcing him to make a decision on whether to pack up and leave or stay and take his chances of maybe taking two cocks at once. He usually let someone fuck him here on Saturdays, but this doubling business still had him unsure. Their game was moving closer to him, and the blond was flashing him smiles, working on making contact. Keith had seen this before and knew that this was how they moved in on a target.

Keith was about to make a decision when he saw both of them turn and look up at the wooden stairs leading down from the parking lot next to Larson's summer home on the bluff. He let his attention sweep that way too—past the tableau of Larson now being on his back and holding the waist of the young black guy riding his cock—to the top of the stairs, where a young Asian guy—probably Indian—was standing, looking tentatively down at the beach. He was wearing baggy swimming shorts and had a towel and what looked like a pair of water wings tucked under an arm.

After a few hesitant moments, he started to come down to the beach. He was wearing flip-flops on thin legs with strongly defined muscles. They had strength in them; they just looked sinewy. A soccer player, Keith thought.

The two hunks conversed between themselves momentarily at a volume that Keith could almost, but not quite, hear, and then, the blond having given Keith a wink and a "later" smile, they recommenced their beach ball passing game and moved back along the beach, getting closer to where the Indian was spreading out his towel.

The new arrival wasn't tall. Certainly not as tall as Long; more the height of Thick. But he was even thinner than Long was. Keith thought more in terms of wiry than thin, though, as the guy had real good muscle tone. He just was willowy and had long, thin legs, with little meat on the bones. He obviously hadn't realized this was a nudist beach, because he was wearing baggy swimming shorts, emphasizing the thinness of this body—and looking at the other guys but then looking away in apparent slight embarrassment.

He was standing between his blanket and the surf line, nervously eyeing the water and letting his hands prod and knead the inflated water wings like he wasn't really sure how to put them on. He did have inflatable plastic things around his ankles, though, which made him look like a gangly kid. Long had the beach ball and was going back to sit on his towel, arms hugging knees, and watching Thick go to work.

Thick sidled up to the Indian. "Going for a swim with those things?" He was gesturing at the water wings.

"I want to swim, yes," the Indian answered in precise, but somewhat accented English. "But I've never lived near the ocean. I can't swim."

"This isn't exactly the ocean," Thick said with a broad smile. "I think you'd have to get all the way out to the middle before you couldn't touch bottom. You don't really need those wings."

"I think I would be scared without them. There may be deeper places. And I might not be able to float."

"Yeah, you don't look like you have an ounce of body fat on you and might not float too good," Thick said. "Nice body, though. But you're wearing a suit. Do you know what kind of beach this is?"

The Indian was shaking his head back and forth in little dips, which Keith could tell was confusing Thick but that Keith knew was an Indian gesture of "yes." "Yes, I know. Mr. Larson invited me. He has known me." Considering the strange word arrangements of his sentences, Thick probably couldn't be sure that this meant what he'd literally said either. But the way Thick's body relaxed told Keith that this admission was all the permission he needed to target the guy.

The mention of Larson caused both of them, and Keith too, to look over at Larson's private beach. He was embracing the black guy's back close in to his chest, and, with the black guy raised a bit on his knees, Larson was fucking up into his ass at a fast pace.

As the Indian was looking at that too, The Indian's face reddened up, but he neither looked away nor packed up and left the beach. Thick chose to more assuredly interpret what he said and gestured as acknowledgment that the Indian knew what this beach was for—and that he took cock.

Larson didn't invite anyone to use his beach in the summer who didn't give or take cock—and who wouldn't take it from Larson on demand.

"Maybe you'd have enough confidence if you had a few swimming lessons," Thick said.

"I have thought of taking lessons, but I never have had the time," the Indian answered.

"Well, if you have the time today, my friend over there and I could maybe give you lessons in a few basic strokes." Thick drew the Indian's attention to Long and smiled and waved, and Long raised his hand and gave a minimal response. Keith could see the Indian's eyes slit when he saw Long, who was sitting with his legs bent and was squatting close enough to the towel that his cock head reached the towel and turned up, almost winking at the Indian.

Maybe the Indian isn't as innocent as he's coming across, Keith thought.

"I think my friend and I could teach you a few good strokes," Thick said. He had an arm around the Indian's shoulders and they were walking slowly toward the water. The water wings had dropped to the sand next to the Indian's towel. He still had the bloated anklets on, though. They were orange and made plastic rubbing sounds as he walked. Keith almost wanted to laugh.

Keith watched for a bit as Thick and the Indian stood in water up to their knees and Thick was showing the Indian how to position and move his arms in swimming strokes. There was a lot of hands-on work and Thick had gotten hard. The Indian couldn't have not noticed that. Well, he's on his own, Keith thought, and went back to reading his Kindle and turned onto his belly, facing away from the water, deciding that it was time for sun on the back.

When he turned back to lie on his back and took his attention away from the Kindle, he saw that Thick was in business. The Indian was floating on his back—his torso actually looking like it was floating, but from Thick's stance, it was possible that Thick's arms were under the Indian's back, supporting him in the water. The Indian's arms were spread straight out from his side and they looked like they were floating. The Indian's legs were spread and floating on top of the water— at least the inflated anklets were working a charm. Thick was standing between the Indian's thighs, and from the wave patterns in the water, it was fairly evident that Thick's cock was buried in the Indian's ass and that the blond was pulling the Indian on and off his cock. What were doing the best job of floating were the Indian's baggy swimming shorts. They were floating on the surface of the pond all by themselves and off to the side, remaining afloat all by themselves with the big air bubble inside them.

Keith wondered what stroke Thick had told the Indian this was.

He noticed movement out of the corner of his eye up the beach and saw Long languidly unfolding himself, rising, and slowly sauntering toward the water line. He was at least half hard. In following Long with his eyes, Keith's attention went to Larson's private beach. It was empty now except for a mussed-up beach blanket. But up on the bluff on the house's porch overlooking the water, Keith could see that Larson was sitting on a chair and the black guy was in his lap, facing away from him, and moving his hips up and down on Larson's cock with the leverage of his feet. Larson had an arm around his waist and both appeared to be watching what was going on in the pond while they languidly fucked. They'd been fucking since before Keith had come to the beach, what, an hour or more ago now? That was the Larson Keith remembered.

Keith tore his attention away from that action and went back to reading his Kindle. He was a little concerned for the Indian, whether or not this was really what he'd come here for, and whether he was getting into more than he bargained for, but Keith didn't want to get involved. He thought he really should just pick up his blanket and leave, but he had just a bit more to read in this chapter. He got to the end of the chapter and it had one of those cliff hangers that bugged him about what a character he liked was going to do to get out of trouble, if, indeed he did. So Keith kept on reading.

It was the sounds coming across the water that arrested Keith's attention and made him look up. The Indian was being quite vocal. At first Keith thought he was in distress as he was using curse words that Keith wouldn't have thought an Indian would even know. But as Keith paid more attention to the words, he realized that the Indian was enjoying himself and most of what he wanted his tormenters to do with themselves, he wanted them to do to him.

The three were plastered together in the water, the surface level of which reached just below where the obvious action was taking place. The tableau was familiar to Keith. Long was behind the Indian, leaning back, his arms crossed and embracing the Indian under the Indian's pecs. Keith had no doubt that Long had his cock snaked up the Indian's channel. Thick was plastered in front of the Indian, holding the Indian's thin, long legs up and spread from his body. Thick's buttocks were making waves in the water behind him as he took long, slow strokes inside the Indian's channel on top of Long's stationary cock. The Indian was clutching the tips of Thick's shoulder blades with his white-knuckled hands. His head was thrown back into Long's shoulder, and his mouth was hanging open. He was practically yodeling.

Up on the bluff, the young black guy's back was arched down to the floor of the porch, with his arms spread on the porch over his head. Larson was gripping his waist and pulling him on and off his cock.

Keith had enjoyed Larson using that position on him. With a sigh, he went back to his chapter in the Kindle. The character he identified with had been trapped by the villain and was being rough fucked. Other members of the villain's gang were gathering around, watching, talking dirty about what they were going to do when they got their turn. Keith's hand went to his cock and encased it. He squeezed it and rubbed a thumb on the piss slit. He could feel himself going hard, cum welling up deep inside him.

He had no idea how much time had transpired, but it came as a shock when he felt a hand brush away the hand he was encasing his cock with and felt the sensation of a warm and moist mouth coming down over his cock and hands clutch his buttocks. He looked down the line of his body and saw the blond buzz cut. Thick was sucking his cock. Thick's hands glided up his torso and latched onto his pecs.

The head Keith was getting was good immediately. Very, very good. There was no fighting it. He let his arms flop to the side and his Kindle sank into the sand next to him. Looking over toward and beyond it, he saw that Long and the Indian were on Long's blanket. The Indian was on knees and elbows, chest pushed into the blanket and his head turned toward Keith, his eyes wide open. Long was crouched over his hips and feeding his cock inside the Indian in long, deep strokes.

Keith was no longer watching the story or even reading a story; he was part of the story. Up on the bluff Larson and the black guy had disappeared. Maybe into the house to rest and then start again. Keith had every reason to believe that Larson could stroke all day.

Moaning as Thick pushed a rolled-up towel under the small of his back, turning his pelvis up, and started to lick from his balls down his perineum to his hole, Keith's hands went back to his own cock. He arched his back and groaned as Thick's tongue pushed into his channel, moistening and opening him. One of Thick's hands was scrounging around inside a beach bag laying off to the side and came out with a small bottle of lubricant and a bundle of condom packets that were attached in a string. He raised the bundle before Keith's eyes and let it open and cascade down.

Thick lifted his head up, smiled, and whispered. "All of these. We've been saving you. By popular vote, this is your day."

Keith groaned again. That was so much like what the villain in his novel had said as he was tying the protagonist's wrists to posts. "All of these," the villain was saying, sweeping his hand in a gesture that took in all of the salivating gang members hunched around them and pulling at their cocks.

Thick was standing in a crouch, lifting Keith's pelvis to his and fucking Keith in quick, efficient strokes when the Indian came over and crouched down at Keith's side and gave him a look of sympathy or some sort of brotherhood. Long was settling on his haunches nearby and watching. The Indian encased Keith's cock in his hand and then leaned over and took it in his mouth. After a few minutes of what Keith considered very expert sucking, the Indian murmured something to Thick, who went down on his knees, bringing Keith's back down on the ground, but not skipping a beat in the stroking. The Indian rolled a condom on Keith's cock; straddled Keith's belly, facing him; skewered himself on the hard dick; and raised and lowered himself on the staff as he leaned over, put an arm under Keith's neck, palmed his cheek, lowered his forehead to Keith's, and looked intently into Keith's eyes.

Keith, who had never been particularly fond of Indians, was embarrassed at the intimacy of this, and would have shrunk away from the Indian when he began kissing him on his face— his cheeks and eyelids and ears—and tried to groan disapproval when the Indian reached the mouth, but he found his tongue being sucked into the Indian's mouth and sucked there just like it was a cock. The sensation was so sensual and such a surprise, that Keith's hips jerked and he ejaculated in the Indian's channel.

Sometime during all of that the thick cock was replaced by a long cock, and Keith realized there had been a change of the guard. Whereas Thick fucked in short, staccato bursts, Long fucked in long, deep strokes.

After Keith had come in the Indian, Thick pulled him off Keith's cock, swung the Indian around by his belly, crawled off a couple of yards with him in tow, and started doggy fucking him. Long was crouched over Keith and looking down into his eyes, giving him a dark, sensual half smile while he stroked. He gripped Keith's knees with his hands, pushing them out and bringing them back in the rhythm of the fuck. Then he went back on his haunches and pulled Keith's buttocks up on his thighs, with Keith's torso streaming down in front of him. He was reaching deeper inside. Keith groaned and crossed his legs behind Long's back, holding him as deep inside as he could.

The deep fuck. What he melted to was the deep fuck.

Keith looked over at the wooden staircase up to the parking lot. Larson and the black guy, still naked, were at the bottom of the stairs, arms around each other and starting to move up the beach toward him. There was also someone new there—a man, a bulky body-builder type—at the top of the stairs. He too appeared to be naked. Keith closed his eyes and turned his head away, wanting all of his senses to go to Long's cock working deep inside him.

He felt Long jerk and shudder and come deep inside him. When Long withdrew and was rising from the sand, Keith opened his eyes and watched him move away, toward Thick and the Indian. Thick was on his back, under the Indian, fucking up into him from behind. Long crouched between the Indian's legs and was rubbing his cock on the Indian's balls, perineum, and inner thighs, waiting for it to engorge enough to double the Indian again. When he moved out of the way, another man was standing there, leering down at Keith and snapping the latex edge of the Maxim condom encasing a huge cock crowned with a thick cock ring. A leather strap tightly bound the root of the cock.

Stan. Stan, the bartender, had shown up.

Stan was sitting, leaning back on his elbows on the sand, legs slightly apart. Keith was sitting on his cock, the two facing each other, his legs on either side of Stan's torso, knees bent, leveraging off his toes. His arms were stiff-armed behind and under him, the heels of the palms buried in the sand on either side of Stan's slightly spread legs. Stan was holding Keith's body suspended over his with strong hands gripping his waist. Both were rotating their pelvises, in opposite directions, Stan's cock ring kissing every part of Keith's undulating channel walls.

Stan was teaching Keith the Kamasutra Butterfly position.

He had already told Keith he'd be taking him home to show him so much more that night. Keith had moaned but had not objected. He loved the feel of the cock ring inside him.

All of the others were gathered around them in a close circle on the otherwise deserted beach. Thick and Long had the Indian between them, both of their hands fondling his cock and balls as he had the cock of each in a hand. Across from them, Larson and the black guy were stretched out in reverse, the black guy on top of Larson, and 69ing.

Keith couldn't shake the sensation that they were all in a waiting pattern. Waiting for the end of the Butterfly lesson so that they each could have another go at Keith. He moaned at the prospect that Thick and Long's specialty was yet to come for him.

This, with summer drawing to a close. What new heights of languid-fucking pleasure could he have achieved if the summer had started this way and heightened in swimming lesson sensuality from that point, he wondered. Perhaps next summer.

The Chance Café

What a neat idea, Ted thought. He'd been down
Lexington a couple of times a week all semester from his room
to his classes at the university and he hadn't even noticed the
Chance Café, down on the lower level under a hippy New Age
gear store.

A cyber café, he quickly figured out from a scan of the
membership agreement, where you could hook up with other
guys in cyber space in comfort. It was sort of a closed men's
club—a dating service, where you checked in at the membership
desk—really a private little room—the first time, and someone
actually took the measurements himself and filled in the vital
information on your club Web site profile and took your picture
for posting. Then one could be quite sure who they were talking
to and what they looked like and how they measured up. It
wasn't subject to personal exaggeration—at least on physical
attributes.

It was a closed site only accessible from the other
Chance Cafés, wherever they were, and when you wanted to
browse the members' pages of those currently on line and chat
with them one-on-one, they had cubicles where you could do
that—very privately, other than the open door from the
corridor. So, if the conversation got hot, you could comfortably
get hot too.

The whole issue of false advertising had been what had
turned Ted off about any of these Internet dating services, and

he certainly didn't think he had anything to be ashamed of in his own vital statistics, so there was nothing that bothered him about either having a hunky guy gather his statistics—which had led to a proposition that Ted had politely fended off—or having these statistics placed on a profile with his picture—as long as it was a very, very private club and he'd be talking with some guy safely off in Cleveland somewhere.

Ted had fucked with guys before—well, a couple of times. But he'd always found the fantasy of cyber chat and of dirty talk with a guy in cyber space as so much more arousing than the actual fuck, and a good background for masturbating. Plus, he had this imaginary picture of the guy who would be fucking him—a muscle-bound hunk who would overpower him and sink an extra-long dick in him—and none of Ted's actual coupling partners had lived up to that in any way. He was going to a somewhat geeky school. Very good academically, but most of the men students were the indoor, quiet type who felt well fucked only by a complicated computer program.

But Ted had to laugh at that thought as he stood in the little room off the reception area of the Chance Café and had his dick measured. Here he was not very far from choosing to be fucked by a computer rather than a real man himself.

Ted had been sorely tempted to take the guy checking his stats up on his proposition. He was a nicely bulked-up Scandinavian type with a broad smile and a very nice thick cock of his own, which he had been quite proud to show Ted for comparison purposes while he was measuring and propositioning him.

"I've got my own nice little private cubicle right back here," the attendant had said. "I can hook into a live sex session on my computer, and you can watch it while I bend you over and fuck you deep. How about it?"

Ted had looked at what the guy was packing and was intrigued by the thick gold ball he had pierced to the underside of the cock right under the rim of his bulb. That alone sent little chills up Ted's spine. Nothing like the fucking he'd done in small study apartments with the other computer geeks. He wondered how that gold ball would feel running up and down his inner channel. But Ted was just too shy to more than fantasize about how that might feel.

Alone in the booth and with his still-to-be-completed profile backlit on the screen before him, Ted couldn't get the image of the attendant's gold ball-enhanced cock out of his mind. Why did he shrink from being cocked with something as exotic as that? He knew he wanted more than he'd been getting. That was why he'd checked out this cyber café and continued with the membership procedure after he heard what it was all about. He could find stuff to wank to in the privacy of his own room.

He was here because he wanted to kick it up a level—wanted to masturbate in a more public venue—and to something that stepped it all up a notch—to the fucking words of someone in another Chance Café somewhere, sitting, as he was, in a semiprivate booth in front of a computer with a Web cam. Actually being able to see each other, each other forming the words, as they sat there and masturbated themselves to the fucking words of the other guy in some distant club.

What the hell, Ted, thought, and he threw all caution to the wind. He registered under the name of teddybear4u and tapped in likes and dislikes that described a submissive for muscle hunks. In truth that was his fantasy, so why should he hold back? It was all fantasy anyway. No pretty boys for him. He wanted to see a thug on the screen. And cock? The bigger the better. And, still thinking of that gold bar on the underside of the attendant's cock, he specified that he liked thick cock rings and toys. And forceful. Yes, forceful—don't take no for an answer.

Ted pushed the submit button and laid back in the chair, eyes closed. Waiting to see what, if anything came up in a match. He heard the ding in less than a five-minute wait, but he had no idea what it was.

"Scoot your chair back and take your shirt off."

What? Ted heard the voice, but he had no idea where it was coming from. It seemed to be coming from the computer. He opened his eyes and then he opened them very wide indeed. His profile was no longer what was appearing on the screen. What he saw was a biker type all leathered out and sitting in a chair away from the video cam wherever he was recording from. It was a cubicle much like the one Ted was in.

That was fast, Ted thought. It was intriguing what the system matched him up with in such a short time. And it was a bit surprising how his profile requests had been interpreted. But from the way his cock was hardening, the match up must have been done well.

Bulky, hard pecs, bulging biceps. Not fat, but a good hard belly that had seen its share of beer. Dark. The overall visage of darkness and danger. Black curly hair, covering pecs and moving down the sternum and belly into a pubic bush from which protruded a thick cock hanging down between spread thighs at the front of the desk chair. A thick silver cock ring—just as Ted had ordered. The guy was wearing a black leather hat, a black leather vest that didn't close across his chest, and black shiny boots that reached up almost to his knees. Nothing else, except an insistent, mocking stare.

As Ted watched, the guy leaned forward toward the screen and took his cock in a beefy hand and repeated in a gruff, commanding voice, "Scoot back in the chair and take off your shirt. Now!"

Meekly, a chill of thrill going down his spine, Ted pushed his chair back and lifted his T-shirt over his head.

"Aw, nice little chicken," the computer screen muttered. "Straighten up and lean back in the chair. Now run your hands up your chest. Yes, like that. Finger your nipples. Make them puff out for me. Now!"

Another ding from the computer and it went to split screen. Another hulky hunk. More a bodybuilder this time. Red hair, freckles, lightly tanned hairless flesh where the first guy was dark and hairy. A perfectly sculpted body. Squared-jawed chiseled features on a thick neck. Completely naked and sitting away from the video cam as the first guy was—both guys with computer mouses in their hands on long cords. Heavy-muscled spread thighs, big balls resting on the vinyl of the desk chair seat, stubby little cock in repose, but thick, and crowned with a big gold stud with a ruby-colored gem in the center. This one had already started. He had his hips rolled up and his hand was slowly working a long purple dildo into his hole.

Ted was reacting to the first guy. The second guy just sat there and smiled and worked at himself. Ted was on screens to two other booths somewhere. He was momentarily stunned not only that he had so quickly attracted this attention but that the technology existed to link this way in the first place. This could be a triangulated encounter across the American continent.

"I said Now!" the first voice commanded. Ted started playing with his tits, as commanded. He found it arousing—and more arousing because he was being ordered to do it by a bruising hulk—and not the least so because another guy was watching him do it. Not reality, but close enough to make his cock hard.

"Strip off those pants." The commanding voice again. "Now!"

Ted rushed to comply. It was getting pretty tight in there anyway. He flipped his loafers off with toe on heel and then stood and stripped down his jeans and briefs.

"No, don't sit yet. Turn around."

Ted did so, slowly.

"Now bend down and spread those cheeks."

"What?" Ted asked, shocked at how quickly this was going.

"You heard him. Bend and spread those cheeks." This was the first utterance from the redhead. Higher register voice, but no less commanding, dominating.

Ted turned and bent over and spread his butt cheeks apart.

"Very nice butt and puckered hole," the first guy said. "Been fucked before? Are you a virgin? The hole doesn't look like it's been used."

"No, not really," Ted answered in a choked voice. "I've done it. But not often, no."

"Nice. It'll be a close fit. Run your finger across the hole," the other guy commanded. "Yes, like that. Nice pucker." Ted could hear heavy breathing. It was coming from that second screen.

"Pretty tight. Ever been doubled?" The first voice chimed in.

"Doubled?" Ted asked, confused.

"Two dicks working you at the same time."

"Oh. No." Answered with hesitation.

"Nice. As good as virgin." The second voice commenting.

"OK, turn around and sit down again. Now!" The leather guy commanding. "OK. Here's how this is going to go down. Me and Red here are goin' come in there and give you a fuckin'. Got that?"

A pause and then Ted squeaked out a "Yes." This was so realistic. These guys were going to do him well with just their words. And calling the other guy Red. It was just like they knew each other.

"Yes, what, pretty boy? Yes, sir, don't cha mean?"

"Yes . . . yes, sir," Ted responded in a breathy little voice.

"See this?" the leather guy was saying. He was waving his cock at Ted. It had gotten really big and the cock ring was wobbling back and forth. "You're gonna suck this while Red here is spiking you and then I'm gonna attach a nice toy to this here ring and give you the thrill of your life. You like toys, don't cha? Your profile says you do."

"Look at Red now, pretty boy. See what he's growin' for you."

Ted's eyes went over to the other side of the screen and got real big. Red's cock was no longer stubby. It had lengthened out alarmingly. And Red had that purple dildo real far up his ass too. Ted couldn't help but gasp with his eyes bugged out. Red looked real pleased with himself.

"Jerk your meat slowly while we talk to you here, boy," the leather man commanded. And Ted took up his cock in his hand and started to pull on it slowly. He was trembling all over. God, this was a great fantasy.

"Red, tell him what you're going to do with that cock."

"Lean over and open the drawer of the desk under the computer," Red commanded. "You should find a couple of nice things there."

Ted did so and found another purple dildo, just like the one Red was using and a bottle of lube and a stack of condoms. Wow, these clubs are organized, he thought. They are all fully stocked—and the users know that they are.

"Lube up the old purple pleasurer," Red continued. "Do it to your satisfaction. It's going to be in your ass."

Ted covered it real well with the lube.

"Now your hole. And put your legs out wide and role your bum up. I wanna watch this."

Ted did as instructed, and he got a little thrill at the sound of the heavy breathing in stereo from the split computer screen. He was lost in this new experience. It was helping him lose some shyness about opening up. He thought he might get a little more adventuresome in who he responded to on campus now.

"Now put the tip of that purple guy at your entrance and move it around, working it in just enough that your channel gets a taste of it. Lay back and close your eyes. Think of it as my cock. My cock with this here ruby eye in it about to give you a fuck you'll never forget."

Ted widened his stance and propped the heels of his socked feet up on the edge of the computer desk and laid back in the chair, the back of which had give in it, and closed his eyes. He was holding the dildo to his hole and moving it around in a little circular motion, letting it sink in a bit farther with every couple of rotations. He was sighing and moaning now. He'd never done this. He'd have to buy himself one of these. The dildo wasn't all that thick. It felt sort of like Stewart when he was fucking him. Ted knew he could handle this.

"Now, think of me between your legs, right where you are. I've got my cock at your hole just like that. Can you feel the ruby?"

"No." Ted was being truthful. And his voice had a tinge of regret to it; he wanted to feel the ruby.

"Well, you will. Imagine it for now, though. It's slowly working its way in until your muscle grabs it and pulls it in nicely. Happening?"

"Yessss," Ted moaned. His sphincter had caught the bulb of the dildo and drawn it in. He could feel a straight shot up his chute. His walls were actually rippling in anticipation of the journey.

"I'm gonna fuck your mouth while Red's fucking your tail." A gruff, lower-toned voice. The leather guy now. "Keep your hand on the dildo, but put the thumb of your other hand in your mouth and suck it. That's my cock, getting ready for when Red's finished with your hole."

Ted felt his body going into the rhythm of an undulating motion, going with the fuck. He had managed this a couple of times with Stewart. And striving for this feel was the only reason he kept going back to Stewart. And these two were fucking him just as well with only words across cyber space. He was making slurping sounds with the sucking of the thumb. He'd never sucked a man before. He wondered now what that felt like and decided he'd try it sometime for real.

"Now slowly sink the purple guy all the way in," Red was saying. "That's what I do. I let my partner feel all of me at first. Do it. Now!"

Ted slowly pushed the dildo deep inside him. He was breathing raggedly and shuddering at the exertion. More than once he stopped, and Red commanded him to continue.

When he had bottomed. "All the way out and all the way back in now. Feel me. Open your eyes and see me in the screen."

Ted did so and moaned. Red had lengthened out to at least the size of the dildo, but thicker.

"Now close your eyes and pull it out again—but not all the way. Rest the tip on your prostate. You can find that, can't you? Now slowly rub across it—and think of that ruby eye making love to your spot. Yes. I like the way you move against it. Don't let up. I don't want you to stop until you've creamed yourself."

Ted's other hand had moved to his cock and he was stroking himself.

"Did I tell you you could take that thumb out of your mouth?" The leather guy. Booming voice, cutting across Ted's heightening arousal.

"No, sir," Ted squeaked.

"Three fingers now. Three fingers in your mouth," the leather guy commanded. "Open your eyes and look at me."

When Ted did so, he saw that the leather guy's heavy cock was at full staff now.

"Three fingers aren't enough to be me, but they'll have to do now," the leather guy declared. "No, shut your eyes and don't open them again until you've shot off. I want to hear heavy breathing, moaning, and groaning."

Ted didn't have to be instructed to do this. God what a great masturbation session. This club was great!

Soon, silence reigned with only the sounds of moans and sighs from inside Ted's cubicle backdropped by heavy breathing that sounded so real that it sounded like it was in the room with Ted rather than over the computer. Ted was working the head of the dildo on his prostate and sucking on three fingers and moving his body in the universal rhythm of the full-body fuck.

As Ted ejaculated, though, there suddenly was a flurry of activity in his cubicle. His heels were being swept off the edge of the computer desk, the chair he was sitting in was being leaned back on its back two legs, and his body was being thrown back.

Ted's eyes popped open and he only had time to see a flash of bulging muscle on smooth, freckled skin thrust itself between his legs, when his head was forced back and he had a swarthy-skinned cock with a big silver cock ring being forced between his lips.

Leather guy and Red. Both right here in the room with him; not a cyber space away in some sister club to the Chance Café.

Red pulled the dildo out of Ted's ass with a slurp and replaced it with his own cock, which started its long journey up Ted's channel. The dildo hadn't been anything like this, really. This was thicker and that ruby eye was gliding along Ted's wall, sending ripples of pleasure all around his pelvis.

But Ted didn't have a great deal of time to think about what Red's sheathed cock was doing to his channel. Ted's mouth was busy trying to take in the leather guy's cock. This was something Ted hadn't done before, and the leather guy wasn't giving him much time or space to figure out what was expected of him.

For the next fifteen minutes, while Ted was tilted back on the desk chair in his cubicle and worked up a second helping of cum, Red's ruby eye was rubbing across his prostrate, demanding more cum, and the leather guy's cock was exploring every inch of Ted's inner cheek walls and upper throat, silver ring occasionally clicking on teeth.

Then, when Ted and Red had come almost simultaneously, Red dove his cock to the bottom again and held, while Ted, in fascination, watched the leather guy roll on a condom with a little something special on the end. It had a clip that latched onto the leather guy's silver cock ring through the head of the condom. And running off this clip were five thin ribbon streamers, about a foot in length and all a different color.

Red picked Ted up from the chair and lapped him in a half-standing, half-crouched position, while the leather guy moved around behind Ted, crouched down, and began working his cock in on top or Red's in Ted's hole. Ted panted and groaned at the stretching of his hole and the feel of two men inside him. This didn't last long—just long enough for Red and the leather guy to show that it could be done.

And then Red had withdrawn from Ted's channel, Ted was lowered back into the chair, the Red came around to hold his shoulders down, while the leather guy replaced him and started fucking Ted deep, swirling those streamers around on his inner channel walls and rubbing that thick cock ring up and down deep inside Ted.

Ted had no trouble coming for a third time.

Later when Ted was alone in his cubicle and contemplating getting up from the floor where he had fallen after being released from his third ejaculation, his mind slipped back into gear and he began to wonder how he had slipped over from self-administered fantasy to full threesome fuck.

The attendant was standing at the door, looking at Ted with some concern.

"What? How? But it was all supposed to be on computer," Ted muttered.

"On the computer only?" The attendant asked. And then he laughed. "You mean you thought . . .? You didn't read all of the provisions in the membership contract, did you? You thought you were just connected to some sort of cyber space file. That's not the way this works, fella. When you log on here, you're connected to other guys right here in the club at any given time."

The Rapino Brothers

(Excerpt from the Clint Folsom mystery series novel Death to the Past in Clint Folsom Compendium 2)

I had gotten what I needed to know at the Silver Screen Underground nightclub within the first hour I'd been there. But I couldn't just get up and leave—from the looks of the goons standing by the door to the reception room Jesse and I'd been ushered to, I wouldn't have been permitted to leave—I'd just have to play this out and get out of here when I could and get a couple of related problems here wrapped up. What I really needed to do was to get to a telephone to talk to Lieutenant Kahn in private. Fat chance of that happening for a while, though.

The Rapino brothers had a pretty nifty idea with this new nightclub, I thought. The Gallery had been a struggling Broadway stage theater on Broadway and West 45th Street that had reopened as a movie theater. It had a great location, and it had a huge basement with a warren of rooms that had once been used as dressing and wardrobe and set and prop storage rooms but that no longer were needed for that. The Rapinos had bought the theater building and installed a nightclub in the basement space with separate party and theater venues for separate tastes in vintage movies. Some of the venues were rumored to be decidedly racy, and an elevator could take aroused partygoers up beyond the legitimate movie house to floors above where there were rooms for more private partying—along with space for whatever illegal gang purposes the Rapinos had going at the time.

I thought that naming a movie-based nightclub in the basement of a movie theater the Underground Silver Screen was a straightforward clever idea. But I didn't know the half of it.

Word had gone out on the street that the Rapinos wanted to hire someone appropriate to manage the nightclub, and I had snatched that information from the air from my street contact, Larry, when he'd given me a ride back to Manhattan from Brooklyn. My sometimes name, Clint Sloan—or rather my parents' classic movie star names—had gotten me an interview for the job.

While I was being kept waiting, the youngest of the Rapinos—and the only one we didn't have a police blotter on—Stefano, had been sent out to keep me occupied. He said he'd only stopped by on his way to class. He was a sophomore at Colombia and was studying American history. He said he wanted to be a professor. Stefano seemed quite a nice young man, and I could believe that he was the Rapino that the rest of them were trying to keep out of the business and wanted to have a start in some other line of work.

He was also a strikingly good-looking young man. Sultry dark looks, with dark, curly hair and a slim, but well-worked body. It was said that he was a son from the patriarch's last wife and must have gotten most of his good looks from his mother, because the mug shots of his two surviving older brothers, Mario and Drago, showed guys who were considerable more thuggish in looks. Not ugly, just dangerous looking. And big; not fat, just big.

And, speaking of looking dangerous, Drago was standing at a door, decked out in a dark blue silk robe and gesturing to me. "Mr. Sloan, is it?"

I nodded and rose. Jesse started to move from where he was standing nearby.

"Your man can stay here," Drago said. Jesse sat in the seat I had vacated, beside the young Stefano Rapino.

I was about to leave—to work my way, along with Jesse, out of the nightclub. Stefano had already revealed what I wanted

266

to know. But Drago's appearance had cut off any chance of that happening. So, I went with the flow.

When we had chitchatted while we were waiting, Stefano had told me about his school and I told him about my life in Hollywood, going from the reality of my childhood to an imaginary story I spun of still being in Hollywood. I'd made a few references to his family and its businesses, but he appeared genuinely open on the legitimate businesses the Rapinos conducted—and equally genuinely ignorant of their gangland activities. I got what I wanted, though, when I asked him why he was here. What I had been fishing for was how much he knew of what went on here in this club, but what I got was far more.

"I'm waiting for my ride—back to Colombia. I don't come here much, but my brothers are busy getting ready for a trip, and they wanted me to come here to get some instructions on what I could do while they're gone. They're really straight laced. They don't give me much rope."

Not enough rope to figure out what they're up to is what I thought. But what I said was, "A trip? Both of them?"

"Yeah. A big deal, I gather. Not just them; they're taking some of their associates too. They say it's a big convention. In Chicago."

"Chicago?" I couldn't help repeating. Bingo, I thought. That's what Hank was trying to convey to me by leaving Ron Price's name and telephone number for me. Ron was in the Chicago police. The Scarlottis had retreated to Chicago. And now the Rapinos were going to follow them there. There would be blood on the streets. Not on New York's streets, thank god. But that wasn't much comfort if Hank had gone to Chicago with the Scarlottis. He would be directly in the line of fire.

I had what I'd come for. It was time to beat a retreat. But then there was Drago in the doorway, beckoning to me. I'd have to carry through with the charade.

Drago led me down a wide passageway with richly carpeted floor, walls and ceiling. I suppose the public explanation was that it protected patrons down here from the sound of the movie theater above—but that sound protection went both ways. I wondered if the sound of a gunshot from down here would be heard in the theater above. The floor of the passage was sloped and was, purposely, I'm sure, reminiscent of a movie theater corridor. Posters from classic movies hung in glass cases along the wall.

I watched Drago's butt as we walked. I had every reason to believe he was naked under that robe. I had thoroughly researched these guys. I knew what a job audition with them would entail. He had a good, big butt, though. In fact, he was very solidly built. Like a heavy-weight prize fighter. Not tall, nor fat, but thickish and built—big. I had experience in the equipment that a man built like that would have, and I felt an itch of anticipation. His head was shaved. From the back he looked like a prize fighter entering the ring. I had few doubts who would be in the ring with him.

He turned at a doorway and motioned me through it. The door shut with a solid thud behind us.

We were in a room that was maybe thirty by fifty feet, and looking from the door we were facing a semicircle wall at the back. To my right, covering nearly the whole, two-story wall against the outer corridor was a flat movie screen. The room was in semidarkness and a movie was playing. A long, curved, whitish couch followed the curve of the wall, facing the movie screen. The couch was deep enough for even the tallest person to recline on.

Reclining on the couch, in the middle of the curve of the room, was Mario Rapino. I would have known him from his mug shots. But I also recognized him because I'd seen him in person, but from afar, at the Colorado dude ranch I'd been sent to to protect a novelist from being murdered by him. He hadn't gotten a look at me there—I hoped—and he didn't kill the novelist. As it turned out, I did that myself.

Mario was the oldest of four brothers. Drago was the next oldest. It was the sex-and-snuff murder of the third brother, Lorenzo, which Mario had come west to revenge. Stefano, who I had just met, was by far the youngest one—the one I believed, and hoped, was out of it all.

In contrast to Drago's near baldness, Mario was hirsute—and he had a profusion of salt-and-pepper hair, including, still, on his head. He shared a build with his brother, Drago. Thick, but not fat, barrel-chested, powerful muscles, the thighs of a soccer player. I knew all of this, because, like Drago, he was wearing a dark silk robe. But unlike Drago, he was reclining on the couch with his robe full open and his hand encasing a mean-looking erect cock.

"My brother, Mario," Drago said as we entered the small theater.

"Sir," I said. I gave no notice to Mario masturbating himself. I knew this for the test it was.

"So, you think you might want to manage our little club here?" Mario said. I could hear him fine. The sound on the movie was almost nonexistent. I was standing facing him, so, at that point I had no idea what was playing.

"Yes, sir. I've managed clubs in California."

"So my sources said."

I blessed the strength of my connections in Hollywood—based on the lingering legend of my actor parents.

"And your parents were . . ."

"Scott Sloan and Laura Lake."

"Ah, yes, that's would be a big plus. Come here and stand in front of the screen in front of me, please."

I walked over to the center of the room.

"Ah, yes, the resemblance is striking," Mario said when I was standing in front of him.

I took a peek at the screen. It was a John Holmes movie, one I recognized. He was playing some sort of Arabian potentate, and he was fucking a muscle-bound young blond with what some, fancifully, I thought, had reported to be a fourteen-inch dong. The movie was a colorized version of a black and white porn classic. While I was moving to the center of the room, Drago went over to the couch, about ten feet from Mario. He sat, let the robe open across his lap, and he fisted a cock that looked bigger than his brother's.

"When you called, I believe my associate was quite explicit about the requirements of the job. Exactly what I expect in the way of loyalty from my employees."

"Yes, sir."

"Then strip down for me, please. I want to see what your qualifications are."

I did so and stood there in a model's casual stance. I could see that the cocks on both brothers were on the rise.

"Tell me, Clint Sloan, son of Scott Sloan. Do you give good fuck?"

"Yes, I think I do," I answered.

"Yes, I think you might. Your father certainly did."

I didn't know what to think about that. He was too young for my father. Mario wasn't more than ten years older than I was. Of course, who knows where Mario might have been in those days. For all I knew, he was one of the young, hopeful studs my father and his lover, the movie idol, Gordon Fields, had kept around the pool area at our ranch to entertain them and their friends.

"Come here, Clint," Mario said in a low, hoarse voice. As I moved to the couch and went down on it with my knee, Drago moved over to where, when Mario had taken my wrist and pulled me down, I was wedged between them. The two immediately began to work my body with their hands, exploring and gliding and pulling and pushing.

I could see the movie straight on now. I was puzzled. It was the same John Holmes movie I'd seen in stolen videos when I was young—and yet it wasn't. Holmes was more forceful in his fucking than I remembered. And the young blond was younger than I'd thought. And he didn't seem to be as willing. The movie was all about a slave being taken by an Arabian potentate, but in the movie I remembered, the blond was more in to it and Holmes wasn't giving him the whole fourteen inches (or whatever). In this version everything was bigger, more, and approaching brutality—and Holmes was stroking to the root. This wasn't the same version I'd seen.

Drago pulled my face down into his lap, and I gave him head. Mario's tongue was at my hole.

The movie had changed when I found myself leaning out beyond the bottom edge of the couch, chest bowed out toward the movie screen, ass skewered on Drago's dick, feet hooked on his shoulders on either side of his head, and his fists gripping my wrists and pulling back like my torso was an archery bow. He was rocking my ass on his dick and I was enjoying the deep fuck. From the sounds he was making, he obviously was too.

I was doing fine before they segued into another movie. The young blond from the first movie couldn't have been any more finished from Holmes's fucking than if he was dead—for all I knew maybe he was.

This new—or rather, old—movie, though. This was something else together. It opened up with one man, shirtless and all bronzed muscle, in the woods, holding an ax, and being approached by another, younger, equally hunky shirtless man. They kissed, the younger man bending the older one back, mastering him, his hand going to the older man's basket.

Gordon Fields—going down on my father, Scott Sloan. I was in shock. It was the last film they did, *High Timber*, but then it wasn't. There was no way this scene was in the original movie. The original movie was a grade A blockbuster that played in the best movie theaters across the country. This one was male porn.

"What do you think?" Mario was saying, his voice pleasant, his hand rubbing the small of my back as Drago continued to pull me back and forth on his cock. "As soon as we received your call, I sent down to the vault. This is one of my favorite movies. The original was *High Timber*. This remix was titled *Big Timber*. Fields fits the 'big' part, don't you think? Look at them."

Look at them? I couldn't take my eyes off the screen. When had they filmed this? I'd been there, up at Theo Klein's cabin for the early shoots—before they took the crew up into Northern California for the high timber shots. I'd even had a small part in that movie. A movie of two men, in the high timber, struggling for ascendance. The older foreman, the young interloper. But the message more psychological than sexual. At least in the original movie—the original parallel to two males, one the established stud bull, the other a young claimant, the two vying for dominance in the herd; the pornographic version, one male fighting for sexual domination over the other.

On the screen, my father, vanquished in the struggle for ascendance, was on the small of his back on a tree stump. Gordon was hunched over him, They were both naked and Gordon was fucking my father hard.

"Come on over here, baby," Mario whispered. "Sit on this. No, facing the screen. I don't want you to miss where this movie goes."

He pulled me over into his lap, facing the screen. Drago moved away and sat on the edge of the couch, watching Mario and me and stroking his cock. I lowered my channel on Mario's cock, as he groaned and I gave him the moan I knew he wanted. I was still thinking of the movie on the screen. I was remembering back twenty-one years—to a conversation I overheard on the patio at my parents' ranch by the pool. The producer, Theo Klein, and the director, Charles Tilton. They were whispering, but I could hear them, Tilton was trying to convince Klein to make an underground gay male cut of *High Timber*. Klein wasn't agreeing with him, but even at the time he seemed to be warming up to the idea. The undercurrent of homosexuality ran deep in films in those days—it was like hedonist Hollywood was thumbing its nose at the puritanical American movie audiences. Movies of that era were rife with an undercurrent of sexual innuendo. I had to admit that it was not such a big step from *High Timber* to the *Big Timber* version.

And now I knew that there was a similar double entendre to the name of the nightclub, the "Underground" in Underground Silver Screen taking on a whole new meaning.

"Watch this, baby," Mario murmured. "This blew me away when I first saw it. I couldn't wait to get you in here for this audition."

"Oh, my god," I exclaimed. I hadn't been prepared for this. My eighteenth birthday. I'd been there at the cabin in the mountains. A bit part in the original movie—but this, this I'd never imagined. And it fit right in with the recut of the movie, just like it belonged there.

So much in shock, I was like a rag doll as Mario hooked his legs inside mine and spread me, embraced my chest in his arms and pulled me back onto his reclined body, his cock deep inside me, his hips rhythmically playing me, his lips next to my ears, whispering a commentary of the me of twenty-one years earlier getting fucked on the screen.

My eyes were glued to the screen. All these years and I had no idea an underground film had been made. I couldn't take my eyes off

Fields as he moved over me—the me on the screen—and gathered up my thighs and hooked them on his hips—the young stud, having vanquished the old monarch, moving in to claim dominance over the rest of the herd. We were in the cabin. In Theo's cabin. It fit right in with the high timber setting. Rustic furniture in the cabin, me, on the bed, just in a flannel shirt unbuttoned and open wide on my young, heaving, eighteen-year-old chest. And boots. The timber boots, set wide and high over my body. The film cut flawless to the scene of Fields fucking my father on the tree stump—moving farther down the line in the herd.

Only my second time—right after Klein. My eyes so wide in fear and want, my mouth opening to a silent scream. I felt him again—after all these years. I knew exactly from the expression on my screen face when he first entered me. Such a big dick. And I felt it all over again. The pain of it—the glorious release of it. I had waited so long. Bigger, much bigger than Klein. I panted with the panting youth on the screen.

Mario's hand began to glide over my chest and belly as I panted—misunderstanding probably that I was panting with the me on the screen, not with the Mario who lay under me on the couch facing the screen. Holding me to his chest. Arms embracing my chest; legs between mine, holding mine spread. Cock inside me. Slow pumping me as we watch me being fucked—for only the second time—on the screen.

Field's hips beginning to move. It had taken so long, so very long for him to get it all inside me. I moaned on the screen. Deeper. He was moving deeper inside me with each thrust. Only my second time. But the pleasure beginning to win out. I wanted him inside me. Just as I wanted Klein inside me. Klein sitting there, stroking himself. Murmuring to the me on the screen. Telling me how much he'd like to join Fields. Telling me maybe someday.

I couldn't see the screen for a moment. Something was blotting out that world of the past. Drago. Naked. Crouching over me. Kissing me on the lips and then Mario.

"My brother," Mario whispers in my ear. "He cannot wait. He wants us both. He asks please."

"Yes," I whispered. Someday. Today was someday. There have been somedays before. This was blowing me away. I had thought I had what I wanted before I walked into this room. But now, now I was getting what I wanted.

"Oh, god. Oh, shit." I writhed away from the cock head, entering on top of that of his brother's. But Drago held my hips steady and grunted his determination. He was in an inch. I could see the

273

screen again over his shoulder. Fields getting serious with the me on the screen now. Nearly all the way out, then slow in, out to the edge of the glans. Thrust! I scream on the screen. I screamed on the couch, as Drago became impatient and pushed all the way in, sliding in on top of his brother's cock. Fields no long seemed that big. Mario and Drago had done this before, I could tell.

Well, so had I.

Drago bigger than Mario. Drago wanted to power fuck. "Oh, Fuck."

On and on; one withdrawing as the other thrust. Sandwiched between sweating, grunting beef, the two engaged with each other as much as with me, trying to work their cocks in unison inside me, withdrawal met with thrusts, as the hard shafts slid over each other, and my mouth agape, my fingers digging into Drago's shoulders, anticipating each thrust with a shudder, feeling them ejaculate almost in unison.

Oh, yes, they both had done this before.

"We'll let you know," Mario said, all business, as I redressed.

I bet you will, I thought. But that phone no longer will work when you do call.

Trawler Initiation

On a shrimp boat trawler well out to sea, you and a big muscle-bound bruiser of questionable intellect are telling me, while we are taking a coffee break in the trawler I'd signed on for my sophomore summer in college, that the senior crew all have privileges with the new guy. Just an initiation—like crossing the equator for the first time. But more fun.

What privileges and fun for who? I think, fear rising from my gut. I'm leery about this because I can tell that my being in college grates on these guys. I've heard about being taken down a notch or two.

I'd been avoiding the bruiser because I didn't like the way he looked at me. But you've been nothing but friendly to me and have shown interest in who I was, why I was spending the summer working on a trawler, how old I was, did I screw all of the coeds—stuff like that. This, though. This, here and now, doesn't seem friendly—or maybe it seems too friendly. It has got me off balance.

You say you know I take cock because I'd been with the captain in his cabin the previous night and the bruiser heard how well I liked the captain's cocking. He says the captain was crowing this morning, saying he'd won the crew poll on who would be first. And he was hinting about something else that you've been quizzing me about that was something I don't want to think about let alone have whispered around to the other guys.

275

Would it make any difference if I told you that the captain had gotten me drunk, and that I'd never done it before, and that, other than the soreness, I wouldn't be half aware that I had done it last night? Somehow I don't think you'd care—or that the bruiser would care either. And the captain said he wouldn't tell anyone if I came to his cabin again tonight. And he said it in such a way for me to understand that it wasn't really a request—out here on the open water, where it's just those of us on this trawler.

Flustered, I say I don't know what to say. What I'm thinking is how the bruiser heard. The captain's cabin isn't anywhere near the quarters for the rest of the crew. But what I say is that I'm not easy like that, and will think about it.

I'm trying to remain calm—cool. Trying to cool man my way out of the cabin. But if they'd seen me riding the captain's cock that second time last night they'd have a right to think I sniffed after it anywhere I could get it. I'd just been letting loose. And he'd gotten me drunk. Three months on the sea completely free from the constraints of land and college. And the captain was a stud and a half and he wore practically nothing, just a Speedo—just like all of us when we are out to sea. It was just a fling. Just a summer madness to mark the end of the school term. And he got me drunk. I'd thought about it, yes, and I'd fantasized about it when I was thinking of signing onto the trawler, because I'd heard what could happen on these isolated vessels out on the open water. But I'd never done it before last night.

And the third time. Well, I don't want to even think about that.

I wasn't even sure all I'd done that night, I was so drunk. It had to be just the captain. But that third time, when he'd been on his back and I was straddling his hips and riding his cock—I was never as confused and drunk as at the time. It seemed that hands were all over me. He was holding my waist and lifting and lowering me on his cock, but he also had the palms of his hands covering my pecs, his thumbs thrumming my nipples. And when he pushed my thighs out with his and pitched me forward onto his torso, it felt like he had doubled in size inside me, stretching me, and moving like there were two cocks inside me. And virile—the man came twice, almost in succession. I barely could walk from the cabin as I heard him laughing and talking to himself—in stereo. It wasn't just because I was woozy from the drink. That third fucking. Nothing before had stretched me like that.

You laugh and wink at Big Jim as if there is some joke I'm not privy to, and then you say, "Felt like double the size, eh?" and turn to the bruiser and say, "What do you think, Big Jim? Right here on the table?"

The bruiser giggles, stands, and pops the biggest cock I've ever seen out of his Speedo. I'd been eyeing his basket for days, wondering who would be up to taking it that big. That was part of why I'd been staying away from him. In shock, I stand. You reach out and grip my forearm, but I brush your hand away and lurch for the hatch out to the deck.

I hear you both laugh as you start in pursuit. I make it only about thirty feet, into the bow and below the bridge. The bruiser pounces on me and brings me down on a coil of rope. I land on top of him, and he snakes heavily muscled arms around mine, pinning me to his chest. You lean down and pull my Speedo off my legs. The bruiser's legs then lace in between mine, and he lifts and spreads his legs, so that mine spread and lift as well. I feel his thick, hard cock in the small of my back, snaking almost all the way up to my shoulder blades, it seems. I start to hyperventilate, but I know that won't help, so I start taking breaths in large gulps.

You are standing, looking down at me, and smiling. You push your Speedo to below your balls, showing that you're hard for me too. You go down on your knees between my legs, and I cry out as you slowly work your way into my ass.

I struggle, but it's useless, the bruiser is too strong for me. And the struggling only helps you move deeper inside me. I whimper as you stroke and stroke and stroke. I'm determined not to cry, though, to take it and then get as far away from here as possible. But what is far away on a trawler on the open seas?

Seeing that the captain has come out onto the deck of the bridge above us, I call out to him. He smiles and waves, takes a swig from his coffee cup, and turns and calls to the mate to join him. I see that he's pushed his Speedo down and is stroking his cock. No relief there. The black guy, Horace, who provides a lot of the muscle on moving cargo, has come up from the stern, hearing that something's going on. He's wearing a big grin and comes and stands beside us. He's got his cock in his hand.

"Relax kid," you say. "It's just the new guy initiation. When everyone's had a piece, we'll let you choose your two favorites for the rest of the voyage. Maybe they'll both enjoy you at once." You, the black guy, and the bruiser laugh.

I feel you jerk and come and then you are out of me and helping the bruiser free his cock from between his groin and my back. You are helping the bruiser find my hole with his staff. And when he has and I feel like I'm being split asunder, I start screaming anew. The mate is next to the captain on the bridge deck now. They are embracing and kissing and have taken possession of each other's cocks.

I can't stop complaining loudly from having the largest cock in the world pumping inside me. This isn't anything like the captain's. It isn't anything like I had from either the captain or you.

"Scream all you want, kid," the bruiser says in my ear in a hoarse voice. "There's empty ocean in every direction you can see from here, and we'll be out here for three months. And," he giggles, "a screamer makes me horny. And when I'm horny, I can go all day."

I believe him. I moan, starting to calm down, because the pain is turning into pleasure and I'm taking the biggest cock in the world. I'm taking the biggest dick in the world. I can't believe I'm managing the biggest dick in the universe. I'm wondering if it can get deeper from a different position. I shudder. I don't want to know that. But . . . but, of course I do want to know that. I'm taking the biggest dick in the world.

"Sweet ass," bruiser whispers. "And you like it. I can tell you like it. You wanna bunk with me tonight? I'll show you tricks you never knew. Maybe Horace can join us. You'll like that, kid. I can tell."

I'm thinking of the captain. I've got to go there tonight. But will he keep me all night? And, if not, will the bruiser be waiting for me? Can I take it? Maybe I'll need to be drunk tonight. Three months. Oh, fuck.

God he can fuck. God he can fuck.

I look up to see the captain and mate coming down the stairway, cocks in hand, smiling. I can barely hear what the captain is saying. "Great lay. Tight ass. Had him three times last night. I can tell you what he likes. And Bill here and I can tell you what he'll take."

"For sure?" Captain, "You really did?"

"We really did," the captain answers.

"Holy shit," I hear you say, and they you're telling the big bruiser, "Put him on your cock again, Big Jim."

"Right-o," Big Jim declares, and he's pulling me on top of him again, entering my channel with his cock, pushing way up into me. And using his thighs to spread mine. Tilting me up. And there you are again, holding your cock in your hand, pushing your knees inside Big Jim's thighs.

The bulb of your cock is at my hole.

"No," I moan. "I . . . I can't take both."

"Sure you can, son," and you laugh. "Both the captain and the first mate had you the other night. You can do it. It will become your specialty on this voyage. You'll love it."

"Oh, god, oh shit?" I cry out as the bulb presses inside me, on top of Big Jim's buried cock.

"I can't. I can't," I moan.

"You can and you are."

And you are right. You are inside me, pushing in on top of Big Jim's staff. And you both begin to stroke. I writhe under you, first in pain, but then in greater arousal. My memory is kicking in. I wasn't really so drunk that I didn't know there were two men fucking me in the captain's cabin. It was just strange and . . . so forbidden.

My fingers are dug into your shoulders and you lean in to me for a deep kiss while your hands grip my thighs and push them further apart, giving your cock purchase to stroke me hard and deeper.

Big Jim comes, then me. And last, you. We collapse together, the rest of the crew gathered around us and grinning down at us.

I can handle two men at once. I've done it twice already. I wonder how many more times on the cruise. But it doesn't matter. I can do it.

You are pulling me up off of Big Jim, handing me off to two other of the crew. They are licking their chops and grinning at me. "Whadya say, Jake," one is saying to the other. "Let's do him in the rope locker."

I moan.

Uncle Carl

"My name is Nario. You are Mr. Armstead?"

"Yes. I was expecting my uncle."

"He could not come. I'm am his boy."

Yes, I'll just bet you are, I thought. But then he clarified, if not enough to make a difference to me.

"I am his houseboy. Welcome to Naples, Mr. Armstead."

"Call me Harry, please. Is it far from here to Positano?"

"No, not too far. The worst part will be getting through the airport traffic. Then it is a very pleasant ride, a scenic ride down the Amalfi coast. Your uncle has picked a very beautiful spot to live in."

And a very beautiful houseboy, I thought. But then I knew he would. Some things never change. I certainly didn't think Uncle Carl would change for anyone. He always expected the world to change for him. Not in this respect, of course—him being here in Italy rather than back in England with the rest of the family—well, most of the rest of the family. That's what I had been sent here to do. I had come to try to get Gordon to come home.

Nario was certainly a cute little trick. Small and deeply tanned—the olive Mediterranean complexion. Curly black hair, a beautiful androgynous face, with a winsome smile. His mincing steps as he preceded me to the baggage claim gave him away. Just like my uncle liked them. Didn't do a thing for me, though.

281

Better here than in England, of course. We'd been well through that. But this was one of the reasons I was here. I was charged to tell Carl he could come home now—if he had given up the ways that had gotten him exiled. Seeing who he'd hired as a houseboy, though, made me think that part of the mission was a lost cause.

I wondered if Nario too was some important person's favorite son—someone who could dismember Carl at will if he found out what was happening to his precious child. Not that Carl picked them underage, mind you. He just went for the danger of a powerful backlash.

I was on edge and disgruntled. I hadn't told anyone the whole of why I was here. I had only told Uncle Carl that the family wanted me to talk to him—and then only through telegrams. He had said that my plane would be met. He didn't say he wasn't meeting it, though.

As we left the airport, I briefly had the fearful thought that Uncle Carl wasn't even at his exile villa in Positano. He flitted all over the world. He was a portrait photographer of choice by the rich, famous, royal, and, when he needed the money, the want-to-bes. He could go anywhere but England. And if our circle of friends could be trusted to have their collective ears to the ground, he was even wanted back in England. Despite everything. In fact, I wouldn't be surprised to find that the well-heeled in London had greased the skids to just make his trouble go away so that he could return.

And return he could, my family had discerned. And it was one of the two legs of mission I'd been sent here to accomplish. But whereas I hadn't defined these to Carl, I also hadn't told my family all of the reasons I was willing to be the messenger.

If they knew what I knew—indeed, all that Uncle Carl knew—they wouldn't have sent me. Not in a million years.

The drive in the Fiat down the coast of Italy from Naples did quite a bit to assuage my nervousness and pique. And when we crossed the mountains surrounding the sea side town of Positano, west along the rugged coast from Salerno, and descended into the semicircle of old dwellings holding onto the mountainside for dear life, I was completely captivated.

I could understand why Uncle Carl had chosen this escape hatch. And I could understand why he might not want to leave here to return to England.

The Fiat wound its way down a few levels through narrow streets and hair-pin curves until he came to a white stuccoed villa wedged between two ochre ones. It appeared to be mainly only one story, with a large, fully windowed room at one side on the top, opening out onto an open veranda, with a bougainvillea-covered loggia as a buffer between the room and the open air.

This would be a perfect art studio for painting, I thought. And then the dread hit me that perhaps it was. There was a semicircular drive tucked into the narrow stretch of front courtyard between the front of the villa and the cobblestoned road. The courtyard was ringed by a high stuccoed wall, with just an opening at one end into the vehicle turnaround, an identical one at the other end for the vehicle exit, and a iron-gated pedestrian entrance between.

Nario pulled into the turnabout and moved all the way around so that the nose of the car almost spilled out onto the roadway again.

Uncle Carl was at the door, beaming at me and rubbing his hands. He hadn't aged hardly any in the four years since I'd last seen him. Still looking disingenuously benign and almost grandfatherly—he was my father's older brother. A happy smile on his face. He may have put on a bit of weight, but he always had been the stalwart, solid-body type. I knew that he was deceptively strong and that most of what looked like the beginnings of fat was actually muscle. I trusted that he still took his long morning walks and had a weight room tucked around the villa somewhere. Although where it might be was a mystery to me. The villa didn't look very large.

When he ushered me into the main room, however, while Nario struggled getting my luggage out of the boot of the car and carrying it in, I began to learn that the exterior presentation of the villa was deceiving.

We were on only one of five floors of the villa, he told me, as I walked straight to the large windows at the back of the room and marveled at the panoramic sight down the slope of the

283

town, to the harbor below, and out into the Golfo di Salerno. This view alone was worth the trip.

This floor was largely one room, with a square section in the front corner for the kitchen. On the town side of that room was the dining L. To my right was a spiral staircase leading up and down. The room was richly appointed with old English furniture and oriental rugs purloined from the family estates in England. In contrast to this, however, was the artwork covering the three walls not covered with glass and overlooking the harbor.

All of the celebrities who Uncle Carl had photographed over the years—indeed, was still photographing—but the blown up art photos on his walls were all of meltingly beautiful and androgynous youths—in the nude. The photographs were provocative and just this side of pornographic—an edge that I had known Uncle Carl to cross in his art but, in this, at least, he had shown a bit of discretion in his life. I was to find that the next level down in the house, Carl's photograph studio, and the one below it, housing four bedrooms and two baths, he had not held back on the photographs.

I was to be shocked—although I told myself that I shouldn't be—to see that he still displayed some photographs I remembered well. Ones the authorities must have found quite damning when they had come for Uncle Carl in his wing of Armstead Rest just outside Cambridge. How Carl was able to get the sons and daughters of some of the richer and more powerful to pose for him like this was beyond me. But, then, who was I to question his powers and his infatuation with danger?

The floor at the bottom of the house contained a laundry, a dark room, storage, a well-stocked wine cellar, and Nario's small bedroom and bath. Both this level and the bedroom level had no view, being blocked by the back wall of the villa immediate down the steep slope from Carl's villa.

"You didn't show me the roof," I said to Carl as we sat out on the full-width balcony between the house and the harbor view on the living-room level—which made the floors below it deeper than the two upper levels. Nario had served us drinks and disappeared after Carl told him he'd be down in the studio shortly.

"That's Edward's domain," Carl said. "I rarely go up there, and he rarely comes down in my studio."

"You still meet in the bedroom?"

"Yes, we're still together."

"I thought Edward was in the gaol," I said. "He didn't have the connections you do."

"He was for a while, but I made your father get him out. Edward shouldn't fare worse than I did just because I came from position and money and he didn't. Now, if you can take care of yourself for a while—"

"Where is Edward, Uncle Carl? For that matter, where is Gordon? I came to try to convince him to come back to England. The family is worried. Nationals are coming up. He needs to prepare for them."

"Gordon is of age. He can make his own decisions where he goes."

"Only barely. And mentally he's still a child. You know that. His entire life is figure skating. If he can't go to nationals or doesn't do well there, it will crush him. You know that. And I know he's of age. That's why I'm not asking you to return him. I want to talk to him."

"He's in Milan. Edward has taken him there."

"You . . . let . . . Edward take Gordon anywhere?" I was close to hyperventilating. Gordon was my younger brother. He was a vision on ice, but he didn't have a clue what to do with himself.

"I'm sure the family knew what Gordon was doing here. On his nineteenth birthday, he made a beeline for Italy." Carl raised his hand, staving off what he knew would be a scathing reply from me. It was all tied up with what had sent Carl scurrying for an Italian exile. The scandals had involved our family as much as anyone else's. "Gordon has been keeping up with his practice," Carl said. "He's skating at the Milan Skating Club. That's where Edward took him. There are only four facilities good enough for his preparation. They are all in the Milan region. He and Edward should be back tomorrow. I cabled that you were coming. I surmised that it was to take Gordon back to England. Both he and I know the nationals are looming."

"Seeing that Gordon makes the nationals in London is only one of my family missions, Carl. The other one involves you directly."

"Me?"

"Yes. Father believes it's safe for you to come home now. The two young men . . . their families have emigrated to Australia. They are no longer a problem."

"Good lord, how much did that cost Adrian? That MP was quite the news hound at the time. And to have left his future in politics—"

"He is ambitious enough to stake his future in Australia. You made sure that his family name would always be linked to a sordid scandal if he'd remained in London."

"Well, I must say, your father must love his older brother dearly to arrange for me to come home. It's quite a noble gesture after he robbed me of the barony and—"

"We could hardly have the head of household guiding the family from prison, Uncle. You fucked your own way out of the barony, I do believe."

Carl laughed. "What a bald—and appropriate—way to refer to it, Nephew. You always were good with your tongue."

I winced. "Well, the family can tolerate your return. And England seems to be clamoring for it. I do believe even the queen is ready to sit for you."

"Return? Why in heaven's name would I return? Look around. Why would I leave this paradise and go back to an ungrateful England?"

"You didn't leave much room for England to be grateful. And, yes, now that I'm here, I can see why you'd want to stay. Nario is quite a pretty little trick. Some Italian count's son, I assume?"

"He's Sicilian?"

"Sicily. You mean Mafia? And his family doesn't know he's here?"

Carl just smiled.

"So, you haven't changed," I said. I swept my arm toward the room behind us. "And he seems to be staring at us from various places on three walls in your living room. This, I suppose is what his uncles will see when they come in, guns blazing."

"You should see the ones in the bedroom," Carl said with a little cackle of self-congratulation. "In fact, Nario is waiting for me now. Downstairs in my studio. If you are interested, by all means come downstairs and watch me work. If not, I see you have brought a book. Stay up here and read. There is no finer backdrop for reading on a balcony anywhere to be found in the world. Oh, mercy me. Why should I want to leave Positano?"

With a bit of effort that provided me the first evidence of the passage of four years in my uncle's later middle age, Carl hoisted himself from his chair and descended the spiral staircase. I gave reading a chance to grip me, but it was no use. I had to know if Carl had changed at all. I rose from the chair and quietly descended the staircase and went to the beaded curtain that separated the landing of the floor below from Carl's huge photography studio.

Carl was finishing up positioning the lights so that they shone on Nario, naked, and sitting provocatively in an antique, red velvet-upholstered slipper chair on a damask-draped platform.

I dug my nails into the palm of my hands and shivered as I saw Carl disrobe, pick up a camera, and move around the chair, taking photos of Nario from various positions. Nario knew how to pose, and he had a beautiful, if diminutive, body. The gazes he gave for the camera under long, fluttering eyelashes were sensual while still having an edge of youthful innocence. How old was Nario, I wondered? Was Carl pushing his usual modus operandi and skating on thin ice even here in Italy? Thus far, as far as I knew, he hadn't breached the age divide. But he certainly liked them young looking—and naïve and with powerful relatives with short tempers.

I decided, with bitter remembrances, that this really was Carl's problem. And Edward's as well. I presumed that Nario was old enough to know what he was doing—and that he knew enough not to be bragging on the streets of Sicily about what he was doing.

I watched Carl's dangling cock become less dangly and more upright as he moved around Nario. I should have moved away from the beaded curtain when, as I knew would be the case, I saw Carl moving in on Nario. I wanted to look away, but I couldn't, as Carl put the camera down, moved Nario to where his chest lay on the top of the back of the slipper chair, with his arms swaying down toward the floor on the other side, nudged Nario's thigh in a wider stance, and began to fuck him slowly and languidly from behind. Carl had picked up the camera again and directed Nario to turn his head to him, and Carl took close-ups of Nario's face as he was being fucked.

Carl was long and thick and Nario was small—just as Carl liked them—and Nario's expressions were an emotional mix of pain and passion and longing.

Carl had amazing stamina for a man his age. Nario was clearly exhausted before Carl was done with him. After ejaculation, Carl turned Nario around in the chair so that he was slumped in a sitting position, with his legs splayed wide and his arms artfully arranged in an seemingly natural askew position behind his head, one arm behind his neck, showing his hairless armpit and pulling his pecs tight and the other arm draped behind the back of the chair.

Nario's facial expression in post-total fuck was priceless, although Carl was sure to put a big price tag on it. These were Carl's most infamous studies in the art underground—the photos that brought him the most money—the splayed out body of a completely fucked young man, showing facial expressions of mixed satisfaction, violation, and exhaustion—and evoking the reaction of "Isn't that?" Carl reveled in the viewer's revelation of what young celebrity or well-connected youth that was. There was never a question of what had happened to the subject of these photographs right before they were taken.

"You can return to your reading now, Harry," Carl called out to me when he had taken the photographs he wanted to take. "I'm finished now. As you can see, I haven't changed, and I have no reason to leave this paradise—or the beauties they provide me."

Carl wasn't finished with Nario. I knew he wouldn't be if he had remained true to form. Going down on his knees between Nario's thighs in the chair, recharged, and a new postcoital pose in mind, Carl grasped Nario's legs and lifted and spread them, and thrust his cock inside Nario's rolled up buttocks again. Nario moaned and clasped his hands around Carl's neck. Carl kissed him on the mouth. I turned and left as Nario began to burble in Italian.

I went to the room where Nario had taken my luggage, one floor down. It was on the front of the house and only had a couple of half windows opening to the side. The view was of an ochre stuccoed wall of the adjacent villa, not more than eight feet away. There were other curtained areas around the walls of the shape of windows, giving an illusion that the room would be airy if they were open. I pulled aside one of the curtains and then another, and then I quickly closed both, my stomach threatening to give dry heaves. The photographs were some of the very explicit nudes Carl photograph—none of them of a single subject. I recognized the model for most of them, and I was shocked in the recognition. I fled the room and went back to the balcony two flights up and forced myself to read from my book.

Dinner was late, with just the two of us, Carl and me, at the table and Nario buzzing around us, giving full service, but not giving any hint at the full service he'd given earlier in the day. The food was gourmet. I heard activity in the kitchen, so I surmised there was a cook out there. I heard humming in a woman's register, so I surmised that the cook lived out. I had never known Carl to allow a woman to spend a night under his roof. The wine also was first rate. And there were at least three bottles of it served and emptied before I voiced my weariness from short flights and interminable waits in lounges and passenger check lines between London and Naples, and declared my intent to go to bed and read a bit before going to sleep.

I did not mention the photographs in my room. I believed that more than once Carl was on the edge of bringing them up. I could tell by that mischievous little smile he had. But he said nothing. There was more silence than discussion, but what discussion there was was of the art world. I had started life in an art auction house. I was surprised to find that Carl was well versed in what was being sold and for how much.

"For Edward's sake," he said. "Someday he will be discovered."

Not likely, I thought. But I didn't say as much. Edward's art was insipid. That had always surprised me because I had found Edward to be intense and forceful. I would have expected broad, telling strokes in oil from him, rather than the washed-out watercolors of sailboats. Of course there was Edward's private collection. His rendering of the same theme that drove Carl's life—the search for the perfect depiction of the face of a handsome young man right after being fucked by the artist. That art of Edward's was, technically, excellent. And it sold well. But it wasn't going to be sold in the reputable, high stakes auction houses, and it wasn't going to make his public reputation.

Both Carl and Edward had overextended themselves in those months in England before the authorities got on to them. Both moaned of having found the perfect subject and rendered their individual modes of art perfectly—but only with one youth, the son of a duke. In search of regaining this, they had been sloppy in their techniques of developing subjects, and it had caught up with them.

I had trouble sleeping, and part of that was because of my curiosity of what Edward was up to, painting wise. I eventually realized I wasn't going to be able to sleep until I satisfied that question. I quietly got out of bed and padded up the two flights to Edward's studio at the top of the house.

He had never been a neat person in his studio. Chaos reigned here and it took me a few minutes to focus on what was where. I wanted to see canvases, the sheets of rice paper he liked to use for his water colors. There were plenty of the latter around. The harbor below was the subject of many of those, and Positano obviously had been a good influence on his work. Many of these were vibrant and the strokes bold and sure. Several, I thought were good enough for the auction houses. I didn't know if I would say anything about that, though. I found Edward foreboding and overwhelming. The distance between us these last four years had been perfectly fine with me.

Edward was a ruggedly handsome man of towering height and muscular build. He was a good ten years younger than Uncle Carl. Carl had taught him in art school. He'd taught him art and then he had taught him how to fuck, and, finally, he had taught him how to share. Of the two, though, I had always thought of Edward as the more cruel and dangerous lover of men.

I found a couple of canvases, with cloths over them. I uncovered one, and my hand began to tremble. I quickly uncovered two more.

I, of course, knew it. I knew it before I had come. The whole family had known it. They were just pretending it wasn't so. I pretended too, but of all of them, I had the most reason to accept reality.

The paintings were all of Gordon—my younger brother—and they were all nudes of his splayed body and various positions of surrender. And the faces of all revealed without a doubt, that his visage had been captured right after he'd been fucked.

I didn't want to look at them. I covered them and quickly left the studio and descended the spiral staircase. As I reached the bedroom level, I heard the sounds. I knew what they were, of course. They hadn't even bothered to close the door. The door led into the master bedroom, which was dominated by a king-sized poster bed. Carl and Edward's bed, I knew. Nario was lying in the center of the bed, legs running up either side of Carl's chest, as Carl, buttocks pistoning, fucked Nario deeply. There was a camera on the bed beside them. I was sure that Carl knew enough about the working of light and shadows even to be able to collect excellent photographs this late at night.

Edward dropped off Gordon at the entrance the next day and then drove on to somewhere else. I didn't ask where he had gone or how long he would be gone. And Carl didn't volunteer the information. I thought perhaps that Edward was staying down in the town for as long as I was there. If so, he was being thoughtful—and perhaps he was changing, that his months in the goal had changed him somehow. But then I thought of those paintings of Gordon in his studios, and I realized that Edward had not changed a bit. My father was a violent man. If he knew for sure . . . even though they were brothers . . .

For the first time I began to wonder what my father's real motives were for wanting Uncle Carl to return to England as well as Gordon.

Gordon seemed relieved to see me. I think he only needed someone in the family to come to him and tell him that he needed to return to England and pick up his quest for the figure skating gold again.

He assured me that he had been diligent in practicing on the ice—and had spent more time in Milan than here. I believed him, but then I knew how fast Edward could paint. I wanted to ask him if our uncle, Carl, had also photographed him as Edward had painted him. But I really didn't want to know the answer to that—and it wouldn't have changed anything if he had.

I showed Gordon his return air ticket to London the next day, and he didn't argue. He just went off to pack.

"I assume we'll be sitting together," he said as he stood from the patio table on the balcony and prepared to leave.

"No, we won't be travel together," I answered. "I have family business in Naples, as well. I'll be following on the weekend. But I will be at the airport to see you off safely."

That seemed to satisfy him. And I knew I'd have to be there to see him off. He was still such a child in mind. Large airports confused him. There would be a family car and chauffeur on the London end to meet him. To meet us both, as a matter of fact, but the family business in Naples was something I hadn't actually told the family about.

I had trouble sleeping that night too. The sounds of sex from the master bedroom were louder, more insistent that night. And I heard more than two voices. Curious, I left my bed and padded out into the corridor. As the night before, the master bedroom door had been left ajar. It was almost as if Carl was taunting me, teasing me.

I went into the shadow cast by the door, to a place where I could see the bed. The light in the room was glaring. Spots were directed to the bed. Nario, naked, was moving around the bed with both a video and a still camera in his hands. I nonsensically wondered if Carl was teaching him photography—and, if so, how good he was.

Carl was lying on his back in the center of the bed. I could hardly see him, because my view was obstructed by the broad back of a somewhat younger man, who was facing Carl and straddling his legs. Edward, I suddenly realized. But that wasn't what had me mesmerized. There, sandwiched between them, back to Edward and hunched over the chest of Carl, his eyes squinched up in a mix of agony and ecstasy. My brother, Gordon.

All three men were naked. Both Carl's and Edward's cocks were inside Gordon.

I nearly burst in on them. But I didn't. Gordon was of age now, and I had known what I'd find when I got here—well, most of it. I would have guessed that Carl or Edward was fucking Gordon, or even both. I would not have guessed that they were doing it together, fucking him at the same time in the same channel. But then, I should have guessed that as well, I suppose.

Tomorrow. I'd put Gordon on a plane tomorrow. And then no more would be said about it. The family need know nothing about. I had protected them from this earlier—or so I argued myself into believing now, rationalizing away all thoughts that Gordon's and my father or the rest of the family already knew. I would protect them from the truth now, if I could. Gordon wouldn't talk. He would probably go on to be with men, but that was his choice. I had known for some time that he would do that.

I went back to my room, closed the door, climbed into bed, and buried my head under the pillows. Mercifully, in an hour or two—or three—I managed to drift off to a restless sleep.

* * * *

I got home from the airport in Naples after dark the next day. The planes had all been late and the airport was chaos. Gordon walked around at my side, glassy eyed, and acting like a frightened rabbit.

I said nothing to him about what I had seen the previous night. He said nothing either to indicate what had happened, but

I got the impression that Carl and Edward had gone farther with him in the night than ever before, because he was quiet and somewhat distant, and obviously was anxious to get out of the villa and on his way back to England.

Neither Carl nor Edward saw us off—or appeared at breakfast or lunch. They were both in their separate studios. No doubt, I reasoned each working hard to capture the previous night's work in their art. I heard humming from both studios when I passed, so I gathered they were very pleased with themselves.

Nario served me a solitary dinner at the dining room table. Again the food was excellent and the wine was flowing. Neither Carl nor Edward appeared.

I went to bed early. I left the door open to my room, and before I stripped down and climbed up onto the bed, I went around and opened the drapes that had been covering all of the photographs. I laid down on the bed and moved my gaze around the room, taking in all of the photographs in turn, remembering. Waiting.

Carl was the first to appear. Naked. Smiling.

"The photographs were a nice touch, don't you think?" he asked. He laughed, walked over to the foot of the bed, grasped my ankles, and pulled me down to him. I had become hard looking at the photographs. He came to me hard as well. While waiting, I had lubed my channel well, so without preliminaries, Uncle Carl splayed my legs, moved between my thighs, and began fucking me.

"Just like our early days," he murmured. "You are still as beautiful as you were then, when those photos were taken."

I raised my hands to his gray-haired, hairy chest and let my fingers play in the silkiness of him. Searching for and find his nipples and rubbing them to hear him groan—just as he had all those years ago.

My eyes went to each photograph on the wall that I could see. Me, a young me—the son of a duke. A younger Carl and Edward as well. Fucking—or immediately after being fucked. After being fucked by both of them—together, sharing my channel.

"You were always perfection, my little bird," Carl was murmuring as he plowed me deep. "Never since have we been able to capture the perfection—the released innocence and awakening to the cock of men—of that summer of photos of you."

Edward was in the room now. And Nario as well. Nario had a video camera at the ready and a still camera in his other hand. Carl pulled out of me and reached for the camera. Edward put his hand behind the edge of the curtain of one of the photographs and strong lights came on, focused on the bed.

I knew then that Carl had started to prepare for me as soon as I'd sent him the telegram that it was me who was coming to fetch Gordon. He had known why it was me—why I would have volunteered to do that.

There was, of course, no family business in Naples. And I had no idea whether I would be returning to the weekend or not. Now, after having Carl's cock inside me again after so many years, I rather thought not—that I wouldn't be catching a plane back to London on the weekend.

Edward took up the position Carl had vacated. I cried out as he thrust inside me. He was younger, longer, thicker, more vigorous—crueler—then Carl was. No—pant, pant, moan—I would not be returning to London on the weekend.

Edward was digging into my chest, twisting my nipples, and I was howling. He slapped me on the face and told me to be quiet. I whimpered, but I didn't really want him to stop punishing me. I deserved punishment. I had come to Carl. So, so young. I had seen him fuck young men in his studio—my friends, sons of famous people. I wanted that too. I was the son of a duke. Surely he'd want me too. He hadn't refused me. He told me that I was just the beautiful, androgynous body that he wanted for his art. Edward had agreed.

I had wanted Carl, not Edward. but Edward had taken me first, repeatedly, cruelly, gloriously, while Carl had fired off those shots on the wall. And then an assistant had taken the camera and both Edward and Carl . . .

"Oh, god, oh holy shit. Fuck me Edward. It's been so long." I rose up to his chest, reaching down for his buttocks, holding him deep inside me. I bit him on the nipple and he screamed, pushed me down onto the bed and backhanded me across the face, whipping my head to the side. I felt blood in my mouth.

"Get that dazed look," Edward cried out.

"Got it," Carl answered, his voice excited.

Carl moved around us, snapping off photographs. Nario was beside and behind him, holding the whirring video camera.

I lurched up to Edward's chest again. He was pumping, pumping, pumping. God, he was virile. And so big.

I grabbed his head between my hands and brought his lips to mine, letting him taste the blood he had released. He shuddered and lifted me up off the bed, roughly, turned me, and slammed me down into a club chair. I was draped over the back of the chair, totally spent and exhausted after he had finally finished pumping me from behind.

"Yes! That's the look. Perfection," Carl cried out, full of exhilaration, as he moved around me, in post-fuck exhaustion, snapping off shots of my face. Edward reached over and turned me in the chair, and my body just slid down the chair and onto the floor, Carl firing off stills the entire time.

"Both of us now," Carl said with an excited voice.

I knew what was coming. It's how they always ended their sessions with me—even that first one—the one where I thought I was going to die. And didn't care if I did as long as they kept fucking me. It's how they ended their session with Gordon the previous night.

Carl was on his back on the bed. His cock was standing at full attention. Edward pulled me up from the floor and carried me over to the bed, and laid me stretched out on top of Carl, my shoulder blades on his chest. I whimpered, as Edward took hold of Carl's cock and moved it to my channel and helped guide it in. Carl was embracing my torso in his arms and kissing my neck and nibbling on my ear.

Nario was taking all of the photographs now.

Edward knelt between my thighs, working my cock with a hand and cupping and squeezing my balls, as Carl fucked up into me from underneath. When I had come for Edward, he moved in between my thighs, positioned his cock with his hand,

and slowly entered me, the underside of his cock on top of Carl's already encased cock.

I panted and huffed and cried out for the fuck. Remembering how good it had been. Both of them. Making love to me, making love to each other. I had never risen to such heights since.

Edward began to pump me seriously.

Oh, God! No, I wasn't going to be returning to London on the weekend. Thank god I hadn't aged so much in the past years that they no longer wanted me.

"If father saw you doing this, he'd kill you!" I cried out as I ejaculated.

"Yes, I know he would," Carl answered with a cackle. "Isn't it delicious?"

Wait for Carnival

Ned Harrington had patiently waited for his young protégé. Ned had known for years that he wanted Devin; he'd known for more than a month he could have him. But everything had to be right, just right.

Ned and Devin's father, John Treadwell, had been long-time lovers. The Harringtons and Treadwells were among the first families of Charleston, South Carolina. Ned and Devin had gone to private school together; Ned had been John's best man. And the night before John took Helene to the matrimonial bed, Ned took John in the backseat of a Cadillac convertible. They initially had tried to stay away from each other after John Treadwell had wed, but their resolve was weak, and within a couple of years they had begun surreptitiously meeting for sex.

When Devin was six, John's wife, Helene, died in an airplane crash on her way to her usual summer retreat in Paris; John followed along behind her five years later in what would have been a suspicious hunting accident covering a suicide if Charleston society hadn't closed ranks around its own. John's death left Devin Treadwell an orphan. It also revealed that the Treadwells had been living well beyond their means for decades. Ned Harrington swept in and covered the family's debt and bundled Devin off to the same private school he and Devin's father had attended.

John wasn't nearly as successful in life as Ned was, and Ned had carried the Treadwells for years financially. He didn't give John and Helene money directly, but he made sure that business came their way and that the Treadwells could hold up their head at the forefront of old-line Charleston families.

Ned mourned the passing of John, but in Devin he had the spitting image of John. Patrician Greek god looks, a ready smile, natural athletic ability, curly light-brown hair, and an innate interest in men. Ned would not have disagreed with anyone who said bisexual preferences were inherited. The Harrington and Treadwell men loved their woman, but a good many of them loved their men as well. And the Harringtons and Treadwells had been linked in this way for generations. Ned had been initiated into male-male sex by his own father in the family's hunting lodge in the Great Smokey mountains and before that evening was over he had been taken as the lover of Devin's father, John. as well in a threesome. It was almost inevitable he himself one day would seduce Devin.

Charleston society was one that was not as unique as the local patricians liked to suppose. It was all prim and proper and almost antiseptic on the surface, but underneath it was teeming with sexuality and a wild bent toward hedonism. In truth this was the same with many an isolated, highly stratified cast system, though.

Devin, the orphan Ned had taken on to raise as his own, worshipped Ned, and Ned figured it was only a matter of time till he could relive his love affair with John Harrington through his mirror-image son. But Ned wanted to do it right, and he wanted to do it away from the searching eyes and wagging mouths of the insular old-family culture of Charleston. And he wanted the taking to be special. Once he'd made love to Devin, he wanted to have Devin with him forever, taking the "spitting image" place of his true love, John.

All of Ned Harrington's carefully and well-laid plans for Devin almost were blown to the winds early on, however. Shortly after Devin's eighteenth birthday, the two of them had gone up to the Harrington family's hunting lodge in the Great Smokeys. After a day of hunting deer, weary and tired but with Devin exhilarated about the stag he had bagged, the two drank a bit too much. Ned had always assumed that he would have to prepare Devin for him and methodically seduce him when it came time to take him.

Thus, he was taken by surprise when Devin put the moves on him, begging Ned to make love to him. Ned had showered and was sitting in the lounge of the lodge just in his sleeping shorts and a light robe. Devin appeared naked, told Ned he had wanted to be taken by him for years, stating that he now was of an age to make this decision for himself, and sinking between Ned's thighs and burying his face in Ned's crotch.

This put Ned into such a sense of shock that he failed to react immediately. And within minutes, he was too weak and defenseless to the unexpected onslaught to resist Devin pushing the waistband of his sleeping shorts below his balls and taking his cock in his mouth. Devin's sucking technique was wholly unpracticed, but Ned was so taken with him—and had been for so long—that this hardly mattered in his arousal and the quickening of his cock. He lay back in his chair and moaned deeply as Devin sucked him hard.

Periodically Devin pulled his mouth off Ned's cock long enough to beg his mentor to make love to him, to fuck him properly.

Ned came back to his senses just as Devin was taking charge and was coming down into Ned's lap and holding the older man's cock in position to penetrate his ass. He rose and pushed Devin off him and backhanded the young man across the cheek, sending him onto his ass on a bear rug in front of a roaring fire in a deep stone fireplace. Standing over the young man, looking so wounded and so vulnerable and yet so desirable and still desiring of what Ned could give him, Ned had to steel himself with all of his might. This was the same bear rug, and an identical roaring fire, where his father had pushed a cushion under his belly and fucked him for the first time and then invaded his mouth with his cock while Devin's father, John, turned him, Ned's butt cheeks raised on the cushion, and came in between his spread thighs and fucked him as well. It was where John, lying on his back on the bear rug, had pulled Ned down on his cock and then Ned's father, straddling John's thighs, had worked his cock into Ned's channel above John's, and had pumped his own son in double penetration while kissing John passionately over Ned's shoulder.

Then, spent and whimpering but filled with arousal, Ned had sat on the floor, his back against the warm stones of the fireplace, and watched John put on a show of just how intensely and masterly he could fuck Ned's father. Ned had been taken into John's bed that night and shown just how filling and satisfying man sex could be. In one night, Ned had experienced it all.

"Have you done this before? With other men? Have you been fucking other men?" Ned roared at Devin in indignation. All of his plans, all of his careful work, and someone else had slipped in and taken this little bastard. The ultimate betrayal. A betrayal of all that John and he had been to each other.

Ned wasn't reasoning well; he was acting as if supposition were reality—and he was holding Devin up to standards he'd never enunciated to Devin. If Devin had been sexually active with men already, this was something he had done naturally. He had made no pledge of constancy to Ned; Ned had never asked him to do this, never demanded it of him. Now he was looking up at the man he worshipped with dismay, confusion, and deep embarrassment.

"No . . . no . . . never . . . never with anyone else. I've always wanted it to be you. I knew you went with men . . . I've always wanted that for me. Not just any man. You . . . never before. I wanted you to be the first."

Ned believed him, relief rushing in, the program salvaged. The awkward way Devin had sucked him was evidence he was telling the truth. And the young man looked so startled and contrite and openly shocked.

"I'm sorry, son. I never expected that you'd make the first move. I've always wanted you too. But it has to be special the first time. I'll think of some way to make it special. Something we'll always remember. And we'll always be together."

Ned had sunk to the bear rug and had taken a now trembling and sobbing Devin into his arms. They both immediately slipped into renewed arousal, and Ned took Devin's lips with his and they kissed passionately and deeply.

302

Instinctively they each moved to take the cock of the other in their hands, and Ned permitted this much intimacy, a mutual masturbation to a shared climax with soft moaning and sighing. But no further than this. Beyond this, although the two came together regularly over the next couple of weeks, Ned would not permit the lovemaking to go farther for now. In fact, he wouldn't again, in those months building up to the full taking, let Devin touch his cock. Instead, he would take Devin in his arms and stretch out behind him and hold Devin tight, one hand playing his nipples and the other stroking Devin's cock relentlessly until the young man had ejaculated for him.

"I'll think of something special," he murmured as they lay entwined before the dying fire that first night.

"Please do it soon," Devin whimpered. "I don't know how long I can hold out. This isn't enough. I want you inside me." And then he gasped and began to groan and grind his pelvis against Ned's flank, as Ned took his cock in his fist again and masturbated him in vigorous and relentless strokes to a second ejaculation.

* * * *

Ned Harrington was perplexed about how he could make the taking of Devin special until one day, when he was walking down Charleston's Queen Street, he stopped at a corner for a light change and turned and looked in the window of a travel agency.

They were advertising special rates on travel to Carnival in Rio de Janeiro. Just the thing, Ned thought, and when Devin next lay stretched out in the arms of Ned and being stroked to completion—and begging, in vain, for Ned to move their lovemaking to a whole new level—Ned told him where they would be this time next week—fucking in a suite at the Mar Ipanema hotel in Rio and enjoying the sounds from outside of the annual Samba parade making its way to the Sambadrome.

Devin was delighted to hear this plan.

Ned Harrington was a world traveler and thus he completely misjudged how overwhelmed Devin, who had never been abroad, would be by the sights and sounds and sensations of Carnival in Rio. Ned's idea was to have Devin completely devoted to and in thrall to him and only him in this foreign environment. But from the very beginning—starting in the airport itself, where a group of young, hunky Brazilian men honed in on Ned and Devin and swept them up in the gaiety of Carnival—Devin started to spin away from Ned. The Brazilian men were preparing a float for the gay procession in the Samba Parade, and they declared that Devin would be perfect at the top of the float—and that, yes, of course, there would be a place for Ned as well.

From there the whole trip careened out of Ned's control. The Brazilians dashed all over town, Devin in tow, gathering materials for their float and costumes for Devin and Ned. The theme of the float was the Arabian nights, and both Devin and Ned were to be outfitted in diaphanous harem pants and turbans and nothing else but greased up torsos to accentuate their musculature. And the float needed to be prepared as well.

For two nights, Ned made careful preparations in the Mar Ipanema suite for a ritualistic deflowering of his young protégé. Devin was always working on the float with the boisterous Brazilian hunks, though. The preparations for Carnival had put Devin in high heat, so it wasn't a question of not wanting to lose his virginity to Ned—and, in fact, every time Ned appeared to check on Devin and on the progress of the preparation of the float, Devin begged Ned to take him off in a corner of the warehouse and relieve his virginity forthwith. But Ned was a stubborn man, and he had it in his head to do this in luxury and in a way that would always be memorable to them both.

At last he gave up and decided that it would have to wait for the concluding night of Carnival, when the parade was completed.

The day of the parade arrived, and all was in readiness. Ned was on the first level of the float, arm in arm with two of the Brazilian studs, while Devin was at the very center, top of the float, surrounded by several nearly naked Brazilian men. All were laughing and gay, and the Brazilians were passing around bottles of Cachaca, the local strong sugarcane rum, as the float started out in the Samba Parade, headed for the Sambadrome.

But the float never made it to that destination. The drunker the revelers on the float became and the more intense the gaiety along the parade route was, the hornier the Brazilian men got.

Ned was horny too. He looked up at the greased up, youthfully beautiful, nearly naked Devin at the top center of the float and he ached for him. He could hardly wait to get Devin alone in the hotel suite.

Sensing the heat rising off the handsome American, the two Brazilians at his side went into heat themselves. The float began to waver, the driver now being heavily under the influence of the Cachaca. The first Ned sensed something was unusual was as the float was staggering off the parade route and into a secluded park area to the west of the Sambadrome. And then he realized that his harem pants had been lowered and that one of the hunky Brazilians was beginning to suck his cock.

Ned recoiled and started to move out of the grasp of the young Brazilian making love to his cock, but this only pushed him into the encircling arms around his waist of the other strong and large-built Brazilian who was kneeling behind him and had inserted his tongue in the crease between Ned's ass cheeks.

Ned looked up wildly at the top center of the float—just in time to see Devin's ass channel being breached by the chubby cock of one of four Brazilians near him. One of the Brazilians was crouched behind Devin and holding him up in the air, while two at each side of Devin were hold his thighs wide and the fourth Brazilian was hunched between Devin's thighs and slowly feeding his cock inside the young American.

"Nooooo," Ned cried out, but the noise of the crowd was too loud for anyone to hear him, and the hedonist festivities were at too high a level of anyone to care.

As Ned watched in horror, he realized that it wasn't just the Brazilian between Devin's thighs who had his cock inside Devin. The Brazilian holding him from the back was already saddled. And Devin was writhing in pleasure at the double attention.

Devin was having a ball. Laughing and swigging from a bottle of Cachaca and egging the Brazilians on. Wanting to be fucked. Having been put off by Ned too long in the losing of his virginity.

Over the next hour, Devin's ass entertained the vigorous cocks of four virile Brazilian studs, two by two in mix and match progression, all five lost in the hilarity and freedom of the Carnival Rio, while Ned, looking helplessly on at the ruination of all his careful planning, was being fucked from behind by his own two Brazilian companions, in succession. Ned was shuddering, unable to take his eyes off Devin.

"You want some of that too, don't you?" one of the men paying attention to Ned asked.

"No, no. I just. Oh, fuck! Oh, SHIT!"

The two attending Ned hadn't waited for his answer. Standing facing each other, they were both stuffing their cocks in his channel at the same time. Ned was suspended in air, his legs hooked on the hips of the man facing him, his thighs held up and wide by the hands of the man behind him. The man in front of him was palming his buttocks and spreading the cheeks, making the channel as wide as he could to accommodate the two cocks. Ned grunted and groaned and pleaded as the two cocks pushed in to their limit. By the time they were pumping him, he was reduced to whimpers and moans.

But he was moving with them too, clawing the shoulder blades of the Brazilian facing him and moving his channel on his own, so that the two inside him only had to stand and hold and he was the one doing the pumping. He was lost in his memories of his father and John, the times they had engaged in three-way love, connecting in a double penetration of his channel.

"Yeah, that's what you wanted," on the Brazilians said, and Ned was too far gone with the ultimate fuck to disagree. He wasn't able to break away until all three had come. Finished with him, the Brazilians let him sink to the ground and stepped away, clapping each other on the back and searching for the bottles of liquor that had been stashed around the float.

Ned staggered to the ground and hobbled toward the other float. He waved for Devin to try to do the same, but Devin just waved a friendly smile at his benefactor and smiled broadly as several Brazilian men who had been at the lower edges of the float now start mounting the tiers for their own turn with the highly receptive and achingly handsome young American man.

The two Brazilians from his own float hailed Ned. "Ready for another round?" one of them called out.

Ned fled the scene. He waited at the hotel for two days for Devin to return to him. But at the end of that time, he decided he was waiting in vain—and the interest he had had in Devin had waned anyway when Devin was no longer pure and just beyond his reach. Ned left Rio never to see Devin again, although he continued sending checks regularly. He had simply waited too long.

~

About the Author

Habu is one of the pen names of a former supersonic spy jet pilot, intelligence agent, male model, movie actor, and diplomat. A wild youth in South East Asia was spent enjoying whatever sexual opportunities came his way, and much of his gay male writing is about recalling incidents from those days and inventing ones he'd perhaps have liked to experience. He now leads a very quiet and ordinary happily married family life.

An American, he is a published mainstream novelist and short story writer under another name and in another dimension of his life. He has written or cowritten (with Sabb) approaching 1,000 published short stories and over 100 published erotica e-books, primarily of gay fiction but also memoir, straight fiction and ménage fiction.

His hand and creative writing can be seen in stories and books by habu, sr71plt, Dirk Hessian, Shabbu, and Stephen Kessel—among unrevealed others that might surprise readers.

The fictionalized GM memoir *Flying High, Diving Deep* is loosely based on his life experiences. He can be found at the adults only gay male site www.BarbarianSpy.com, which he shares with Sabb.

Our authors always like to receive feedback, and appreciate it when readers post reviews at Goodreads and other sites.

BarbarianSpy

FOR LITERARY HEAT

Not all books listed below may currently be on release.
* indicates the book is available in paperback and e-book.

BOOKS BY DIRK HESSIAN

Xtreme Erotica

The King's Men
Shores of Tripoli
Prophecy of Noto
Pretender's Fate

General Erotica/Romance

Fire Down the Valley*
Constantinople*
The Beautiful Way*
Blue and Gray
Colonel's Treasure
Beginning of Time
Labyrinth

BOOKS BY HABU

Gay Erotica

Memoir Faction

Flying High, Diving Deep*

Xtreme Erotica

Apyko: The Greek Pimp
Visits of the Schlange
Second Coming: Emile La Cour Unleashed
Vortex: Sacrificed by Curiosity*
Dark Angel Sounding *(in e-book & included in Sounding:Ultimate Control Paperback)**
Sounding: Ultimate Control *(Print Only)**
Sounding Five *(in e-book & included in Sounding:Ultimate Control paperback)*

General Erotica

Romance

Snowy, Snowy Nights (Christmas Romance)
Four Coins
Lower Than the Heart
Brambleton

Gotta Keep Trying
Finding Amnad
Platres Conclave
Other Novels/Novellas
Cruising Gigolo
Prepared in Cape Verdi
Gilded Cage
House on Park
Anything for Ambition
Dance of the Ravishers
Hard Knocks U*
My Neighbor's Spa*
Man's Man: Tales of a High Priced Gay Hooker*
Trip Money
Clint Folsom Mysteries Compendium Volume 1*
Death to Blonds - Stolen Judgment (Clint Folsom Mystery)
Clint Folsom Mysteries Compendium Volume 2*
The Indian Doctor
Sailorboy
Home to Fire Island
Choke Hold
Gay Erotica Anthologies
Spy Tales 001*
Spy Tales 002*
Doubled*
Doubled Again*
Tails in the Tropics*
Tails in the Med*
Tails in the West*
Rough Riders*
Grab Bag 1*
Grab Bag 2*
Grab Bag 3*
Grab Bag 4*
Grab Bag 5*
Beyond the Beaded Curtain*
Habu's Christmas Balls
The Sporting Life*
Fetish Galore!*
Literary Gay Erotica
Cairo Surrender*
The Handyman*

Homeward Bound
Journey to Mirage*
Menage Erotica
Cruising Gigolo
13 Ways for Halloween
Luther*
The Indian Prince
Literary GLBT Fiction
Summer of Denial
BOOKS BY SHABBU
Finding Jason
Dirty Pool
Operation Black Jade
Cigars!*
Angel in the Barn
Gayly Complicated*
Despoiling David
The Tree of Idleness*
I Met a Man
The Interview
Rough Road to Happiness
BOOKS BY SABB
Hiring in Hollywood
The Legend of Holleystone Grange
Surprise Encounters
She is He
Wrong Man
Loyal to his King
Barbarian Tales - Book One - Traveler's Tales*
Barbarian Tales - Book Two - Journeys Begin*
Barbarian Tales - Book Three - The Inheritance*
Barbarian Tales - Book Four - Road to Persepolis*